JN011826

大修館
シェイクスピア双書
第2集

THE

TAISHUKAN

SHAKESPEARE

2nd Series

大修館書店

ペトルーチオ（アントン・レッサー）とキャタリーナ（アマンダ・ハリス）
ビル・アレグザンダー演出、ロイアル・シェイクスピア劇場 (1992)
Photo by Reg Wilson © RSC

ウィリアム・シェイクスピア

じゃじゃ馬ならし

William Shakespeare

THE TAMING OF THE SHREW

前沢浩子

編注

大修館シェイクスピア双書 第2集（全8巻）について

　大修館シェイクスピア双書 第1集（全12巻）の刊行が始まったのは1987年4月。その頃はシェイクスピア講読の授業を行う大学もまだ多く、双書はその充実した解説と注釈において（手頃な値段という点においても）、原典に親しむ学生の心強い味方となり、教員の研究・教育に欠かせないツールとなった。

　そうした時代に比べれば、シェイクスピアよりも実用英語という経済性偏重の風潮もあって、シェイクスピア講読の科目を有する大学は数えるほどになったが、双書が役割を終えたわけでは全くなかった。そのことは発行部数からもよくわかる。2010年代になっても双書のほとんどは継続的に増刷を続けており、例えば『ロミオとジュリエット』の総発行部数は15,000に届く勢いだ。英文学古典の注釈書としてはかなりの部数と言える。

　これは大学の教員や学生のみならず、多くの一般読者にも双書が届いているからに他ならない。実際、周囲を見回せば、通信教育、生涯学習講座、地域のカルチャー・センター、読書会や勉強会でシェイクスピアの原典を繙く人は少なくない。そういう読者に双書が選ばれているのだとすれば、その主な理由は第1集編集委員会の目指した理念が好意的に受け取られているからだろう。

　原文のシェイクスピアをできるだけ多くの人に親しみやすいものにすること。とは言え、入門的に平易に書き直したりダイジェスト版にしたりするのではなく、最新の研究成果に基づいた解説や注釈により、原文を余すところなく読み解けるようにすること。そのために対注形式を取り、見開き2ページで原文と注釈を収めて読みやすさを重視すること。後注や参考文献により学問的な質を高く保ちつつ、シェイクスピアの台詞や研究の面白さを深く理

解できるようにすること。こうした第1集の構想が、第2集においてもしっかりと受け継がれていることは言うまでもない。また、表記の仕方などを除いて、厳密な統一事項や決まりなどは設けず、編集者の個性を十分に発揮していただく点も第1集と同様である。

　一方、重要な刷新もある。第1集では Alexander 版（1951）のテクストを基本的にそのまま用いたが、当時と比べれば近年の本文研究は大きな進展をみせ、現在 Alexander 版は必ずしも使いやすいテクストではない。むしろ編者が初期版本の性質を見極めた上で、そこからテクストを立ち上げ、様々な本文の読みを吟味しつつ編集作業を行う方が（負担は増すものの）、意義ある取り組みになるのではないか。そうした考え方に基づいて第2集では大きく舵を切り、各編者がテクストすべてを組み上げた。そのため作品によっては本文編集に関する注釈を煩雑に感じる読者もおられようが、注釈に目を通していただくと、問題になっている部分が実は作品の読みを左右する要なのだとご納得いただけると思う。

　第2集の企画を大修館編集部の北村和香子さんにご検討いただいたのは 2017 年秋。無謀とも思える提案に終始にこやかかつ冷静沈着に耳を傾け、企画全体を辛抱強く推し進めて下さった。第2集8巻の作品選定は大いに悩んだが、第1集『ハムレット』で編者を務めた河合祥一郎氏からのご提言もいただき、喜劇・悲劇・歴史劇・ローマ劇・ロマンス劇からバランスよく作品を選ぶことができた。ご両名にこの場を借りて心から御礼を申し上げる。「さらに第2期、第3期と刊行をつづけ、やがてはシェイクスピアの全作品を網羅できれば」という初代の思いが次に繋がることを願いつつ、あとは読者諸氏のご支援とご叱正を乞う次第である。

　　大修館シェイクスピア双書　第2集　編集者代表　　井出　新

まえがき

　大学院に入ってしばらくして、小津次郎先生のゼミで『じゃじゃ馬ならし』について発表する機会があった。シェイクスピア研究のとば口に立ったばかりの私は、出版されてまだ数年だった第2アーデン版の解説といくつかの論文を読み、それらで得た知識の断片を組み合わせて「シェイクスピアはペンブルック伯一座を経て宮内大臣一座に加わったのではないか」という内容の報告をした。小津先生は静かに「肝心のバーベッジが出てこないね」と短くコメントされただけだった。解説をなぞっただけの発表の底の浅さを見透かされたことに、当然と思いながらも、私は少ししょげた気分になった。

　その頃だったと思うが、小津先生から「研究は事実をブルドーザーでかき集めることではなく、事実と事実の間をコンシート（conceit）で結ぶことだよ」と言われたことがあった。"Conceit"と聞いて、ジョン・ダンの形而上詩の「奇想」――飛躍した難解な比喩――を連想した私は意表を突かれ、どこか腑に落ちないまま"conceit"という言葉にかすかな違和感を覚えていた。

　それから40年ほどの年月が過ぎて、あらためて『じゃじゃ馬ならし』に取り組み、ひとつの作品を編むことは、議論の整理や事実の検証の上に立って、そこから自分の想念を組み立てていく創造的営為であることを実感した。大衆劇場の平土間に立ち並ぶ観客の喝采や野次、大陸ヨーロッパから続々と流入する新しい文化、日常を不安と恐怖に陥れるペストの流行、運や流行に左右される劇団経営、そうした大きな絵の中に酔っぱらいのスライや、威勢の良いペトルーチオとキャタリーナを登場させる。古版本に紛れこんだ役者の実名や、セリフの中の凝った言葉遊び、もろも

ろの小さな材料を繋ぎ合わせて大きな絵を完成させるには、まさに"conceit"と呼ぶべき大胆な機知が必要だ。40年を経てようやく恩師の言葉の意味を理解できた。

　本書は40年前のそんなナイーブな私自身を読者のひとりとして想定している。辞書と首っ引きで遅々としたスピードで読むうちにドラマとしての面白さなどわからなくなってしまう。私はそんな不出来な学生だった。初学者でも楽しめるように、できるだけ細かく注は付けたが、シェイクスピアを原文で読む楽しみは、連なる言葉の躍動感の中で個々の語が本来持っている意味が鮮やかに際立ってくるところにあると思う。シェイクスピアの面白さは英語の面白さだ。英語を日本語に置き換えるよりも、英語でパラフレーズする方がその面白さへの近道であると考え、そのような注釈が多くなっている。

　1980年前後から、『じゃじゃ馬ならし』はフェミニズム批評の格好の材料になってきた。しかし先鋭化した理論は、ときに議論の精緻さを追求するあまり、自己完結的な抽象性を帯びてしまうことがままある。一方で、舞台の上の『じゃじゃ馬ならし』はドタバタ騒ぎと見下されようと、女性差別の産物と批判されようと、怒鳴ったり、罵ったり、殴ったり、身体性たっぷりの喜劇として繰り返し楽しまれてきた。ジェンダーをめぐる政治的課題と、民衆的笑いが共存するのが『じゃじゃ馬ならし』だ。この混在の魅力を、多くの人が本書から読みとってくださることを願っている。

　本書の編注に際しては、数多くの先行の版本、研究書、翻訳を参考にさせてもらった。中でも大場建治先生の岩波文庫『じゃじゃ馬馴らし』は、本文の校訂においても、作品成立をめぐる議論においても、学術研究の範を示してくださり、負うところが特に大きい。悠然と前を行く師の背中をはるか彼方に見ながら、後ろから懸命に追いかける思いだった。改めて感謝申し上げる。

　また遅々として進まぬ仕事ぶりを、辛抱強く見守ってくださった大修館書店の北村和香子氏にも心より御礼申し上げる。デジタル技術が飛躍的進歩を遂げ、必要な情報や欲しいコンテンツが即座に入手できる今日にあって、ゆっくりと時間をかけてシェイクスピアの原文を読む経験は、また新たな意義を持つだろう。このような時代にシェイクスピア双書の出版を実現してくださった大修館書店にも敬意と謝意を表したい。

　2023年　春

前沢浩子

目次

挿絵リスト

凡例・略語表

1. 凡例

(1) 本文

　本書のテクストは 1623 年に出版されたシェイクスピアの全集（First Folio、以下「二つ折本」または「F1」とする）を底本として、現代綴りへの変更、ト書きや話者表示および句読法の整理修正を行ったものである。こうした編纂作業に際しては、第 3 アーデン版、ケンブリッジ版をはじめとする複数の校訂本を参照した。二つ折本は Early English Books Online (EEBO) に収録されたものを利用した。また付録として収録した *The Taming of A Shrew* からの抜粋は、The Malone Society Reprints, vol. 160（1998）を底本とし、Roy Miller 編のケンブリッジ版等を参考にして編纂した。

(2) 登場人物一覧

　二つ折本における登場人物名は一貫性を欠いている。キャタリーナは頭書きでは Kate だが、'Katerina'、'Katherina'、'Katherine' とさまざまな呼ばれ方や表記が混在している。スライも頭書きでは Sly だが、ト書きでは 'Beggar' となっている。本書ではそれらを登場人物一覧にある名前で統一した。キャタリーナに関してはイタリアを舞台としていることを考慮して Katherina とした。他の登場人物も含め、名前の発音はイタリア語風な英語とするのが、現在は最も一般的であり、本書でもそれを反映した発音記号を付した。

(3) 注釈

　語注は右ページでの対注とし、歴史背景などの説明は後注とすることを原則としたが、スペースの関係で必ずしもその限りではない。後注とするものは該当箇所に「⇒後注」と記した。

　幕・場・行数の表示にはアラビア数字を用いた。たとえば 2.1.315 は第 2 幕第 1 場 315 行を指す。ト書きのうち ［ ］ で示されている箇所は、二つ折本にないことを表す。

　ト書きに関する注釈は、直前の行数の後にト書きの中の行数をつけて示す。例えば 47.2. は本文 47 行目に加えられたト書きの 2 行目である。0.1. は本文が始まる前のト書きである。

　シェイクスピアの作品名、登場人物名、その他の人名、作品名の日本語表記は、原則として『シェイクスピア辞典』（研究社）に拠る。またイタリアの地名の日本語表記に関しては、英語での呼び方を原則とした。たとえば Padua はイタリア語でのパドヴァではなく、パデュアとした。ただしロンバルディアやピサのように日本で長く定着している地名についてはイタリア語での呼び方を選んだ。

2. 略語表

Capell	*Mr William Shakespeare his Comedies, Histories, and Tragedies*, ed. Edward Capell, 10 vols (1768)
Collier	*Works of William Shakespeare*, ed. J. P. Collier, 8 vols (1842-44)
EEBO	*Early English Books Online*
F1	The First Folio of Shakespeare (1623)
F2	The Second Folio of Shakespeare (1632)
Knight	*The Pictorial Edition of the Works of Shakespeare*, ed. Charles Knight, 8 vols (1838-43)
Malone	*The Plays and Poems of William Shakespeare*, ed. Edward Malone, 10 vols (1790)
OED	*The Oxford English Dictionary Online*
Pope	*The Works of Shakespeare*, ed. Alexander Pope, 6 vols (1723-5)
Rowe	*The Works of Mr William Shakespear*, ed. Nicholas Rowe, 6 vols (1709)
RSC	Royal Shakespeare Company
A Shrew	*The Taming of A Shrew*
The Shrew	*The Taming of the Shrew*
SQ	*Shakespeare Quarterly*
Sisson	*William Shakespeare: The Complete Works*, ed. C. J. Sisson (1954)
Theobald	*The Works of Shakespeare*, ed. Lewis Theobald, 7 vols (1733)
Warburton	*The Works of Shakespeare*, ed. William Warburton, 8 vols (1747)

大修館シェイクスピア双書　第2集

じゃじゃ馬ならし

THE TAMING OF THE SHREW

解　説

1.　作品の成立まで

　他のシェイクスピア作品同様、いや他の作品以上に、『じゃじゃ馬ならし』のテクストと成立年代と材源の問題は、相互に絡み合っている。従来の研究では、成立年代の推定について、大きな幅があり、最も早いものでは 1589 年、最も遅い時期を取るものは 1604 年だ[1]。前者に従えばこの喜劇は、劇作を始めたばかりの無名の作家が書いた最初の作品であり、後者を主張する研究者は、十分に経験を積んだ人気劇作家が若い頃の習作を自ら書き直した作品とみなす。

　この推定範囲の幅の広さの最大の要因は、1594 年に出版された四つ折本 *The Taming of A Shrew*（以下 *A Shrew* と記す）と 1623 年の F1（第一・二つ折本）に収録された *The Taming of the Shrew*（以下 *The Shrew* と記す）の不明確な関係だ。*A Shrew* の四つ折本には作者名はない。登場人物名はスライとキャタリーナ（ケイト）を除いて異なっており、舞台もイタリアとギリシアで違っているが、筋書きにも言葉遣いにも共通する要素は多く、どちらかがどちらかに影響を与えていることは確実だ。だとしたらどちらが先か。あるいはこの 2 つより前に、原型となる作品があったのか。2 つの前後関係の推定は、成立年代の議論に直接つながっている。

---

[1] 1589 年と推定するのは、第 2 アーデン版（1981）の編者 Brian Morris。一方 Eric Sams は *The Real Shakespeare*（1995）で若い時の作品を自ら書き直すのがシェイクスピアの真の姿だったとして 1603 年以降の改作を示唆する。

　A Shrew は表紙に「ペンブ
ルック伯一座によってたびたび
上演」されたと印刷されており、
この劇団の活動期間から 1592-
93 年に上演されたものと判断
できる。*A Shrew* を *The Shrew*
から派生したものと考えるのな
ら、*The Shrew* の成立は 1592
年より前ということになる。一
方、*A Shrew* が先行作品であり、
The Shrew はそれを材源とし
て書かれたと考えれば、*The*
Shrew は 1593 年以降の成立の
可能性が高い。2 つの版の本文

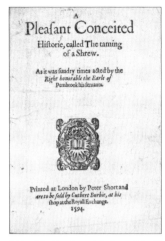

図 1　*The Taming of A Shrew* 四つ折
本（1594 年）の表紙
Huntington Library 所蔵

そのものの比較に加え、当時の劇団の興行の記録、テクストに紛
れこんだ役者の実名、他のシェイクスピア作品との関連など、複
数の要素が絡み合い議論は極めて複雑に錯綜（さくそう）している。

　ここではそうした複雑な議論を少しでもわかりやすくするため
に次のような作業仮説を立ててみよう。念のため繰り返すが、あ
くまでもこれは「作業仮説」だ。

1.1　仮説——*The Taming of the Shrew* の成立まで

　「シェイクスピアは 1587 年にストラットフォードにやってきた
劇団女王一座に役者として加わりロンドンに出て、役者をしなが
ら劇作もするようになっていた。女王一座のレパートリーにはヘ
ンリー五世やリチャード三世の時代を描いた歴史劇があった。リ
ア王と 3 人の娘の年代記もあった。シェイクスピアはそれらの劇
に役者として関わった。

　1588 年に一座の人気道化タールトンが死ぬと、女王一座は弱体化し、何人かの役者はストレンジ卿一座に移っている。役者とともにいくつかの戯曲もストレンジ卿一座のレパートリーに移っていく。役者として劇団に加わったシェイクスピアも、やがて劇作にも才能を発揮し、ヘンリー六世の治世を描いた芝居が評判になった。1592 年 3 月から 6 月までの間、ストレンジ卿一座は『ハリー六世』という芝居を上演している。

　だが 1592 年夏、ロンドンでペストの死者が増え、劇場は閉鎖を命じられた。劇団は人数を絞って地方巡業に出ざるを得なかった。女王一座も小さなペンブルック伯一座へと再編成して、旅に出る。シェイクスピアはロンドンに残り、長編詩『ヴィーナスとアドーニス』『ルークリース陵辱』を書いて青年貴族サウサンプトン伯に献呈し、またいくつものソネットを書いて上流階級の若者たちの間で回し読みされていた。一方、ペンブルック伯一座は地方興行がうまくいかず、追いつめられた役者たちは持っていた戯曲を出版者に売り払わざるを得なくなった。その中に *A Shrew* があった。

　1594 年春、ようやくペストが収束して劇場が再開されたとき、女王一座とストレンジ卿一座のメンバーが、新たに宮内大臣ヘンリー・ケアリーを庇護者として劇団を作り直す。シェイクスピアもかつての仲間たちとともにこの劇団の主要メンバーとなる。この新しい劇団のためにシェイクスピアは新しい喜劇を書いた。素材にしたのは、ペンブルック伯一座の *A Shrew* だ。旅興行に適した 11 人の役者で上演できる 1,500 行ほどの短い喜劇を、シェイクスピアは大幅に書き換えた。6 月にロンドンの南の郊外サリー州にあるニューイントン・バッツ座で上演されたこの喜劇が *The Shrew* である。」

　もしこの仮説の通りであれば、*The Taming of the Shrew* の成立年は 1594 年ということになる。

1.2　実証の限界

　さてこの仮説を検証してみよう。実はこの仮説に対する否定的な材料は数多くある。まず *A Shrew* の前にその元になる戯曲があったことはほぼ間違いない。*A Shrew* のト書きには 'Simon' という役者の名前が混入している箇所がある。おそらく 1592 年 8 月に亡くなったサイモン・ジュエル（Simon Jewell）という役者を指すと考えられる。だとすればペストの流行前にジュエルが出演していた Shrew 劇があったはずだ。

　また『悪党を見分けるコツ』（*A Knack to Know a Knave*）という作者不詳の戯曲に *A Shrew* および *The Shrew* と共通の言葉遣いが多く見つかっている。『悪党を見分けるコツ』は 1592 年 6 月に「新作」としてストレンジ卿一座が上演している。『悪党を見分けるコツ』が Shrew 劇から言葉の借用をしたのであれば、このことも 1592 年以前の Shrew 劇の存在を示唆している。

　1594 年 6 月のニューイントン・バッツ座での上演の記録を *The Shrew* と考えることにも反論の余地がある。興行主フィリップ・ヘンズロウが 1594 年 6 月 11 日に 9 シリングの収入とした記録には 'the tamiynge of A shrowe' と表記されている。果たして冠詞ひとつに関係者たちがどれほど気を配っていたかは不明だが、このヘンズロウの記録が *The Shrew* ではなく *A Shrew* を指す可能性は否定できない。またヘンズロウの記録には新作を示す 'ne'（=new）という付記がない。もしもニューイントン・バッツの上演が *The Shrew* だったとしても、1594 年の時点では新作ではなかった可能性がある。

　さらに *A Shrew* とともにペンブルック伯一座が手放した他の

戯曲との関連も問題となる。ヘンリー六世の治世を描いた『ヨーク、ランカスター両名家の抗争・第1部』と『ヨーク公リチャードの実話悲劇』という四つ折本が 1594-95 年に出版された。これらの四つ折本は 1623 年の全集に含まれた『ヘンリー六世』第2部、第3部の亜流と考えられている。もともとあったシェイクスピアの戯曲を改作して崩れたテクスト、いわゆる「悪い四つ折本」だ。それと同じ関係を、*A Shrew* と *The Shrew* の間に想定することは十分に合理的だ。*A Shrew* を *The Shrew* から派生した「悪い四つ折本」と捉える立場は 1920 年代のピーター・アレグザンダーから始まり、20世紀後半にはそれが主流となっている[2]。

　こうした推論の積み重ねから、*The Shrew* はシェイクスピアがペストの流行以前に（おそらく）女王一座のために書いていたもので、*A Shrew* はそれをペンブルック伯一座の旅興行のために、改作した戯曲であろうと考え、*The Shrew* の成立年代を 1590-92 年と推定する研究者が多い。[3]

1.3　推論の可能性

　こうした研究は、複数のテクスト中に見出せる言葉遣いの異同、同時代の文書に残る記録など、微小な事実の粘り強い検証の上に成り立っている。20世紀以降の文学研究が科学的指向を強め、実証性を重んじてきた成果である。ただし、自然科学研究が検証のための再現性や反復性を重視するのに対し、シェイクスピア研究はあくまで見出した小さな事実の上に推論を重ねるしかない。1592 年以前に、*A Shrew* に先立つ Shrew 劇はほぼ確実に存在し

---

[2] Peter Alexander, '*The Taming of the Shrew*,' *TLS* (16 September 1926).

[3] 最新の版本である第3ケンブリッジ版（2017）の編者 Ann Thompson も *A Shrew* を *The Shrew* の「悪い四つ折本」とみなし、*The Shrew* の成立を 1590-92 年と推定している。

たとして、それがシェイクスピアの二つ折本の *The Shrew* であったと判断する決定的な証拠は、実のところない。*A Shrew* の元になったのは別のすでに失われた戯曲だと推測することも十分に可能なのだ。

　女王一座（あるいはストレンジ卿一座）に、『原じゃじゃ馬』（*Ur-Shrew*）と呼べる作品があって、それをペンブルック伯一座の旅興行用にしたのが *A Shrew* だったという説を支持する研究者も少なくない。このように失われた作品を想定すれば辻褄の合う部分は出てくる。ジュエルが登場したのは『原じゃじゃ馬』で、『悪党を見分けるコツ』も『原じゃじゃ馬』から言葉を借りて書かれた。シェイクスピアが『原じゃじゃ馬』に出演していた、あるいは劇作に関わった可能性もある[4]。

　第3アーデン版（2010年）の編者バーバラ・ホジドンは、*The Shrew* の編集者は「未解決事件の再調査を命じられた刑事」のようだと述べている[5]。この *A Shrew* と *The Shrew* をめぐる案件については、どこまで追求しても、確実な事実はつかみ得ない。迷宮のような研究史を振り返り、ホジドンは *The Shrew* と *A Shrew* の関係について新たな視点を提示している。2つの作品を、どちらかがもう一方の材源あるいは亜流とする直接の前後関係で関連づけるのではなく、1590年代前半以降、上演条件に合わせた Shrew 劇が複数書かれ、改変されてきた、その流動的な状況の中でそれぞれ独自に成立した作品とホジドンは捉える。ホジドンはさらなる証拠がない限り確実な成立年代の断定は不可能であると断念しながらも、*The Shrew* が *A Shrew* よりも後、1594年

---

[4] この『原じゃじゃ馬』説の支持者には、オックスフォード版（1982）の編者 H. J. Oliver やペンギン版（1968）の編者 G. R. Hibbard などがいる。

[5] Barbara Hodgdon, ed. *The Taming of the Shrew* (London: Mehuen, 2010), 7.

に成立した可能性に議論の余地を残している。

1.4　解釈の必要性

　18世紀末にシェイクスピア学の礎を築いたエドマンド・マローン以来、19世紀までの編者や研究者の多くは、*A Shrew* を *The Shrew* の材源と捉えてきた。その判断の根底にあるのは、2つの作品の優劣の判断だ。*A Shrew* と *The Shrew* の作品としての質にははっきりとした差がある。大場建治が「水が川下から川上に流れることはありえない」と断言するように、優れたものから劣ったものが作られるという流れは、いかにも不自然と感じられる[6]。関連する事実の発掘と検証、それに基づく推論の後でなお、*A Shrew* と *The Shrew* の関係をめぐる議論は、最終的には作品の内側に入っての解釈と比較に立ち返らざるを得ない。

　この2つの作品の最大の違いはじゃじゃ馬キャタリーナをならす本筋ではなく、キャタリーナの妹の結婚をめぐる副筋の方だ。*A Shrew* のキャタリーナには2人の妹がいる。旅興行の少人数用の上演台本を作るのに、妹の数を1人から2人に増やすとは考えにくいという単純なひっかかりもある。それよりもはっきりと違うのは副筋の恋愛騒動の設定だ。*A Shrew* も *The Shrew* も、古典喜劇プラウトゥスの再現をめざしたアリオストーのイタリア語喜劇を翻案したジョージ・ギャスコインの『取り違え』（*Supposes*）を材源としている。偽物の父親を仕立てて急場をしのごうとするという展開など共通するところは多い。だが *A Shrew* では下の妹に恋をした貴族の息子が商人と身分を偽って求婚するという筋書きになっている。*A Shrew* の身分違いの恋という設定は、ギャスコインの『取り違え』と重なり合う。『取

---

[6] 大場建治訳、編注『じゃじゃ馬馴らし』（岩波書店、2008年）, 241.

り違え』では高貴な生まれの男が、召使いに身分をやつして恋する女を手にいれる。この身分違いの恋という設定は *A Shrew* の副筋は *The Shrew* を介さずに『取り違え』から直接取り込んでいる要素と考えることが可能だ。

こうした設定以上に違うのは、喜劇性の差とでも言うべき、劇作法の違いだ。*A Shrew* の 2 人の妹たちは混乱というほどの混乱もなく親友同士の 2 人の男とめでたく結ばれる。2 人の妹たちが競い合うようにして、それぞれの愛の強さを語る場面がひとつのクライマックスだ。そこで語られる台詞には、ギリシア・ローマ神話への言及や誇張した表現が散りばめられている。クリストファー・マーロウの詩行の、模倣か剽窃かあるいはパロディかと思われるような、大げさな恋愛詩のやりとりが続く。

一方の *The Shrew* では、ビアンカひとりに 3 人の求婚者が群がり、オウィディウスからの引用や音楽理論を用いた高度なワードゲームのような言語遊戯を通して、騙しあい、ライバルを出し抜こうとする。この副筋だけを比較すれば、*A Shrew* と *The Shrew* は、まったく別の作品と受け止めるのが自然であろう。

The Shrew にはむしろ、1594 年以降に書かれた他のシェイクスピアの喜劇との共通点が多く見出せる。1594 年 12 月にグレイズ・イン法学院で上演された『間違いの喜劇』とは、偽物のせいで本物が門前払いを食わされる場面がそっくりだ。ペトルーチオとキャタリーナの丁々発止のやりとりは、『空騒ぎ』のベネディックとビアトリスの原型のようだ。

そもそもキャタリーナとビアンカという対照的な女 2 人の組み合わせは、『間違いの喜劇』のエイドリアーナとルシアーナ、『夏の夜の夢』のヘレナとハーミア、『空騒ぎ』のビアトリスとヒーローなど、シェイクスピアお得意のパターンだ。やがて『お気に召すまま』のロザリンドとシーリア、『十二夜』のヴァイオラと

オリヴィアへとつながる喜劇の女性登場人物たちの系譜を考えれば、個性の違う2人の少年俳優を念頭において、その違いを生かした軽快な喜劇を次々と書いていった宮内大臣一座の座付き作者シェイクスピアの姿が浮かび上がってくる。キャタリーナとビアンカは、この系譜の最初に位置するのではないだろうか。成立年代の考察には、事実の検証、推察とともに、最終的にはこうした解釈が入らざるを得ない。

1.5 「作者不詳」から「シェイクスピア」へ

冒頭の作業仮説に戻ってみよう。シェイクスピアがいつストラットフォードからロンドンに来たかも、最初にどこの劇団に入ったのかも、ペストの流行期に果たしてロンドンにいたのか、旅興行に一緒に行ったのかも、確たる根拠となる資料はない。1580年代の終わりから1594年まで、商業演劇が首都ロンドンの娯楽として定着しようかという時代、劇団の離合集散やペストの流行による劇場閉鎖という動乱期にいたのが若き日のシェイクスピアだ。田舎町ストラットフォード出身の無名の役者についての記録が残っているはずもない。

その無名の役者が次第に劇作に関わったとしても、劇団仲間たちとの共同作業だった可能性はきわめて高い。18世紀の全集編者ウォーバートン（Warburton）以来、*The Shrew* はシェイクスピアの単独作ではなく、他の作家の手が入っていると考える編者、研究者は少なくない。近年ではデータ化されたテクストを使った言語学的分析から、クリストファー・マーロウを共作者とする説が有力となっている[7]。

The Shrew はシェイクスピアが単独で一気に書き上げたものではなく、揺れ動く劇団の状況に合わせて書き改められながら、次第に今あるような形に変容していったその産物なのではないだ

ろうか。1580 年代の終わり、無名の役者シェイクスピアが所属していた劇団に Shrew 劇はあった。シェイクスピアが台詞を書いた部分もあったのかもしれない。1592 年には、旅興行用の少人数用の台本が書かれて、ペンブルック伯一座が演じた。その後、1594 年の劇場再開に合わせて、さらに書き直しがされた。この数年をかけたプロセスの中で、Shrew 劇はシェイクスピアの劇作手法をよりはっきりと示す喜劇 *The Shrew* へと変容してきたのではないか。

　戯曲の、特に初期のシェイクスピアの作品の「成立年代」はそもそもどこか特定の年に限定できるものではなく、戯曲は劇団という共同作業の現場で、姿を変えながら、ある形を取るようになるものであろう。その間にシェイクスピア自身も無名の存在から、宮内大臣一座の主要メンバーという明確なプロフィールがはっきりしてくる。*The Shrew* の成立をめぐる、18 世紀以来 21 世紀までの錯綜した議論は、そのような流動的状況の一瞬を捉えようとしてきた、無数の努力の集積だ。だが *The Shrew* の成立は特定の年へと限定するのではなく、流動する興行条件の中で、数年をかけて変容してきた戯曲の複数のテクストの混成の結果と捉える方が実態に近いのではないだろうか。

2.　不完全なテクスト

　四つ折本の *A Shrew*（1594 年）と二つ折本 *The Shrew*（1623 年）の不明瞭な関係は、テクストの編纂にも影響を与えてきた。*A Shrew* のテクストが、誰が、いつ、どのように関わって出来た

---

[7] John V. Nance, 'Early Shakespeare and the Authorship of *The Taming of the Shrew*', in Rory Loughnane and Andrew J. Power (eds), *Early Shakespeare, 1588-1594* (Cambridge: Cambridge UP, 2020), 261-83.

ものなのか確定できぬまま、18世紀以来の編纂者たちは、二つ折本 *The Shrew* テクストの欠落や混乱を四つ折本 *A Shrew* で補ってきた。シェイクスピア全集の最初の編纂者であるニコラス・ロウは *A Shrew* を参照して、*The Shrew* のテクストにト書きを加え、台詞の頭書き（speech prefix）の混乱を修正した。本書も含め、現代に至る版本の多くは、このロウの校訂のいくつかをそのまま踏襲している。その点で *The Shrew* のテクスト編纂には、*A Shrew* のテクストが利用され続けてきたと言える。

　二つ折本の *The Shrew* のテクストの最大の欠落はスライの消失と考える編纂者も多い。*The Shrew* では冒頭に登場したスライが第1幕第1場の後で一瞬登場した後、そのまま消えてしまう。*A Shrew* ではところどころでスライのコメントが挟まれ、最後も眠りから覚めたスライが最高の夢を見たと語るエピローグで締めくくられる。詩人でシェイクスピア全集の編集もしたポープ（Pope）は *A Shrew* にあって *The Shrew* にはないスライの登場場面5箇所をすべて、*The Shrew* に挿入してこの欠落を埋めた。王政復古期から18世紀にかけての編纂は、このように不足部分を補い、狭雑物や乱れを除去して、シェイクスピアのテクストを改善することを目指していた。一方でマローン（Malone）は、*A Shrew* をシェイクスピアの作ではないと判断し、スライの登場場面を取り除いて、1623年の二つ折本に近いテクストへと回帰している。

　現代の版本では *The Shrew* の編纂者たちのほとんどが、*A Shrew* のスライの登場場面のみを抜き出して巻末の付録として収めている。本書も参照資料として、同様の抜き書きを付録に収めている。だが第3アーデン版の編者ホジドンはあくまで、*The Shrew* と *A Shrew* はそれぞれに独立した別個の戯曲という立場にたち、*A Shrew* のファクシミリ版を全編そっくり付録として

いる。*A Shrew*のスライ登場場面だけを抜き出す作業は、*The Shrew*の欠落を補うために2つのテクストを合成させるという発想につながる可能性を持つ。ホジドンはその発想を避け、並行して存在する自立した作品として全編収録という選択をしているのだ。

　テクストの合成を避けたとしても、それでも*The Shrew*におけるスライの消失が「欠落」なのかどうかという問題は残る。*The Shrew*は開口一番、スライの'I'll feeze you, in faith.'「お前なんかやっつけてやる」という威勢の良い捨て台詞で始まる。*A Shrew*の冒頭では酒場の給仕人に毒づかれて追い出されたあと、一人になったスライが'Tilly vally! By crisee, Tapster, I'll feeze you anon!'「バカ言うんじゃねえ。まったく、給仕人よ、すぐにやっつけてやるからな」と、負け惜しみを言う。給仕人とスライの小競り合いで平凡に始まる*A Shrew*と、酔っ払いの怒鳴り声1行でドラマに引き込む*The Shrew*の勢いの差の違いを、さすがシェイクスピアの手腕とほめそやすこともできるのだが、それよりも注目すべきはこの'feeze'という見慣れない一語だろう。*OED*は'I'll feeze you'という脅し文句の数少ない用例として*The Shrew*を引用しているが、めったに使われないこの言葉が*A Shrew*と*The Shrew*に共通して使われているのは偶然であるはずがない。

　このスライの発する'feeze'という言葉は、どちらが先にせよ、2つの作品の間に明らかに強い影響関係があることを示している。これだけ濃厚な結びつきを示すスライの登場場面が、*A Shrew*では終幕にもあり、*The Shrew*では途中消失するというのは、やはり考えにくい。その欠落を*A Shrew*のテクストで補うことの是非は置いておいて、*The Shrew*のスライの登場場面は、もともとなかったのではなく、どこかで失われてしまったと考える

方が妥当であろう。

　The Shrew のテクストの不完全さを示唆するのはスライの途中消失だけではない。*The Shrew* には「ホーテンシオ問題」と呼ばれる不可解な点がある。第3幕第2場、花婿ペトルーチオの遅刻や奇妙奇天烈な服装を弁護するトラーニオの台詞があるが、これは本来、ペトルーチオの親友ホーテンシオの台詞だった可能性があると考えられている。また第4幕第5場、たまたま旅の道中で出会ったヴィンセンシオに、ペトルーチオとホーテンシオはビアンカとルーセンシオがすでに結婚したと告げているが、これは劇の展開上、辻褄が合っていない。ルーセンシオとビアンカの秘密結婚はまだ実行されていないし、そもそも第4幕第2場でトラーニオ扮するルーセンシオはホーテンシオとともにビアンカの不誠実さに呆れ果て、ビアンカになど二度と求婚しないと誓いあっている。そのルーセンシオがビアンカと結婚したとホーテンシオが断言できるはずがない。

　こうした筋書き上の食い違いをテクストの瑕疵とみなすか、あるいは観客には気にならない、いやむしろ取り違え満載のスピーディな劇の展開をさらに加速させる効果とみなすかは、解釈の範囲の問題かもしれない。ホーテンシオは喜劇的効果のためにご都合主義的に利用された脇役に過ぎないとも考えられる。しかし第3幕第1場や第4幕第2場など、ホーテンシオの台詞の頭書きの乱れが集中していることを考え合わせると、どこかの段階でホーテンシオの人物造形に改変が加えられ、その結果として筋書きの齟齬が生じてしまったという可能性が高い。

　1623年の二つ折本の *The Shrew* の印刷所原本の性質も、この問題に関連してくる。散見されるト書きの乱れから、舞台での上演を経ていない原稿が印刷に使われたのではないかと推定されている。また明らかな印刷上エラーの多さは、清書を経ていない草

稿からの印刷の可能性を示唆している。作者自身の草稿なのか、筆耕による清書原稿なのかを断定することは難しいが、上述の「スライの消失」や「ホーテンシオ問題」を考え合わせると、印刷の原本として使われた原稿は、戯曲のいずれかの時点での完成形を示すものではなく、何回かの改変を部分的に反映した原稿の寄せ集めだった可能性もある。3人の植字工が関わった *The Shrew* の組版には、工程の途中で中断期間があったことが明らかにされている[8]。原本となる原稿が最初から最後まで一通り揃っていなかった可能性もある。

　The Shrew が、一気に完成形に至ったのではなく、1590 年代前半に何回かの改変を経ながら徐々にシェイクスピア喜劇としての形をなしたとするなら、1623 年に印刷所に回された原稿も、そのプロセスを反映した、いくつかの段階に書き加えられたり、書き直されたりした原稿で、しかも部分的には寄せ集めだったのかもしれない。二つ折本の *The Shrew* は一編の戯曲の完成形を示すテクストではなく、作品成立の経緯を反映させた不完全なテクストとして読まれるべきであろう。

3.　批評史

　The Shrew と *A Shrew* の関係についての議論をひとまず終えたところで、ここからは『じゃじゃ馬ならし』という邦題に戻ろう。20 世紀前半までさかのぼると、『じゃじゃ馬ならし』は決して評価の高い喜劇だったとは言えない。よく知られているように、ジョージ・バーナード・ショーは『じゃじゃ馬ならし』の終幕は「不愉快」で，「隣に女性がいれば、良識ある男性は恥じいらざる

---

[8] Charlton Hinman, *Printing and Proof-Reading of the First Folio of Shakespeare* (London: Oxford UP, 1963), vol. 2. 446-62.

を得ない」と書いた。詩人 W. H. オーデンも「シェイクスピア唯一の失敗作」と呼んでいる[9]。20世紀半ばまで、この劇は単なる笑劇（ファルス）として軽視されるか、あるいは真剣な議論の対象とはされない傾向があった。

　その傾向に歯止めをかけ、『じゃじゃ馬ならし』擁護に回る議論の方向性は2つあった。ひとつは歴史的な相対化によって、この劇の地位回復を図ろうとする試みだ。チョーサーの「バースの女房」をはじめ、中世の説話やチューダー朝のインタールードあるいはバラッドには、気性や言葉遣いの荒い女が、暴力的に制裁され、従順な妻へと飼い慣らされていくモチーフは数多く見出せる。広い意味でこれらは『じゃじゃ馬ならし』の間接的な材源と言える。その系譜の中においてみれば、ペトルーチオが抜きん出て横暴な人物とは言えない。これらの物語に出てくる妻を叩いたり監禁したりする夫たちに比較してみれば、ペトルーチオのキャタリーナに対する振る舞いには、知性や人間らしさを読み取れると『じゃじゃ馬ならし』を擁護する[10]。

　もうひとつの擁護論は、キャタリーナやペトルーチオの演劇的自意識によってこの劇の喜劇性を解明しようとする立場だ。2人は「じゃじゃ馬ならし」というゲームのプレーヤーであり、食事や睡眠を奪うというペトルーチオの暴力性もロール・プレイングであり、終幕のキャタリーナの長演説にも、従順な妻を巧みに演

[9] 1897年、ショーはギャリックの改作『キャサリンとペトルーチオ』を観たあとで、このようにシェイクスピアの『じゃじゃ馬ならし』を批判しながら、それでもギャリックの寸劇よりはマシと *Saturday Review* に書いている。G. B. Shaw, *Shaw on Shakespeare*, ed. Edwin Wilson（New York: Books of Library Press, 1971）, 187-88. W. H. Auden, *Lectures on Shakespeare*（New Jersey: Princeton UP, 2000）, 63-64.

[10] Anne Barton, *The Riverside Shakespeare*（Boston: Houghton Mifflin, 1974）, ed. Blakemore Evans, 138.

じる楽しみを見出す[11]。この議論には、スライというナイーブな観客の存在を考慮に入れることで、いっそう重曹的な視点が与えられる。演劇が現実のメタファーとして強く機能し、イリュージョンと現実が相互に作用しあっていたシェイクスピアの劇場で、スライは自らも領主の役を演じながら、劇と現実の区別のつけられない観客として「じゃじゃ馬ならし」を見ている[12]。メタ・シアターという切り口から見てみれば、ともすれば次元の低いジャンルと見なされる笑劇という特質には、リアリズムを欠く人工性ゆえにより巧妙な喜劇的仕掛けを見出せる可能性がある。分の悪かった『じゃじゃ馬ならし』も、こうして次第にポジティブな読み直しがなされるようになった。

　1960年代以降、フェミニズムの台頭は白人男性作家シェイクスピアの作品を、女性の視点から読み直すことに直結した。延々と妻の従順を説いたうえに、夫の足元にひれ伏そうとさえするキャタリーナを、フェミニストの旗手でもあったジャーメイン・グリアは、意外なほど好意的に解釈している。キャタリーナは手に負えない女になることによって自己実現を目指し、彼女の強烈な個性に価値を見出すペトルーチオとの結婚は、欺瞞（ぎまん）に満ちたビアンカの結婚より純正なものであり、新たな結婚観を提示しているとグリアは評価する[13]。一方、シェイクスピアに関するフェミニズム批評の端緒を切ったジュリエット・デュシンベリーは、2人の関係に懐疑的だ。チューダー朝の結婚観は男女相互の精神的結びつきを重視する方向に次第に変化していったことを指摘しなが

[11] Alexander Leggatt, *Shakespeare's Comedy of Love* (1974; London and New York: Routledge, 2005)

[12] Ann Righter, *Shakespeare and the Idea of the Play* (London: Chatto and Windus, 1962), 104-06.

[13] ジャーメン・グリア『去勢された女』（ダイアモンド社、1976）下巻287-88.

ら、キャタリーナの現実離れした従順さに真偽の定まらぬ曖昧さを見てとっている[14]。

さらに 1980 年代以降、フェミニズムや歴史主義の理論が先鋭化されるのに従い、『じゃじゃ馬ならし』に対する批評は、にわかに活性化してくる。フェミニストとしてのコッペリア・カーンの視点は「男らしさ」というファンタジーが構築されるメカニズムに向けられた。父権制社会における男性の優越性は、女性の従属という神話に依存して成り立つものであり、男らしさのステレオタイプであるペトルーチオは、男性支配の非合理性を笑劇的に表現して風刺対象になっているとカーンは論じる[15]。

フェミニズム批評の成果も取り込みながら、新歴史主義は歴史を社会的、政治的イデオロギーの動的な集合体とみなし、文学テクストもその一部として、鋭い批判精神を向けるようになった。夫に暴力を振るう悪妻は共同体への侵犯者であるから、村人総出で笑いものにすればいい。カレン・ニューマンは、この「スキミントン」と呼ばれる中世以来のシャリバリ的儀礼に、当時の家族イデオロギーを見る。『じゃじゃ馬ならし』はこのイデオロギーに組み込まれていながら、一方で丁々発止の舌戦でペトルーチオを上回るキャタリーナのレトリックの能力は、強固なイデオロギーを切り崩す可能性を表現しているとニューマンは論じる[16]。

リンダ・ブースも、口うるさい女が社会不安の要因として処罰と嘲笑の対象となり、彼女らの舌が拘禁用の轡（くつわ）で封じ込められて

---

[14] Juliet Dussnberre, *Shakespeare and the Nature of Women*, 3rd edition（New York: Palgrave Macmillan, 2003）, 105-08.

[15] Coppélia Kahn, *Man's Estate: Masculine Identity in Shakespeare*（Berkeley: University of California Press, 1981）, 104-18.

[16] Karen Newman, *Fashioning Femininity and English Renaissance Drama*（Chicago: University of Chicago Press, 1991）, 33-50.

いた近世イングランドの民衆社会の様相を浮かび上がらせた。その歴史が滲（にじ）み出していえる文学テクストが『じゃじゃ馬ならし』であり、キャタリーナに与えられた「口うるさい女（scold）」あるいは「じゃじゃ馬（shrew）」という呼称が、いかに強烈なスティグマであったかをブースは明らかにしている[17]。

　家庭が政治的なイデオロギーだけでなく、経済原則にも支配されていることに着眼したのが、ナターシャ・コルダだ。『じゃじゃ馬ならし』には、持参金、寡婦年金、家財、衣装といった、金とモノについての言及がきわめて多い。妻や娘が夫や父の所有物とみなされていることは、一読すればすぐにわかることだが、キャタリーナの価値が、有用性と結びつく使用価値にあるのではなく、夫の社会的ステイタスを維持するための象徴資本にあるとコルダは読み解く。地主階級であるペトルーチオも結婚によって資産を増やすブルジョア階級の一員にならざるを得ない。キャタリーナの「服従の演説」は経済力を反映する宴会という舞台で、夫の社会階級を象徴的に表現するパフォーマンスとしての価値を持つ[18]。コルダは『じゃじゃ馬ならし』が書かれた初期近代は、家庭が消費と倹約のバランスの上に成り立つ資本形成の場へと変質しつつある時代であったと論じる。

　シェイクスピア作品に現れているジェンダーあるいは家族のポリティクスを論じる際に、しばしば引用されるローレンス・ストーンの家族史では、家父長主義から情愛的個人主義への転換を

---

[17] Lynda E. Boose, 'Scolding Brides and Bridling Scolds: Taming the Woman's Unruly Member', *Shakespeare Quarterly*, 42 (1991), 179-213.

[18] Natasha Korda, 'Household Kates: Domesticating Commodities in *The Taming of the Shrew*', *Shakespeare Quarterly*, 47 (1996), 109-31.

[19] ローレンス・ストーン『家族・性・結婚の社会史－1500年-1800年のイギリス』（勁草書房、1991年）

17 世紀から 18 世紀に見ている[19]。しかし結婚が資産の継承と財産管理の問題であるのか、それとも夫婦や家庭は情愛によって結びつくものか、その二分法によって、前近代から近代への移行を見るという図式のみをストーンの広範な研究から抽出するのは、単純化し過ぎであろう。

娘や妻が家財のひとつであった家父長主義の歴史を批判的に分析し、そこからキャタリーナを愛すべき、あるいは愛されるべき個人として救い出そうとする思考には、ストーンの言う情愛的個人主義を純化して、「純愛イデオロギー」とでも呼ぶべき愛情至上主義を前提としてしまう危惧がある。シェイクスピア喜劇の主題はいずれも愛だが、父や金から完全に解放されているヒロインはいない。それを家父長制という歴史的枠組みだけに遡求させてしまって良いのだろうか。現代の「両性の合意のみに基づいて」いるはずの結婚も、実は政治や経済のネットワークの中に複雑に組み込まれている。自分の価値と相手の価値のマッチングを、恋愛と呼ばずに交換と呼ぶことに抵抗を感じるのは、純愛を特権化する別のイデオロギーが働いているゆえではないか。キャタリーナは、このイデオロギーには縛られていない。男の権力、金、モノにまみれながら奮闘するキャタリーナの姿に、時代や制度を超えた普遍的人間像を見ることは十分に可能なはずだ。

その可能性をフィクションの形で追求しようとしたのが、アン・タイラーの『ヴィネガー・ガール』だ[20]。シェイクスピア劇を現代的に語り直す「ホガース・シェイクスピア」シリーズの1冊として、『じゃじゃ馬ならし』を現代アメリカの大学町を舞台とした小説に書き直している。可愛い妹とは対照的なぶっきら棒な姉

---

[20] Ann Tyler, *Vinegar Girl* (London and New York: Hogarth, 2016)
鈴木潤訳『ヴィネガー・ガール』(集英社、2021 年)

が、父の都合で結婚話を進められてしまうという大筋は『じゃじ
ゃ馬ならし』のままだ。だが主人公ケイトの無愛想ぶりにも関わ
らず、この小説が最終的には甘い恋愛ロマンスに回収されてしま
っているのは、父も結婚相手の男も大学に籍をおく研究者という
金に縁のない職業に設定されていることが理由の1つだろう。金
がない方が愛の純度は高まる。これが近代の資本主義社会を補完
する「神話」であることを、『じゃじゃ馬ならし』は逆照射して
気づかせているのではないか。キャタリーナが滔々と従順を説い
て、賭けに勝ち、父親からもたっぷりと金をもらう。この「ハッ
ピー・エンディング」には、家父長主義にせよ資本主義にせよ恋
愛至上主義にせよ、どれかひとつのイデオロギーには封じ込めら
れない、したたかな多義性がある。この意味で『じゃじゃ馬なら
し』はこれからもなお、未来に開かれた文学テクストとして多く
の批評を呼び込むことになろう。

4.　上演史

　ドタバタ喜劇と低く見られたり、女性蔑視の男の幻想と非難さ
れたりと、批評史における旗色の悪さのわりに、舞台の上では『じ
ゃじゃ馬ならし』は4世紀にわたって、継続して上演され、楽し
まれ続けてきた。シェイクスピアの時代における人気ぶりは、続
編が書かれたことからもうかがえる。ジョン・フレッチャーの『女
の勝利 ── 馴らし屋が馴らされ』(*The Woman's Prize, or The
Tamer Tamed*) は『じゃじゃ馬ならし』の後日譚で、キャタリ
ーナの死後、ペトルーチオが再婚相手のマライアによって暴君ぶ
りを矯正されるという内容だ。『女の勝利』の執筆時期は1611年
ごろと推測されている。『じゃじゃ馬ならし』のペトルーチオの
横暴ぶりが観客にある程度共有されているからこそ、「馴らし屋
が馴らされ」るという続編のオチが面白くなる。実際に、1633

年11月はチャールズ一世の宮廷で『じゃじゃ馬ならし』が上演され、その2日後には『女の勝利』が上演されたという記録が残っている。1631年に出版された *The Shrew* の四つ折本の表紙の「国王一座によってブラックフライアーズ座およびグローブ座で上演された」との記載からも、『じゃじゃ馬ならし』が長期にわたって国王一座のレパートリーのひとつだった可能性を推測できる。

　王政復古期以降19世紀半ば過ぎまでは、『じゃじゃ馬ならし』はそれぞれの時代の求めに応じて大きく改変して上演されてきた。王政復古期の喜劇役者ジョン・レイシーはロンドンを舞台とするドタバタ喜劇『スコットランド人ソーニー』（*Sauny the Scott*, 1667年初演）へと書き直した。服を脱がそうとしたり、歯を抜いたり、あげくのはて埋葬するぞと脅して、妻を暴力的に屈服させる粗野な笑劇で、笑いの中心はレイシー自ら演じた召使いのソーニーだった。この笑劇はさらにジェイムズ・ワースデイルによって歌とダンスをまじえた二幕物のミュージカル笑劇『がみがみ女の矯正』（*A Cure for a Scold*, 1735）に改作されている。

　ハノーヴァー朝の成立を受け、1715年にジャコバイトが反乱を起こしイングランド北西部の町プレストンまで進軍すると、ホイッグの熱心な党員でもあった劇作家チャールズ・ジョンソンは『じゃじゃ馬ならし』のインダクションを利用して酔っ払いの職人スライが登場する政治寸劇『プレストンの靴直し』（*The Cobbler of Preston*, 1716）を書いた。ドルーリー・レイン劇場と競い合っていたリンカーンズ・イン・フィールズ劇場でも、クリストファー・ビュロックが同名の作品を書いて対抗している。

　名誉革命からワーテルローの戦いまでの「長い18世紀」のダイナミックな変化の中で、シェイクスピアはイギリスの国民作家として次第に崇拝の対象へと持ち上げられていく。18世紀演劇

界の大立者であるデイヴィッド・ギャリックは『じゃじゃ馬なら
し』から粗野な部分は削除し、国民作家にふさわしいウィットに
あふれる喜劇『キャサリンとペトルーチオ』（*Catherine and Petruchio*, 1756）へと変身させた。スライの登場するインダクシ
ョンは削除され、ビアンカをめぐる副筋も大幅に単純化された短
い喜劇だ。はつらつとした知性の持ち主のキャサリンと、頑固で
横柄な夫という仮面をかぶった愛情豊かなペトルーチオが、相思
相愛の夫婦になるまでを描いた上品な喜劇になっている。

　19 世紀までギャリックの『キャサリンとペトルーチオ』の人
気は続いた。フィリップ・ケンブル、セアラ・シドンズ、ウィリ
アム・チャールズ・マクリーディ、ヘレン・フォーシット、ヘン
リー・アーヴィング、エレン・テリーといった人気俳優たちも、
多少の改変を加えながら、このギャリックの改作を演じ続けた。
1844 年にはベンジャミン・ウェブスターと J. R. プランシェがヘ
イマーケット劇場で、1856 年にはサミュエル・フェルプスがサ
ドラーズ・ウェルズ劇場で、シェイクスピアの『じゃじゃ馬なら
し』のテクストを復活させた上演を行っている。しかし、それら
は単発的な試みに終わっている。

　本格的にシェイクスピアのテクストが舞台の上に戻ってくるの
は、1887 年にニューヨークの劇場支配人オーガスティン・デイ
リーが自らの劇場で行った上演まで待たなければならない。この
上演はニューヨークでの成功のあと、ロンドンでの公演も主演女
優エイダ・リーンの好演もあって人気を博した。20 世紀に入ると、
それまでの改作や 19 世紀のスペクタクル化された演出への批判
から、シェイクスピア時代の上演に戻る試みが始まる。1895 年
にウィリアム・ポールは当時の詩や衣装を再現するためにエリザ
ベス朝舞台協会を設立した。1913 年には『じゃじゃ馬ならし』
もポールと俳優ジョン・マーティン゠ハーヴィとの協力によって

上演された。

　シェイクスピアの『じゃじゃ馬ならし』のテクストに回帰すれば、ペトルーチオの暴虐やキャタリーナの屈従という、この戯曲の持つ問題性に直面せざるを得ない。18世紀から19世紀まで、笑劇化やテクストの改変によって避けてきた問題に20世紀の演出家や俳優たちはどのように向き合ってきたか、それがそのまま20世紀の『じゃじゃ馬ならし』の上演史となる。一方的な性差別という問題を演出によって「解消」することを目指すか、あるいは逆に「強調」して突きつけるか、その二者択一がおおまかな方向性と言える。

　1953年のジョージ・ディヴァインの演出はスライの枠組みを膨らませ、その枠の中に相思相愛の夫婦が成立する幸せな喜劇を納め込んだ。1960年のジョン・バートンの演出もメタシアターの枠組みの中に問題を溶け込ませている。エリザベス朝の宿屋の中庭を再現し、そこで演じられる喜劇をスライが宿屋のバルコニーから眺めている。その舞台装置が回転して舞台裏があらわになり、いくつかのセリフが楽屋落ちのジョークとして語られ、問題含みの喜劇も役者たちが作り出す美しいイリュージョンになる。

　一方、問題をむき出しにして突きつけたのはチャールズ・マロウィッツだ。マロウィッツはシェイクスピアのテクストに戻ることを超えて、言葉の深層に潜むサブ・テクストをむき出しにすることを目指した。1974年、マロウィッツの『じゃじゃ馬』(*The Shrew*)は、表層のユーモアを剥ぎ取ればこの喜劇がサディスティックな悲劇になりうることを表現した。完全に洗脳されたキャタリーナは、もぬけの殻のようになって服従を語った。

　この解釈の幅の広さと、『じゃじゃ馬ならし』の上演回数の多さは相関していると言える。1961年、ピーター・ホールによってロイアル・シェイクスピア劇団（RSC）が発足して以来、2020

年までの60年間、数年おきに『じゃじゃ馬ならし』は上演され
続け、16人もの演出家がこの劇を手がけている。『リア王』の15
回（演出家は12人）、『夏の夜の夢』の12回と比べてみれば、『じ
ゃじゃ馬ならし』がいかに頻繁に取り上げられるかがわかるだろ
う。その一部を取り上げても、演出の多様性がうかがえる。

　1961年、モーリス・ダニエルズの演出では、ヴァネッサ・レ
ッドグレイヴがキャタリーナに内面性を与えようとした。1973
年のクリフォード・ウィリアムズの演出は、ペストによる劇場閉
鎖で旅に出た役者たちの即興劇という枠組みでの上演だった。
1978年、マイケル・ボグダノフは現代社会に対する問題提起と
して演出した。スーツ姿でマッチョな男性優位性を誇示するジョ
ナサン・プライスのペトルーチオと、その前にひざまずくパオラ・
ディオニオソッティのキャタリーナは、打破すべき男性中心主義
と女性差別の構造を舞台の上で表象した。この上演を見て劇評家
マイケル・ビリントンが『じゃじゃ馬ならし』は二度と上演すべ
きでないと反発したのは、むしろこの劇の問題性をむき出しにで
きた成果であろう[21]。

　1987年のジョナサン・ミラーの演出はマスクをかぶったコメ
ディア・デラルテの役者たちの奏でるルネサンス音楽にのって始
まる時代劇だった。1990年、東京を含むツアーの後、1992年に
ストラットフォードで再演されたビル・アレキサンダーの演出で
は、劇中劇はエリザベス朝に、それを見るスライや領主は現代社
会に設定されるという趣向だ。現代の労働者スライや雇った役者
たちに対する領主や彼の友人たちのあからさまな優越感が、劇中
劇の終幕に向けて揺るがされる。2003年、グレゴリー・ドーラ

---

[21] Michel Billington, 'A spluttering firework', in *The Guardian*, 5 May, 1978, 10.

ンはフレッチャーの『女の勝利―馴らし屋が馴らされ』を同時期に同じ俳優陣で上演した。『じゃじゃ馬ならし』の問いかける問題への答えが『馴らし屋が馴らされ』というわけだ。

RSCの最新の『じゃじゃ馬ならし』は2019年、ジャスティン・オーディバート演出で、主要登場人物の性別をぜんぶまとめて反転させる大胆な試みだった。ペトルーチオはペトルーチア、ルーセンシオはルーセンシアに変えて、この2人の女性がお目当ての夫を獲得するまでを描いている。バプティスタも父親ではなく母親だ。母親たちが支配する母系社会で、エリザベス朝の豪華なコスチュームに身を包んだ女たちが心理的および肉体的暴力で男を従わせる。強要と支配は、男から女であろうと、女から男であろうと同じように問題だ。女性に対する旧弊なジェンダー観の見直しとともに、男らしさもまた問い直すことが求められている時代の『じゃじゃ馬ならし』だった。

日本でも数多くの『じゃじゃ馬ならし』の演出がなされている。

図2　男女を入れ替えた2019年のRSCの公演。演出ジャスティン・オーディバート。Photo by Ikin Yum ©RSC

2010年、松岡和子訳による彩の国さいたま芸術劇場での蜷川幸雄演出は男性俳優だけで演じられた。歌舞伎役者の二代目市川亀治郎（当時）が演じるキャタリーナと、小劇場出身の筧利夫が演じるペトルーチオの舌戦は、まったく異なったセリフ回しのスタイルが激しくぶつかり合う面白さがあり、強烈な印象を残した。

　翻案では、脚本サム・スピーワック、ベラ・スピーワック、作詞作曲コール・ポーターのブロードウェイ・ミュージカル『キス・ミー・ケイト』（Kiss Me Kate, 1948年）がある。『じゃじゃ馬ならし』のミュージカル版の初演をめぐり、離婚したばかりの夫婦の意地の張り合いと和解が、劇中劇とともに進行する。ニューヨークとロンドンでたびたび再演されており、1953年に映画化もされている。日本でも1966年以来、幾度か上演され、1988年には宝塚歌劇団も上演している。

　フランコ・ゼフィレリ監督の映画『じゃじゃ馬ならし』（1967年）は、ハリウッド大スターエリザベス・テイラーとリチャード・バ

図3　男性俳優だけで演じられた彩の国さいたま芸術劇場の『じゃじゃ馬馴らし』（2010年）。演出蜷川幸雄。

ートンが演じるキャタリーナとペトルーチオに焦点を合わせて脚本は単純化されている。ローマで撮影され、ゼフィレリ作品らしくいかにもイタリアという雰囲気の中で繰り広げられる明快で陽気なコメディだ。映画での翻案としては、1999 年のジル・ジュンガー監督『恋のからさわぎ』（*10 Things I Hate about You*）もある。成績優秀で男嫌いの女の子と強引にデートに誘う男の子が次第に愛し合うようになるという学園コメディでヒット作となった。これらの映画は『じゃじゃ馬ならし』にもともと備わっていた大衆娯楽性をうまく利用して成功した例であろう。

　『じゃじゃ馬ならし』は問題劇でもあり、同時に大衆娯楽でもある。ラテン喜劇の伝統を受け継ぐ機知に富む筋書きも、コメディア・デラルテの即興性もあわせ持っている。酔っ払いに一夜の夢を見せたり、じゃじゃ馬を良妻へと仕立て直す民衆的な説話の伝統も引き継いでいる。『じゃじゃ馬ならし』の上演史は、そうした多様な要素を吸収して作られたシェイクスピアの作品から、それぞれの時代に合わせた部分を引き出して新たな表現を与えてきた 400 年の歴史だ。

参考文献解題

1. 校訂本

『じゃじゃ馬ならし』の比較的近年の校訂本のうち主なものを挙げる。Thompson 編のものは1984年に出版された第 2 ケンブリッジ版の 3 回目の改訂である。その点で2010年の Hodgdon の第 3 アーデン版が、本文、解説ともに、先行の数々の校訂本を踏まえた最新の成果と位置付けられる。

Hibbard, G. R., ed., *The Taming of the Shrew* (1968; New York and London: Penguin Random House, 2006). 〔ペンギン版〕

Hodgdon, Barbara, ed., *The Taming of the Shrew*, The Arden Shakespeare, 3rd series (London: Methuen, 2010). 〔第 3 アーデン版〕

Morris, Brian, ed., *The Taming of the Shrew*, The Arden Shakespeare, 2nd series (London: Methuen, 1981). 〔第 2 アーデン版〕

Oliver, H. J., ed., *The Taming of the Shrew*, The Oxford Shakespeare (Oxford: Oxford University Press, 1982). 〔オックスフォード版〕

Thompson, Ann, ed., *The Taming of the Shrew*, The New Cambridge Shakespeare, 3rd edition (Cambridge: Cambridge University Press, 2017). 〔第 2 ケンブリッジ版〕

2. 学習者向け版本

比較的手軽に読める学習者向けの版本も挙げておく。

Bate, Jonathan, and Eric Rasmussen, eds., *The Taming of the Shrew*, The RSC Shakespeare (Basingstoke: Macmillan, 2010). 〔マクミラン版〕 注釈が簡便で、批評史、上演史を含め、わかりやすい解説がついている。

Brady, Linzy, ed., *The Taming of the Shrew*, Cambridge School Shakespeare, 2nd edition（Cambridge: Cambridge University Press, 2014）.
　　平易な注釈と楽しい課題がついていて、シェイクスピア作品への敷居を低くしてくれる、初学者におすすめの版である。

Callaghan, Dympna, ed., *The Taming of the Shrew*, Norton Critical Edition（New York: Norton, 2009）.
　　材源や代表的な批評も収録しているので便利。

3. 基礎資料・事典・辞書類

Chambers, E. K., *The Elizabethan Stage*, 4 vols（Oxford: Clarendon, 1923）.
　　出版から1世紀を経ているが、考証学的なアプローチをする際は今もなお有用な基礎資料集。

Dent, R. W., *Shakespeare's Proverbial Language: An Index*（Berkeley and Los Angeles: University of California Press, 1981）.
　　Tilley の *A Dictionary of the Proverbs in England in the Sixteenth and Seventeenth Centuries*（1950）をもとにシェイクスピア作品に出てくることわざを集めた索引。

高橋康也、大場建治、喜志哲雄、村上淑郎編『シェイクスピア辞典』（研究社、2000）
　　シェイクスピアおよび同時代の演劇に関する基本情報事典。

4. 材源および同時代の劇作品

Bullough, Geffrey, ed., *Narrative and Dramatic Sources of Shakespeare*, 8 vols（London: Routledge and Kegan Paul, 1957）.
　　シェイクスピア劇になんらかの影響を与えた作品を収録した材源研究に関する基本図書。『じゃじゃ馬ならし』は第1巻で扱われている。ただし Bullough は A Shrew を直接の材源としているが、それに

ついては解説でも書いたように諸説あるので要注意。

Fletcher, John, *The Tamer Tamed*, New Mermaids, ed. by Lucy Munro (London: Bloomsbury, 2010).

ジョン・フレッチャーによる『じゃじゃ馬ならし』の続編を読むには New Mermaids 版が手軽で読みやすい。

Miller, Stephen Roy, ed., *The Taming of A Shrew: The 1594 Quarto,* The New Cambridge Shakespeare (Cambridge: Cambridge University Press, 1998).

A Shrew の詳細な注釈、解説つきの信頼できる校訂本。*The Shrew* との関係も慎重に論じている。

5. 本文、初演、*A Shrew* に関する研究

20世紀半ば過ぎまで、『じゃじゃ馬ならし』に関する研究は、文学作品としての内容に関する批評よりも、*A Shrew* との関係あるいは、それと連動して1590年代の劇団事情に関するものが多かった。20世紀後半以降はそうした考証学的研究において、改作や共作の可能性を検証するものが多くなっている。

Alexander, Peter, 'The Original Ending of *The Taming of the Shrew*', *SQ*, 20. 2 (1969), 111-16.

A Shrew を海賊版ととらえ、*The Shrew* にも元々は結末部分があったと論じる。

George, David, 'Shakespeare and Pembroke's Men', *SQ*, 32. 3 (1981), 305-23.

ペンブルック伯一座の地方巡業にシェイクスピアは同行していないと論じる。

Loughnane, Rory, and Andrew J. Power, eds., *Early Shakespeare, 1588-1594* (Cambridge: Cambridge University Press, 2020).

『じゃじゃ馬ならし』は Marlowe との共作であると論じる Nance の研究を含む論集。

Marcus, Leah S., *Unediting the Renaissance: Shakespeare, Marlowe, Milton* (Abingdon: Routledge, 1996).

校訂の歴史の中で隠れてしまった戯曲の本来の姿を解明しようとする試み。

McMillin, Scott, 'Casting for Pembroke's Men: The Henry VI Quartos and *The Taming of A Shrew*', *SQ*, 23. 2 (1972), 141-159.

1594年の四折本からペンブルック伯一座の構成を推定する試み。

Sams, Eric, *The Real Shakespeare* (New Haven and London: Yale University Press, 1995).

シェイクスピア自身による改作の可能性を論じる。

Wells, Stanley, and Gary Taylor, 'No shrew, A Shrew and The Shrew: internal revision in *The Taming of the Shrew*', in *Shakespeare: Text, Language, Criticism: Essays in Honour of Marvin Spevack*, ed. Bernard Fabian and Kurt Tetzeli von Rosador (Hildersheim and New York: Lubrecht & Cramer, 1987), 351-70.

シェイクスピア自身による改作説を提唱し本文研究を大きく軌道修正させた2人が *The Shrew* についても検証する。

6. 批評

『じゃじゃ馬ならし』の文学批評は1980年前後からにわかに活気づく。それ以前の Bradbrook、Barton、Leggatt らの議論は、男女差別的笑劇とみなされがちな『じゃじゃ馬ならし』を演劇として再評価しようとする試みだ。一方、1980年代以降の理論化された批評は、『じゃじゃ馬ならし』を通して16世紀イングランドの家族や結婚についてのイデオロギーを読み解き、ジェンダーと権力についての問題意識を提示するものが多い。

Aspinall, Dana E. ed., *The Taming of the Shrew: Critical Essays* (New York: Routledge, 2002).

劇の成立から20世紀までの歴史を俯瞰する論集。

Barton, Ann, introduction to *The Taming of the Shrew* in *The Riverside Shakespeare,* 2nd edn, ed. G. Blakemore Evans and Harry Levin (Boston: Houghton Mifflin, 1974), 138-41.

短いがバランスの良い解説。『じゃじゃ馬ならし』を好意的に評価する。

Boose, Linda, 'Scolding Brides and Bridling Scolds: Taming the Woman's Unruly Member', *SQ*, 42. 2 (1991), 179-213.

じゃじゃ馬を罰する民衆の歴史とシェイクスピア劇の成立を連動させる論文。

Bradbrook, M. C., 'Dramatic role as social image: a study of *The Taming of the Shrew*', *Shakespeare Jahrbuch*, 94 (1958), 132-50.

同時代の文学伝統と対比させてキャタリーナの人物造形を論じる。

Dolan, Frances. E., 'Household Chastisements: Gender, Authority, and "Domestic Violence"', in *Renaissance Culture and the Everyday*, ed. Patricia Fumerton and Simon Hunt (Philadelphia: University of Pennsylvania Press), 204-28.

キャタリーナの暴力性にも注目し、家庭内におけるジェンダーと暴力の関係を論じる。

Dusinberre, Juliet, *Shakespeare and Nature of Women,* 3rd edition (1975; Basingstoke: Palgrave Macmillan, 2003).

シェイクスピアのフェミニズム批評の端緒を開いた一冊。邦訳は森祐希子訳『シェイクスピアの女性像』(紀伊國屋書店、1994)

Fineman, Joel, 'The Turn of the Shrew', in *Shakespeare and the Question of Theory*, ed. Patricia Parker and Geoffrey Hartman (London: Methuen, 1985), 138-59.

精神分析批評。言語が秩序を転覆させながら回復させるという自己言及的な構造を論じる。

Kahn, Coppélia, *Man's Estate: Masculine Identity in Shakespeare* (Berkley and Los Angeles: University of California Press, 1981).

16世紀の男性優位とその不合理さをペトルーチオは表現していると
論じる。

Korda, Natasha, 'Household Kates: Domesticating Commodities in *The Taming of the Shrew*', *SQ*, 47. 2 (1996), 109-31.

マルクス主義批評。キャタリーナとペトルーチオの関係を階級と経済の視点から説明する。

Leggatt, Alexander, *Shakespeare's Comedy of Love* (1974; London and New York: Routledge, 2005).

キャタリーナもゲームを楽しみながら成長していくと解釈する穏当な喜劇論。

Newman, Karen, *Fashioning Femininity and English Renaissance Drama* (Chicago: University of Chicago Press, 1991).

新歴史主義批評。悪妻矯正の民俗的風習と『じゃじゃ馬ならし』が、同じイデオロギーの枠組み内にあるとする。

Novy, Marianne L., 'Patriarchy and Play in *The Taming of the Shrew*', *English Literary Renaissance*, 9. 2 (1979), 264-80.

言語ゲームの遊戯性と権力ゲームである父権制が結びついていると論じる。

Preeshl, Artemis, *Shakespeare and Commedia dell'Arte* (London and New York: Routledge, 2017).

コメディア・デラルテの手法がどのように取り込まれているかを作品ごとに論じる。

Righter (Barton), Ann, *Shakespeare and the Idea of the Play* (London: Chatto and Windus, 1962).

演劇が現実に及ぼす力を論じる。邦訳は青山誠子訳『イリュージョンの力』(朝日出版社、1981)。

Ryan, Kiernan, *Shakespeare's Comedies* (Basingstoke: Palgrave Macmillan, 2009).

父権支配のイデオロギーを超える喜劇として『じゃじゃ馬ならし』

を読む。

Stone, Lawrence, *The family, Sex and Marriage in England 1500-1800*
（1977; London: Penguin, 1990）.
16-18世紀の家族史についての基本図書。邦訳は北本正章訳『家族・
性・結婚の社会史』（勁草書房、1991）。

Wootton, David, and Graham Holderness, eds., *Gender and Power in
Shrew-Taming Narratives*, 1500-1700（Basingstoke: Palgrave
Macmillan, 2010）.
中世から王政復古期までのじゃじゃ馬矯正の文学を通して女性史を
考察する論集。

Wynne-Davies, Marion, ed., '*Much Ado about Nothing*' and '*The
Taming of the Shrew*', *New Casebooks*（New York: Palgrave, 2001）.
1980年代以降の批評理論の代表的成果を集めた論集。

7. 上演史

　上演史研究のアプローチも多様だ。上演台本や劇評などの一次資料
を検証し、過去の上演を浮かび上がらせて、歴史を俯瞰するものがあ
る。一方でそれらの上演に反映している政治性を読み解こうとするも
のもある。さらに演出家や俳優など制作側の声をまとめたものもある。

Haring-Smith, Tori, *From Farce to Metadrama: A Stage History of the
Taming of the Shrew 1594-1983*（Westport, Connecticut:
Greenwood Press, 1985）.
4世紀にわたる上演史を網羅的に記述している。

Holderness Graham, *The Taming of the Shrew*, Shakespeare in
Performance（Manchester: Manchester University Press, 1989）.
1960-80年代の上演および映像作品を時代背景とともに政治的に批
評する。

McMullan, Gordon, and Lena Cowen Orlin and Virginia Mason
Vaughan, eds., *Women Making Shakespeare: Text, Reception,*

Performance（London and New York: Bloomsbury, 2014）.

シェイクスピアの編纂、受容、上演の歴史と女性との関わりをテーマとする論集。『じゃじゃ馬ならし』上演について３つのエッセイを含む。

Schafer, Elizabeth, ed. *The Taming of the Shrew,* Shakespeare in Production（Cambridge: Cambridge University Press, 2002）.

上演史の詳説とともに、具体的な上演記録を本文への注釈として付す。

Smallwood, Robert, ed., *Players of Shakespeare 4*（Cambridge: Cambridge University Press, 1998）.

1995年にペトルーチオを演じた Michael Siberry を含め、RSC の俳優たちによるエッセイ集。

小林かおり『じゃじゃ馬たちの文化史』（南雲堂、2007）

近現代の上演史と女性史を並行的に論じている。劇評を含む文献一覧も詳細。

8. 邦訳・翻案・映像作品

小田島雄志訳『じゃじゃ馬ならし』（白水社、1983）

大場建治『じゃじゃ馬馴らし』（岩波書店、2008）

松岡和子訳『じゃじゃ馬馴らし』（筑摩書房、2010）

Tyler, Ann, *Vinegar Girl*（London and New York: Hogarth, 2016）.

邦訳は鈴木潤訳『ヴィネガー・ガール』（集英社、2021）

ジョージ・シドニー監督『キス・ミー・ケイト』（1953）

コール・ポーター作曲によるミュージカルの映画化。

フランコ・ゼフィレリ監督『じゃじゃ馬ならし』（1967）

主演はリチャード・バートンとエリザベス・テイラー。

ジル・ジュンガー監督『ヒース・レジャーの恋のから騒ぎ』（1999）

原題 *Ten Things I Hate About You*。アメリカ学園コメディへの翻案。

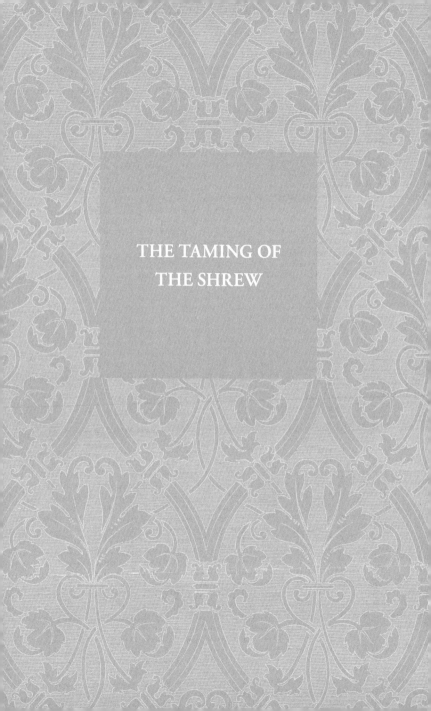

THE TAMING OF
THE SHREW

DRAMATIS PERSONAE

The Induction

CHRISTOPHER SLY, a tinker

HOSTESS, of an alehouse

LORD

BARTHOLOMEW, the Lord's page

HUNTSMEN

SERVANTS

PLAYERS

THE PLAY-WITHIN-THE-PLAY

BAPTISTA MINOLA, a rich citizen of Padua

KATHERINA, elder daughter of Baptista

BIANCA, younger daughter of Baptista

PETRUCHIO, a gentleman of Verona, suitor to Katherina

GRUMIO, Petruchio's servant

LUCENTIO, a gentleman of Pisa, suitor to Bianca

TRANIO, Lucentio's servant

BIONDELLO, Lucentio's servant

HORTENTIO, Petruchio's friend, suitor to Bianca

GREMIO, a rich old man, suitor to Bianca

VINCENTIO, Lucentio's father

A PEDANT, who pretends to be Vincentio

A WIDOW, who becomes Hortentio's wife

CURTIS, Petruchio's chief servant at his country house

NATHANIEL, PHILIP, JOSEPH, NICHOLAS, PETER, Petruchio's domestic servants

A TAILOR

A HABERDASHER

Other Servants, Officer

登場人物

インダクション

クリストファー・スライ [krístəfər sláɪ]　鋳掛屋

居酒屋のおかみ

領主

バーソロミュー [bɑːrθɔ́ləmjuː]　領主の小姓

猟師たち

従者たち

役者たち

劇中劇

バプティスタ・ミノーラ [bæptístə mɪnóulə]　パデュアの富裕な市民

キャタリーナ [kæθəríːnə]　バプティスタの娘（姉）

ビアンカ [biǽŋkə]　バプティスタの娘（妹）

ペトルーチオ [petrúːtʃiou]　ヴェローナの紳士、キャタリーナの求婚者

グルーミオ [grúːmiou]　ペトルーチオの召使い

ルーセンシオ [luːsénʃiou]　ピサの紳士、ビアンカの求婚者

トラーニオ [tráːniou]　ルーセンシオの召使い

ビオンデロ [biɔndélou]　ルーセンシオの召使い

ホーテンシオ [hɔːnténʃiou]　ペトルーチオの友人、ビアンカの求婚者

グレミオ [grémiou]　金持ちの老人、ビアンカの求婚者

ヴィンセンシオ [vɪnsénʃiou]　ルーセンシオの父親

教師　ヴィンセンシオに扮する

未亡人　ホーテンシオと結婚する

カーティス [kə́ːrtɪs]　ペトルーチオのカントリー・ハウスの召使い頭

ナサニエル [nəθǽnjəl]、フィリップ [fílɪp]、ジョセフ [dʒóuzəf]、ニコラス [níkələs]、ピーター [píːtər]　ペトルーチオの召使いたち

仕立屋

帽子屋

その他の召使いたち、警吏

〔**Induction 1**〕

Enter Christopher Sly and Hostess

Sly I'll feeze you, in faith.

Hostess A pair of stocks, you rogue!

Sly You're a baggage, the Slys are no rogues. Look in the
chronicles, we came in with Richard Conqueror: therefore
paucas pallabris, let the world slide. Sessa! 5

Hostess You will not pay for the glasses you have burst?

Sly No, not a denier. Go by, Saint Jeronimy, go to thy cold
bed and warm thee.

Hostess I know my remedy, I must go fetch the thirdborough.

[Exit]

Sly Third, or fourth, or fifth borough, I'll answer him by law. 10
I'll not budge an inch, boy. Let him come, and kindly.

He falls asleep

Wind horns. Enter Lord from hunting, with his train

Lord Huntsman, I charge thee, tender well my hounds.
Breathe Merriman — the poor cur is embossed —
And couple Clowder with the deep-mouthed brach.
Saw'st thou not, boy, how Silver made it good 15
At the hedge-corner, in the coldest fault?
I would not lose the dog for twenty pound.

First Huntsman Why, Belman is as good as he, my lord.
He cried upon it at the merest loss,
And twice today picked out the dullest scent. 20
Trust me, I take him for the better dog.

Lord Thou art a fool. If Echo were as fleet,
I would esteem him worth a dozen such.
But sup them well and look unto them all.
To-morrow I intend to hunt again. 25

First Huntsman I will, my lord.

〔インダクション 1〕あらすじ・・・

　酔っ払いのスライは酒場のおかみさんと言い争った後で、店の前で眠りこんでしまう。そこに狩猟から戻ってきた領主が来あわせ、眠ったままのスライに仕掛けるいたずらを思いつく。スライは精神を病んで 7 年間、自分のことを低い身分だと思い込んでいたけれど、実は殿様なのだという設定にするため、小姓に女装をさせ奥方役をやらせることにする。たまたまやってきた旅役者の一行には、この偽物の殿様に芝居を見せるようにと命じる。

・・・

0. 0. INDUCTION 1　⇒後注

0. 1. *Enter Christopher Sly*　⇒後注

1. feeze = do for, settle the business of (*OED v.*¹3a)「やっつけてやる」というような意。　⇒後注　　**in faith** = truly

2. A pair of stocks　stock は板の穴に両足首をはめさせ晒し者にする刑具。

3. baggage = good-for-nothing woman, strumpet (*OED n.* 6)

4. Richard Conqueror　「征服王リチャード」スライの間違い。　⇒後注

5. *paucas pallabris*　few words という意味のスペイン語の *pocas palabras* と言おうとして、スライは間違えている。　⇒後注

　let the world slide「世の中がひっくり返っても気にしないぞ」という捨て台詞。(*OED n.* P17)　　**Sessa!**　⇒後注　　**6. burst** = broken

7. denier　ごく少額のフランスのコイン「びた一文」　　**Saint Jeronimy**　⇒後注

7-8. go to thy cold bed and warm thee　⇒後注

9. thirdborough　「教区のお役人」　⇒後注

10. by law　「法廷で」

11. boy　「下郎め」という相手を見下した呼びかけ

　and kindly = and welcome（もちろん皮肉で言っている）

11. 2. *Wind horns*　「ホルンを吹け」という命令形のト書き。

12. tender well my hounds　「私の猟犬たちの世話をよくしてくれ」　⇒後注

13-22. Merriman, Clowder, Silver, Belman, Echo　いずれも猟犬の名前。

13. Breathe　「(休ませて) 息を整えさせる」　⇒後注

　embossed　「疲れきって口から泡を吹いている」(*OED v.*²3)

14. couple = to tie or fasten (dogs) together in pairs (*OED v.* 1)

　the deep-mouthed brach　「よく声の通る雌犬」

15. made it good　「手柄をあげた」ここでは獲物の匂いを探り当てたこと。

16. in the coldest fault　「匂いがわからなくなる場所」

19. cried upon it at the merest loss　「すっかり匂いのわからなくなったところで、匂いを嗅ぎ当てて声をあげた」　⇒後注　　**merest** = absolute

22. fleet = swift, fast

24. sup them well　「たっぷり食事を与えてやれ」

LORD   What's here? One dead, or drunk? See, doth he breathe?

SECOND HUNTSMAN   He breathes, my lord. Were he not
    warmed with ale,

This were a bed but cold to sleep so soundly.

LORD   O monstrous beast, how like a swine he lies!   30

Grim death, how foul and loathsome is thine image.

Sirs, I will practise on this drunken man.

What think you, if he were conveyed to bed,

Wrapped in sweet clothes, rings put upon his fingers,

A most delicious banquet by his bed,   35

And brave attendants near him when he wakes,

Would not the beggar then forget himself?

FIRST HUNTSMAN   Believe me, lord, I think he cannot choose.

SECOND HUNTSMAN   It would seem strange unto him when he
    waked.

LORD   Even as a flattering dream or worthless fancy.   40

Then take him up and manage well the jest.

Carry him gently to my fairest chamber

And hang it round with all my wanton pictures.

Balm his foul head in warm distilled waters

And burn sweet wood to make the lodging sweet.   45

Procure me music ready when he wakes,

To make a dulcet and a heavenly sound.

And if he chance to speak, be ready straight

And with a low submissive reverence

Say 'What is it your honour will command?'   50

Let one attend him with a silver basin

Full of rose-water and bestrewed with flowers,

Another bear the ewer, the third a diaper,

And say 'Will't please your lordship cool your hands?'

Some one be ready with a costly suit   55

And ask him what apparel he will wear.

Another tell him of his hounds and horse,

29. a bed but cold 「あまりに冷たいベッド」but は just, absolutely という意味の副詞。

31. thine image = your likeness「お前に似た姿はなんと醜いのか」と呼びかけられているのは Grim death。死のような抽象的なものを擬人化して呼びかけるのはシェイクスピアがたびたび用いる手法。thine は所有格の thy だが、次に image という母音で始まる言葉が続くため音節を区切るために thine という形になっている。

32. Sirs 複数形では自分より身分の低い者たちに対する呼びかけでも使われる。l. 62 の gentle sirs も同様。　　　**practise on**「いたずらをしかける」

34. sweet「良い匂いのする」(*OED adj.* 2a) l. 45 の sweet も同じ意味。

35. banquet「甘いものや果物など、食後に食べる軽食、デザート」(*OED n.* 3)

36. brave「見事に着飾った」

38. cannot choose = is bound to

40. flattering「いい気分にさせてくれる」　　　**fancy** = fantasy

43. wanton = erotic, lascivious　Induction 2, 47-58 で語られるような絵。

44. Balm = bathe, anoint with fragrant oil or liquid　(*OED v.* 2a)
distilled waters「良い匂いをつけた水」l. 52 の rose-water と同様なもの。

45. sweet wood 松やヒノキ科の常緑樹ジュニパーなどを焚き、そのアロマ効果で部屋の空気を浄化した。

46. me ethical dative（心性的与格）。話者の感情を伝えるために添えられる。この用法は近代英語では次第に用いられなくなった。ここでは領主が、音楽の手配をしてくれと召使いたちに依頼する気持ちが反映している。

47. dulcet = sweet, melodious

48. And if and の古い用法で and if の形で「もしも」という条件を示す。an if という形を取ることもある。　　　**straight** = immediately, straight away

49. low = humble　　　**reverence**「深々としたおじぎ」

50. your honour you の代わりに用いられる「ご主人様」という敬称。

52. bestrewed = covered

53. ewer「手洗いや洗面用の水差し」　　　**diaper**「顔や手を拭くための布巾」

54. your lordship l. 50 の your honour と同様の貴族に対する敬称。

55. Some one「召使いの中の誰かひとり」

57. horse 古い英語では horse は複数形も同形であった。ここではおそらく複数の馬のことを言っている。

And that his lady mourns at his disease.
Persuade him that he hath been lunatic,
And when he says he is, say that he dreams, 60
For he is nothing but a mighty lord.
This do, and do it kindly, gentle sirs.
It will be pastime passing excellent,
If it be husbanded with modesty.
FIRST HUNTSMAN   My lord, I warrant you we will play our part 65
  As he shall think by our true diligence
  He is no less than what we say he is.
LORD   Take him up gently and to bed with him,
  And each one to his office when he wakes.

                        [Sly is carried out] Sound trumpets

  Sirrah, go see what trumpet 'tis that sounds — 70

                             [Exit a Servant]

  Belike some noble gentleman that means,
  Travelling some journey, to repose him here.

Enter Servant

  How now! Who is it?
SERVANT   An't please your honour, players
  That offer service to your lordship.

Enter Players

LORD   Bid them come near. — Now, fellows, you are welcome. 75
PLAYERS   We thank your honour.
LORD   Do you intend to stay with me tonight?
SECOND PLAYER   So please your lordship to accept our duty.
LORD   With all my heart. This fellow I remember,
  Since once he played a farmer's eldest son. 80
  'Twas where you wooed the gentlewoman so well.
  I have forgot your name, but sure that part
  Was aptly fitted and naturally performed.

60. he is 「今、自分は確かに狂っている」is の後に lunatic が省略されている。

61. but = except

62. This do 「以上のことをやってくれ」　**kindly** = naturally

63. passing = surpassingly, exceedingly

64. If it be husbanded with modesty 「節度をもってやれば」ここでの husband は manage（管理する）という意味の他動詞。一般的な「夫」という名詞の用法も、もともとは「家の管理者」という意味からきている。

66. As = So that　　**shall** は話者の意思を表す助動詞。ここでは「この男には必ず、こちらが言ったとおりの人間だと思わせてみせますよ」という意思が表明されている。

70. Sirrah 「おい」というような、身分の低い者への呼びかけ。　　**'tis** = it is

71. Belike = perhaps

73. An't = if it　　**your honour** は高位の人に対する敬称。if it please you を丁寧に言った形で「御意にかなえば」という意味。ここでは「（御意にかなえば）申し上げますが」という、召使いの丁重な態度を表している。

73-74. players / That offer service to your lordship 「殿のお役に立ちたいという役者たちでございます」1592 年から 1594 年にかけてペストで劇場が閉鎖していた期間にあたり、役者たちがロンドンを離れて地方巡業をせざるを得なかった。そのような時代背景を、この台詞は反映しているのではないかと推測する研究者もいる。

78. So = if it　　**duty** = services 「私どもの芝居をご覧いただけるのでございましたら」と、役者たちの丁重な態度を表している。

79-85. This fellow I remember *Hamlet* でも旅回りの役者一座がやってきたとき、Hamlet が「この役者のあの役を覚えている」と特定の芝居の話をし始める。Hamlet やこの領主のような高い身分の者に「ひいき」にされる役者がいたことが、こうした台詞からうかがえる。この時代の演劇文化は、王侯貴族の愛顧や庇護と、熊いじめや闘鶏と同列の大衆性が両立する一方で、ピューリタン的志向の強い市民階級からは敵視されていた。

80. Since once = since the time when

81. 'Twas = it was

83. aptly fitted and naturally performed 「役もぴったりで、自然な演技だった」ll. 62-64 で領主は、スライをだますための演技を、自然で (kindly)、節度をもってする (husbanded with modesty) ようにと助言している。Hamlet の役者たちへの演技指導でも、やりすぎを諫め、自然をそのまま映し出す演技をするようにと同じ趣旨のことが語られている。*Shrew* と *Hamlet* の創作年代の間には開きがあるが、シェイクスピアの一貫した演劇理念がこれらの台詞に表れている。

SECOND PLAYER   I think 'twas Soto that your honour means.

LORD   'Tis very true, thou didst it excellent.   85

Well, you are come to me in a happy time.

The rather for I have some sport in hand

Wherein your cunning can assist me much.

There is a lord will hear you play tonight;

But I am doubtful of your modesties,   90

Lest over-eyeing of his odd behavior —

For yet his honour never heard a play —

You break into some merry passion

And so offend him; for I tell you, sirs,

If you should smile, he grows impatient.   95

SECOND PLAYER   Fear not, my lord, we can contain ourselves,

Were he the veriest antic in the world.

LORD   Go, sirrah, take them to the buttery,

And give them friendly welcome every one.

Let them want nothing that my house affords.   100

                              Exit one with the Players

Sirrah, go you to Barthol'mew my page,

And see him dressed in all suits like a lady.

That done, conduct him to the drunkard's chamber,

And call him 'madam', do him obeisance.

Tell him from me — as he will win my love —   105

He bear himself with honourable action,

Such as he hath observed in noble ladies

Unto their lords by them accomplishèd.

Such duty to the drunkard let him do,

With soft low tongue and lowly courtesy,   110

And say 'What is't your honour will command

Wherein your lady and your humble wife

May show her duty and make known her love?'

And then with kind embracements, tempting kisses,

And with declining head into his bosom,   115

84. SECOND PLAYER ⇒後注　　**Soto** ⇒後注

86. you are come = you have come　　**in a happy time**「ちょうど良い時に」

87. The rather for = the more so because「ちょうど良いのはなぜかというと」　**sport**「お楽しみ、娯楽」

88. cunning「技能」ここでは演技力のこと。

89. There is a lord will hear you play　lord と will の間に関係代名詞が省略されている。直訳すると「芝居を聞きたいと思っておられる貴族がいる」。シェイクスピアの時代、芝居は「見る」のではなく「聞く」ものだった。

90. I am doubtful of your modesties　領主は役者たちの演技がやり過ぎになるのを警戒している。　doubtful = apprehensive about

91. over-eyeing = observing　　**his**　l. 89 の a lord つまりスライを指す。

92. yet = before now

his honour　l. 73, l. 78 と同様、he の代わりに用いている敬称。

93. merry passion = fit of laughter　芝居を見たことがないスライの反応を見て、役者たちが笑いを抑えられなくなるのではないかと領主は心配している。

95. impatient = angry

97. veriest antic「この上なく滑稽な人物」　antic = grotesque or ludicrous person

98. buttery = pantry for liquor and food　この領主の台詞は召使いに向けた指示。役者たちに食事を出すようにと言っている。

100. want = lack　　**affords** = offers

101. Barthol'mew my page「小姓のバーソロミュー」Barthol'mew と my page は同格。

102. in all suits = in all respects　ただし suit は「衣服の一そろい」という意味も重ねた語呂合わせ (pun) にもなっている。

104. do him obeisance = show him dutiful respect　この him は小姓バーソロミューを指す。実は小姓だが貴婦人のように扱えと指示している。

105. as he will win my love「小姓が私の寵愛を得たいのなら」

106. bear himself with honourable action「威厳あるふるまいをする」

107-08. Such ... accomplishèd「立派なご婦人たちが夫に対して示すようなふるまいを見たことがあるだろう。そのような威厳あるふるまいをせよ」と領主は小姓に指示している。　accomplishèd = performed　アクセント記号は e の母音を発音して 1 音節にすることを示している。

112. Wherein = in which　　**your lady and your humble wife** は自分のことを指しており、全体として「あなたの従順な妻であるこの私があなた様への崇敬の念 (duty) を示し愛情を示せる」という意味。　　**113. May** = can

115. And ... his bosom「スライの胸に顔をうずめ」

Bid him shed teares, as being overjoyed
To see her noble lord restored to health,
Who for this seven years hath esteemèd him
No better than a poor and loathsome begger.
And if the boy have not a woman's gift   120
To rain a shower of commanded tears,
An onion will do well for such a shift,
Which in a napkin being close conveyed
Shall in despite enforce a watery eye.
See this dispatched with all the haste thou canst.   125
Anon I'll give thee more instructions.   *Exit a servant*
I know the boy will well usurp the grace,
Voice, gait and action of a gentlewoman.
I long to hear him call the drunkard 'husband',
And how my men will stay themselves from laughter,   130
When they do homage to this simple peasant.
I'll in to counsel them. Haply my presence
May well abate the over-merry spleen,
Which otherwise would grow into extremes.   [*Exeunt*]

[INDUCTION 2]

*Enter aloft the drunkard [Sly] with attendants — some with apparel,
basin and ewer, and other appurtenances — and Lord*

SLY   For God's sake, a pot of small ale.

FIRST SERVANT   Will't please your lordship drink a cup of
    sack?

SECOND SERVANT   Will't please your honor taste of these
    conserves?

THIRD SEVANT   What raiment will your honor wear today?

SLY   I am Christophero Sly, call not me 'honour' nor 'lordship'.   5
    I ne're drank sack in my life, and if you give me any conserves,
    give me conserves of beef. Ne're ask me what raiment I'll

118. esteemèd him = thought himself

119. No better than = merely, just the same as

120. a woman's gift 自由自在に嘘の涙を流すのは「女ならではの才能」なので、小姓には無理かもしれないと言っている。

121. commanded = forced

122. for ... a shift = as a makeshift「とりあえずの手段として」

123. napkin = handkerchief **close conveyed** = secretly carried

124. in despite = in defiance of nature「笑いそうになろうとも」

125. dispatched = carried out promptly

126. Anon = very soon, shortly

127-28. well usurp the grace ... of a gentlewoman 「貴婦人の優美さをうまく我がものとする」 **gait and action**「立居振る舞い、身のこなし」

129. long = desire **130. stay** = prevent, stop

131. do homage 「臣下として敬う」

  simple = of poor or humble condition「身分の低い」

132. I'll in = I'll go in **Haply** = perhaps

133. May well abate the over-merry spleen 「笑い転げそうな脾臓(ひぞう)をうまく抑制できる」spleen（脾臓）はシェイクスピアの時代には、激しい喜怒の感情の宿る臓器と考えられていた。over-merry　*OED*はこの用例を初出としており、おそらくシェイクスピアが作った言葉と考えられる。

〔インダクション 2〕あらすじ ……………………………………………

　召使いたちは目が覚めたスライを丁重に殿様として扱い、スライが 15 年間、病気で眠り続け、自分が鋳掛屋だという夢を見ていたと説明する。戸惑っていたスライも、美しい奥方がいると聞かされ、すっかり殿様気分になってしまう。病気の快癒のためにと観劇を勧められ、スライは美しく女装した小姓を妻だと信じて一緒に芝居を見ることになる。

……………………………………………………………………………

0. 1. *Enter aloft* ⇒後注

1. small ale = weak ale　シェイクスピアの時代にもっとも広く飲まれていた酒が ale。ビールに似た麦芽醸造酒だが、ホップが使われていない。

2. sack 「サック酒」辛口の白ワインでおもにカナリア諸島やスペインから輸入されていた。ale よりも sack の方が高級な酒。

3. conserves「果物の砂糖漬け」

4. raiment = clothing

5. Christophero　Christopher を気取ってスペイン語風に発音している。

6. ne'er = never

7. conserves of beef　「牛肉の塩漬け」　果物の砂糖漬けより庶民的な食べ物。

wear, for I have no more doublets than backs, no more
stockings than legs, nor no more shoes than feet — nay,
sometime more feet than shoes, or such shoes as my toes look   10
through the over-leather.

LORD   Heaven cease this idle humour in your honour!
 O, that a mighty man of such descent,
 Of such possessions and so high esteem,
 Should be infusèd with so foul a spirit.   15

SLY   What, would you make me mad? Am not I Christopher
Sly, old Sly's son of Burton Heath, by birth a pedlar, by
education a cardmaker, by transmutation a bear-herd, and
now by present profession a tinker? Ask Marian Hacket, the
fat ale-wife of Wincot, if she know me not. If she say I am   20
not fourteen pence on the score for sheer ale, score me up for
the lyingest knave in Christendom. What, I am not bestraught.
Here's —

THIRD SERVANT   O, this it is that makes your lady mourn.

SECOND SERVANT   O, this is it that makes your servants droop.   25

LORD   Hence comes it that your kindred shuns your house
 As beaten hence by your strange lunacy.
 O noble lord, bethink thee of thy birth,
 Call home thy ancient thoughts from banishment,
 And banish hence these abject lowly dreams.   30
 Look how thy servants do attend on thee,
 Each in his office ready at thy beck.
 Wilt thou have music? Hark, Apollo plays,   *Music*
 And twenty cagèd nightingales do sing.
 Or wilt thou sleep? We'll have thee to a couch   35
 Softer and sweeter than the lustful bed
 On purpose trimmed up for Semiramis.
 Say thou wilt walk, we will bestrew the ground.
 Or wilt thou ride? Thy horses shall be trapped,
 Their harness studded all with gold and pearl.   40

8. I have no more doublets than backs ＝ I have no more doublets than I
have backs 「体の数以上の上着は持っていない」（着た切り雀だから選択の余
地などない） doublets 体にぴったりとした男性用の上着。

9. nay ＝ no 否定文をさらに強めて言おうとするときしばしば使われる副詞。

10. sometime ＝ sometimes **more feet than shoes** 「靴の数より足の数の方
が多い」

11. over-leather 「靴の甲の革部分」前行の or は「すなわち」という意味。as
は such shoes を先行詞とする関係代名詞。「つま先がのぞくような靴」なの
で、そんなものは靴とは呼べず、足の数の方が多いとスライは言う。

12. Heaven cease 祈願文。助動詞 may が省略されている。cease はここでは
stop の意味の他動詞。 **this idle humour** 「こんな無意味な妄想」
humour ＝ temporary disposition ⇒後注

13. O, that 主節が省略された形で、強い驚き、悲しみ、願望などの感情を表
す。ここでは「…するなんて！」という嘆きを表している。

15. be infusèd with so foul a spirit 「こんなにひどい心の病に取り憑かれてし
まっている」spirit は disposition(精神状態) と evil spirit(悪霊) の両方の
意味が重なっている。

17. Burton Heath ⇒後注 **pedlar** 「行商人」

18. cardmaker card は羊毛を梳いて繊維にするための鉄製の道具。
transmutation ＝ change of condition **bear-herd** 熊を見せ物にして地
方を巡る人、熊使い。

19. tinker 「鋳掛屋」村や町を訪ね歩いて、穴の空いた鍋の修理をする職業。
Marian Hacket ⇒後注

20. ale-wife「酒場の女主人」 **Wincot** ⇒後注

21. on the score 「つけがある、借金している」 **sheer ale** ＝ just for ale
score me up for 「…として記録する」

22. lyingest lying （嘘つきの）という形容詞の最上級。 **bestraught** ＝ mad

25. droop 「元気をなくしてうなだれる」

27. As beaten hence 「打ちのめされて追い出されるように」 **As** ＝ As if

28. bethink thee ＝ come to think **29. ancient** ＝ former

32. Each in his office 「召使い各自がそれぞれの職務で」 **beck**「うなずいて
指示を出すこと」

33. Apollo ギリシア・ローマ神話の太陽神、詩歌や音楽をつかさどる。

36-37. the lustful bed ... Semiramis ⇒後注 **lustful** 「欲望をかき立てる」
trimmed up 「しつらえられた」

38. Say ＝ suppose l. 45 の Say も同じ。 **bestrew the ground** 「地面にい
ぐさ（あるいは花かカーペット）を敷きつめる」

39. trapped 「装飾馬具 (trap) を付けてある」

Dost thou love hawking? Thou hast hawks will soar
Above the morning lark. Or wilt thou hunt?
Thy hounds shall make the welkin answer them
And fetch shrill echoes from the hollow earth.

FIRST SERVANT   Say thou wilt course, thy greyhounds are as swift   45
As breathèd stags, ay, fleeter than the roe.

SECOND SERVANT   Dost thou love pictures? We will fetch thee straight
Adonis painted by a running brook,
And Cytherea all in sedges hid,
Which seem to move and wanton with her breath,   50
Even as the waving sedges play with wind.

LORD   We'll show thee Io as she was a maid,
And how she was beguiled and surprised,
As lively painted as the deed was done.

THIRD SERVANT   Or Daphne roaming through a thorny wood,   55
Scratching her legs that one shall swear she bleeds,
And at that sight shall sad Apollo weep,
So workmanly the blood and tears are drawn.

LORD   Thou art a lord, and nothing but a lord.
Thou hast a lady far more beautiful   60
Than any woman in this waning age.

FIRST SERVANT   And till the tears that she hath shed for thee,
Like envious floods o'errun her lovely face,
She was the fairest creature in the world,
And yet she is inferior to none.   65

SLY   Am I a lord, and have I such a lady?
Or do I dream? Or have I dreamed till now?
I do not sleep: I see, I hear, I speak,
I smell sweet savours, and I feel soft things.
Upon my life I am a lord indeed,   70
And not a tinker, nor Christopher Sly.

41. hawking「鷹狩り」　**Thou hast hawks will soar**　hawks と will の間に関係代名詞が省略されている。

43. welkin = sky（文語的な表現）

45. course = to hunt (hares) with greyhounds in view (*OED v.* 1b)　匂いで追いかけさせるのではなく、うさぎの姿を見て追いかけさせた。

46. breathèd stags　「肺活量の多い、息を切らさず走れる鹿」　breathèd = able to withstand physical exertion without getting out of breath (*OED adj.* 1)　**ay** = yes　**roe**「ノロジカ」小型の敏捷な鹿。

47. straight = immediately

48. Adonis　美と愛の女神ヴィーナス (Venus) に愛された美青年。狩りの最中にイノシシに殺され、その血が赤いアネモネの花になった。シェイクスピアの長編物語詩 *Venus and Adonis* は 1593 年に出版され人気を博した。　⇒後注
by a running brook　アドーニスは裸になって小川で水浴びをしようとしている。

49. Cytherea　ヴィーナスの別名。

in sedges hid　「茂みに隠れて」アドーニスをのぞき見している。

50. wanton = play sportively, behave seductively

52. Io　ジュピター (Jupiter, Jove) が霧に身を隠して強姦した娘。その後、アイオーは白い雌牛に変えられた。　⇒後注

53. beguiled = deceived　**surprised** = attacked

54. As lively painted ... done　「行為をそのまま生き生きと描いている」

55. Daphne　太陽神アポロに愛されたニンフ。愛の神キューピッド (Cupid) がアポロには金の矢尻、ダフネには鉛の矢尻で傷をつけたため、ダフネはアポロから逃げ続け、月桂樹の木に変身した。　⇒後注　**wood** = forest

58. workmanly = skilfully, with art

59. nothing but a lord　「殿様にほかならぬ」　but = except

61. in this waning age　「この衰えゆく世にあって」　⇒後注

63. envious = malicious, spiteful　**o'errun** = overran

65. yet = even now「涙のせいで容色が衰えていてもなお」

66. ここからスライの台詞は韻文に変わる。l. 23 までは地元の地名や人名をまじえ庶民的な生活ぶりをむき出しにした散文で語っていたが、領主や召使いたちの話し方に影響され、スライがその気になってきてしまったことを表している。ギリシア神話のエロティックな物語をリアルに描いた絵画の話を聞いた後で、自分に「美しい奥方」がいると聞かされ、スライは餌に食いつく魚のように領主たちのトリックにひっかかる。

69. savours = smell

70. Upon my life「この命にかけても」（絶対に）

Well, bring our lady hither to our sight,

And once again a pot o'th' smallest ale.

SECOND SERVANT   Will't please your mightiness to wash your
hands?

O, how we joy to see your wit restored;   75

O, that once more you knew but what you are.

These fifteen years you have been in a dream,

Or when you waked, so waked as if you slept.

SLY   These fifteen years — by my fay, a goodly nap.

But did I never speak of all that time?   80

FIRST SERVANT   O yes, my lord, but very idle words,

For though you lay here in this goodly chamber,

Yet would you say ye were beaten out of door,

And rail upon the hostess of the house,

And say you would present her at the leet,   85

Because she brought stone jugs, and no sealed quarts.

Sometimes you would call out for Cicely Hacket.

SLY   Ay, the woman's maid of the house.

THIRD SERVANT   Why, sir, you know no house, nor no such
maid,

Nor no such men as you have reckoned up,   90

As Stephen Sly, and old John Naps of Greece,

And Peter Turph, and Henry Pimpernell,

And twenty more such names and men as these

Which never were nor no man ever saw.

SLY   Now Lord be thankèd for my good amends.   95

ALL   Amen.

Enter [Page dressed as a] lady with Attendants

SLY   I thank thee, thou shalt not lose by it.

PAGE   How fares my noble lord?

SLY   Marry, I fare well, for here is cheer enough. Where is my
wife?

72. our lady my ではなく our が使われているのは、スライが王様気分になって royal plural（国王が自らを指す際に用いる一人称複数）を使っているため。次の行の smallest ale という庶民的な安酒とのギャップがコミカルな効果を生み出す。

73. smallest ＝ cheapest

75. wit ＝ mental faculty, understanding

76. knew but ＝ knew only「せめてわかっていただけたら」

77. fifteen years Ind. 1. 118 での領主の指示では、スライが正気を失っていたのは「7 年間」という設定だった。ここでは従者が調子にのって「15 年間」と言っている。

79. by my fay ＝ by my faith「実に、まったく」 **goodly** ＝ fair, fine

80. of ＝ in, during

81. idle ＝ meaningless, futile, silly

83. ye ここでは目上の人に対する丁寧な二人称代名詞として使われている。

84. house ＝ alehouse

85. present her at the leet 「酒場の女主人を裁判で訴える」leet は領主裁判所。

86. she brought ... quarts quart は液体の量を示す単位で、1/4 ガロン。**stone jug** は容量がはっきりしない器。 **sealed quart** はその量が入ることを公式に認められている容器で 1/4 ガロンを示す印（seal）がついている。スライは酒の量をごまかされたと怒っている。

87. Cicely Hacket l. 19 でスライが口にした Wincot の酒場の女主人 Marian Hacket の身内の娘。

89. nor no 強く否定するために使われている二重否定。

90. reckoned up 「名前を並べ立てた」

91-92. Stephen Sly ... John Naps ... Peter Turph ... Henry Pimpernell いずれも Marian Hacket や Cicely Hacket と同様、実在の人物と推測できる。Stephen Sly という人物が Stratford に住んでいた記録は残っている。⇒後注

91. Greece ⇒後注

95. amends 「病気が治ったこと」

97. thou shalt not lose by it 「損はさせないからな、褒美をやるからな」 ⇒後注

99. Marry 驚きや不信などを表す間投詞。By Mary(聖母) が崩れて Marry となった。 **I fare well** 小姓が fare を get along の意味で用いて，How fares my noble lord?(ご体調いかがですか) と挨拶したのに対し、スライは fare を food の意味に取って、I fare well(たっぷりいただいている) と答えている。 **cheer** ＝ food, entertainment

PAGE   Here, noble lord, what is thy will with her?   100

SLY   Are you my wife, and will not call me 'husband'?

  My men should call me 'lord'; I am your goodman.

PAGE   My husband and my lord, my lord and husband,

  I am your wife in all obedience.

SLY   I know it well. — What must I call her?   105

LORD   'Madam'.

SLY   'Al'ce Madam', or 'Joan Madam'?

LORD   'Madam', and nothing else. So lords call ladies.

SLY   Madam wife, they say that I have dreamed,

  And slept above some fifteen year or more.   110

PAGE   Ay, and the time seems thirty unto me,

  Being all this time abandoned from your bed.

SLY   'Tis much. Servants, leave me and her alone.

                  [Exeunt Lord and Servants]

  Madam, undresse you and come now to bed.

PAGE   Thrice noble lord, let me entreat of you   115

  To pardon me yet for a night or two,

  Or if not so, until the sun be set.

  For your physicians have expressly charged,

  In peril to incur your former malady,

  That I should yet absent me from your bed.   120

  I hope this reason stands for my excuse.

SLY   Ay, it stands so that I may hardly tarry so long. But I would be loath to fall into my dreams again. I will therefore tarry in despite of the flesh and the blood.

Enter a Messenger

MESSENGER   Your honour's players hearing your amendment,   125

  Are come to play a pleasant comedy,

  For so your doctors hold it very meet,

  Seeing too much sadness hath congealed your blood,

  And melancholy is the nurse of frenzy.

100. what is thy will = what do you want

102. goodman = husband「亭主」というような庶民的な言葉遣い。

104. I am your wife in all obedience　小姓は領主が Ind. 1. 101-25 で指示したとおりの貞淑な奥方を演じている。この類型化された従順な妻のイメージは、本編の芝居の中でのキャタリーナのじゃじゃ馬ぶりと対照をなす。

107. Al'ce = Alice　Alice も Joan も庶民的な名前で貴婦人にはふさわしくない。

109. Madam wife　領主から Madam だけで良いと助言されたのにも関わらず、スライは Madam wife と奇妙な呼び方をしてしまう。

112. abandoned = banished, rejected (*OED v.* 10)

118. expressly charged = specifically ordered

119. In peril to incur your former malady　「これまでの病気が再発してしまう危険があるので」

120. absent = keep far, abstain

121. stands for = can be accepted as, is valid as

122. it stands　スライは前行の stand を性的な意味と解釈した。興奮したスライはもはや気取っておらず、スライの台詞はここで韻文から散文に戻ってしまう。

tarry = wait

hardly は「待ちきれない」という意味とともに、ペニスが「硬くなっている」という意味を重ね合わせた駄洒落。

123. loath = unwilling, disinclined

124. in despite = in spite

the flesh and the blood　スライの肉体すなわち性的な欲望。

124. 1. *Enter a Messenger*　このト書きは F1 のままであるが、l. 113 で退場した領主が伝令役として登場すると考える編者が多い。1) そもそも劇中劇をスライに見せるのは領主の計画であったこと、2)*A Shrew*では役者たちの到来を告げるのは領主であること、この 2 点がその推定の根拠として挙げられる。

126. Are come = have come　　**pleasant** = merry

127. meet = fitting, suitable, appropriate

128-29. シェイクスピアの時代には、血の流れが滞る (congealed your blood) ことでメランコリーとなり、さらにそれがもとで精神の錯乱 (frenzy) が起きてしまうと考えられていた。

sadness = dejection of mind

nurse = nourisher

Therefore they thought it good you hear a play   130
And frame your mind to mirth and merriment,
Which bars a thousand harms and lengthens life.

SLY Marry, I will. Let them play it. Is not a comonty a
Christmas gambold or a tumbling trick?

PAGE No, my good lord, it is more pleasing stuff.   135

SLY What, household stuff?

PAGE It is a kind of history.

SLY Well, we'll see't.
Come, madam wife, sit by my side,
And let the world slip. We shall ne're be younger.   140

130. hear = should hear　シェイクスピアの時代、芝居は「見る」のではなく、「聞く」ものだった。Cf. Ind. 1. 89

131. frame = conform, adjust

132. bars = prevents

133. comonty　スライは comedy と言おうとして comonty と言い間違えた。

134. gambold = gambol「陽気に跳ね回るダンス」

tumbling trick　「アクロバット、曲芸」

135-36. 小姓の more pleasing stuff（もっと面白い内容のもの）という言葉を聞いて、スライは stuff を「物」という字義通りに受け取り household stuff「家財道具」なのかと聞き返している。

137. history = story

140. let the world slip　もともとは‘Let the world wag’ということわざ。スライは Ind. 1. 5 でも let the world slide と言っており、「なんとかなるさ」というスライの楽観的な気質を表している。

We shall ne're be younger　これもよく使われることわざを元にした台詞。「若いうちが花、これから年はとるばかり」というような、その場を楽しもうとする享楽的な気分を表している。この台詞のあと、F1 には特にスライたちの動きを示すト書きはない。スライたちがどこで劇中劇を見るのかが問題となる。

[ACT I, SCENE I]

Flourish. Enter Lucentio and his man Triano

LUCENTIO   Tranio, since for the great desire I had
    To see fair Padua, nursery of arts,
    I am arrived for fruitful Lombardy,
    The pleasant garden of great Italy,
    And by my father's love and leave am armed   5
    With his good will and thy good company —
    My trusty servant, well approved in all —
    Here let us breathe and haply institute
    A course of learning and ingenious studies.
    Pisa, renownèd for grave citizens,   10
    Gave me my being and my father first,
    A merchant of great traffic through the world,
    Vincentio, come of the Bentivolii.
    Vincentio's son, brought up in Florence,
    It shall become to serve all hopes conceived   15
    To deck his fortune with his virtuous deeds:
    And therefore, Tranio, for the time I study,
    Virtue and that part of philosophy
    Will I apply that treats of happiness
    By virtue specially to be achieved.   20
    Tell me thy mind, for I have Pisa left
    And am to Padua come, as he that leaves
    A shallow plash to plunge him in the deep
    And with satiety seeks to quench his thirst.
TRANIO   *Mi perdonato*, gentle master mine,   25
    I am in all affected as yourself,
    Glad that you thus continue your resolve
    To suck the sweets of sweet philosophy.
    Only, good master, while we do admire
    This virtue and this moral discipline,   30

〔**1. 1**〕**あらすじ**……………………………………………………………

　ルーセンシオは学問の都パデュアに到着したとたんバプティスター家を見かけ、娘のビアンカに一目惚れしてしまう。だが父バプティスタは手におえないじゃじゃ馬のキャタリーナに結婚相手が決まらない限りビアンカの結婚は許さない。ビアンカへの求婚者たちはキャタリーナの結婚相手を探そうとし、ルーセンシオも家庭教師に扮してビアンカに近づこうと計画する。

……………………………………………………………

0. 1. *Flourish*　トランペットのファンファーレ。劇の開始を告げる合図。

1. for = because of

2. fair Padua, nursery of arts　パデュアは北イタリのベネト州の都市。　⇒後注　　arts = liberal arts　⇒後注

3. I am arrived for = I have arrived in　　**Lombardy**　北イタリアのロンバルディア州　⇒後注

5. leave = permission　　**armed** = provided　　**6. good will** = consent

7. approved in all　「あらゆることで優れていると証明済みの」

8. breathe = settle down, pause　　**haply** = with good luck　　**institute** = set up, establish

9. ingenious = befitting a well-born person, 'liberal' (*OED adj.* 6)

10. Pisa　イタリア北西部トスカーナ州の都市。

11. first = before me　父親もピサ生まれということ。

12. traffic = trade, business

13. come of the Bentivolii　「ベンティヴォリ家の血を引く」　⇒後注

14-15. Vincentio's son, ... all hopes conceived　Vincentio's son は Lucentio 自身のことで、次行 become の目的語。「自分に寄せられている期待すべて（all hopes conceived）に応えることが、ヴィンセンシオの息子としてフィレンツェで育った自分にはふさわしい」と言っている。

17. for the time = while

19. apply = pursue, devote myself to　　**treats of** = deals with　　**that** は関係代名詞で先行詞は that part of philosophy。「幸福について議論する哲学」に専念するとルーセンシオは言っている。

19-20. happiness / By virtue ... achieved　⇒後注

23. plash = pool

24. satiety = full gratification

25. *Mi perdonato* = Pardon me　舞台がイタリアであることを強調するために、この場面ではイタリア語が台詞の中に散りばめられている。

26. I am ... yourself.　「私もあらゆる点で、あなたと同じ気持になっています。」　　**affected** = disposed

Let's be no stoics nor no stocks, I pray,
Or so devote to Aristotle's checks
As Ovid be an outcast quite abjured.
Balk logic with acquaintance that you have
And practise rhetoric in your common talk; 35
Music and poesy use to quicken you;
The mathematics and the metaphysics,
Fall to them as you find your stomach serves you.
No profit grows where is no pleasure ta'ne:
In brief, sir, study what you most affect. 40
LUCENTIO   Gramercies, Tranio, well dost thou advise.
If, Biondello, thou wert come ashore,
We could at once put us in readiness
And take a lodging fit to entertain
Such friends as time in Padua shall beget. 45
But stay a while, what company is this?
TRANIO   Master, some show to welcome us to town.

Enter Baptista with his two daughters, Katherina and Bianca;
Gremio a pantaloon, Hortensio suiter to Bianca.
Lucenio [and] Tranio stand by

BAPTISTA   Gentlemen, importune me no farther,
For how I firmly am resolved you know:
That is, not to bestow my youngest daughter 50
Before I have a husband for the elder.
If either of you both love Katherina,
Because I know you well and love you well,
Leave shall you have to court her at your pleasure.
GREMIO   To cart her rather. She's too rough for me. 55
There, there, Hortensio, will you any wife?
KATHERINA   [*To Baptista*] I pray you, sir, is it your will
To make a stale of me amongst these mates?
HORTENSIO   'Mates', maid? How mean you that? No mates for

62

31. Let's be no stoics nor no stocks 「堅物にもでくの棒にもなるな」stoic は「禁欲主義者」、stocks は「鈍感な人間」という意味だが、音が似ている言葉を2つ立て続けに並べて言葉遊びをしている。

32. devote = devoted   **Aristotle's checks** 「アリストテレス流の謹厳さ」checks = restrictions

33. As ... abjured 「オウィディウスを無用のものとして捨て去るほどに」トラーニオはオウィディウスを官能的な愛の詩人として、アリストテレスと対比させている。オウィディウスについては Induction 2. 48, 52, 55 および 3. 1. 28-29 の後注を参照のこと。   As = That   abjured = rejected

34-35. Balk logic ... common talk logic や rhetoric は必須の学問だが、友人との議論で論理学の勉強ができるし、日常のおしゃべりをしながら修辞学の勉強ができると、トラーニオは言っている。1. 1. 2 の後注を参照のこと。balk logic = chop logic, bandy words (*OED v*. 6)

36. quicken = enliven

38. Fall to 「(数学や形而上学)に取りかかる」   **your stomach serves you** 「食欲がわいたときに」 serves = prompts, dispose (*OED v.* 24a)

40. affect = like   **41. Gramercies** = many thanks

42. Biondello ルーセンシオはここには来ていないもう1人の召使いに向かって呼びかけている。   **wert** 主語が thou の時の be の過去形。

come ashore ⇒後注

45. beget = produce   **47. show** = play, entertainment

47. 2. *pantaloon* コメディア・デラルテで類型化された滑稽な役柄。老人なのに好色で、若者たちの恋愛に横槍を入れ、最後には笑い物にされる。

48. importune = urge

50. bestow = give in marriage

54. Leave = permission 「求婚 (court) する許可を与える」と言っている。

55. cart 前行の court の音が似ていることを利用した言葉遊び。carting は荷車 (cart) に乗せて町中を引き回し、見せ物にすること。娼婦やうるさい女に対する罰として行われていた。   **rough** = bad-tempered, harsh

56. will = wish to have, want

58-59. To make a stale ... for you ここでは複数の言葉遊びが組み合わせられている。stale には「エサ、おとり」「下賤な娼婦」「笑い物」の意味がある。mates にも「連中」と「連れ合い、配偶者」の意味が重ね合わされている。さらに2つの言葉が連動して、チェスの stalemate（手詰まり）も連想させる。キャタリーナは「こんな連中の間で私を「笑いもの」/（妹の結婚のための）「おとり」/「娼婦」扱いしようとしている」と父親に不平を言っている。次行のホーテンシオは mate を「配偶者」の意味に取り、「あなたに連れ合いはできない」と断言している。

you

Unless you were of gentler, milder mould.   60

KATHERINA   I'faith, sir, you shall never need to fear:

Iwis it is not halfway to her heart.

But if it were, doubt not her care should be

To comb your noddle with a three-legged stool,

And paint your face and use you like a fool.   65

HORTENSIO   From all such devils, good Lord deliver us.

GREMIO   And me too, good Lord.

TRANIO   [*Aside to Lucentio*] Husht, master! Here's some good
pastime toward;

That wench is stark mad or wonderful froward.

LUCENTIO   [*Aside to Tranio*] But in the other's silence do I see   70

Maids' mild behaviour and sobriety.

Peace, Tranio.

TRANIO   [*Aside to Lucentio*] Well said, master. Mum, and gaze
your fill.

BAPTISTA   Gentlemen, that I may soon make good

What I have said — Bianca, get you in,   75

And let it not displease thee, good Bianca,

For I will love thee ne'er the less, my girl.

KATHERINA   A pretty peat! It is best

Put finger in the eye, an she knew why.

BIANCA   Sister, content you in my discontent.   80

— Sir, to your pleasure humbly I subscribe:

My books and instruments shall be my company,

On them to look and practise by myself.

LUCENTIO   [*Aside*] Hark, Tranio, thou may'st hear Minerva
speak.

HORTENSIO   Signor Baptista, will you be so strange?   85

Sorry am I that our good will effects

Bianca's grief.

GREMIO   Why will you mew her up,

60. mould = constitution, character　もともとは型や枠 (frame, cast) に入れて出来上がった形の意味。人やものの性質という意味でも使う。(*OED n.*³ 1)

62. Iwis = certainly, indeed

it is not halfway to her heart「そんなこと (結婚) なんて本心から程遠い」キャタリーナは自分のことを her と他人事のように言っている。

63. her care = her chief concern

64. To comb your noddle with a three-legged stool　「脳天を椅子でガツンと叩いてやる」という意味のことわざ。　comb = to beat, thrash (*OED v*¹. 3) noddle = head

65. paint your face　「顔を（ひっかいて血だらけにし）真っ赤に染めてやる」ll. 64-65 は stool と fool という同じ音で終わる二行対句 (couplet) である。

66. good Lord deliver us　「神様が守ってくれますように」という祈願文。助動詞 may が省略されている。

68. Husht = hush　「静かに」という間投詞。

pastime = entertainment　　**toward** = about to take place

69. wonderful froward = incredibly perverse　wonderful はここでは副詞。

71. sobriety = modesty

72. Peace = be silent

73. Mum = be silent

your fill = as much as you like

74-76.「すでに申し上げたとおりにしたいので」と言いかけたところで話を中断し、ビアンカに家に入りなさいと命じている。

78. peat = pet, spoilt child

79. Put finger in the eye　「（目に指をつっこんで）嘘の涙を出す」という意味のことわざ。前に to が省略されている。「口実を思いついたら泣きまねすれば一番効果的だわ」と皮肉を言っている。

an = if

81. pleasure = command, will

subscribe = submit

84. Minerva　ミネルヴァ、古代ローマの知恵の女神。ここではもちろんビアンカのことを言っている。

85. strange = unfriendly, cold

86. effects = causes, produces

87. mew her up = shut her up

Signor Baptista, for this fiend of hell,
And make her bear the penance of her tongue?

BAPTISTA Gentlemen, content ye: I am resolved. 90
Go in Bianca. [*Exit Bianca*]
And for I know she taketh most delight
In music, instruments and poetry,
Schoolmasters will I keep within my house
Fit to instruct her youth. If you, Hortensio, 95
Or, Signor Gremio, you know any such,
Prefer them hither, for to cunning men,
I will be very kind, and liberal
To mine own children in good bringing up.
And so farewell. — Katherina, you may stay, 100
For I have more to commune with Bianca. *Exit*

KATHERINA Why, and I trust I may go too, may I not? What,
shall I be appointed hours, as though, belike, I knew not
what to take and what to leave? Ha! *Exit*

GREMIO You may go to the devil's dam. Your gifts are so good 105
here's none will hold you. — Their love is not so great,
Hortensio, but we may blow our nails together and fast it
fairly out. Our cake's dough on both sides. Farewell. Yet for
the love I bear my sweet Bianca, if I can by any means light
on a fit man to teach her that wherein she delights, I will wish 110
him to her father.

HORTENSIO So will I, Signor Gremio. But a word, I pray.
Though the nature of our quarrel yet never brooked parle,
know now, upon advice, it touches us both — that we may yet
again have access to our fair mistress and be happy rivals in 115
Bianca's love — to labour and effect one thing specially.

GREMIO What's that, I pray?

HORTENSIO Marry, sir, to get a husband for her sister.

GREMIO A husband? A devil.

HORTENSIO I say a husband. 120

88. for = because of　　**this fiend of hell** はキャタリーナのことを指している。

89. 最初の her はビアンカ、2つ目の her はキャタリーナ。「キャタリーナの口の悪さのせいで、ビアンカに辛い思いをさせるなんて」と言っている。

90. ye　二人称の代名詞 thou の複数形。ここではビアンカの求婚者たちを指している。

93-95. music, instruments and poetry　⇒後注

94. Schoolmasters = private tutors（*OED n.*^{l} 1c）

95. Fit = well qualified, becoming

97. Prefer = recommend　　**cunning** = knowledgeable, skilful

98-99. liberal ... bringing up　「我が子に良い教育をするためなら、金に糸目はつけない」　　liberal = bounteous

101. commune = talk over together, discuss（*OED v.* 1b）

103. shall I be appointed hours　「何時になったら何をしろと指図されるの？」　　**belike** = as it seems, I suppose

104. Ha!　驚きや怒りを表す間投詞。「冗談じゃないわ！」とキャタリーナは怒って退場する。

105. dam = mother　悪魔の母親は悪魔よりも凶悪なものとされ、手に負えない女の代名詞でもあった。キャタリーナはその仲間になれるとグレミオは言っている。　gifts（天賦の才）はもちろん皮肉。

106. here's none will hold you　none と will の間に関係代名詞 that が省略されている。　　**Their love**　⇒後注

107. but we may = that we cannot　　**blow our nails** = wait, waste time, to be unable to do anything useful（*OED n.* P2b）

107-08. fast it fairly out「そろって仲良く我慢する」fast out は「禁欲して過ごす」　　fairly = peacefully

108. Our cake's ... both sides.　直訳すると「われわれ2人とも、ケーキが生焼けでふくらまなかった」となるが、つまり「2人とも運が悪い」という意味。'My cake is dough' ということわざを下敷きにしている。前行の blow our nails もことわざ。グレミオにことわざを使った台詞が多いのは、いかにも老人らしい印象を与えるため。

109-10. light on = come upon　　**110. wish** = recommend

113. yet never brooked parle　「これまでは交渉などできなかったが」　　brook = tolerate　　parle = parley, conversation

114. upon advice　「熟慮して」　　advice = consideration, reflection　　**touches** = affect, concern　　**that** = so that

116. labour and effect　「なんとかして実現する」labour（= endeavour to bring about）も effect（= produce）も one thing を目的語とする他動詞。

118. Marry　Induction 2. 99 を参照。

Gremio   I say a devil. Think'st thou, Hortensio, though her
father be very rich, any man is so very a fool to be married to
hell?

Hortensio   Tush, Gremio; though it pass your patience and
mine to endure her loud alarums, why, man, there be good   125
fellows in the world, an a man could light on them, would
take her with all faults, and money enough.

Gremio   I cannot tell, but I had as lief take her dowry with
this condition: to be whipped at the high cross every morning.

Hortensio   Faith, as you say, there's small choice in rotten   130
apples. But come, since this bar in law makes us friends, it
shall be so far forth friendly maintained till by helping
Baptista's eldest daughter to a husband we set his youngest
free for a husband, and then have to't afresh. Sweet Bianca!
Happy man be his dole. He that runs fastest gets the ring.   135
How say you, Signor Gremio?

Gremio   I am agreed, and would I had given him the best
horse in Padua to begin his wooing that would thoroughly
woo her, wed her, and bed her, and rid the house of her.
Come on.   *Exeunt* [*Gremio and Hortensio*]   140

Tranio   I pray, sir, tell me, is it possible
That love should of a sudden take such hold?

Lucentio   O Tranio, till I found it to be true,
I never thought it possible or likely.
But see, while idly I stood looking on,   145
I found the effect of love-in-idleness,
And now in plainness do confess to thee
That art to me as secret and as dear
As Anna to the Queen of Carthage was,
Tranio, I burn, I pine, I perish, Tranio,   150
If I achieve not this young modest girl.
Counsel me, Tranio, for I know thou canst;
Assist me Tranio, for I know thou wilt.

124. Tush 「ちぇっ」というようなじれったさを表す間投詞。

pass = exceed

125. alarums もともとは「出撃の合図の音」を指すが、ここでは比喩的に「けたたましい声」のことを言っている。

126. an = if

would この前に関係代名詞の that が省略されている。先行詞は good fellows。

127. with all faults 「難あり」「責任は買主」という意味で'WAF'と略され広く使われているが、もともとは家畜の売買の際に用いられた用語。「じゃじゃ馬」であるキャタリーナには、劇中、繰り返し動物の比喩が用いられる。

128. had as lief = would as willingly

129. high cross 市場十字。市場として使われる町の中心の広場に建てられた目標の建造物。イングランドでは鞭打ち刑の場として広場が使われた。

130-31. there's ... apples 「悪いものばかりで選択肢がない」という意味のことわざ。

131. this bar in law 娘たちの結婚については父バプティスタが決定権を持っているという「法律上の障害」。

131-32. it shall be so far forth friendly maintained 「友好的に事態を進めよう」

134. have to't afresh 「あらためて求婚争いを再開しよう」

135. Happy man be his dole 直訳すると「幸せ者」が彼の運命 (dole) でありますようにという意味だが、そのあとに続く文と合わせて「勝者に幸せを。強いものが勝つ」と、ことわざを連発して言っている。

ring 女性性器を表す隠語としてしばしば用いられる。

137. would = I wish

139. woo her, wed her, and bed her 結婚するまでのプロセスを表す決まり文句。そのあとにホーテンシオは rid という1音節で似た音の言葉をつなげて言葉遊びをしている。

142. of a sudden = suddenly

146. love-in-idleness 植物のパンジー。パンジーの花の汁には恋心をかきたてる力があるという言い習わしがあった。*A Midsummer Night's Dream* 第2幕第1場で、オーベロンがこの花の力を利用する。

148. secret 「腹心の」(intimately trusted) という意味の形容詞。

149. Anna カルタゴ文明を築いた賢明な女王ディドは英雄アエネアスと恋に落ちるが、アエネアスはディドを捨てて去ってしまう。アンナとディドは姉妹同士でアンナはディドの相談相手だった。

TRANIO   Master, it is no time to chide you now.
Affection is not rated from the heart.   155
If love have touched you, naught remains but so:
Redime te captum quam queas minimo.

LUCENTIO   Gramercies, lad. Go forward. This contents;
The rest will comfort, for thy counsel's sound.

TRANIO   Master, you looked so longly on the maid,   160
Perhaps you marked not what's the pith of all.

LUCENTIO   Oh yes, I saw sweet beauty in her face,
Such as the daughter of Agenor had
That made great Jove to humble him to her hand
When with his knees he kissed the Cretan strand.   165

TRANIO   Saw you no more? Marked you not how her sister
Began to scold and raise up such a storm
That mortal ears might hardly endure the din.

LRUCENTIO   Tranio, I saw her coral lips to move,
And with her breath she did perfume the air.   170
Sacred and sweet was all I saw in her.

TRANIO   [*Aside*]   Nay, then 'tis time to stir him from his trance.
— I pray, awake, sir. If you love the maid,
Bend thoughts and wits to achieve her. Thus it stands:
Her elder sister is so curst and shrewd   175
That till the father rid his hands of her,
Master, your love must live a maid at home,
And therefore has he closely mewed her up
Because she will not be annoyed with suitors.

LUCENTIO   Ah, Tranio, what a cruel father's he!   180
But art thou not advised he took some care
To get her cunning schoolmasters to instruct her?

TRANIO   Ay, marry, am I, sir — and now 'tis plotted.

LUCENTIO   I have it, Tranio.

TRANIO   Master, for my hand,
Both our inventions meet and jump in one.   185

155. rated = scolded, driven away by chiding

156. naught = nothing

  but = except

  so は次の行の内容を指す。

157. *Redime ... minimo* 当時のグラマー・スクールで教科書として使われていた William Lily の文法書からの引用。英訳は 'Free yourself from captivity at the lowest ransom you can.'

158. This contents 「今言ってくれたことには満足している」

159. The rest will comfort 「助言の続きにも満足するだろう」

  sound = reliable, based on a good judgement

160. longly 「長い間 (for a long time)」と「うっとりと (longingly)」と2つの意味を兼ねている。

161. marked = noticed

  pith of all = essential part, main point

163-65. the daughter of Agenor フェニキア（現レバノン）の王アゲノールの娘エウロペ（Europa）のこと。エウロペの美しさに、最高神ゼウス (Zeus = ローマ神話の Jove) は魅せられる。ゼウスは白い牡牛に変身し、背にエウロペを乗せてクレタ島 (Crete) まで泳いで渡った。

168. din ひどくやかましい騒音。

171. Sacred and sweet was all I saw in her. この行の文章の主語は all。 all と I の間に関係代名詞 that が省略されている。

174. Bend thoughts and wits 「頭脳と知恵をふりしぼってください」 bend = direct to a task

175. curst = perverse, bad-tempered

  shrewd = sharp of tongue, shrewish

177. your love = Bianca

  live a maid 未婚のまま暮らす

178. closely = securely

  mewed her up = confined her

179. Because = in order that, so that

  annoyed with = troubled by (*OED v.* 2a)

181. art thou not advised = are you not aware

182. cunning = knowledgeable, skilful

183. 'tis plotted 「策略ができました」この直前のダッシュは、黙って考えをめぐらしている「間」を表現している。

184. for my hand = for my part

185. Both our inventions meet and jump in one 「私たち2人の考えついたことはぴったり重なります」 meet = agree jump = coincide

LUCENTIO   Tell me thine first.

TRANIO   You will be schoolmaster,
   And undertake the teaching of the maid.
   That's your device.

LRUCENTIO   It is. May it be done?

TRANIO   Not possible: for who shall bear your part
   And be in Padua here Vincentio's son,   205
   Keep house and ply his book, welcome his friends,
   Visit his countrymen and banquet them?

LUCENTIO   *Basta*, content thee, for I have it full.
   We have not yet been seen in any house,
   Nor can we be distinguished by our faces   195
   For man or master. Then it follows thus:
   Thou shalt be master, Tranio, in my stead,
   Keep house and port and servants as I should.
   I will some other be, some Florentine,
   Some Neapolitan, or meaner man of Pisa.   200
   'Tis hatched, and shall be so. Tranio, at once
   Uncase thee. Take my coloured hat and cloak.
                    [*They exchange clothes*]
   When Biondello comes, he waits on thee,
   But I will charm him first to keep his tongue.

TRANIO   So had you need.   205
   In brief, sir, sith it your pleasure is,
   And I am tied to be obedient —
   For so your father charged me at our parting:
   "Be serviceable to my son", quoth he,
   Although I think 'twas in another sense —   210
   I am content to be Lucentio,
   Because so well I love Lucentio.

LUCENTIO   Tranio, be so, because Lucentio loves,
   And let me be a slave t'achieve that maid
   Whose sudden sight hath thralled my wounded eye.   215

188. device = plot

  May = can

189. bear = play

190. And be in Padua here Vincentio's son,「ヴィンセンシオの息子としてパデュアに滞在する」

191. Keep house「主人として客人を迎える」

  ply his book = apply himself to his studies

192. his countrymen「同郷（ピサ）の人たち」

  banquet = treat with a feast

193. *Basta* = enough（イタリア語）

  I have it full　「それはもう十分に考えてある」

198. port = social position, state, style of living

200. meaner = poorer

201. hatched = devised, planned

202. Uncase thee = take off your outer garment

  my coloured hat and cloak　シェイクスピアの時代の召使いは青い制服を着ていることが多かった。ここでは青ではない、主人らしい色のついた服装を身につけろと言っている。

203. waits on = serves

204. charm ... his tongue　「（魔法をかけるように）説得して黙らせる」

205. So had you need.　この1行は4音節で短い。「その必要があるでしょうねえ」とトラーニオは言っているが、その理由を詳しく語るわけではなく、次行の In brief（「ようするに」）という言葉とも話のつながりも良くない。そのためここで台詞の削除があったのではないかと考えられる。

206. sith = since

207. tied = bound

208. charged = ordered, commanded

209. serviceable = diligent in service

210. 'twas in another sense　「こんな仕事は（お父上の）念頭になく別の意味でしたが」

215. Whose sudden sight　「その姿を見たとたんに」

  thralled = enslaved

Enter Biondello

Here comes the rogue. Sirrah, where have you been?

BIONDELLO   Where have I been? Nay, how now, where are you?
Master, has my fellow Tranio stolen your clothes, or you
stolen his, or both? Pray, what's the news?

LUCENTIO   Sirrah, come hither. 'Tis no time to jest,   220
And therefore frame your manners to the time.
Your fellow Tranio here, to save my life,
Puts my apparel and my countenance on,
And I for my escape have put on his,
For in a quarrel since I came ashore   225
I killed a man, and fear I was descried.
Wait you on him, I charge you, as becomes,
While I make way from hence to save my life.
You understand me?

BIONDELLO   I, sir? Ne're a whit.

LUCENTIO   And not a jot of 'Tranio' in your mouth.   230
Tranio is changed into Lucentio.

BIONDELLO   The better for him. Would I were so too.

TRANIO   So could I, faith, boy, to have the next wish after:
That Lucentio indeed had Baptista's youngest daughter.
But, sirrah, not for my sake but your master's, I advise   235
You use your manners discreetly in all kind of companies.
When I am alone, why, then I am Tranio,
But in all places else your master Lucentio.

LUCENTIO   Tranio let's go.
One thing more rests that thyself execute: 240
To make one among these wooers. If thou ask me why,
Sufficeth my reasons are both good and weighty.   *Exeunt*

The Presenters above speaks

FIRST SERVANT   My lord, you nod. You do not mind the play.

216. Sirrah 「おいおい」「こら」というようなじれったさを表す、目下の者への呼びかけ。

217. how now 「いったいどうしたんですか」という驚きを表す表現。

218. fellow = fellow servant

219. Pray = please

221. frame = fit, adapt

223. countenance = appearance, manner

225. came ashore ⇒ l. 42 の後注

226. descried = recognized, identified

227. as becomes 「（主従関係として）ふさわしいように」

229. Ne'er a whit = not in the lease　a whit は「ごくわずか」という意味。否定文で使うのが通例。

230. not a jot of 'Tranio' in your mouth 「トラーニオという名前をわずかでも口にしてはダメだぞ」

232. Would = I wish

233-38. このトラーニオの台詞は F1 では散文として印刷されているが、18 世紀の本文批評家ケイペル (Capell) が荒削りな韻文もどき (doggerel) の調子を読み取り、韻文として行分けした。　⇒後注

233. So could I, faith, boy, to have the next wish after, 「俺がルーセンシオになれるのも、次なる望みを叶えるため」　faith = in faith

236. use your manners discreetly 「俺に対してわきまえた態度を取れ」

240. rests = remains　次に続く関係代名詞 that の先行詞は One thing more.「お前が実行しなければならないことがもう１つ残っている」

241. make = become

242. Sufficeth = it sufficeth that 「それ（that 以下の内容）で十分だ」「それ以上の説明は不要だ」

242. 0. *The Presenters* シェイクスピアの時代の劇場では、劇の説明役や紹介者を presenter と呼んだ。ここではスライらインダクションに登場した人物たちを指している。F1 のト書きでは above と二階舞台の使用が示唆されているが、当時の実際の上演については議論が分かれている。またこの場面を最後にスライが登場しなくなることについても、さまざまな議論がなされている。付録 (p.220-) を参照のこと。

243. nod = sleep　　**mind** = pay attention to

SLY Yes, by Saint Anne, do I. A good matter, surely. Comes
there any more of it?   245

PAGE My lord, 'tis but begun.

SLY 'Tis a very excellent piece of work, madam lady. Would
'twere done.   *They sit and mark*

[ACT I, SCENE II]

Enter Petruchio and his man Grumio

PETRUCHIO Verona, for a while I take my leave

To see my friends in Padua, but of all

My best belovèd and approvèd friend

Hortensio; and I trow this is his house.

Here, sirrah Grumio, knock, I say.   5

GRUMIO Knock, sir? Whom should I knock? Is there any man

has rebused your worship?

PETRUCHIO Villain, I say, knock me here soundly.

GRUMIO Knock you here, sir? Why, sir, what am I, sir, that I

should knock you here, sir.   10

PETRUCHIO Villain, I say, knock me at this gate

And rap me well, or I'll knock your knave's pate.

GRUMIO My master is grown quarrelsome. I should knock
you first,

And then I know after who comes by the worst.

PETRUCHIO Will it not be?   15

'Faith, sirrah, an you'll not knock, I'll ring it.

I'll try how you can *sol-fa* and sing it.

He wrings him by the ears

GRUMIO Help, masters, help! My master is mad.

PETRUCHIO Now knock when I bid you, sirrah villain.

Enter Hortensio

HORTENSIO How now, what's the matter? My old friend   20

244. Saint Anne 聖母マリアの母親。　　**matter** = subject「良い内容だ」と
言ってはいるものの、スライは居眠りをしていた。またこれで芝居が終わりか
と誤解している。スライにとってラテン喜劇風の洗練された喜劇は高尚すぎ
る。

247-48. Would 'twere done. 「早く終わってほしいものだ」　Would = I wish

〔**1. 2**〕**あらすじ**……………………………………………………………………………………
　金持ちの娘と結婚したいと考えているペトルーチオは、ホーテンシオからキャ
タリーナのことを聞き、どんなじゃじゃ馬でも持参金さえあれば問題ないと求婚
を決意する。一方のビアンカへの求婚者たちは、それぞれに策をめぐらす。ホー
テンシオは音楽教師として近づこうとし、グレミオも家庭教師に扮したルーセン
シオを使って言い寄ろうとしている。トラーニオもルーセンシオに扮して、求婚
者の一人として名乗りをあげる。
……………………………………………………………………………………

1. Verona 北イタリアのベネト州西部の都市。ペトルーチオは「ヴェローナ
よ」とこの町に向かって呼びかけている。　⇒後注

2. of all = most important of all

3. approvèd = put to proof, tested　*cf.* 1. 1. 7

4. I trow = I am pretty sure

7. rebused グルーミオ（ペトルーチオの召使い）は abuse を言い間違えて
rebuse と言っている。　⇒後注

8. knock me here この me は ethical dative（心的与格）。Induction 1. 46
を参照。ただしグルーミオは（わざと）me を knock の目的語と受けとって、
「ご主人をひっぱたくなんて」とうろたえ（るふりをし）ている。　⇒後注
soundly「しっかりと」

12. rap これも knock と同様、グルーミオはペトルーチオを叩くことだと受け
とる。　　**pate** = head　この pate は前行の gate と韻を踏んでいる。

13-14. My master is ... by the worst. 行末の first と worst は韻を踏んでい
る。「まず殴れと命じられて、それからひどい目にあうのはお見通しだ」とい
う趣旨のことを、ふざけた口調の二行対句でグルーミオは言っている。

15. Will it not be?「俺の命令通りにならないのか？」

16. an = if　　**ring** ring the bell（呼び鈴を鳴らす）という意味だが、同音異
義語の wring（お前を絞りあげてやる）と重ね合わせた言葉遊び (pun) になっ
ている。

17. *sol-fa*「ドレミファソラシドで歌う」　ring it と sing it も音を合わせた言
葉遊び。

Grumio and my good friend Petruchio? How do you all at
Verona?

PETRUCHIO   Signor Hortensio, come you to part the fray?
Con tutto il cuore ben trovato, may I say.

HORTENSIO   *Alla nostra casa ben venuto, molto honorato signor mio*   25
Petruccio.
Rise, Grumio, rise. We will compound this quarrel.

GRUMIO   Nay, 'tis no matter sir, what he 'lleges in Latin. If this
be not a lawful cause for me to leave his service, look you, sir:
he bid me knock him and rap him soundly, sir. Well, was it fit   30
for a servant to use his master so, being perhaps, for aught I
see, two and thirty, a pip out?
Whom would to God I had well knocked at first,
Then had not Grumio come by the worst.

PETRUCHIO   A senseless villain! Good Hortensio,   35
I bade the rascal knock upon your gate,
And could not get him for my heart to do it.

GRUMIO   Knock at the gate? O heavens, spake you not these
words plain: 'Sirrah, knock me here, rap me here, knock me
well, and knock me soundly'? And come you now with   40
'knocking at the gate'?

PETRUCHIO   Sirrah, be gone, or talk not, I advise you.

HORTENSIO   Petruchio, patience. I am Grumio's pledge.
Why, this' a heavy chance 'twixt him and you —
Your ancient, trusty, pleasant servant Grumio.   45
And tell me now, sweet friend, what happy gale
Blows you to Padua here from old Verona?

PETRUCHIO   Such wind as scatters young men through the
world
To seek their fortunes farther than at home,
Where small experience grows. But in a few,   50
Signor Hortensio, thus it stands with me:
Antonio my father is deceased,

21-22. How do you all at Verona? = How are you and your family at Verona?

23. part the fray 「喧嘩をやめさせる」

24. *Con tutto ... trovato* イタリア語で 'With all my heart, well met!' の意。

25-26. *Alla ... Petruccio.* イタリア語で 'Welcome to our house, much honoured Signor Petruccio.' の意。

27. compound = settle or compose (*OED v.* 6a)

28. 'lleges = alleges　　**in Latin** ペトルーチオとホーテンシオがイタリア語で挨拶をしたのを聞いて、グルーミオはラテン語だと誤解した。筋書きの上ではグルーミオもイタリア人なので、イタリア語とラテン語の区別がつかないのはおかしいが、シェイクスピアはこうした整合性には比較的、無頓着である。筋書き上のつじつま合わせよりも、喜劇的効果の面白さの方を優先している。

31. use = treat　　**for aught** = for anything

32. two and thirty, a pip out 「ずれている、頭がおかしい」という意味と推測できる。one-and-thirty と呼ばれる、数字の合計を 31 にすることを目指すトランプのゲームがある。「32 なので 1 点 (a pip) やりすぎ」という意味ではないかと解釈する説が有力。

33-34. Whom would ... the worst Whom は前の文からの続きでペトルーチオを指す関係代名詞。　　would = wish 「最初に旦那を引っぱたいておいて、ひどい目にあわずにすめばよかったのになあ」という意味。ll. 13-14 と同様に first と worst で脚韻を踏んで自分の言い分を締めくくっている。

35. senseless = foolish

37. for my heart = for my life 「どうしても」という意。

40-41. And come you now with 'knocking at the gate'? 「それで今になって『ドアを叩けと言った』と言い出すんですか？」

43. pledge 「保証人」（法律用語）

44. this' = this is　　**heavy** = regrettable　　**chance** = happening

45. ancient 「長年仕えている」　　**pleasant** = merry

46-47. what happy gale ... old Verona? 「どういう風の吹きまわしで慣れ親しんだヴェローナを離れてパデュアにやってきたんだい？」

50. Where small experience grows 「故郷にいてはたいした経験はできない」という意。　　**in a few** = in short, briefly　⇒後注

And I have thrust myself into this maze,
Happily to wive and thrive as best I may.
Crowns in my purse I have and goods at home,   55
And so am come abroad to see the world.

HORTENSIO Petruchio, shall I then come roundly to thee
And wish thee to a shrewd ill-favoured wife?
Thou'dst thank me but a little for my counsel.
And yet I'll promise thee she shall be rich,   60
And very rich. But thou'rt too much my friend,
And I'll not wish thee to her.

PETRUCHIO Signor Hortensio, 'twixt such friends as we
Few words suffice; and therefore, if thou know
One rich enough to be Petruchio's wife —   65
As wealth is burden of my wooing dance —
Be she as foul as was Florentius' love,
As old as Sibyl, and as curst and shrewd
As Socrates' Xanthippe, or a worse,
She moves me not, or not removes at least   70
Affection's edge in me, were she as rough
As are the swelling Adriatic seas.
I come to wive it wealthily in Padua;
If wealthily, then happily in Padua.

GRUMIO Nay, look you, sir, he tells you flatly what his mind is. 75
Why, give him gold enough and marry him to a puppet or an
aglet-baby, or an old trot with ne'er a tooth in her head,
though she have as many diseases as two and fifty horses.
Why, nothing comes amiss, so money comes withal.

HORTENSIO Petruchio, since we are stepped thus far in,   80
I will continue that I broached in jest.
I can, Petruchio, help thee to a wife
With wealth enough, and young and beauteous,
Brought up as best becomes a gentlewoman.
Her only fault, and that is faults enough,   85

53. this maze = this labyrinth, uncertain business

54. Happily = with luck

wive and thrive　「結婚して金持ちになる」当時のことわざ 'First thrive and then wive', あるいは 'It is hard to wive and thrive both in a year' を踏まえた台詞。

56. am come abroad = have come abroad

57. come roundly to thee　「君に率直な話をする」 roundly = plainly

58. wish = recommend　　**shrewd** = shrewish, unruly

ill-favoured　通常は「器量が悪い、不美人だ」という意味だが、l. 83 ではキャタリーナは beauteous と形容されているので、ここでの ill-favoured は「気性が激しい」という意味であろう。

59. Thou'dst = you would　　**but** = only

64. suffice = are enough, sufficient

66. burden　「低音部のメロディ、伴奏」

67. Be she as foul as was Florentius' love　「フロレンティウスの恋人ほどの不美人であろうとも」フロレンティウスは John Gower (c.1330-1408) の物語詩 *Confessio Amantis*（『恋人の告白』）に登場する騎士。醜い老婆に助けられて謎を解き、死を免れたが、その老婆と結婚しなければならなかった。

68. Sibyl　ギリシア神話に出てくる巫女シビュラ。手に握った砂の粒の数だけの年数の命をアポロンから与えられた。

69. Xanthippe　ソクラテスの妻クサンティッペは悪妻の代表として有名。夫を常に口汚く罵っていたとされるが、悪妻ぶりは史実ではなく、後世に誇張されたもの。

70. She moves me not　「私の決意は動かない」

71. Affection's edge　「私の想いの鋭さ、強さ」

73. wive it　「妻を娶る」この it は wive が動詞であることを示す役割をしており、何かを指し示してはいない。

75. flatly = plainly　　**his mind** = his opinion

77. aglet-baby　留ひもやリボンの先に重りとして付けられた小さな、人形の形をした飾り。　　**old trot**　「醜い老婆」

78. though she have as many diseases as two and fifty horses　1. 1. 127 と同様に市場で売買される馬に女性を喩えている。「病気だらけの売り物にならない馬みたいだったとしても」という意味。

79. nothing comes amiss　「なんの問題もない」　　**so** = if

80. since we are stepped thus far in　「ここまで踏み込んだからには」

81. that = what　　**broached in jest**　「ふざけて話し始めた」

84. becomes　「似つかわしい、ふさわしい」

Is that she is intolerable curst,

And shrewd and froward so beyond all measure

That, were my state far worser than it is,

I would not wed her for a mine of gold.

PETRUCHIO   Hortensio, peace. Thou know'st not gold's effect.   90

Tell me her father's name and 'tis enough,

For I will board her though she chide as loud

As thunder when the clouds in autumn crack.

HORTENSIO   Her father is Baptista Minola,

An affable and courteous gentleman.   95

Her name is Katherina Minola,

Renowned in Padua for her scolding tongue.

PETRUCHIO   I know her father, though I know not her,

And he knew my deceasèd father well.

I will not sleep, Hortensio, till I see her,   100

And therefore let me be thus bold with you

To give you over at this first encounter,

Unless you will accompany me thither.

GRUMIO   I pray you, sir, let him go while the humour lasts. O'

my word, an she knew him as well as I do, she would think   105

scolding would do little good upon him. She may perhaps

call him half a score knaves or so. Why, that's nothing; an he

begin once, he'll rail in his rope-tricks. I'll tell you what, sir,

an she stand him but a little, he will throw a figure in her face

and so disfigure her with it that she shall have no more eyes   110

to see withal than a cat. You know him not, sir.

HORTENSIO   Tarry, Petruchio, I must go with thee,

For in Baptista's keep my treasure is.

He hath the jewel of my life in hold,

His youngest daughter, beautiful Bianca,   115

And her withholds from me and other more —

Suitors to her, and rivals in my love —

Supposing it a thing impossible,

86. intolerable = intolerably 　　 **curst** = bad-tempered

87. froward = difficult to deal with, perverse

beyond all measure = exceedingly, excessively

88. were my state ... it is 「私の経済状況が今よりはるかに悪いとしても」if が
省略されて語順が倒置している。

92. board 「乗りこむ」もともとは海戦で他の船を襲撃することを指す言葉。こ
こではセクシャルな意味も匂わされているので、「襲ってやる」と訳しても良
いだろう。　　 **chide** = scold

93. crack 「爆音を轟（とどろ）かせる」

95. affable = good-natured, friendly

101-02. let me be thus bold ... this first encounter 「会って早々だが失礼させ
てくれ」　　 **give you over** = leave you

103. thither = to that place　ここではキャタリーナのところに行くことを指
している。

104. the humour 「（そのガミガミ女と結婚するという）気まぐれな気分」

104-05. O' my word = On my word「誓ってもいいが」

105. an = if

106. do little good = be little useful, have little useful effect

107. half a score = ten

that's nothing 「そんなもの（ごろつき呼ばわり）は無意味だ」　　 **an** = if

108. in his rope-tricks ⇒後注

109. stand = resist

throw a figure in her face 「面（ばり）と向かって罵詈雑言を投げつける」この
figure は a figure of speech（比喩的表現）の意。

110. disfigure = deform　前行の figure の意味を文字通りの「形」という意味
にずらし、「（罵詈雑言を顔に向かって投げつけられたせいで）顔形が崩れてし
まう」と言っている。

110-11. no more eyes to see withal than a cat そのまま訳すと「猫同然に目
が見えなくなってしまう」という意味だが、なぜ「猫」なのか判然としない。
猫が互いにひっかきあって、目が見えなくなってしまうというイメージではな
いかという推測する研究者もいる。

113. keep ここでは名詞。「大事にとっている」(keeping) という抽象的な意味
か、「塔の中の保存庫、要塞」(castle keep) のいずれか。

114. hold = keeping, custody

116. other more = others besides

118. it l. 120 の That 以下の内容を指す。

For those defects I have before rehearsed,
That ever Katherina will be wooed.   120
Therefore this order hath Baptista ta'en,
That none shall have access unto Bianca
Till Katherine the curst have got a husband.

GRUMIO   'Katherine the Curst'!
A title for a maid of all titles the worst.   125

HORTENSIO   Now shall my friend Petruchio do me grace,
And offer me disguised in sober robes
To old Baptista as a schoolmaster
Well seen in music, to instruct Bianca,
That so I may by this device at least   130
Have leave and leisure to make love to her
And unsuspected court her by herself.

Enter Gremio and Lucentio disguised [as Cambio]

GRUMIO   Here's no knavery. See, to beguile the old folks, how
the young folks lay their heads together. Master, master, look
about you. Who goes there, ha?   135

HORTENSIO   Peace, Grumio, it is the rival of my love.
Petruchio, stand by a while.

GRUMIO   A proper stripling and an amorous.

[Petruchio, Hotensio and Grumio stand aside]

GREMIO   O, very well, I have perused the note.
Hark you, sir, I'll have them very fairly bound —   140
All books of love, see that at any hand —
And see you read no other lectures to her.
You understand me. Over and beside
Signor Baptista's liberality,
I'll mend it with a largess. Take your paper too,   145
And let me have them very well perfumed,
For she is sweeter than perfume itself

119. rehearsed = related

121. order = measures

　ta'en = taken

126. do me grace = do me a favour

129. seen = qualified, skilled

130. may = can

131. make love to her = court her, woo her　make love は現代とは違う意味。

133. Here's no knavery 「汚い手なんて使っていないね」という意味だが、もちろんグルーミオは皮肉で言っている。

　beguile = deceive

133-34. See, to beguile the old folks, how the young folks lay their heads together 若者が老人を騙<だま>して恋を成就させるというのは、喜劇の基本的なパターン。また、lay their heads together は当時のことわざに出てくる表現。皮肉やことわざを口にすることで、グルーミオには客観的なコメンテーターとしての道化の視点が与えられている。

136. Peace = be silent

138. proper stripling = handsome youth　グレミオは老人なので、これもグルーミオの皮肉。

　amorous 「好色な、色っぽい」

139. the note 家庭教師に扮したルーセンシオから提出された「本のリスト」と考えられる。

140. have them very fairly bound 「これらの本 (them) は美しく装丁してもらおう」この当時、本は製本されない状態で売られていた。

141. see that = see to that「恋愛関係の本に限ることに気をつけろ」

　at any hand = in any case

142. read no other lectures = give no other lessons　read = teach lectures はここでは個人レッスンの意味。

144. liberality 「気前良く報酬を払ってくれること」

145. mend it with a largess 「たっぷり祝儀を上乗せしよう」

　your paper l. 139 の the note のこと。

146. them ルーセンシオが選んだ本を指す。

To whom they go to. What will you read to her?

LUCENTIO   Whate'er I read to her, I'll plead for you
  As for my patron, stand you so assured,   150
  As firmly as yourself were still in place —
  Yea, and perhaps with more successful words
  Than you, unless you were a scholar, sir.

GREMIO   O this learning, what a thing it is!

GRUMIO   [Aside]   O this woodcock, what an ass it is!   155

PETRUCHIO   [Aside]   Peace, sirrah.

HORTENSIO   [Aside]   Grumio, mum. — God save you, Signor
  Gremio.

GREMIO   And you are well met, Signor Hortensio.
  Trow you whither I am going? To Baptista Minola.
  I promised to inquire carefully   160
  About a schoolmaster for the fair Bianca,
  And by good fortune I have lighted well
  On this young man, for learning and behaviour
  Fit for her turn, well read in poetry
  And other books, good ones, I warrant ye.   165

HORTENSIO   'Tis well, and I have met a gentleman
  Hath promised me to help me to another,
  A fine musician to instruct our mistress.
  So shall I no whit be behind in duty
  To fair Bianca, so beloved of me.   170

GREMIO   Beloved of me, and that my deeds shall prove.

GRUMIO   [Aside]   And that his bags shall prove.

HORTENSIO   Gremio, 'tis now no time to vent our love.
  Listen to me, and if you speak me fair,
  I'll tell you news indifferent good for either.   175
  Here is a gentleman whom by chance I met,
  Upon agreement from us to his liking,
  Will undertake to woo curst Katherine,
  Yea, and to marry her, if her dowry please.

149. plead = make an emotional appeal

150. stand you so assured 「そう思って安心していてください」というのが表向きの意味だが、stand には男性器を想像させる意図も隠されている。若い女に言いよる年寄りを笑い物にするという喜劇の伝統にのっとっている。

151. as yourself were still in place = as if you yourself were present all the time   still = always

154-55. O this leaning ... what an ass it is! グレミオが「おお、学問とはなんと素晴らしきもの」と言ったのに対し、グルーミオは「おお、このでくのぼうはなんと愚かなもの」と、同じ文型を繰り返して皮肉っている。woodcock（ヤマシギ）はワナにかかりやすくすぐ捕まるので、だまされやすい愚か者の代名詞になった。

157. mum = silence 「黙れ、静かに」という意味の間投詞。グルーミオに静かにするように注意してから、ホーテンシオとペトルーチオはグレミオに近づいて挨拶をする。

158. you are well met 「これはよいところでお会いしました」

159. Trow you = Do you know

162-63. lighted ... / On = came across, met by chance

164. Fit for her turn 「彼女にぴったりな」   her turn = her needs

167. help me to another = assist me in obtaining another teacher

169. no whit 「少しも…ない」

170. of = by

171. Beloved of me me に強勢が置かれる。「いやいや、私こそが愛しているんだ」という意。   that   prove の目的語。

172. his bags shall prove bags に強勢が置かれる。「行動ではなくて、財布の力で証明するんだろう」という意。bags は money-bags のこと。

173. vent = express

174. speak me fair = speak courteously to me

175. indifferent good for either = equally good for each of us

177. Upon agreement from us to his liking 「彼（ペトルーチオ）が望む条件に我々2人が合意すれば」ここまでの台詞の中ではペトルーチオは何も条件を提示していない。しかしこの後、ll. 209-10 でペトルーチオがキャタリーナに求婚するための費用は、ホーテンシオとグレミオが引き受けることが語られる。

179. if her dowry please 「もしキャタリーナの持参金の金額が満足のいくものであれば」

GREMIO   So said, so done, is well.   180
   Hortensio, have you told him all her faults?
PETRUCHIO   I know she is an irksome brawling scold.
   If that be all, masters, I hear no harm.
GREMIO   No, say'st me so, friend? What countryman?
PETRUCHIO   Born in Verona, old Antonio's son.   185
   My father dead, my fortune lives for me,
   And I do hope good days and long to see.
GREMIO   O sir, such a life with such a wife were strange.
   But if you have a stomach, to't a God's name.
   You shall have me assisting you in all.   190
   But will you woo this wildcat?
PETRUCHIO   Will I live?
GRUMIO   Will he woo her? Ay, or I'll hang her.
PETRUCHIO   Why came I hither but to that intent?
   Think you a little din can daunt mine ears?
   Have I not in my time heard lions roar?   195
   Have I not heard the sea, puffed up with winds,
   Rage like an angry boar chafèd with sweat?
   Have I not heard great ordnance in the field,
   And heaven's artillery thunder in the skies?
   Have I not in a pitchèd battle heard   200
   Loud 'larums, neighing steeds and trumpets' clang?
   And do you tell me of a woman's tongue,
   That gives not half so great a blow to hear
   As will a chestnut in a farmer's fire?
   Tush, tush, fear boys with bugs.
GRUMIO   For he fears none.   205
GREMIO   Hortensio, hark.
   This gentleman is happily arrived,
   My mind presumes, for his own good and yours.
HORTENSIO   I promised we would be contributors
   And bear his charge of wooing whatsoe're.   210

180. So said, so done, is well　「おっしゃったとおりに実現すれば結構なことだ」

182. irksome = disgusting, loathsome (*OED adj.* 2)　シェイクスピアの時代に、irksome は現代よりも意味が強く、激しい嫌悪を表す言葉だった。

184. say'st me so　「まさか、本当ですか」という驚きの表現。現代の you don't say! に相当する。　　**What countryman?** = Where are you from?

187. I do hope ... to see　「末長く幸せに暮らしたい」

188. such a life with such a wife　life と wife で音をそろえた言葉遊び。
were = would be

189. if you have a stomach, to't a God's name　「もしもその気があるのなら、ぜひおやりなさい」　stomach = inclination, disposition　　a = on

191. Will I live? = Certainly!

192. Will he ... hang her　「旦那がその女に求婚するかだって？　もちろんさ。でなきゃ、その女を俺が絞首刑にしてやる」　　**Ay** = Yes　このグルーミオの台詞は当時のことわざ 'Better be half hanged than ill wed'（ひどい結婚をするなら首くくられかける方がマシ）に基づいていると推定されている。*Twelfth Night* のフェステも Many a good hanging prevents a bad marriage（首くくられたおかげでひどい結婚をしなかったやつがたくさんいる）と、似た表現をしている (1. 5. 18)。

193. but = except

194. daunt = intimidate, dispirit　　**mine ears**　my ではなく mine になっているのは、次の ears が母音で始まるため。

197. chafèd = angered, irritated

198. ordnance = cannon, artillery　　**field** = battlefield

200. pitchèd battle　「陣営を整えた戦場」

201. 'larums = alarums (出撃の合図)

205. Tush　「ちぇ！」じれったさや叱責の気持ちを表す間投詞。
fear boys with bugs　「子供をお化けで脅しなさい」　fear = frighten　bugs = hobgoblin

208. My mind presumes ... yours　My mind presumes（私が思うに）は挿入句。「（ペトルーチオが来てくれて、）ご本人のためにもなるだろうし、あなた（ホーテンシオ）にも有益ですね」と言っている。ペトルーチオがキャタリーナに求婚するのはグレミオにとっても有益なことなので、最後の yours を ours に改訂する編者もいる。F1 のとおり yours を採り、ここでグレミオはペトルーチオの求婚費用をホーテンシオだけに押し付けようとしていると解釈する編者もいる。その解釈に従えば、次の台詞であわててホーテンシオは、費用は 2 人の折半と言い出すという流れになる。

210. charge = expenses

GREMIO And so we will, provided that he win her.

GRUMIO I would I were as sure of a good dinner.

Enter Tranio brave [disguised as Lucentio], and Biondello

TRANIO Gentlemen, God save you. If I may be bold,
  Tell me, I beseech you, which is the readiest way
  To the house of Signor Baptista Minola?   215

BIONDELLO He that has the two fair daughters — is't he you
  mean?

TRANIO Even he, Biondello.

GREMIO Hark you, sir, you mean not her to —

TRANIO Perhaps him and her, sir. What have you to do?   220

PETRUCHIO Not her that chides, sir, at any hand, I pray.

TRANIO I love no chiders, sir. Biondello, let's away.

LUCENTIO [*Aside*] Well begun, Tranio.

HORTENSIO   Sir, a word ere you go.
  Are you a suitor to the maid you talk of, yea or no?

TRANIO And if I be, sir, is it any offence?   225

GREMIO No, if without more words you will get you hence.

TRANIO Why, sir, I pray, are not the streets as free
  For me as for you?

GREMIO   But so is not she.

TRANIO For what reason, I beseech you?

GREMIO For this reason, if you'll know,   230
  That she's the choice love of Signor Gremio.

HORTENSIO That she's the chosen of Signor Hortensio.

TRANIO Softly, my masters. If you be gentlemen,
  Do me this right: hear me with patience.
  Baptista is a noble gentleman,   235
  To whom my father is not all unknown,
  And were his daughter fairer than she is,
  She may more suitors have, and me for one.
  Fair Leda's daughter had a thousand wooers,

212. 1. *brave* = finely dressed

213. If I may be bold 直訳すると「厚かましくさせていただけるのなら」という意味だが、「失礼ながら」程度の意味。主人のルーセンシオに扮し紳士然とした服装で登場したトラーニオは、言葉づかいも紳士的になっている。

214. readiest = shortest

216-17. is't he you mean? もちろんビオンデロはトラーニオがバプティスタの家に向かっていることは知っている。ここでは周囲の人間にそれを伝えるためにあえて「娘さんが2人いる、その人のことですよね」と念を押していると考えられる。

219. to ― このあとにグレミオはwooと言葉を続けようとした。「娘に求婚するつもりじゃないでしょうね」と言いかけたところを、トラーニオに遮られる。

219-27. sir トラーニオ、グレミオ、ペトルーチオ、ホーテンシオは、この会話の中で互いをいちいちsirと呼びあっている。わざとらしく丁重な話ぶりから、求婚のライバル同士であることを意識して、お互いに警戒しあっている様子が浮かび上がる。

220. What have you to do? = What is it to do with you?

221. at any hand = in any case

222. chiders = quarrelsome women, scolds

223. ere = before

226. hence = from here 「ここから立ち去ってくれれば問題ない」とグレミオは言っている。

228. so is not she soは前行のfree for me as for youを指す。

231. choice = chosen

232. chosen of = chosen by

233. Softly = gently

234. Do me this right 「これから申し上げる正当な扱いをしてほしい」

236. all = entirely

237. were his daughter ifが省略されていることによる倒置。

239. Fair Leda's daughter 「レダの美しい娘」とは世界一の美女とされるヘレネのこと。スパルタの王妃レダを見染めたゼウスは、白鳥に姿を変えてレダに近づき身籠らせ、ヘレネが生まれた。

a thousand wooers は同時代の劇作家 Christopher Marlowe の *Doctor Faustus* の中の有名な台詞 Was this the face that launched a thousand ships? の影響を受けていると推測される。

Then well one more may fair Bianca have,   240
    And so she shall. Lucentio shall make one,
    Though Paris came in hope to speed alone.
GREMIO   What, this gentleman will out-talk us all.
LUCENTIO   Sir, give him head. I know he'll prove a jade.
PETRUCHIO   Hortensio, to what end are all these words?   245
HORTENSIO   Sir, let me be so bold as ask you,
    Did you yet ever see Baptista's daughter?
TRANIO   No, sir, but hear I do that he hath two:
    The one as famous for a scolding tongue
    As is the other for beauteous modesty.   250
PETRUCHIO   Sir, sir, the first's for me; let her go by.
GREMIO   Yea, leave that labour to great Hercules,
    And let it be more than Alcides' twelve.
PETRUCHIO   Sir, understand you this of me, in sooth:
    The youngest daughter whom you hearken for   255
    Her father keeps from all access of suitors,
    And will not promise her to any man
    Until the elder sister first be wed.
    The younger then is free, and nor before.
TRANIO   If it be so, sir, that you are the man   260
    Must stead us all, and me amongst the rest,
    And if you break the ice and do this feat,
    Achieve the elder, set the younger free
    For our access, whose hap shall be to have her
    Will not so graceless be to be ingrate.   265
HORTENSIO   Sir, you say well, and well you do conceive;
    And since you do profess to be a suitor,
    You must, as we do, gratify this gentleman,
    To whom we all rest generally beholding.
TRANIO   Sir, I shall not be slack; in sign whereof,   270
    Please ye we may contrive this afternoon
    And quaff carouses to our mistress' health,

242. Paris トロイの王子パリス。　⇒後注

　in hope to speed alone「ただひとり成功することを願って」ここでの speed は「成功する」という意味の動詞。

243. out-talk = overcome in talking　ギリシア神話を引用しながら自分の立場を主張するトラーニオの雄弁ぶりに舌を巻いている。　⇒後注

244. give him head「手綱をゆるめる、馬を勝手に走らせる」

　jade「駄馬、スタミナのない馬」「勝手に走らせておけば、すぐにくたびれて動かなくなりますよ」と言っている。　⇒後注

251. let her go by = leave her alone, pass without challenge

252. leave that labour to great Hercules「その大仕事はヘラクレスに任せておけ」

253. And let it be more than Alcides' twelve　Alcides は Hercules の別名。ヘラクレスはとうてい不可能と思われる 12 の試練を課され、それを見事に成し遂げた。グレミオは、キャタリーナへの求婚は、ヘラクレスの 12 の偉業よりも大変だと言っている。

254. understand you this of me, in sooth「これからする話をしっかり理解してほしい」　sooth = truth

255. hearken for　seek to win あるいは inquire after のいずれかの意味。

257. promise her = betroth her（*OED v.* 4a）

261. Must stead us all　Must の前に who を補って考える。　stead = help

264. whose hap shall be to have her = he whose good fortune it shall be　it はその後に続く to have her を指す。

265. Will not so graceless be to be ingrate　Will の主語は前行の whose。「幸運にも彼女を手に入れた男は、必ずやあなたに感謝します」という意味。

　graceless = ill-mannered, lacking in decency　　ingrate = ungrateful

　ll. 260-65 のトラーニオの台詞は上品ぶるあまり、但し書きや繰り返しの多い、もったいぶった口調になっている。

266. Sir, you say well　トラーニオに向かってお世辞を言いながら、ペトルーチオの求婚費用を分担させようとする台詞。　　**conceive** = understand

268. gratify = reward, compensate

269. generally = collectively, without exception（*OED adv.* 3a）

　beholding = indebted, obliged

270. slack = slow, backward　　**in sign whereof**「ぐずぐずしていないことを示すために」whereof は「それについての」という意味の関係副詞。

271. Please ye = If it please you（よろしければ）　　**contrive** = spend, wear away（*OED v.*²）

272. quaff carouses「乾杯する、一気飲みする」

And do as adversaries do in law,
Strive mightily, but eat and drink as friends.

GRUMIO AND BIONDELLO

O excellent motion! Fellows, let's be gone.   275

HORTENSIO   The motion's good indeed, and be it so.

Petruchio, I shall be your *ben venuto*.   *Exeunt*

273. as adversaries do in law 「法廷で競い合う者たちと同じように」

275. motion 「動議」 前のトラーニオの台詞で法廷闘争の喩えが出てきたのを
受けて、続けて法律用語を使っている。

277. *ben venuto* イタリア語で welcome。自分はペトルーチオを歓迎する立場
なので、ペトルーチオの食事代は自分が払うとホーテンシオは言っている。

[ACT II, SCENE I]

Enter Katherina, and Bianca [with her hands tied]

BIANCA   Good sister, wrong me not, nor wrong yourself,
　　To make a bondmaid and a slave of me.
　　That I disdain. But for these other goods,
　　Unbind my hands, I'll pull them off myself,
　　Yea, all my raiment, to my petticoat,　　　　　　　　　5
　　Or what you will command me will I do,
　　So well I know my duty to my elders.
KATHERINA   Of all thy suitors here I charge thee tell
　　Whom thou lov'st best. See thou dissemble not.
BIANCA   Believe me, sister, of all the men alive　　　10
　　I never yet beheld that special face
　　Which I could fancy more than any other.
KATHERINA   Minion, thou liest. Is't not Hortensio?
BIANCA   If you affect him, sister, here I swear
　　I'll plead for you myself but you shall have him.　　15
KATHERINA   O, then belike you fancy riches more:
　　You will have Gremio to keep you fair.
BIANCA   Is it for him you do envy me so?
　　Nay then, you jest, and now I well perceive
　　You have but jested with me all this while.　　　20
　　I prithee, sister Kate, untie my hands.
KATHERINA   If that be jest, then all the rest was so.　　*Strikes her*

Enter Baptista

BAPTISTA   Why, how now, dame, whence grows this insolence?
　　Bianca, stand aside. Poor girl, she weeps.
　　Go ply thy needle, meddle not with her.　　　　　25
　　For shame, thou hilding of a divilish spirit,
　　Why dost thou wrong her that did ne're wrong thee?
　　When did she cross thee with a bitter word?

〔**2. 1**〕あらすじ···

　キャタリーナの乱暴ぶりにバプティスタが頭を悩ませているところに、ビアンカの求婚者たちがやってくる。ペトルーチオはキャタリーナの求婚者として名乗りをあげ、音楽教師に扮したホーテンシオを娘たちの家庭教師として紹介する。グレミオも学者に変装したルーセンシオを家庭教師として提供する。トラーニオもルーセンシオを名乗って、ビアンカに求婚したいと申し出る。持参金の条件に納得したペトルーチオは、さっそくキャタリーナに求婚するが、互いに相手の言葉を鋭く切り返す激しい舌戦となり、結局、ペトルーチオは強引に結婚式の日取りを決めてしまう。グレミオとトラーニオは財力を競い合い、でまかせを言ってトラーニオが勝つものの、保証人として父親を連れてくるようバプティスタに条件を出される。

···

0. 1. [*with her hands tied*]　⇒後注

2. bondmaid ＝ slave girl

3. goods ＝ possessions

4. Unbind my hands ＝ If you unbind my hands

5. raiment ＝ clothes

　petticoat ＝ underskirt

9. dissemble ＝ lie, conceal your intentions

12. fancy ＝ like, love

13. Minion ＝ spoilt darling「この甘ったれ女！」といったところ。

14. affect ＝ like, love

15. but you shall have him ＝ if you shall not have him otherwise「自分から彼を手に入れようとしないなら」

17. fair ＝ finely dressed

18. envy ＝ hate　シェイクスピアの時代の用法では、「うらやましい」という意味より強い感情を表した。

20. but ＝ only

23. dame ＝ mistress, madam

　whence ＝ from where「いったい何の原因から」

　insolence ＝ rudeness, bad manners

25. ply ＝ work with

　meddle not with ＝ have nothing to do with

26. hilding ＝ worthless person

28. cross ＝ contradict, provoke

KATHERINA   Her silence flouts me, and I'll be revenged.

Flies after Bianca

BAPTISTA   What in my sight? Bianca, get thee in.   *Exit [Bianca]*   30

KATHERINA   What, will you not suffer me? Nay, now I see
   She is your treasure, she must have a husband.
   I must dance barefoot on her wedding day,
   And, for your love to her, lead apes in hell.
   Talk not to me. I will go sit and weep   35
   Till I can find occasion of revenge.   *[Exit]*

BAPTISTA   Was ever gentleman thus grieved as I?
   But who comes here?

Enter Gremio, Lucentio [as Cambio] in the habit of a mean man;
   Petruchio with [Hortensio as Litio; and] Tranio
   [as Lucentio], with his boy [Biondello] bearing a lute and books

GREMIO   Good morrow, neighbour Baptista.

BAPTISTA   Good morrow, neighbour Gremio. God save you,   40
   gentlemen.

PETRUCHIO   And you, good sir. Pray, have you not a daughter
   Called Katherina, fair and virtuous?

BAPTISTA   I have a daughter, sir, called Katherina.

GREMIO   You are too blunt. Go to it orderly.   45

PETRUCHIO   You wrong me, signor Gremio, give me leave.
   —I am a gentleman of Verona, sir,
   That hearing of her beauty and her wit,
   Her affability and bashful modesty,
   Her wondrous qualities and mild behaviour,   50
   Am bold to show myself a forward guest
   Within your house, to make mine eye the witness
   Of that report which I so oft have heard.
   And for an entrance to my entertainment
   I do present you with a man of mine,   55
   Cunning in music and the mathematics,

29. flouts = mocks, insults

　be revenged = take revenge

31. suffer me = let me have my own way

33. dance barefoot on her wedding day　妹が先に結婚してしまうと、姉は妹の結婚式の日に裸足で踊るものとされ、'To dance barefoot'は妹に先を越されるという意味のことわざになった。

34. lead apes in hell　子供のいない女は、天国で子供の手をひく代わりに、地獄で猿の手をひくという言い伝えがあった。

36. occasion of = opportunity for

37. grieved = afflicted

38. 1. *in the habit of a mean man*　「貧しい男の身なりで」この劇では服装や服飾が経済力や社会的地位を可視化するものとして繰り返し利用されている。1. 1. 201-02 でルーセンシオはトラーニオに自分の coloured hat and cloak を着させている。

38. 2. *Hortensio as Litio*　ホーテンシオが扮した音楽家の名前は F2 では Licio と綴られており、Rowe をはじめとしてそちらに従う版も多い。また材源となった Gascoigne の *Supposes* ではルーセンシオの父親にあたる人物の召使いが Litio という名前である。

45. blunt = abrupt, brusque

　orderly = in due order　ペトルーチオのあまりにも単刀直入な話の切り出し方をグレミオはたしなめている。

46. give me leave　「失礼ながら」「申し訳ないが 'You wrong me' と言い返させてもらうよ」という意味。

49. affability = friendliness, kindness

50. wondrous qualities = marvellous nature

51. forward = eager, ardent

54. for an entrance to my entertainment　「迎え入れていただくことへの謝礼として」　entrance=entrance fee　entertainment=hospitable reception

56. Cunning = skilled

　music and the mathematics　音楽と数学は古代ギリシア・ローマ時代に自由市民として身につける学問 (liberal arts) 7 科目の中に含まれていた。リベラル・アーツの中でも、音楽と数学は幾何学および天文学とともに quadrivium（四科）を構成し、trivium（文法、修辞、論理の三科）の上位に位置づけられていた。1. 1. 2 の後注参照。

To instruct her fully in those sciences,
Whereof I know she is not ignorant.
Accept of him, or else you do me wrong.
His name is Litio, born in Mantua.   60

BAPTISTA   You' re welcome, sir, and he for your good sake.
But for my daughter Katherine, this I know:
She is not for your turn, the more my grief.

PETRUCHIO   I see you do not mean to part with her,
Or else you like not of my company.   65

BAPTISTA   Mistake me not; I speak but as I find.
Whence are you, sir? What may I call your name?

PETRUCHIO   Petruchio is my name, Antonio's son,
A man well known throughout all Italy.

BAPTISTA   I know him well. You are welcome for his sake.   70

GREMIO   Saving your tale, Petruchio, I pray,
Let us that are poor petitioners speak, too.
Baccare, you are marvellous forward.

PETRUCHIO   O, pardon me, Signor Gremio, I would fain be
doing.

GREMIO   I doubt it not, sir. But you will curse your wooing.   75
— Neighbor, this is a gift very grateful, I am sure of it. To
express the like kindness, myself, that have been more kindly
beholding to you than any, freely give unto you this young
scholar that hath been long studying at Rheims, as cunning
in Greek, Latin and other languages as the other in music   80
and mathematics. His name is Cambio. Pray, accept his
service.

BAPTISTA   A thousand thanks, signor Gremio. Welcome, good
Cambio. — But, gentle sir, methinks you walk like a stranger.
May I be so bold to know the cause of your coming?   85

TRANIO   Pardon me, sir, the boldness is mine own
That, being a stranger in this city here,
Do make myself a suitor to your daughter,

57. sciences 「科学」という意味ではなく、「学問分野」という意味で用いられている。

59. Accept of = accept

60. Mantua イタリアのロンバルディア州の都市マントヴァ。*Romeo and Juliet* ではロミオはヴェローナを追放されマントヴァに行く。

61. he 後ろに is welcome を補って読む。

62. for = as for

63. She is not for your turn 「あなたのお役には立ちません」 turn = use, purpose

65. you like not of my company 「私と付き合うことがお嫌なのですね」

67. Whence = from where
What may I call your name? = What is your name? call と name で意味が重複しているが、このように類義語が反復されるような口調は、年寄りが使う古めかしい言い方とされている。

71-73. この3行は F1 では散文として印刷されているが、ll. 74-75 の2行が doing と wooing で脚韻を踏んでおり、l. 75 までは韻文が続いているととらえる方が適切と判断し、18 世紀以来、多くの版が韻文として編集している。

71. Saving = with no offence to, with respect for 「お話をさえぎって申し訳ないが」という意。

72. poor petitioners = humble suitors poor は謙遜するためにつけられている形容詞であって貧しいわけではない。

73. *Baccare* stand back を意味する擬似ラテン語。 ⇒後注

74. I would fain be doing 「はやくしたいものですから」という意。 fain = eagerly, willingly doing には求婚を急ぐというだけではなく、「はやくやりたい」という性的な意味もほのめかされている。

76-85. F1 では韻文として印刷されているが、リズムが不自然なため、おそらく割り付けを調整するため植字工が適宜、改行したものと推測される。

76. grateful = agreeable, welcome

77. like = same

77-78. myself, that have been more kindly ... any 「私は他の誰よりも恩義を受けておりますから」 kindly = affectionately

79. Rheims フランス北東部の町ランス。1547 年に大学が創設された。

81. Cambio イタリア語で「交換」を意味する。召使いと立場を交換し、家庭教師に変装するルーセンシオにはふさわしい名前。

84. you walk like a stranger 「よそよそしく話の輪から離れていらっしゃいますね」とトラーニオに向かって話しかけている。

86. the boldness 次行以下で語られる、よそ者でありながら求婚者として名乗り出ることを指している。

Unto Bianca, fair and virtuous.
Nor is your firm resolve unknown to me   90
In the preferment of the eldest sister.
This liberty is all that I request:
That, upon knowledge of my parentage,
I may have welcome 'mongst the rest that woo,
And free access and favour as the rest.   95
And toward the education of your daughters
I here bestow a simple instrument
And this small packet of Greek and Latin books.
If you accept them, then their worth is great.
BAPTISTA Lucentio is your name? Of whence, I pray?   100
TRANIO Of Pisa, sir, son to Vincentio.
BAPTISTA A mighty man of Pisa. By report,
I know him well. You are very welcome, sir.
[*To Hotensio and Lucentio*] Take you the lute, and you the set
    of books.
You shall go see your pupils presently.   105
Holla, within!

Enter a servant

           Sirrah, lead these gentlemen
To my daughters, and tell them both
These are their tutors. Bid them use them well.
                    [*Exeunt Servant, Hortensio, Lucentio*]
We will go walk a little in the orchard
And then to dinner. You are passing welcome,   110
And so I pray you all to think yourselves.
PETRUCHIO Signor Baptista, my business asketh haste,
And every day I cannot come to woo.
You knew my father well, and in him me,
Left solely heir to all his lands and goods,   115
Which I have bettered rather than decreased.

89. fair and virtuous l. 43 でペトルーチオはキャタリーナについて同じ表現を使っている。にわか紳士に扮しているトラーニオは、耳にした常套句をちゃっかりそのまま模倣していると解釈できる。

91. In the preferment of = in giving priority to

93. upon knowledge of = when you know about

94. 'mongst = among

96. toward = as a contribution to

97. simple instrument 「つまらない楽器ですが」と謙遜している。具体的にはリュート。

100. Lucentio is your name? ここまでにバプティスタにルーセンシオの名前を伝える台詞はないので、この台詞をいかすために様々な演出が工夫されている。トラーニオから渡された本を見て、そこにルーセンシオの名前が記されているのを見て、「ルーセンシオというお名前ですね?」と聞くというのがその1例である。トラーニオが渡した名刺を見ながらという演出もある。

102. mighty = important, influential

102-03. F1 では A mighty man of Pisa by report, / I know him well というパンクチュエーションになっている。だが後に他人をヴィンセンシオとしてバプティスタに紹介するという展開上、バプティスタはヴィンセンシオと面識がないことは確実である。そのため 18 世紀以降、ほとんどの編者が By report I know him well と校訂している。

105. presently = immediately

106. Holla 「おーい」と呼びかける言葉。ここでは奥 (within) にいる召使いを呼び出している。

109. orchard = garden

110. dinner シェイクスピアの時代には、午前 11 時頃に食べる dinner が 1 日の主たる食事だった。

passing = extremely

111. so = welcome

112. asketh = requires, demands (*OED v.* 23a)

113. every day I cannot come to woo バラッド 'The Wooing of John and Joan' からの引用。メロディをつけて歌われ、このフレーズは繰り返し部分に使われていたので、よく知られていた。

112-25. Signor Baptista ... on either hand ⇒後注

Then tell me, if I get your daughter's love,
What dowry shall I have with her to wife?
BAPTISTA   After my death, the one half of my lands,
And in possession twenty thousand crowns.   120
PETRUCHIO   And for that dowry I'll assure her of
Her widowhood, be it that she survive me,
In all my lands and leases whatsoever.
Let specialties be therefore drawn between us,
That covenants may be kept on either hand.   125
BAPTISTA   Ay, when the special thing is well obtained,
That is, her love, for that is all in all.
PETRUCHIO   Why, that is nothing, for I tell you, father,
I am as peremptory as she proud-minded,
And where two raging fires meet together   130
They do consume the thing that feeds their fury.
Though little fire grows great with little wind,
Yet extreme gusts will blow out fire and all.
So I to her, and so she yields to me,
For I am rough and woo not like a babe.   135
BAPTISTA   Well mayst thou woo, and happy be thy speed.
But be thou armed for some unhappy words.
PETRUCHIO   Ay, to the proof, as mountains are for winds,
That shakes not though they blow perpetually.

Enter Hortensio [as Litio] with his head broke

BAPTISTA   How now, my friend? Why dost thou look so pale? 140
HORTENSIO   For fear, I promise you, if I look pale.
BAPTISTA   What, will my daughter prove a good musician?
HORTENSIO   I think she'll sooner prove a soldier.
Iron may hold with her, but never lutes.
BAPTISTA   Why, then thou canst not break her to the lute?   145
HORTENSIO   Why, no, for she hath broke the lute to me.
I did but tell her she mistook her frets

120. in possession 「結婚時に持たせるものとして」 **twenty thousand crowns** crown は王冠のマークが刻印してある硬貨。1 クラウンは 5 シリング、または 1/4 ポンド。2 万クラウンは当時の職人の日当に換算して 10 万日分。この金額で馬なら 600 頭、牛なら 2,600 頭が買えた。

122. widowhood 「寡婦相続」 **be it that** = if **survive** = outlive

123. In all my lands and leases whatsoever バプティスタからの莫大な持参金に呼応して、こちらも「土地、借地権すべて」と大きく出ている。

124. specialties = special legal contracts

125. covenants = formal agreements（証書、約款）

128. father もちろん father-in-law の意味だが、それとてキャタリーナの意向を聞く前に使うのは、早急に過ぎる。それをすっとばして father と呼びかけるところに、ペトルーチオの自信満々な態度がうかがえる。

129. peremptory = determined, resolved

132-33. Though little fire ... and all 'A little wind kindles, much puts out the fire' ということわざを元にしている。ペトルーキオは自分を extreme gusts に喩え、キャタリーナという燃え盛る炎でも吹き消してみせると豪語している。

134. So I to her = So I behave to her

136. Well mayst ... thy speed この may(st) は祈願を表す助動詞。「君がそんなふうに求婚をして、その結果が幸せなものでありますように」と、バプティスタは祈願の言葉をペトルーチオに贈っている。 **speed** = outcome

137. unhappy = pernicious, inauspicious 前行の happy との対比。

138. to the proof 前行の be thou armed（武装しておけ）という言葉を受けて、proof armour（どんな武器も受け付けない鎧〈よろい〉）と同じほどに準備しておきますと答えている。

139. shakes = shake 主語（関係代名詞の先行詞）は mountains である。

139. 1. *broke* = injured, bleeding

141. I promise you = I assure you

143. prove a soldier 前の行でバプティスタが will my daughter prove a good musician?（うちの娘は立派な演奏者になれそうですか）と聞いたのに対し、prove という言葉を become と put to the test の二重の意味で使って答えている。「お嬢さんは立派な兵士になれますよ」と同時に「お嬢さんは兵士ごときははねかえしますよ」と言っている。

144. Iron 「鉄の武器」 **hold with her** = stand up to her handling

145. break her to the lute 「リュートを弾くところまで手なずける」break は tame と同様、動物を「ならす、しつける」を意味する。(*OED v.* 14a)

146. broke the lute to me = broke the lute on me

147. frets リュートのフレット。指板を区切るための凸部。

And bowed her hand to teach her fingering,
When, with a most impatient devilish spirit,
'Frets call you these?' quoth she, 'I'll fume with them,'   150
And with that word she struck me on the head,
And through the instrument my pate made way,
And there I stood amazèd for a while,
As on a pillory, looking through the lute,
While she did call me rascal fiddler   155
And twangling Jack, with twenty such vile terms,
As had she studied to misuse me so.

PETRUCHIO   Now, by the world, it is a lusty wench.
I love her ten times more than e'er I did.
O, how I long to have some chat with her!   160

BAPTISTA   [*To Hortensio*]   Well, go with me, and be not so
discomfited.
Proceed in practice with my younger daughter.
She's apt to learn and thankeful for good turns.
Signor Petruchio, will you go with us,
Or shall I send my daughter Kate to you?   165

PETRUCHIO   I pray you do. I'll attend her here —

Exeunt all but Petruchio

And woo her with some spirit when she comes.
Say that she rail, why then I'll tell her plain
She sings as sweetly as a nightingale.
Say that she frown, I'll say she looks as clear   170
As morning roses newly washed with dew.
Say she be mute and will not speak a word,
Then I'll commend her volubility
And say she uttereth piercing eloquence.
If she do bid me pack, I'll give her thanks   175
As though she bid me stay by her a week.
If she deny to wed, I'll crave the day
When I shall ask the banns and when be married.

148. bowed = curved, bent

150. Frets キャタリーナは frets を楽器の部位ではなく、vexations の意味に
ずらして受け取った。

 fume = be in a rage *cf.* fret and fume で「プンプン怒る」という意味。

152. pate = head   **made way** = made a hole through the lute

154. pillory 「さらし台」板の穴に首と両手をはさんで罪人をさらし者にした刑
具。*cf.* Induction 1. 2

155. rascal = rogue, good-for-nothing

 fiddler 「バイオリン弾き、フィドル（弦楽器）奏者」という意味とともに、
「ペテン師」の意味もある。

156. twangling Jack twangling は（楽器の）弦を弾くという意味。Jack は
男に対する蔑称。まとめて「弦楽器野郎」というような意味。

 twenty 具体的な数字ではなく、数が多いことを示している。ここでは「汚
い言葉を無数に並べ」という意味。

157. As had she = as if she had   **studied** = practised   **misuse** = abuse

158. lusty = lively, high-spirited, merry

161. discomfited = disheartened

162. Proceed in practice = carry on your lessons

163. apt = ready   **good turns** = kind actions

166. attend = wait for

167. 文章は前行から続いているが、ペトルーチオはバプティスタとホーテンシ
オがいなくなって一人になったことを確かめてから、この行を話し始める。こ
れからじゃじゃ馬キャタリーナに対抗する方法を一人語るが、観客に自分の本
音を共有させる一種の独白である。

168. Say = suppose

169. nightingale ナイチンゲールはヨーロッパ産のツグミ科の鳥。美しい声で
鳴くことから、美声の象徴となっている。

170. clear = serene, calm

173. volubility = great fluency of language (*OED n.* 6)

174. piercing = moving

175. pack = leave, be gone 「荷物をまとめてさっさと出ていけ」という意味。

177. deny = refuse

 crave = beg to know, ask to be told or informed (*OED v.* 2c)

178. ask = announce, publish (*OED v.* 1d)   **banns** 「結婚予告」

But here she comes, and now, Petruchio, speak.

Enter Katherina

Good morrow, Kate, for that's your name, I hear.   180

KATHERINA Well have you heard, but something hard of
hearing:

They call me Katherine that do talk of me.

PETRUCHIO You lie, in faith, for you are called plain Kate,

And bonny Kate, and sometimes Kate the Curst,

But Kate, the prettiest Kate in Christendom,   185

Kate of Kate Hall, my super-dainty Kate,

For dainties are all Kates, and therefore, Kate,

Take this of me, Kate of my consolation:

Hearing thy mildness praised in every town,

Thy virtues spoke of, and thy beauty sounded,   190

Yet not so deeply as to thee belongs,

Myself am moved to woo thee for my wife.

KATHERINA 'Moved', in good time! Let him that moved you
hither

Remove you hence. I knew you at the first

You were a movable.

PETRUCHIO   Why, what's a movable?   195

KATHERINA A joint stool.

PETRUCHIO   Thou hast hit it. Come sit on me.

KATHERINA Asses are made to bear, and so are you.

PETRUCHIO Women are made to bear, and so are you.

KATHERINA No such jade as you, if me you mean.

PETRUCHIO Alas, good Kate, I will not burden thee,   200

For knowing thee to be but young and light —

KATHERINA Too light for such a swain as you to catch,

And yet as heavy as my weight should be.

PETRUCHIO 'Should be'? Should — buzz.

KATHERINA   Well ta'en?, and like a buzzard.

179. Petruchio ⇒後注

180-271. ⇒後注

180. Kate Kate は Katherine の愛称。 ⇒後注

181. Well have you heard, but something hard of hearing heard と hard は
シェイクスピアの時代には発音が同じだったため、この 1 行は pun（語呂合
わせの言葉遊び）になっている。 something = somewhat

182. that 関係代名詞で先行詞は They。

184. bonny = fine ⇒後注

186. Kate Hall ⇒後注 **super-dainty** = extremely beautiful

187. dainties are all Kates dainties には「おいしい食べ物」(delicacies) の
意味もある。Kate と同音の cate にも「おいしい食べ物」の意味があり、言
葉遊びになっている。

188. consolation = comfort

190. sounded praised aloud（声高に称賛する）という意味と、次行の
deeply を引き出す fathomed（深さをはかる）と意味を重ねた言葉遊び。

191. not so deeply as to thee belongs 「君にふさわしいほどには」 belongs
= is appropriate

192. moved = compelled

193. in good time = indeed, forsooth

194. Remove 前行の move と組み合わせた言葉遊び。

195. movable portable item（動かせる家財道具）という意味と changeable
（心変わりする男）とを重ねた言葉遊び。

196. joint stool joiner（指物師、建具屋）が作ったスツール。

hit it 「的を射た、あたっている」

197. Asses are made to bear 「ロバ（ばか）は人を乗せるもの」 ⇒後注

199. jade 「スタミナのない駄馬」性的スタミナがないという意味も重ねている。

200. burden 「上にのしかかる (lie heavy on)」という意味と「責任追求する
(accuse)」という意味を兼ねている。

201. light 「ほっそりしている (slender)」という意味と「尻が軽い
(promiscuous)」という意味を兼ねている。キャタリーナは次行でさらに「す
ばしこい (quick)」の意味にずらしている。

202. swain = bumpkin（無骨な田舎者）

203. as heavy as my weight should be 「私は自分の社会的地位 (my weight)
にふさわしい重み (heavy) を持っている」と言っている。鋳造の喩え。軽い
コインは偽物。

204. be ⇒後注

ta'en = taken **buzzard** 「よれよれの鷹」 ⇒後注

PETRUCHIO	O slow-winged turtle, shall a buzzard take thee?	205
KATHERINA	Ay, for a turtle, as he takes a buzzard.	
PETRUCHIO	Come, come, you wasp, i'faith, you are too angry.	
KATHERINA	If I be waspish, best beware my sting.	
PETRUCHIO	My remedy is then to pluck it out.	
KATHERINA	Ay, if the fool could find it where it lies.	210
PETRUCHIO	Who knows not where a wasp does wear his sting?	

In his tail.

KATHERINA	In his tongue.	
PETRUCHIO	Whose tongue.	
KATHERINA	Yours, if you talk of tales, and so farewell.	
PETRUCHIO	What, with my tongue in your tail? Nay, come	

again.

Good Kate, I am a gentleman —

KATHERINA	That I'll try.	215

She strikes him

PETRUCHIO	I swear I'll cuff you if you strike again.	
KATHERINA	So may you lose your arms.	

If you strike me, you are no gentleman,

And if no gentleman, why, then no arms.

PETRUCHIO	A herald, Kate? O put me in thy books.	220
KATHERINA	What is your crest, a coxcomb?	
PETRUCHIO	A combless cock, so Kate will be my hen.	
KATHERINA	No cock of mine; you crow too like a craven.	
PETRUCHIO	Nay, come, Kate, come, you must not look so	

sour.

KATHERINA	It is my fashion when I see a crab.	225
PETRUCHIO	Why, here's no crab, and therefore look not sour.	
KATHERINA	There is, there is.	
PETRUCHIO	Then, show it me.	
KATHERINA	Had I a glass, I would.	
PETRUCHIO	What, you mean my face?	
KATHERINA	Well aimed of such a young one.	

205. turtle = turtle-dove（キジバト）。キジバトは誠実な愛の象徴。

206. Ay, for a turtle ... a buzzard 意味の不明瞭な1行。Dover Wilson の解釈を受け入れ、「ええ、私のことを誠実な妻 (turtle-dove) と思うのは、キジバトがブンブン羽音をたてる虫 (buzzard) を飲み込むようなものでしょう」と解するのが有力。この解釈だと次の行の wasp につながりやすい。

207. wasp 「ハチ」 怒りっぽい人の代名詞。'As angry as a wasp' ということわざにもなっている。　　**208. waspish** = angry

213. tales tails と同音であることを利用した言葉遊び。「現実離れした話ばかりしているのなら」という意味と、「お尻（tails）の話ばかりするのなら」という意味を兼ねている。F1 は tales となっているが、tails とする版もある。どちらにしても同じ意図の言葉遊びとなる。

214. with my tongue in your tail ⇒後注

again back と once again の両方の意味。前者の「戻ってくれ」と後者の「もうひと勝負しよう」の両方を一度に言っている。

215. try = test　　**216. cuff** = hit

217. lose your arms 「gentleman の印である coat of arms（紋章）を失ってしまう」と「（自分を捕まえている）腕 (arms) をゆるめる (loosen)」の意味を兼ねている。

220. herald 「紋章官」　　**books** = books of heraldry（gentleman の紋章を登録する記録簿）「君が紋章官なのかい？　僕の紋章を登録しておくれ」という意味。また in a person's good books で「気に入られる」という意味もあるので、ここではペトルーチオはキャタリーナに「僕を気に入ってくれ」とも言っている。

221. crest 紋章の盾の部分の上についている飾り。同時にキャタリーナは「鳥のトサカ」という意味も重ねている。　　**coxcomb**「道化がかぶる鳥のトサカの形をした帽子」あなたは道化（バカ）だ、と言っている。

222. combless = peaceable, harmless　おそらくシェイクスピアの造語。(*OED adj.*)　　**cock** 前行の coxcomb からの連想で cock が出てきているが、cock は penis の隠語でもある。　　**so** = provided that

223. craven 「闘鶏で負ける弱い鶏」

225. crab = crab-apple 酸っぱい (sour) 種類のリンゴ。「根性曲がり、気難し屋」の代名詞でもある。「酸っぱそうなリンゴを見れば酸っぱい顔になる」と言いながら、「ペトルーチオみたいな難しい相手を前にしてはこんな難しい顔になる」とキャタリーナは言っている。

228. Had I if が省略された倒置。　　**glass** = looking glass, mirror

229. Well aimed of such a young one 「未熟者にしてはうまく的にあたったわね」 of = by　young = inexperienced

PETRUCHIO   Now, by Saint George, I am too young for you.   230

KATTHERINA   Yet you are withered.

PETRUCHIO   'Tis with cares.

KATHERINA   I care not.

PETRUCHIO   Nay, hear you, Kate. In sooth you scape not so.

KATHERINA   I chafe you if I tarry. Let me go.

PETRUCHIO   No, not a whit. I find you passing gentle.

   'Twas told me you were rough and coy and sullen,   235

   And now I find report a very liar,

   For thou art pleasant, gamesome, passing courteous,

   But slow in speech, yet sweet as springtime flowers.

   Thou canst not frown, thou canst not look askance,

   Nor bite the lip as angry wenches will,   240

   Nor hast thou pleasure to be cross in talk,

   But thou with mildness entertain'st thy wooers,

   With gentle conference, soft and affable.

   Why does the world report that Kate doth limp?

   O sland'rous world! Kate like the hazel twig   245

   Is straight and slender, and as brown in hue

   As hazelnuts and sweeter than the kernels.

   O, let me see thee walk. Thou dost not halt.

KATHERINA   Go, fool, and whom thou keep'st command.

PETRUCHIO   Did ever Dian so become a grove   250

   As Kate this chamber with her princely gait?

   O, be thou Dian, and let her be Kate,

   And then let Kate be chaste and Dian sportful.

KATHERINA   Where did you study all this goodly speech?

PETRUCHIO   It is extempore, from my mother-wit.   255

KATHERINA   A witty mother, witless else her son.

PETRUCHIO   Am I not wise?

KATHERINA   Yes, keep you warm.

PETRUCHIO   Marry, so I mean, sweet Katherine, in thy bed.

   And therefore, setting all this chat aside,

230. Saint George イングランドの守護聖人。 **young** = strong 前行の
キャタリーナの使った young をわざと別の意味に使っている。

232. scape = escape

233. chafe = to heat or ruffle in temper, to vex, irritate (*OED v.* 5)

234. passing = extremely

235. coy = of distant or disdainful demeanour (*OED adj.* 3)

236. very = absolute

237. pleasant = merry **gamesome** = playful

238. slow in speech 「おっとりしたしゃべり方で」

239. askance = with a expression of contempt or disapproval (*OED adv.* 1b)

241. cross in talk 「口答えする、反論する」 cross = combative, perverse

242. entertain'st = receives

243. conference = conversation

245. hazel 「ハシバミ」 カバノキ科の低木。

246. brown in hue = dark-complexioned ⇒後注

247. the kernels 「(ヘーゼルナッツの)実」

248. halt = limp l. 244 の limp とともに、ペトルーチオが馬の品定めをする
ようにキャタリーナの歩き方を見ていることを示している。

249. whom thou keep'st command 「(私にではなく)雇っている召使いに命令
しなさい」 keep = employ whom の先行詞は省かれている。

250. Dian ローマ神話に出てくる月の女神ダイアナ。真っ白な月は純潔の印で
あり、ダイアナは処女性の象徴。狩猟の女神でもある。

become = suit, adorn

251. gait = manner of walking

253. sportful = lively, merry 同時に純潔の象徴である Dian との対比で
amorous, wanton という意味もほのめかされている。

254. study = learn by heart 「(ローマ神話を引き合いに出すような)そんな
ご立派な台詞をどこで覚えたの」と皮肉を言っている。

255. extempore = improvised (アドリブ)

mother-wit = natural intelligence

256. A witty mother, witness else her son 「母親には知恵があったのでしょう
ね。そうでなければ息子はまるで知恵なしだわ」

257. Am I not wise? / Yes, keep you warm このやりとりは 'He is wise
enough that can keep himself warm'(凍え死なない程度の知恵があれば十
分)ということわざからきている。ペトルーチオは最小限度の知恵しかないと
キャタリーナは言っている。

Thus in plain terms: your father hath consented   260
That you shall be my wife, your dowry 'greed on,
And will you, nill you, I will marry you.
Now, Kate, I am a husband for your turn,
For, by this light whereby I see thy beauty,
Thy beauty that doth make me like thee well,   265
Thou must be married to no man but me,
For I am he am born to tame you, Kate,
And bring you from a wild Kate to a Kate
Conformable as other household Kates.

Enter Baptista, Gremio, Tranio

Here comes your father. Never make denial;   270
I must and will have Katherine to my wife.
BAPTISTA   Now, Signor Petruchio, how speed you with my
    daughter?
PETRUCHIO   How but well, sir? How but well?
    It were impossible I should speed amiss.
BAPTISTA   Why, how now, daughter Katherine, in your dumps?   275
KATHERINA   Call you me daughter? Now I promise you
    You have showed a tender fatherly regard
    To wish me wed to one half lunatic,
    A madcap ruffian and a swearing Jack
    That thinks with oaths to face the matter out.   280
PETRUCHIO   Father, 'tis thus: yourself and all the world
    That talked of her have talked amiss of her.
    If she be curst, it is for policy,
    For she's not froward, but modest as the dove;
    She is not hot, but temperate as the morn;   285
    For patience she will prove a second Grissel,
    And Roman Lucrece for her chastity.
    And to conclude, we have 'greed so well together
    That upon Sunday is the wedding day.

261. 'greed = agreed

262. will you, nill you = whether you will or not

263. for your turn = to fit your need　l. 63 ではバプティスタがペトルーチオに She is not for your turn と言っている。turn は need（必要性、欲求、要望）という意味だが、「性的な欲求」という意味も匂わされている。

264. whereby = by which

266. but = except

267. I am he am　he と am の間に関係代名詞 who を補って読む。　he = the man

268. wild Kate　音が似ていることによる wild cat と重ね合わせた言葉遊び。

269. Conformable = compliant, obedient　**household** = domestic, homely

270. Never make denial = Don't refuse me

272. how speed you = how are you getting on　speed = succeed, progress

274. speed amiss = not make good progress

275. in your dumps = low-spirited, downhearted

277. have showed　当時の英語では show の過去分詞は showed と shown の両方が使われていた。

278. lunatic　「気の狂っている」　語源は「月」を意味するラテン語の *luna*。月の満ち欠けが狂気の原因だと考えられていた。

279. madcap = eccentric, reckless　**swearing**　「口汚い」swear = use offensive language　**Jack** = knave, ill-mannered fellow

280. oaths = swearing, cursing　**to face the matter out** = to get his own way by effrontery　「汚い言葉を吐き散らして傲慢な態度をとれば意を通せると思っている」

282. amiss = wrongly, inappropriately

283. for policy　「戦略のため」

284. froward = perverse, wayward

285. hot = angry, violent　**morn** = morning

286. a second Grissel　グリセルダ (Griselda) は忍耐強い妻の鑑。ボッカチオの『デカメロン』、Geoffrey Chaucer の *The Canterbury Tales* の中の The Clerk's Tale に登場する。侯爵が妻の忍耐を試そうと、子供を殺したり、離婚すると言い出すが、グリセルダはすべてを従順に受け入れる。

287. Roman Lucrece　古代ローマの伝説中の貞淑な妻ルクレティア。夫の不在中に国王の息子に凌辱され自殺する。シェイクスピアはこの話を長編の物語詩 *The Rape of Lucrece* (1594) として書き上げている。

KATHERINA I'll see thee hanged on Sunday first.   290

GREMIO Hark, Petruchio, she says she'll see thee hanged first.

TRANIO Is this your speeding? Nay, then, good night our part.

PETRUCHIO Be patient, gentlemen. I choose her for myself.

If she and I be pleased, what's that to you?

'Tis bargained 'twixt us twain, being alone,   295

That she shall still be curst in company.

I tell you, 'tis incredible to believe

How much she loves me. O, the kindest Kate,

She hung about my neck, and kiss on kiss

She vied so fast, protesting oath on oath,   300

That in a twink she won me to her love.

O, you are novices! 'Tis a world to see

How tame, when men and women are alone,

A meacock wretch can make the curstest shrew.

Give me thy hand, Kate. I will unto Venice   305

To buy apparel 'gainst the wedding day.

Provide the feast, father, and bid the guests.

I will be sure my Katherine shall be fine.

BAPTISTA I know not what to say, but give me your hands.

God send you joy, Petruchio! 'Tis a match.   310

GREMIO AND TRANIO Amen, say we. We will be witnesses.

PETRUCHIO Father, and wife, and gentlemen, adieu.

I will to Venice. Sunday comes apace.

We will have rings, and things, and fine array,

And kiss me, Kate, 'We will be married o'Sunday.'   315

Exit Petruchio and Katherina

GREMIO Was ever match clapped up so suddenly?

BAPTISTA Faith, gentlemen, now I play a merchant's part,

And venture madly on a desperate mart.

TRANIO 'Twas a commodity lay fretting by you;

'Twill bring you gain, or perish on the seas.   320

BAPTISTA The gain I seek is quiet in the match.

116

290. hanged 「絞首刑になる」

292. speeding = success　トラーニオは l. 274 でペトルーチオが 'It were impossible I should speed amiss'「私が首尾よく進められないなんてありえません」と豪語したので、わざとこの言葉を使っている。

good night our part = goodbye to our share in this business 「これで私たちの出番もありませんね」

295. 'Tis = It is　it の指す内容は次行の That 以下。　　**'twixt** = between

twain = two

296. still = always　　**in company** = in public

300. vied = redoubled, increase in number by repetition (*OED v.* 6a) 元々はトランプで「賭け金を上げる」という意味。　　**protesting** = proclaiming

301. in a twink = in a winkling of an eye

302. O, you are novices! 「皆さんわかっていませんね」 novices = beginners　　**'Tis a world** = It is worth a world (すごいことですよ)

304. meacock = mild, timid

306. 'gainst = against = in preparation for

307. bid = invite

308. fine = finely dressed

309-311. バプティスタが 2 人の手を取って、祈りの言葉を唱え、グレミオとトラーニオが証人となることで、婚約の正式な手続きがなされたと考えられる。シェイクスピアの時代の慣習法では、このようにして婚約 (pre-contract) が成立すると、拘束力が発生し、別の人とは婚約や結婚はできなくなる。

312. wife　前行の儀式で婚約が成立したので、ペトルーチオはさっそくキャタリーナを wife と呼んでいる。

313. apace = quickly, swiftly

314. array = outfit, attire, dress (*OED n.* 11a)

315. kiss me, Kate ⇒後注　　**We will be married o'Sunday**　当時流行していたバラッドで使われていた歌詞をペトルーチオは引用している。

316. clapped up = settled, fixed up

317-21.　この数行には当時、隆盛ぶりが目立つようになってきた海洋貿易に関する言葉が多用されている。バプティスタは不安要素の大きな娘の結婚を、いちかばちかのリスクと背中合わせの海洋貿易に比較している。

317. merchant 「貿易商人」

318. venture 「投機する」

desperate mart 「リスクのある市場」 mart = market

319. commodity 「商品」キャタリーナを商品に喩えている。

fretting （商品が）ダメになって価値が下がる (decaying) という意味とプリプリ怒る (irritating) の意味を重ねている。

117

GREMIO   No doubt but he hath got a quiet catch.

   But now, Baptista, to your younger daughter:

   Now is the day we long have lookèd for.

   I am your neighbour and was suitor first.   325

TRANIO   And I am one that love Bianca more

   Than words can witness, or your thoughts can guess.

GREMIO   Youngling, thou canst not love so dear as I.

TRANIO   Greybeard, thy love doth freeze.

GREMIO   But thine doth fry.

   Skipper, stand back. 'Tis age that nourisheth.   330

TRANIO   But youth in ladies' eyes that flourisheth.

BAPTISTA   Content you, gentlemen, I will compound this strife.

   'Tis deeds must win the prize, and he of both

   That can assure my daughter greatest dower

   Shall have my Bianca's love.   335

   Say, Signor Gremio, what can you assure her?

GREMIO   First, as you know, my house within the city

   Is richly furnishèd with plate and gold,

   Basins and ewers to lave her dainty hands;

   My hangings all of Tyrian tapestry;   340

   In Ivory coffers I have stuffed my crowns,

   In cypress chests my arras counterpoints,

   Costly apparel, tents and canopies,

   Fine linen, Turkey cushions bossed with pearl,

   Valance of Venice gold in needlework,   345

   Pewter and brass, and all things that belongs

   To house or housekeeping. Then at my farm

   I have a hundred milch-kine to the pail,

   Six score fat oxen standing in my stalls,

   And all things answerable to this portion.   350

   Myself am struck in years, I must confess,

   And if I die tomorrow this is hers,

   If whilst I live she will be only mine.

322. a quiet catch　もちろん皮肉でキャタリーナのことを「おとなしい獲物」と呼んでいる。catch は前行の match と韻を踏んでいる。　catch = something valuable gained or won, a prize (*OED n.*² 6a)

328. Youngling = inexperienced young man

　dear　「高い金を払って」(expensively) という意味と「大切に」(affectionately) という意味を兼ねている。

329. freeze, fry　年老いたグレミオと若いトラーニオが、同じ fr で始まる言葉で、互いに相手を「凍結する」「焼け焦げる」と揶揄している。

330. Skipper = flighty fellow, irresponsible youth (*OED n.*¹ 1b)

330-31. nourisheth, flourisheth　ここも l. 329 と同様、2 人が似ている言葉を使いながらの応酬。

332. Content you = calm down　　**compound** = settle, resolve

333. deeds　「行動」(actions) という意味と「証書」(legal deeds) の意味を兼ねている。deeds と must の間に that を補って読む。

　he of both = the one of you two

334. That　関係代名詞で先行詞は前行の he。

　dower　「寡婦産」夫が亡くなったときに妻に与えられる財産。

336. assure = guarantee

338. plate　「金や銀の食器」

339. ewers　「水差し」　　**lave** = wash, bathe

340. hangings　「カーテンや壁にかけるタペストリー」　　**Tyrian**　フェニキア（現在のレバノン）の都市テュロスは真紅の染料で有名だった。

341. coffers = chests　　**stuffed** = stored　　**crowns**「クラウン硬貨」*cf.* l. 120

342. arras counterpoints　「アラス織（つづれ織）のベッドの上掛け」

343. tents and canopies　「ベッドの天蓋の枠組みとそこにかけるカーテン」

344. Turkey = Turkish　　**bossed** = studded, ornamented

345. Valance ... needlework　valance は天蓋から吊るされたカーテンの縁飾り。それにヴェニス産の金糸の刺繍がほどこされている。

346. Pewter and brass　pewter は錫を主成分とする合金。「白目」とも呼ばれる。brass は真鍮。ここではそれらの金属製品を指している。

　belongs　先行詞は all things で複数だが関係代名詞 that につられて単数扱いとなっている。

348. milch-kine　「乳牛」kine は cow の複数形の古い形。

　pail　「ミルクを入れる桶」

349. stall = stable, cattle-shed

350. all things answerable to this portion　「今述べた相続分 (portion) に見合う (answerable) ものすべて」

351. struck in years = old

TRANIO That 'only' came well in. Sir, list to me:
 I am my father's heir and only son.   355
 If I may have your daughter to my wife,
 I'll leave her houses three or four as good
 Within rich Pisa walls as any one
 Old Signor Gremio has in Padua,
 Besides two thousand ducats by the year   360
 Of fruitful land, all which shall be her jointure.
 What, have I pinched you, Signor Gremio?
GREMIO Two thousand ducats by the year of land?
 [*Aside*] My Land amounts not to so much in all.
 —That she shall have, besides an argosy   365
 That now is lying in Marseillis' road.
 [*To Tranio*] What, have I choked you with an argosy?
TRANIO Gremio, 'tis known my father hath no less
 Than three great argosies, besides two galliasses
 And twelve tight galleys. These I will assure her, 370
 And twice as much whate're thou offer'st next.
GREMIO Nay, I have offered all. I have no more,
 And she can have no more than all I have.
 [*To Baptista*] If you like me, she shall have me and mine.
TRANIO Why, then the maid is mine from all the world 375
 By your firm promise. Gremio is out-vied.
BAPTISTA I must confess your offer is the best,
 And let your father make her the assurance,
 She is your own; else, you must pardon me.
 If you should die before him, where's her dower? 380
TRANIO That's but a cavil. He is old, I young.
GREMIO And may not young men die as well as old?
BAPTISTA Well, gentlemen, I am thus resolved:
 On Sunday next, you know
 My daughter Katherine is to be married.   385
 Now on the Sunday following shall Bianca

354. That 'only' came well in 「ちょうど良いところで 'only' とおっしゃいましたね」次行で自分が only son であることを言おうとしているから。

list = listen

358. rich Pisa walls 「豊かなピサの街をとりまく城壁」rich は Pisa を修飾している。

360-61. two thousand ducats by the year / Of fruitful land 「実り豊かな土地から得られる、毎年 2,000 ダカットの収入」ducat はヴェニスの金貨。1 ダカットは 9 シリングほどの価値があった。*The Merchant of Venice* でアントーニオが肉 1 ポンドを担保に借りた金額は 3,000 ダカット。

361. jointure 「寡婦給与財産」

362. pinched = troubled, afflicted

365. That she shall have, besides 「先ほど言ったものを彼女にあげよう。そのほかに…」   **argosy** 大型の商船。

366. in Marseillis' road 「マルセイユの安全な停泊地」road は海岸から遠くない投錨地、停泊地。

367. choked 先ほどトラーニオから have I pinched you と言われたのに対抗して、have I choked you と言っている。

369. galliasses 「ガレアス船」16-17 世紀に地中海で用いられた 3 本マストの高速大型船。

370. tight = water-tight

galleys 「ガレー船」両側に 20 本ほどのオールがついている大型船。奴隷や罪人にこがせた。

376. out-vied トランプゲームの用語。賭け金をつりあげる (vie) ことを競い合い、相手に競い勝ったという意味。*cf.* l. 300

378. assurance 「保証人」

379. else = otherwise（お父さんに保証人になってもらわなければ）

381. but = only

cavil = frivolous objection (*OED n.* 1)

Be bride to you, if you make this assurance.
If not, to signor Gremio.
And so I take my leave, and thank you both.   *Exit*
GREMIO   Adieu good neighbour. — Now I fear thee not.   390
Sirrah, young gamester, your father were a fool
To give thee all and in his waning age
Set foot under thy table. Tut, a toy!
An old Italian fox is not so kind, my boy.   *Exit*
TRANIO   A vengeance on your crafty withered hide!   395
Yet I have faced it with a card of ten.
'Tis in my head to do my master good:
I see no reason but supposed Lucentio
Must get a father called supposed Vincentio,
And that's a wonder. Fathers commonly   400
Do get their children, but in this case of wooing,
A childe shall get a sire, if I fail not of my cunning.   *Exit*

391. gamester = gambler

  were = would be

393. Set foot under thy table 「お前に飯を食わせてもらう」経済的に自立できなくなり息子の提供する食卓で食事をしなければならなくなるという意。

  Tut 「ちぇ」いらだちや軽蔑を表す間投詞。

  toy = nonsense　次行の boy と韻を踏んでいる。

394. An old Italian fox is not so kind 'An old fox cannot be taken by a snare' ということわざをもとにした老人の狡猾さを表す表現。

396. have faced it with a card of ten 「はったりをかましてしまった」トランプのゲームで弱い 10 点の手持ち札しか持っていないのに、それで相手の強いカードに立ち向かってしまったという意。　card of ten = a playing card worth ten points (the value of the lowest-scoring cards in the game of primero) (*OED n.*^{2} P1)

397. 'Tis in my head = I have a plan

398. I see no reason but 「…しない理由はない」つまり、「必ずしなければ」という意味。　but = that ... not

398-399. supposed Lucentio, supposed Vincentio supposed は「偽物の」（そう思われているけれど実際は違う）という意味。ここで supposed という言葉が繰り返し使われているのは、ビアンカをめぐる筋書きの材源として、シェイクスピアが Goscoigne の *Supposes* を利用したことの反映と考えられる。

400. wonder = miracle

401. get = beget, breed

402. sire = father

  if I fail not of my cunning 「もし俺が知恵の使い方を間違えなければ」

  fail of = miss, miscarry

[ACT III, SCENE I]

Enter Lucentio [as Cambio], Hortentio [as Litio] and Bianca

LUCENTIO   Fiddler, forbear. You grow too forward, sir.
　Have you so soon forgot the entertainment
　Her sister Katherine welcomed you withal?
HORTENSIO   But, wrangling pedant, this is
　The patroness of heavenly harmony.   5
　Then give me leave to have prerogative,
　And when in music we have spent an hour,
　Your lecture shall have leisure for as much.
LUCENTIO   Preposterous ass, that never read so far
　To know the cause why music was ordained!   10
　Was it not to refresh the mind of man
　After his studies or his usual pain?
　Then give me leave to read philosophy,
　And while I pause, serve in your harmony.
HORTENSIO   Sirrah, I will not bear these braves of thine. 15
BIANCA   Why, gentlemen, you do me double wrong
　To strive for that which resteth in my choice.
　I am no breeching scholar in the schools:
　I'll not be tied to hours nor 'pointed times,
　But learn my lessons as I please myself.   20
　And to cut off all strife, here sit we down.
　— Take you your instrument; play you the whiles;
　His lecture will be done ere you have tuned.
HORTENSIO   You'll leave his lecture when I am in tune?
LUCENTIO   That will be never. Tune your instrument.   25
BIANCA   Where left we last?
LUCENTIO   Here, Madam.
　[*Reads*] 'Hic ibat Simois, hic est Sigeia tellus,
　Hic steterat Priami regia celsa senis.'
BIANCA   Conster them.   30

〔**3.1**〕あらすじ……………………………………………………………………

　ルーセンシオとホーテンシオは家庭教師に扮してビアンカに近づき、自分の気持ちを伝えようとする。ルーセンシオはオウィディウスの一節を翻訳するふりをして自分の正体と恋心を伝える。ホーテンシオは音階の説明の中に結婚を申し込む言葉を書き込む。

··

1. Fiddler, forbear ... sir　前の場面で音楽教師に扮したホーテンシオはキャタリーナにリュートの指使いを教えようとしてひどい目にあった。ここでも同じようにビアンカの手を取って教えているので、ルーセンシオがそれを阻止しようとしている。　forbear = stop, give way

2. entertainment = reception　　**3. withal** = with

4. this　ビアンカを指して「この方は」と言っている。

6. leave = permission　　**prerogative** = priority, precedence

8. lecture = lesson　　**leisure** = time of which you can freely dispose

9. Preposterous　前に (pre) くるべきものが後に (post) 来てしまっている、というこの言葉の元々の意味で使っている。科目の順番を間違えていることを非難している。

10. ordained = found, established

12. usual pain = customary labour

14. serve in = serve up　「料理をお出ししろ」に近い、見下した言い方。

15. braves = defiant behaviour「偉そうな態度」

17. resteth in my choice = is for me to choose

18. breeching scholar = a young boy still subject to the birch (*OED n.* 2b)「ムチで叩かれる生徒」　breeching = whipping　scholar = pupil

19. 'pointed = appointed

22. the whiles = in the meanwhile

23. ere = before

25. That will be never　前行のホーテンシオの when I am in tune は「楽器のチューニングが終わったら」の意味だが、ルーセンシオはそれをわざと文字通りに「僕の調子が良いときに」の意味にずらしている。

28-29. オウィディウスの書簡詩集『ヘロイデス』の中のペネロペがオデュッセウスに宛てた手紙の一節。英訳は下記のとおり。

　　　Here ran the river Simois; here is the Sigeian land
　　　Here stood the lofty palace of old Priam.

シモエイスの川が流れる Sigeian land はトロイアのことを指す。そこに老王プリアモス王の堂々たる宮殿が建っていた。　⇒後注

30. Conster = construe, translate

LUCENTIO *'Hic ibat'*, as I told you before; *'Simois'*, I am
Lucentio; *'hic est'*, son unto Vincentio of Pisa; *'Sigeia tellus'*,
disguised thus to get your love; *'Hic steterat'*, and that
Lucentio that comes a-wooing; *'Priami'*, is my man Tranio;
'regia', bearing my port; *'celsa senis'*, that we might beguile the 35
old pantaloon.

HOETENSIO Madam, my instrument's in tune.

BIANCA Let's hear. [*He plays*] O fie! The treble jars.

LUCENTIO Spit in the hole, man, and tune again.

BIANCA Now let me see if I can conster it. *'Hic ibat Simois'*, I 40
know you not; *'hic est Sigeia tellus'*, I trust you not; *'Hic steterat
Priami'*, take heed he hear us not; *'regia'*, presume not; *'celsa
senis'*, despair not.

HORTENSIO Madam, 'tis now in tune. [*He plays again*]

LUCENTIO   All but the bass.

HORTENSIO The bass is right; 'tis the base knave that jars. 45
[*Aside*] How fiery and forward our pedant is!
Now, for my life, the knave doth court my love.
Pedascule, I'll watch you better yet.

BIANCA In time I may believe, yet I mistrust.

LUCENTIO Mistrust it not, for sure Aeacides 50
Was Ajax, called so from his grandfather.

BIANCA I must believe my master; else, I promise you,
I should be arguing still upon that doubt.
But let it rest. — Now, Litio, to you.
Good master, take it not unkindly, pray, 55
That I have been thus pleasant with you both.

HORTENSIO [*To Lucentio*] You may go walk, and give me
leave a while.
My Lessons make no music in three parts.

LUCENTIO Are you so formal, sir? Well, I must wait —
[*Aside*] And watch withal, for, but I be deceived, 60
Our fine musician groweth amorous.

126

34. a-wooing　a- は動きの方向性や強さを加味する接頭辞。

　'Priami', is my man Tranio　プリアモスはトロイアの王であるが、ここでは「プリアモスは私の召使いトラーニオ」と聞こえ、滑稽さが生まれている。

35. port = status, style

36. old pantaloon　グレミオのこと。pantaloon については 1. 1. 47. 2 の注を参照。

38. fie　不快や非難を表す間投詞。　　　**treble**　高音部（音楽用語）。

　jars = sounds discordant

39. Spit in the hole　弦の調節をする糸巻き (peg) がすべらないように、差し込み部分 (peg hole) に唾をつけろと言うべきところを、ルーセンシオは楽器について無知なため、響孔 (sound hole) に唾をしろと言ってしまっている。また同時に、ことわざの 'Spit in your hands and take better hold' （手に唾つけてしっかり持て）をもじってからかっているとも考えられる。

44. but = except

45. Hortensio　⇒後注

45. base knave　base は bass と音が似ていることを利用した言葉遊び。もちろんここでは「うるさいのはコイツのほうだ」とルーセンシオのことを言っている。

48. Pedascule = little pedant　-cule は「小さい」ということを表す接尾辞。軽蔑の意味をこめて「学者もどきめ」と言っている。

50-51. Mistrust it not　「あなたの言うことは信頼できないわ」と言うビアンカの台詞を受け、「僕の言うことを信頼して」と言っている。同時にホーテンシオの耳には、オウィディウス『名婦の書簡』の続きを引用しながら、「この内容は確かです」と聞こえるように言っている。　　　**Aeacides**　アイアキデスはゼウスの血をひく善良な国王アイアコス (Aeacus) の子孫につけられた父称。　　　**Ajax**　アイアス、トロイア戦争で活躍した英雄のひとりで、確かにアイアコスの孫である。

52. master = tutor

53. still = always

56. pleasant with you both　「両方ともにいい顔をする」　後回しにされて不機嫌になっているホーテンシオに向かって言い訳をしながら、同時にルーセンシオにも謝っている。八方美人のビアンカの抜け目のなさがうかがえる台詞。

57. give me leave = please leave us alone

58. music in three parts　「三声部の音楽」　音楽用語を使いながら、ホーテンシオは邪魔だからいなくなれとルーセンシオに向かって言っている。

59. formal = Unduly precise or ceremonious, stiff (*OED a.* 8)

60. withal = at the same time　　　**but** = unless

HORTENSIO   Madam, before you touch the instrument
    To learn the order of my fingering,
    I must begin with rudiments of art,
    To teach you gamut in a briefer sort,   65
    More pleasant, pithy and effectual
    Than hath been taught by any of my trade;
    And there it is in writing fairly drawn.
BIANCA   Why, I am past my gamut long ago.
HORTENSIO   Yet read the gamut of Hortentio.   70
BIANCA   [*Reads*]
    '*Gamut* I am, the ground of all accord,
    A *re,* to plead Hortensio's passion.
    B *mi,* Bianca, take him for thy lord,
    C *fa ut,* that loves with all affection.
    D *sol re,* one clef, two notes have I,   75
    E *la mi,* show pity, or I die.'
    Call you this gamut? Tut, I like it not.
    Old fashions please me best. I am not so nice
    To change true rules for odd inventions.

Enter a Messenger

MESSENGER   Mistress, your father prays you leave your books   80
    And help to dress your sister's chamber up.
    You know tomorrow is the wedding day.
BIANCA   Farewell, sweet masters both, I must be gone.
                            [*Exeunt Bianca and Messenger*]
LUCENTIO   Faith, mistress, then I have no cause to stay.   [*Exit*]
HORTENSIO   But I have cause to pry into this pedant.   85
    Methinks he looks as though he were in love.
    Yet if thy thoughts, Bianca, be so humble
    To cast thy wandering eyes on every stale,
    Seize thee that list. If once I find thee ranging,
    Hortensio will be quit with thee by changing.   *Exit* 90

63. order ＝ method

64. rudiment ＝ first principles

65. gamut 「音階」　**in a briefer sort** ＝ in a quicker way

66. pithy ＝ concise, to the point　**effectual** ＝ effective

68. drawn ＝ written down

71. *Gamut* **I am**　音階を意味する gamut の語源はラテン語の *gamma ut* である。中世の音階の一番低い音の名称は *gamma*、基音の名称は *ut* だったことから、*gamma ut* となり、それが短縮されて gamut となった。ここでは語尾の ut の意味に戻り、「私は基音」と言っている。ut は現在のドレミのド。

　the ground of all accord ＝ the basis of all harmony　このホーテンシオの音階には、楽典上の知識にさらに、細かい言葉遊びが組み込まれている。

72-76.　A, B, C, D, E および re, mi, fa, sol, la は、いずれも下から上への音階順。　⇒後注

72. *A re*　'Array' と聞こえ、各音に向かって「整列してホーテンシオの思いを訴えよ」と命じていると解釈できる。

73. *B mi*　'Be my' と聞こえ、「僕のビアンカになっておくれ」と解釈できる。

74. *C fa ut*　ll. 75-76 の *D sol re, E la mi* とともに、C がド、D がレ、E がミにあたることを示している。ll. 72-73 と同様の言葉遊びが秘められているのかもしれないが、判然としない。全体としてドからラまでの 6 音からなる中世・ルネサンス音楽のヘクサコードと呼ばれる音階を表記している。

　that　関係代名詞で先行詞は前行の him。

75. one clef, two notes have I　意味の曖昧な 1 行。表面の意味は「ト音記号はひとつで音符はふたつ」だが、「愛はひとつだけれど、僕はホーテンシオとリチオと 2 つの顔を持つ」という意味が隠れているのではないかと推測する研究者もいる。性的なほのめかしで one vagina and two testicles という意味ではないかと推測する研究者もいる。

78. Old ＝ established　**nice** ＝ capricious

79. change ＝ exchange　**true** ＝ legitimate　**odd**　⇒後注

80-82. Mistress, ... day　⇒後注

85. pry into ＝ spy into

87. humble ＝ vulgar

88. stale ＝ decoy, bait　鷹狩りの用語で、鷹を誘い込むための「おとり」。

89. Seize thee that list ＝ Let anyone who wants you catch you　**list** ＝ wish　**ranging** ＝ straying　鷹がどこかに行ってしまうという意味だが、ここでは移り気な女の比喩として使われている。「フラフラどこかに行ってしまうような女なら」と言っている。

90. quit with　requited（お返ししてやる）という意味と rid of（さっさといなくなる）の意味を兼ねている。　**changing**　「別の女にのりかえること」

[ACT III, SCENE II]

Enter Baptista, Gremio, Tranio [as Lucentio], Katherina, Bianca,
[Lucentio as Cambio] and others, attendants

BAPTISTA   Signor Lucentio, this is the 'pointed day
That Katherine and Petruchio should be married,
And yet we hear not of our son-in-law.
What will be said? What mockery will it be
To want the bridegroom when the priest attends   5
To speak the ceremonial rites of marriage?
What says Lucentio to this shame of ours?

KATHERINA   No shame but mine. I must forsooth be forced
To give my hand, opposed against my heart,
Unto a mad-brain rudesby full of spleen,   10
Who wooed in haste and means to wed at leisure.
I told you, I, he was a frantic fool,
Hiding his bitter jests in blunt behaviour.
And to be noted for a merry man,
He'll woo a thousand, 'point the day of marriage,   15
Make feasts, invite friends, and proclaim the banns,
Yet never means to wed where he hath wooed.
Now must the world point at poor Katherine
And say, 'Lo, there is mad Petruchio's wife
If it would please him come and marry her.'   20

TRANIO   Patience, good Katherine, and Baptista too.
Upon my life, Petruchio means but well,
Whatever fortune stays him from his word.
Though he be blunt, I know him passing wise;
Though he be merry, yet withal he's honest.   25

KATHERINA   Would Katherine had never seen him though.
                              Exit weeping [followed by Bianca]

BAPTISTA   Go, girl. I cannot blame thee now to weep,
For such an injury would vex a very saint,

〔**3. 2**〕**あらすじ**……………………………………………………………………………

結婚式に遅れてやってきたペトルーチオは、病気だらけの駄馬に乗り、花婿にふさわしくないボロボロの古い衣装で登場する。結婚式でも大声で怒鳴りちらし、神父を殴り、大騒ぎをして皆を戸惑わせた上、祝宴には出ずに、嫌がるキャタリーナを引き連れて強引に旅立ってしまう。その間、トラーニオは誰か別の男をルーセンシオの父親に仕立ててビアンカとの結婚を認めさせてしまおうと計略をめぐらす。

……………………………………………………………………………………………………

1. 'pointed = appointed

4. What will be said? = What will people say?

5. want = lack

7. Lucentio もちろんバプティスタはここでトラーニオに向かって話しかけている。ビアンカの婚約相手として身内の恥をどう思うか聞いている。

8. but = except　　**forsooth** = indeed, in truth

10. rudesby = insolent, unmannerly fellow　　**spleen** = changeable temper　spleen はもともと「脾臓(ひぞう)」で、憂鬱や大笑いなど激しい気分を宿すところと考えられていた。*cf.* Induction 1. 133

11. Who wooed ... at leisure ことわざ 'to marry in haste and repent at leisure' をもじっている。

12. frantic = insane, lunatic

14. to be noted for = in order to be celebrated as, to be known as
merry = humorous, facetious

16. banns 「結婚予告」*cf.* 2. 1. 178

19. Lo = look

20. If it would ... marry her 「(狂人ペトルーチオの妻と呼ばれるのも)ペトルーチオが結婚する気になればの話だけどな」

21-25. トラーニオがペトルーチオのことをよく知っている人物として極めて好意的に語るのは不自然なため、この台詞は本来はホーテンシオのものだったのではないかと推測されている。

22. means but well 「悪意は絶対にない」　but = except

23. fortune = chance, accidental event　　**stays** = prevents

26. Would = I wish

27. to weep = for weeping

28. very = absolute

Much more a shrew of impatient humour.

Enter Biondello

BIONDELLO   Master, master, news! And such old news as you   30
never heard of!

BAPTISTA   Is it new and old too? How may that be?

BIONDELLO   Why, is it not news to hear of Petruchio's coming?

BAPTISTA   Is he come?

BIONDELLO   Why, no, sir.   35

BAPTISTA   What then?

BIONDELLO   He is coming.

BAPTISTA   When will he be here?

BIONDELLO   When he stands where I am and sees you there.

TRANIO   But say, what to thine old news?   40

BIONDELLO   Why, Petruchio is coming in a new hat and an old
jerkin; a pair of old breeches thrice turned; a pair of boots
that have been candle-cases, one buckled, another laced; an
old rusty sword ta'en out of the town armoury, with a broken
hilt and chapeless; with two broken points; his horse hipped   45
— with an old mothy saddle and stirrups of no kindred —
besides, possessed with the glanders and like to mose in the
chine, troubled with the lampass, infected with the fashions,
full of windgalls, sped with spavins, rayed with the yellows,
past cure of the fives, stark spoiled with the staggers, begnawn   50
with the bots, swayed in the back and shoulder-shotten, near-
legged before, and with a half-cheeked bit and a headstall of
sheep's leather, which, being restrained to keep him from
stumbling, hath been often burst and now repaired with
knots; one girth six times pieced, and a woman's crupper of   55
velour, which hath two letters for her name fairly set down in
studs, and here and there pieced with packthread.

BAPTISTA   Who comes with him?

BIONDELLO   O, sir, his lackey, for all the world caparisoned like

29. humour 「気性」 Induction. 2. 12 の後注参照。

30. old news ⇒後注

34. Is he come? = Has he come?

40. what to = What about, what of

42. jerkin 「短い上着」 ⇒後注　　**breeches** 「ひざ丈のズボン」

　thrice turned 「3 回裏返した」 ⇒後注

43. candle-cases 古くて履けなくなったブーツを蠟燭(ろうそく)を入れる容器として使っていた。それをまたブーツとして履いている。　　**one buckled, another laced** 「片足は金属のバックルで留めていて、もう一方は靴紐で留めている」

44. ta'en = taken　　**town armoury** 「町の兵器庫」

45. chapeless 「(刀剣の) さや (chape) がない」 *OED* で引用されている唯一の用例。シェイクスピアの造語の可能性が高い。　　**points** ズボンを上着に留めるための紐、ズボン吊り。　　**hipped** 臀部(でんぶ)の関節の不具合で足を引きずっている。

46. stirrups of no kindred 「両側の鐙(あぶみ)はちぐはぐ」 kindred は「同種、同族」

47. glanders 馬の病気の「鼻疽(びそ)」。あごに腫れができ鼻汁をたらす。

　like to = likely to　　**47-48. mose in the chine** ⇒後注

48. lampass 馬の病気の「口蓋腫」。　　**fashions** 馬の病気の「馬鼻疽腫」。

49. windgalls 「球腱軟腫」けづめの上にできる腫瘍。

　sped with = ruined by　　**spavins** 馬の病気の「飛節肉腫」。

　rayed = disfigured　　**yellows** 「黄疸(おうだん)」

50. fives 馬の病気で「顎下腺肥大」。　　**stark** = utterly

　staggers 馬の病気で「暈倒病(うんとう)」。千鳥足になったり卒倒したりする。

50-51. begnawn with = eaten away by

51. bots 「ウマバエの幼虫」馬の消化器に寄生する。　　**swayed in the back** 「脊柱が湾曲している」　　**shoulder-shotten** 「肩が脱臼している」

51-52. near-legged before 「前脚がX脚になっている」 *OED* では唯一の用例。

52. a half-cheeked bit 「くつわ (bit) の横の部品 (cheek) がはずれかけている」　**headstall** 「おもがい」くつわを固定するために馬の頭につける緒。

53. sheep's leather 豚や牛の皮に比べて弱い。

　restrained 「(手綱をひいて) 引っ張る」

55. one girth six times pieced 「腹帯 (girth) は 6 回つぎはぎがしてある」　**woman's crupper** 「女ものの尻がい」鞍を安定させる紐で、普通は革製。

56. velour 「ベロア」ビロードのような布。

56-57. two letters ... in studs 「女性の名前の 2 つのイニシャルが、美しく鋲(びょう)で留めつけられている」

57. here and there ... packthread 「どこもかしこも紐で繋ぎ合わせてある」

59. lackey 「下僕、従僕」　　**caparisoned** = dressed, fitted out

the horse; with a linen stock on one leg and a kersey boot-   60
hose on the other, gartered with a red and blue list; an old hat
and the humour of forty fancies pricked in't for a feather; a
monster, a very monster in apparel, and not like a Christian
footboy or a gentleman's lackey.

TRANIO   'Tis some odd humour pricks him to this fashion.   65
Yet oftentimes he goes but mean-apparelled.

BAPTISTA   I am glad he's come, howsoe'er he comes.

BIONDELLO   Why, sir, he comes not.

BAPTISTA   Didst thou not say he comes?

BIONDELLO   Who? That Petruchio came?   70

BAPTISTA   Ay, that Petruchio came.

BIONDELLO   No, sir, I say his horse comes with him on his
back.

BAPTISTA   Why, that's all one.

BIONDELLO   Nay, by Saint Jamy,   75
I hold you a penny,
A horse and a man
Is more then one,
And yet not many.

Enter Petruchio and Grumio

PETRUCHIO   Come, where be these gallants? Who's at home?   80

BAPTISTA   You are welcome, sir.

PETRUCHIO   And yet I come not well.

BAPTISTA   And yet you halt not.

TRANIO   Not so well apparelled as I wish you were.

PETRUCHIO   Were it better, I should rush in thus.   85
But where is Kate? Where is my lovely bride?
How does my father? Gentles, methinks you frown,
And wherefore gaze this goodly company
As if they saw some wondrous monument,
Some comet or unusual prodigy?   90

60. stock = stocking　　**kersey**　きめ粗い毛織物。

60-61. boot-hose　靴下の上にはく保護用のストッキング。

61. list = strip of cloth

62. the humour of forty fancies pricked in't for a feather　意味が不明瞭な一節。おそらく凝りに凝った奇妙な飾りを指すものと思われる。for a feather（羽飾りの代わりに）とあるので、「40色のリボン (forty fancies) を留めつけている (pricked)」と推測する研究者もいる。

65. 'Tis some odd humour pricks him　humour と pricks の間に that を補って考える。　odd humour「奇妙な気分」*cf.* l. 29　pricks = spurs, urges

66. but mean-apparelled　「粗末な身なりで」　but = only

67. howsoe'er = howsoever（どんな格好であろうと）

71. Ay = yes

74. all one = the same thing

75-79.　おそらくバラッドの一部ではないかと想像されるが、もとのバラッドは残っていない。

75. Nay = no　　**Saint Jamy**　おそらく聖ヤコブ (Saint James the Great) のことではないかとされる。

76. hold = bet

80. gallants = fine gentlemen

82. yet I come not well　バプティスタが 'You are welcome' と言ったのに対し、'I come not well' と返答している。「あまり歓迎されていないようですな」という意味か、「へんなかっこうで来まして」という意味かのいずれか。

83. yet you halt not　前行のペトルーチオの come not well を「来てはいるが元気ではない」という意味にずらして、「いや、ちゃんと歩いておられますよ」と切り返している。

85. Were it better, I should rush in thus.　「もっと良い服装で来たとしても、こうして慌ただしく入らせていただくでしょう。」　⇒後注

87. Gentles = gentlemen　　**methinks** = it seems to me

88. wherefore = why　　**goodly** = fine

89. wondrous monument　「驚くべき予兆、兆候」　monument = portent

90. comet　流星は不吉なことが起こる予兆と考えられていた。

　prodigy = omen

135

Baptista   Why, sir, you know this is your wedding day.

First were we sad, fearing you would not come,

Now sadder that you come so unprovided.

Fie, doff this habit, shame to your estate,

An eyesore to our solemn festival.   95

Tranio   And tell us what occasion of import

Hath all so long detained you from your wife

And sent you hither so unlike yourself?

Petruchio   Tedious it were to tell, and harsh to hear.

Sufficeth I am come to keep my word,   100

Though in some part enforcèd to digress,

Which at more leisure I will so excuse

As you shall well be satisfied withal.

But where is Kate? I stay too long from her.

The morning wears, 'tis time we were at church.   105

Tranio   See not your bride in these unreverent robes;

Go to my chamber, put on clothes of mine.

Petruchio   Not I, believe me. Thus I'll visit her.

Baptista   But thus, I trust, you will not marry her.

Petruchio   Good sooth, even thus: therefore ha' done with

   words.   110

To me she's married, not unto my clothes.

Could I repair what she will wear in me

As I can change these poor accoutrements,

'Twere well for Kate and better for myself.

But what a fool am I to chat with you,   115

When I should bid good morrow to my bride,

And seal the title with a lovely kiss!   *Exit [with Grumio]*

Tranio   He hath some meaning in his mad attire.

We will persuade him, be it possible,

To put on better ere he go to church.   120

Baptista   I'll after him and see the event of this.

          Exit [followed by Gremio, Biondello, and attendants]

93. unprovided = unprepared, improperly dressed

94. doff = take off, throw off

  habit = clothing, outfit

  estate = social status, rank

95. solemn festival = ceremonious occasion

96. occasion of import = important event, serious circumstances

99. were = would be

100. Sufficeth = it would be enough that

101. digress 「計画からずれる」という意味と「道をずれて遠回りする」という意味とを重ねている。

102. Which 関係代名詞で前行の内容を指す。「ずれてしまったことについてはあとからゆっくり言い訳をする」と言っている。

103. withal = with

105. wears = is passing

106. unreverent = disrespectful

110. Good sooth = yes indeed

  ha' done with words 「もう話はそれまでにしてください」 ha' = have

112. Could I repair what she will wear in me 直訳すると「私の体の一部で彼女がこれから使い続ける部分を修繕できるのであれば」という意味になる。Could I ... と倒置しているのは if が省略されているため。wear は wear out, use up の意味。「服を立派にするように、あそこも立派にできれば」というような性的なジョーク。

113. accoutrement = items of apparel (*OED n.* 1a)

117. seal the title 「印章を押して権利を確実にする」seal は公文書などに蠟をやわらかくして垂らし、そこに印を押し付けること。ここでは「愛の印」という比喩的な意味に、「契約」としての結婚という直接的な意味の連想が重ね合わせられている。

  lovely = loving

118. meaning = intention, purpose

119. be it possible 「もし可能なら」

120. ere = before

121. event = outcome

TRANIO [*To Lucentio*] But, sir, to love concerneth us to add
    Her father's liking, which to bring to pass,
    As I before imparted to your worship,
    I am to get a man — whate're he be 125
    It skills not much, we'll fit him to our turn —
    And he shall be Vincentio of Pisa,
    And make assurance here in Padua
    Of greater sums than I have promisèd.
    So shall you quietly enjoy your hope 130
    And marry sweet Bianca with consent.

LUCENTIO Were it not that my fellow schoolmaster
    Doth watch Bianca's steps so narrowly,
    'Twere good, methinks, to steal our marriage,
    Which once performed, let all the world say no, 135
    I'll keep mine own, despite of all the world.

TRANIO That by degrees we mean to look into,
    And watch our vantage in this business.
    We'll overreach the greybeard Gremio,
    The narrow-prying father Minola, 140
    The quaint musician, amorous Litio,
    All for my master's sake, Lucentio.

Enter Gremio

    Signor Gremio, came you from the church?

GREMIO As willingly as e'er I came from school.

TRANIO And is the bride and bridegroom coming home? 145

GREMIO A bridegroom, say you? 'Tis a groom indeed,
    A grumbling groom, and that the girl shall find.

TRANIO Curster than she? Why, 'tis impossible.

GREMIO Why, he's a devil, a devil, a very fiend.

TRANIO Why, she's a devil, a devil, the devil's dam. 150

GREMIO Tut, she's a lamb, a dove, a fool to him.
    I'll tell you, Sir Lucentio: when the priest

122. But, sir, to love この行から主人ルーセンシオと2人だけになって話しかけるので、sir と呼びかけているのだが、直前にトラーニオは「ペトルーチオを説得して着替えさせる」と言っており、話の切り替えがやや唐突である。But で始まることも、会話の途中から始まっていることを示唆している。　⇒後注　**concerneth us** = it concerneth us, it is essential for us

123. liking = approval　前行の love に加えて父親の承認を取ることが重要だと言っている。

bring to pass = bring about　関係代名詞 which は「父親の承認を取ること」を指している。「それを実現する (bring to pass) には」という意味。

124. As I ... F は As before となっている。そのままでも imparted を過去分詞ととらえれば意味は通るが、Pope はより韻律がスムーズになるように I を加えた。この場合 imparted は過去形。本書はこれを踏襲する。

126. skills = matters　　**turn** = need, purpose

130. enjoy your hope = get your wish

131. consent ビアンカの父親バプティスタの同意。

132. Were it not if が省略されている。

133. steps = actions　　**narrowly** = closely, inquisitively

134. 'Twere = it would be　　**steal our marriage** = marry secretly

135. let all the world say no 「みんながダメだと言っても」

138. watch our vantage = look out for a favourable opportunity

139. overreach = out wit, outdo 「先を越す」

140. narrow-prying = watchful, suspicious

141. quaint = cunning, clever

144. As willingly as e'er I came from school ことわざ 'With as good a will as ever I came from school' をもじっている。すぐにことわざを使うのは老人グレミオの癖。

146. groom groom はもともと boy, male servant という意味。ここではその見下した意味で「下郎」と言っている。

147. grumbling 「ブツブツ言っている、機嫌の悪い」grumbling groom と冒頭の音を合わせている。こうした工夫を alliteration（頭韻）と呼ぶ。

148. Curster = more curst, more bad-tempered

150. dam 「動物の母親、母獣」

151. Tut いらだちや軽蔑を表す間投詞。　　**be a fool to** = be inferior to in every way, be nothing when compared to (*OED n.¹* P2b)

152. Sir Lucentio ここでの Sir は貴族の地位を示すためではなく、敬意をこめた呼びかけ方として使われている。

152-53. when the priest ... his wife 「神父がキャタリーナにこの人の妻になるかと聞くはずのタイミングで」

Should ask if Katherine should be his wife,
'Ay, by gogs-wounds', quoth he, and swore so loud
That all amazed the priest let fall the book,   155
And as he stooped again to take it up,
This mad-brained bridegroom took him such a cuff
That down fell priest and book, and book and priest.
'Now take them up', quoth he, 'if any list.'

TRANIO   What said the wench when he rose again?   160

GREMIO   Trembled and shook, for why he stamped and swore
As if the vicar meant to cozen him.
But after many ceremonies done,
He calls for wine. 'A health!' quoth he, as if
He had been aboard, carousing to his mates   165
After a storm, quaffed off the muscadel
And threw the sops all in the sexton's face,
Having no other reason
But that his beard grew thin and hungerly
And seemed to ask him sops as he was drinking.   170
This done, he took the bride about the neck
And kissed her lips with such a clamorous smack
That at the parting all the church did echo.
And I seeing this came thence for very shame,
And after me, I know, the rout is coming.   175
Such a mad marriage never was before.
Hark, hark, I hear the minstrels play.

Music plays
Enter Petruchio, Katherina, Bianca, Hortensio [as Litio],
Baptista, [Grumio and ohters]

PETRUCHIO   Gentlemen and friends, I thank you for your
   pains.
I know you think to dine with me today,
And have prepared great store of wedding cheer,   180

154. by gogs-wounds = by God's wounds　しばしば zounds と省略される強い誓いの言葉。「ちくしょう」というような、いまいましさを表現するののしりの言葉としても使われる。教会で使うのにはふさわしくない。

155. all amazed　「すっかりうろたえて」

157. took him = struck him, gave him (*OED v.* 5b)

cuff = a blow with a fist

159. take them up　them は「神父と聖書」を指すと考えるのが妥当であろう。ただし「キャタリーナのドレス」を指すと解釈する研究者もいる。シェイクスピアの時代には、結婚式が終わると出席していた若者たちが花嫁の周りにやってきて、花嫁のドレスにつけられたリボンの飾りを引っ張って取るという風習があった。この解釈に従えば、ペトルーチオは「（式は済んだから）取っていいぞ」と言っている。

if any list = it anyone wants to

161. for why = because

162. cozen = cheat

163. many = various

165. aboard = on board ship

carousing to = drinking toast to and with

166. quaffed off = drank up

muscadel　当時の結婚式で出される甘いワイン。

167. sops　ケーキかパンを甘いワインに浸したもの。当時の結婚式の伝統的しきたりのひとつ。

sexton　「寺男」鐘つきや墓掘りなど教会の用務を引き受ける。

169. But = except

hungerly = sparsely, in a hungry-looking way（貧相な）

170. ask him sops = ask him for sops

172. smack　「ぶちゅっ」というキスする時の音。

173. at the parting　「唇と唇が離れる時に」

175. rout = company of guest

177. Hark = Listen

minstrels = musicians

179. think = expect

180. cheer = food and drink

But so it is, my haste doth call me hence,

And therefore here I mean to take my leave.

BAPTISTA Is't possible you will away tonight?

PETRUCHIO I must away today before night come.

Make it no wonder. If you knew my business, 185

You would entreat me rather go than stay.

And, honest company, I thank you all

That have beheld me give away myself

To this most patient, sweet and virtuous wife.

Dine with my father, drink a health to me, 190

For I must hence, and farewell to you all.

TRANIO Let us entreat you stay till after dinner.

PETRUCHIO It may not be.

GREMIO Let me entreat you.

PETRUCHIO It cannot be.

KATHERINA Let me entreat you.

PETRUCHIO I am content.

KATHERINA Are you content to stay? 195

PETRUCHIO I am content you shall entreat me stay,

But yet not stay, entreat me how you can.

KATHERINA Now, if you love me, stay.

PETRUCHIO Grumio, my horse.

GRUMIO Ay, sir, they be ready: the oats have eaten the horses.

KATHERINA Nay then, 200

Do what thou canst, I will not go today,

No, nor tomorrow, not till I please myself.

The door is open, sir, there lies your way,

You may be jogging whiles your boots are green.

For me, I'll not be gone till I please myself. 205

'Tis like you'll prove a jolly surly groom

That take it on you at the first so roundly.

PETRUCHIO Kate, content thee. Prithee be not angry.

KATHERINA I will be angry. What hast thou to do?

181. so it is = the situation is as follows

182. take my leave = say goodbye

183. will away　動詞 go が省略されている。次行も同じ。

185. Make it no wonder = Don't be surprised

187. honest = honourable, respectable

188. beheld = witnessed

191. must hence　動詞 go が省略されている。

197. not stay = not content to stay

　entreat me how you can = no matter how much you entreat me

198. horse = horses　17 世紀まで horse は複数形としても使われた。次行の they からも複数であることがわかる。

199. the oats have eaten the horses　意味の不明瞭な一節。グルーミオはうっかり間違えて、主語と目的語を逆にしてしまったのか、あるいはわざと逆にしてあてこすりめいた皮肉を言おうとしているのか。「食い過ぎるほどに食って動けなくなっている」、あるいは「逆に餌に食われるほどひどい駄馬だ」と言おうとしているのかもしれない。

204. You may be jogging whiles your boots are green　ことわざ 'Be jogging while your boots are green' をもじっている。迷惑な客を追い払う意味で使われ、「靴が新しいうちに走ってくださいな」という意味。green は new の意味。ペトルーチオがぼろぼろの古靴を履いていることへの皮肉にもなっている。

206. like = likely

　jolly = arrogant, overbearing

　surly = sullen, bad-tempered

　groom = base fellow　*cf.* l. 146

207. That　関係代名詞で先行詞は you。

　take it on you = assume lofty airs（偉そうになんでも自分で引き受ける）

　at the first = from the start　　**roundly** = plainly, outspokenly

209. What hast thou to do? = what has it to do with you?

— Father, be quiet. He shall stay my leisure. 210

GREMIO   Ay, marry, sir, now it begins to work.

KATHERINA   Gentlemen, forward to the bridal dinner.

I see a woman may be made a fool

If she had not a spirit to resist.

PETRUCHIO   They shall go forward, Kate, at thy command. 215

— Obey the bride, you that attend on her.

Go to the feast, revel and domineer,

Carouse full measure to her maidenhead,

Be mad and merry, or go hang yourselves.

But for my bonny Kate, she must with me. 220

— Nay, look not big, nor stamp, nor stare, nor fret.

I will be master of what is mine own.

She is my goods, my chattels; she is my house,

My household-stuff, my field, my barn,

My horse, my ox, my ass, my anything, 225

And here she stands. Touch her whoever dare,

I'll bring mine action on the proudest he

That stops my way in Padua. — Grumio,

Draw forth thy weapon, we are beset with thieves.

Rescue thy mistress if thou be a man. 230

— Fear not, sweet wench, they shall not touch thee, Kate.

I'll buckler thee against a million.

Exeunt Petruchio, Katherina [and Grumio]

BPTISTA   Nay, let them go — a couple of quiet ones.

GREMIO   Went they not quickly, I should die with laughing.

TRANIO   Of all mad matches never was the like. 235

LUCENTIO   Mistress, what's your opinion of your sister?

BIANCA   That being mad herself, she's madly mated.

GREMIO   I warrant him, Petruchio is Kated.

BAPTISTA   Neighbours   and   friends,   though   bride   and

bridegroom wants

For to supply the places at the table, 240

210. Father, be quiet　父親に口を出すなと言っている。
stay my leisure = wait until I am ready　助動詞 shall は話者キャタリーナ
の意思を示すので、「私が行くまで行かせないわ」という意味になる。

211. it begins to work = things are beginning to happen「発酵が始まった」
という醸造のイメージ。「ブツブツ騒ぎ始めたぞ」という意。

217. revel = make merry, have fun
domineer = revel, feast riotously (*OED v.* 2)

218. Carouse full measure = drink plentifully　　**maidenhead** = virginity
「花嫁の初夜を祝って存分に乾杯してください」という意。

219. mad and merry　mad = boisterous, high-spirited　mad and merry は
頭韻 (alliteration) を踏んでいる。　　**or go hang yourselves**　「それがいや
なら首くくれ」、つまり「お嫌でしたらくたばっちまえ」というような軽口。
or = otherwise

221. look not big = don't puff out your chests, don't make yourself look
bigger（威嚇するような態度は取るな）　big = haughtily, pompously,
boastfully (*OED adv.* 3)

222-32.　周囲にいる男たちに、「ケイトに手を出すな」とわざと芝居じみた口
調で脅している。キャタリーナを家財道具や家畜と同列に扱う乱暴さは、ペト
ルーチオの計画された演出と解釈できる。

223. chattels = properties, possessions
224. household-stuff = household goods
225. my ox, my ass, my anything　⇒後注
227. bring mine action　法律用語としての action で「訴訟を起こす」という
意味と体を使った action で「叩きのめしてやる」という意味を兼ねている。
my ではなく mine となっているのは action が母音で始まるため。
he = man

228. stops my way = stands in my way
229. beset with = surrounded by
232. buckler = shield, defend
233. a couple of quiet ones　もちろん皮肉で言っている。
234. Went they not quickly = if they had not gone quickly
235. never was the like　the like が主語。「あの2人のようなカップルは今まで
にいなかった」
237. That = I think that, I am of the opinion that
238. Kated　前行の mated と韻を踏んでいる。Kate を動詞化して「ケイトに
なってしまった」「ケイト化されてしまった」という意。
239. wants = lacks, is missing
240. For to supply = to fill

You know there wants no junkets at the feast.

[*To Tranio*] Lucentio, you shall supply the bridegroom's
   place,

And let Bianca take her sister's room.

TRANIO   Shall sweet Bianca practise how to bride it?

BAPTISTA   She shall, Lucentio. Come, gentlemen, let's go.   245

Exeunt

241. there wants no junkets = there is no lack of sweetmeats

242. supply = fill

243. room = seat at the table

244. bride it　「祝宴で花嫁役をする」　bride = act as a bride (*OED v.*[1] 2)

[ACT IV, SCENE I]

Enter Grumio

GRUMIO   Fie, fie on all tired jades, on all mad masters, and all
foul ways! Was ever man so beaten? Was ever man so rayed?
Was ever man so weary? I am sent before to make a fire, and
they are coming after to warm them. Now were not I a little
pot and soon hot, my very lips might freeze to my teeth, my   5
tongue to the roof of my mouth, my heart in my belly, ere I
should come by a fire to thaw me. But I with blowing the fire
shall warm myself, for, considering the weather, a taller man
than I will take cold. Holla, ho, Curtis!

Enter Curtis

CURTIS   Who is that calls so coldly?   10

GRUMIO   A piece of ice. If thou doubt it, thou mayst slide
from my shoulder to my heel with no greater a run but my
head and my neck. A fire, good Curtis.

CURTIS   Is my master and his wife coming, Grumio?

GRUMIO   O ay, Curtis, ay, and therefore fire, fire, cast on no   15
water.

CURTIS   Is she so hot a shrew as she's reported?

GRUMIO   She was, good Curtis, before this frost. But thou
know'st winter tames man, woman, and beast, for it hath
tamed my old master, and my new mistress, and myself,   20
fellow Curtis.

CURTIS   Away, you three-inch fool! I am no beast.

GRUMIO   Am I but three inches? Why, thy horn is a foot, and
so long am I at the least. But wilt thou make a fire, or shall I
complain on thee to our mistress, whose hand — she being   25
now at hand — thou shalt soon feel, to thy cold comfort, for
being slow in thy hot office?

CURTIS   I prithee, good Grumio, tell me how goes the world?

〔**4. 1**〕あらすじ···

　凍える寒さの中、悪路で泥だらけになりながらペトルーチオとキャタリーナが屋敷に向かっている様子をグルーミオが召使い仲間に伝える。グルーミオの予告通り、屋敷に到着したペトルーチオは横暴に怒鳴り続け、キャタリーナや召使いたちを狼狽（ろうばい）させる。キャタリーナ以上の癇癪（かんしゃく）を見せつけ、食事も睡眠も与えないのが、じゃじゃ馬をおとなしくさせる自分の方法だと、ペトルーチオは独白する。

···

1. ⇒後注　　**jades**「駄馬」

2. foul ways「ぬかるんだ道」　　**rayed** = dirtied with mud　*cf.* 3. 2. 49

4. were not I = if I were not

4-5. a little pot and soon hot　ことわざ 'A little pot is soon hot'（小さい奴はすぐ怒る）を下敷きにしている。グルーミオは hot の「怒りっぽい」という意味に「（温度が）熱い」という意味を重ねて、「俺がすぐに熱くなるチビでなければ体のあちらこちらが凍りつく」と言っている。

7. come by = get

8. taller「背が高い」という意味以外に、シェイクスピアの時代には「強健な」という意味もあった。「（俺みたいなチビは熱くなれるが）俺よりでかい男は風邪をひくぞ」と言っている。

9. Holla「おーい」という呼びかけ。

10. Who is that　that の後に関係代名詞の who を補って読む。
　　coldly「寒そうな声で」という意味と「冷淡な声で」という意味を重ねている。

11. A piece of ice「全身氷の塊だ」　　**slide** = slip

12. run = a distance covered by running (*OED n.*² 1b)「頭から首まで動くだけで、一気に肩から踵（かかと）まで滑り下りられる」と言っている。

15. ay = yes

15-16. fire, fire, cast on no water「火を起こせ、水をかけるな」　⇒後注

19-22. winter tames ... beast　グルーミオはことわざ 'Winter and wedlock tame both man and beast' をもじっている。ことわざ通りなら最後は beast だが、その代わりに「俺と相棒カーティス」とグルーミオは言っている。それに対して、カーティスは「俺は beast じゃねえぞ」と言い返す。

23. horn　妻を別の男に寝取られると、亭主の頭に角が生えると言われていた。「お前の角の長さは 1 フィートもある」とグルーミオはからかっている。

24. so long am I「俺の身長もそれくらいの長さはあるぞ」と言いながら、お前の女房を寝取れるぞとからかっている。

25. complain on = complain about

26. to thy cold comfort「（叩かれて）悲しい思いをするぞ」と言っている。

27. hot office = duty of fire-making

GRUMIO   A cold world, Curtis, in every office but thine, and
therefore, fire. Do thy duty, and have thy duty, for my master   30
and mistress are almost frozen to death.

CURTIS   There's fire ready, and therefore, good Grumio, the
news.

GRUMIO   Why, 'Jack boy, ho boy!' and as much news as wilt
thou.   35

CURTIS   Come, you are so full of cony-catching.

GRUMIO   Why, therefore fire, for I have caught extreme cold.
Where's the cook? Is supper ready, the house trimmed, rushes
strewed, cobwebs swept, the servingmen in their new fustian,
the white stockings, and every officer his wedding garment   40
on? Be the Jacks fair within, the Jills fair without, the carpets
laid, and everything in order?

CURTIS   All ready, and therefore, I pray thee, news.

GRUMIO   First know my horse is tired, my master and mistress
fallen out.   45

CURTIS   How?

GRUMIO   Out of their saddles into the dirt, and thereby hangs
a tale.

CURTIS   Let's ha't, good Grumio.

GRUMIO   Lend thine ear.   50

CURTIS   Here.

GRUMIO   There.   [*He boxes Curtis's ear*]

CURTIS   This 'tis to feel a tale, not to hear a tale.

GRUMIO   And therefore 'tis called a sensible tale, and this cuff
was but to knock at your ear and beseech listening. Now I   55
begin: *Imprimis,* we came down a foul hill, my master riding
behind my mistress.

CURTIS   Both of one horse?

GRUMIO   What's that to thee?

CURTIS   Why, a horse.   60

GRUMIO   Tell thou the tale. But hadst thou not crossed me,

30. have thy duty = earn your reward 'Do thy duty and take thy due' と
いう言い習わしをもじっている。

34. 'Jack boy, ho boy' 輪唱曲 'The devil is dead' の冒頭の歌詞 'Jack
boy, ho hoy, news' を引用している。「ニュースと言えば例の歌」といった
ところ。

34-35. as wilt thou = as you wish

36. cony-catching cony-catching は「詐欺、ペテン」という意味。さらにこ
こでは catching に「輪唱」という意味を重ねて言葉遊びをしている。「輪唱
曲の歌詞ばかりで、話をケチるやつ」というような意。

38. trimmed = prepared, put into order

38-39. rushes strewed 客人を迎える準備として、新鮮なイグサを床にまいて
いた。ハーブ類をまくこともあった。匂いを消したり、害虫を除去する目的が
あった。

39. fustian 綿または麻の丈夫な布で仕事着に使われた。

40. officer = servant

41. the Jacks fair within, the Jills fair without Jack は男、Jill は女の代名詞
なので、Jacks と Jills は男の召使いたちと女の召使いたちを意味している。
同時に jacks は革製の酒を飲むジョッキ、jills と同音の gills は金属製の酒の
量を図る器。fair within, fair without は「内側、外側をきれいにしておけ」
という意味。　　**carpets** この時代には床にひくものではなく、「テーブルク
ロス」を指す。

47-48. thereby hangs a tale 「そこでいろいろあってね」という決まり文句。

49. ha't = have it

50-53. here と hear が同じ発音、さらに両方とも訛って h の音が脱落すると
ear と発音の区別がつかなくなる。言葉の混乱が、ドタバタ喜劇の効果を高め
ている。

54. sensible tale 「話が通っている」という意味と「体で感じることができる
話」という意味を重ね合わせた言葉遊び。

　　cuff = blow

55. but = only

56. *Imprimis* ラテン語「第1に」「第1項」　グルーミオはわざと堅苦しい法
律用語を使ってふざけている。

　　foul = muddy

58. of = on

61. Tell thou the tale 「お前が話せよ」

　　hadst thou not = if thou hadst not

　　crossed = interrupted

thou shouldst have heard how her horse fell, and she under her horse; thou shouldst have heard in how miry a place, how she was bemoiled, how he left her with the horse upon her, how he beat me because her horse stumbled, how she waded 65 through the dirt to pluck him off me, how he swore, how she prayed that never prayed before, how I cried, how the horses ran away, how her bridle was burst, how I lost my crupper — with many things of worthy memory, which now shall die in oblivion, and thou return unexperienced to thy grave. 70

CURTIS   By this reckoning he is more shrew than she.

GRUMIO   Ay, and that thou and the proudest of you all shall find when he comes home. But what talk I of this? Call forth Nathaniel, Joseph, Nicholas, Philip, Walter, Sugarsop and the rest. Let their heads be slickly combed, their blue coats 75 brushed, and their garters of an indifferent knit. Let them curtsy with their left legs, and not presume to touch a hair of my master's horsetail till they kiss their hands. Are they all ready?

CURTIS   They are.   80

GRUMIO   Call them forth.

CURTIS   Do you hear, ho? You must meet my master to countenance my mistress.

GRUMIO   Why, she hath a face of her own.

CURTIS   Who knows not that?   85

GRUMIO   Thou, it seems, that calls for company to countenance her.

CURTIS   I call them forth to credit her.

GRUMIO   Why, she comes to borrow nothing of them.

Enter four or five Servingmen

NATHANIEL   Welcome home, Grumio.   90

PHILIP   How now, Grumio.

JOSEPH   What, Grumio.

63. miry = muddy

64. bemoiled = covered with mud

68. bridle 「馬勒」面繋、轡、手綱からなる、馬の頭部につける道具。

  burst = broken   **crupper** 「尻がい」鞍から馬の尾に回してかける皮ひも。

69-70. この2行には、memory, die, oblivion, grave という死者に関する言葉が多用されており、もったいぶった口調になっている。全体としての意味は「多くの記憶すべき事柄があれど、今や忘却のかなたに消えていくのみにて、汝はそれらを知ることなく土へと帰っていく」といったところ。

69. of worthy memory = worth remembering

71. By this reckoning 「この計算からすると」、つまり「聞いた話から推量すると」という意。

  shrew この言葉は今日ではおもに女性に用いられるが、「がみがみやかましいやつ」という意味で男女ともに用いられていた。

72-73. that thou ... home that は find の目的語で、前の台詞の内容（ペトルーチオの方がキャタリーナより怒りっぽいこと）を指す。「ペトルーチオが戻ったらそれがわかるよ」と言っている。

72. proudest = most self-assured

73. what = for what, why

74. Nathaniel, Joseph, Nicholas, Philip, Walter, Sugarsop ⇒後注

75. slickly = sleekly

  blue coat 召使いは通常、青い制服（お仕着せ）を着ていた。*cf.* 1. 1. 202

76. indifferent 「目立たない (modest)」あるいは「ちぐはぐでない (matching)」のいずれかの意味。

77. curtsy with their left legs 右足を引いて左足を前にして膝を曲げてお辞儀をする。利き足の右を前にすることは、目上の人に対して失礼とされた。

78. kiss their hands 自分自身の手にキスをすることは、敬意を表す動作。その動作をするまでは、主人の馬にも触れてはいけないと注意している。

83. countenance カーティスは「敬意を表する (pay respect to)」のつもりでこの言葉を用いたが、グルーミオは（わざと）文字通りに「顔 (face)」の意味に受け取って、「彼女には顔はあるぞ」と答えている。

86. that 関係代名詞で先行詞は Thou。

88. credit カーティスは誤解を解くため、「敬意を表する (honour)」の意味でこの言葉に言い換えたが、グルーミオはさらに（わざと）「信用取引をする (provide credit for)」の意味に受け取っている。

NICHOLAS   Fellow, Grumio.

NATHANIEL   How now, old lad.

GRUMIO   Welcome, you. — How now, you? — What, you? —   95
Fellow, you. — And thus much for greeting. Now, my spruce
companions, is all ready, and all things neat?

NATHANIEL   All things is ready. How near is our master?

GRUMIO   E'en at hand, alighted by this. And therefore be not
— Cock's passion, silence! I hear my master.   100

Enter Petruchio and Katherina

PETRUCHIO   Where be these knaves? What, no man at door
To hold my stirrup nor to take my horse?
Where is Nathaniel, Gregory, Philip?

ALL SERVINGMEN   Here, here sir, here sir.

PETRUCHIO   'Here sir, here sir, here sir, here sir!'   105
You logger-headed and unpolished grooms!
What, no attendance? No regard? No duty?
Where is the foolish knave I sent before?

GRUMIO   Here sir, as foolish as I was before.

PETRUCHIO   You peasant swain, you whoreson malt-horse
drudge!   110
Did I not bid thee meet me in the park
And bring along these rascal knaves with thee?

GRUMIO   Nathaniel's coat, sir, was not fully made,
And Gabriel's pumps were all unpinked i'th'heel.
There was no link to colour Peter's hat,   115
And Walter's dagger was not come from sheathing.
There were none fine but Adam, Rafe, and Gregory;
The rest were ragged, old, and beggarly.
Yet, as they are, here are they come to meet you.

PETRUCHIO   Go, rascals, go, and fetch my supper in.   120

Exeunt Servingmen

[*Sings*]   'Where is the life that late I led?

95-96. 召使いの一人一人に挨拶をしている。

96. spruce = smart in appearance「きびきびしている」(brisk) という意味合いも含まれているかもしれない。

98. All things is ready　主語は All things で複数だが、グルーミオの台詞の is all ready につられて、動詞は is になっている。

99. E'en = even

　alighted by this　「もう今頃は馬を降りている」　this = this time

100. Cock's passion　by God's Passion の崩れた形。 be not のあとに何か言おうとした瞬間にペトルーチオたちが入ってくる音がして、慌てている。

102. stirrup　「鐙（あぶみ）」馬から降りる時に押さえておいてもらうと降りやすい。

106. logger-headed = thick-headed, stupid (*OED adj.* 1)

　unpolished = rude

　grooms = servants, male attendants (*OED n.¹* 3)

110. peasant swain = country bumpkin

　whoreson = bastard

　malt-horse drudge　「のろま」malt-horse は麦芽製造業で石臼を回すために使われた鈍重な馬。

111. park　「猟園」貴族や大地主の館に付属する広大な敷地。

114. pumps = light shoes

　unpinked　pink は「皮に小さな飾り穴をあける」ことを言う。ゲイブリエルの靴に飾りをほどこす作業がまだ終わっていなかったと、グルーミオは言い訳をしている。

115. link　松やにを塗ったたいまつを燃やしてできる黒い塗料。

116. sheathing　＜sheathe = fit a sward with a sheathe (*OED v.* 1) ここでは剣に合わせた鞘（さや）を用意する作業が間に合わず、剣がまだ届いていなかったと言い訳をしている。

117. fine = properly-dressed

118. old = wearing old clothes, shabby (*OED adj.* 3c)

120. rascals = rogues

121-22.　バラッドの出だしの歌詞であることは明らかだが、そのバラッド自体は残っていない。コール・ポーターはブロードウェイ・ミュージカル『キス・ミー・ケイト』の中で独身時代の自由な恋愛を懐かしんで主人公が歌う歌に作り直している。

Where are those — '
Sit down, Kate, and welcome. — Soud, soud, soud, soud.

Enter Servants with supper

Why, when, I say? — Nay, good sweet Kate, be merry.
—Off with my boots, you rogues! You villains, when?   125
[*Sings*] 'It was the friar of orders grey,
   As he forth walkèd on his way —'
Out, you rogue! You pluck my foot awry.
Take that, and mend the plucking of the other.
—Be merry, Kate. — Some water, here. What, ho!   130

Enter one with water

Where's my spaniel Troilus? Sirrah, get you hence,
And bid my cousin Ferdinand come hither. —
One, Kate, that you must kiss and be acquainted with.
—Where are my slippers? Shall I have some water?
Come, Kate, and wash, and welcome heartily.   135
—You whoreson villain! Will you let it fall?
KATHERINE Patience, I pray you. 'Twas a fault unwilling.
PETRUCHIO A whoreson, beetle-headed, flap-eared knave!
Come, Kate, sit down, I know you have a stomach.
Will you give thanks, sweet Kate, or else shall I?   140
—What's this? Mutton?
FIRST SERVANT   Ay.
PETRUCHIO   Who brought it?
PETER   I.
PETRUCHIO 'Tis burnt, and so is all the meat.
What dogs are these? Where is the rascal cook?
How durst you villains bring it from the dresser
And serve it thus to me that love it not?   145
There, take it to you, trenchers, cups, and all.
You heedless joltheads and unmannered slaves!

123. Soud この言葉の意味は不明瞭。イライラした気持ちを示す間投詞ではないかと考えられる。歌の続きをハミングで歌っているのを、このように書き表したと考える編者もいる。また Food の誤植と考える編者もいる。Secretary hand と呼ばれる当時の筆記体では s が縦長に書かれ、f としばしば読み間違えられた。ただ 'food' という言葉を4回繰り返すのは、台詞としていかにも気が利かない。

124. when 「いつまで待たせるんだ」という苛立ちを示している。

126-27. ll. 121-22 と同様にバラッドの一節。friar of orders grey は灰色の僧服を着たフランチェスコ修道会の修道僧のこと。修道僧が尼僧を誘惑するテーマはバラッドでしばしば歌われたので、この2行もそうしたバラッドの一節ではないかと想像できる。

128. Out 怒りや憤慨を表す間投詞。　　**pluck my foot awry** 「引っ張る方向が違う（足がねじれる）」と文句を言っている。

129. Take that 「これでもくらえ！」と言って召使いを蹴飛ばすか殴るかしているのか、あるいは「こいつを脱がせろ」と言ってブーツをはいた足を突き出しているのかどちらか。

mend = improve　もう一方のブーツはもっと上手く脱がせろと言っている。

130. water 食事の前に手を洗うための水。

131. my spaniel Troilus 「俺のスパニエル犬のトロイラス」　Troilus はトロイアの王子の名前。誠実な Troilus を恋人 Cressida が裏切る悲恋の物語を題材に、シェイクスピアは *Troilus and Cressida* を書いた。

132. cousin Ferdinand ここで名前が言及されるだけで実際は登場しない。

133. One = A cousin

135. wash = wash your hand

136. it おそらく水の入った水盤か水差し。ペトルーチオはわざと召使いの手から落として、怒鳴りつけている。

137. Patience, I pray you この場面での最初のキャタリーナの台詞だが、これまでとは異なり、言葉遣いがずいぶんと丁寧になっている。

unwilling = unintentional, unwilled (*OED adj.* 5)

138. beetle-headed = stupid　beetle は木製の槌。

flap-eared 「耳が垂れている」

139. stomach = appetite

140. give thanks = say grace　どちらが食前の祈りを唱えるかを話している。

142. meat = food

144. dresser 「調理用のキッチンテーブルあるいはサイドボード」または「食事の支度をした人」のいずれか。

146. trenchers 木製の皿

147. joltheads = fools

What, do you grumble? I'll be with you straight.

[Exeunt Servants]

KATHERINE   I pray you, husband, be not so disquiet.

The meat was well, if you were so contented.   150

PETRUCHIO   I tell thee, Kate, 'twas burnt and dried away,

And I expressly am forbid to touch it,

For it engenders choler, planteth anger,

And better 'twere that both of us did fast,

Since, of ourselves, ourselves are choleric,   155

Than feed it with such over-roasted flesh.

Be patient, tomorrow't shall be mended,

And for this night we'll fast for company.

Come, I will bring thee to thy bridal chamber.   *Exeunt*

Enter Servants severally

NATHANIEL   Peter, didst ever see the like?   160

PETER   He kills her in her own humour.

Enter Curtis

GRUMIO   Where is he?

CURTIS   In her chamber,

Making a sermon of continency to her,

And rails and swears and rates that she, poor soul,   165

Knows not which way to stand, to look, to speak,

And sits as one new-risen from a dream.

Away, away, for he is coming hither.   *[Exeunt]*

Enter Petruchio

PETRUCHIO   Thus have I politicly begun my reign,

And 'tis my hope to end successfully.   170

My falcon now is sharp and passing empty,

And till she stoop she must not be full-gorged,

For then she never looks upon her lure.

148. I'll be with you = I'll deal with you right now.

148. 1. このト書きはF1にはない。ペトルーチオが召使いたちを馬鹿だ、間抜けだと罵倒し、「すぐに片をつけてやるぞ」と脅しているので、召使いたちが慌てて逃げ出していくという演出は自然な流れだ。だが全員が退場せずに何人かはステージ上に残りこの後のキャタリーナとペトルーチオのやりとりを遠巻きに眺めているという演出も可能だろう。l. 159 の後に *Enter Servants severally* とあるが、逃げ出した召使いたちが戻ってきて、現場を「目撃」したナサニエル、ピーターの話を聞くのかもしれない。

149. disquiet = upset

150. well = satisfactory   **so contented** 「そんなものだと納得すれば」

151. dried away = dried up

153. engenders choler   当時、主流だった四体液理論では、体液のひとつ choler（胆汁、yellow bile ともいう）は癇癪を起こすと考えられていた。焦げた肉は胆汁を過剰にし、より怒りっぽくさせると言い伝えられていた。

154. fast = refrain from eating

155. of ourselves = by our nature, in ourselves

158. for company = together   こうした台詞にペトルーチオがキャタリーナとともに試練を乗り越えようとする姿勢を読み取り、「ただの暴力亭主」ではないと解釈することもできるが、逆にこの台詞を口先だけの方便と解釈することも可能である。いくつかの演出では、l. 169 で一人登場したペトルーチオがこっそり一人で食べものを口にしている。

159. 1. severally 「一人ずつ」登場するのかもしれないし、「いくつかの方向から（別々のドアから）」登場するのかもしれない。

161. He kills ... humour = he conquers her by outdoing her in bad temper

164. sermon of continency 「抑制、自制を説く説教」

165. rates = scolds, chides   **that** = so that

167. new-risen = newly woken up

169. politicly = cunningly, calculatedly, like a clever politician

171. My falcon ... empty キャタリーナを野生の鷹に喩えている。シェイクスピアの時代には、目を離さずにかまい続けて眠らせず、餌を減らして飢えさせるのが野生の鷹を飼い慣らす方法として知られていた。   **sharp** = eager for prey, hungry (*OED adj.* 4f)   **passing** = extremely

172. stoop 「鷹狩りで鷹が獲物めがけて急降下する」という鷹狩りの用語と、「ぬかづく、屈服する」という意味を兼ねている。

full-gorged = fully fed

173. looks upon = take notice of   **lure** 鷹のトレーニングに使うおとり。「腹一杯食わせると、トレーニング用のおとりに目もくれなくなる」（だからトレーニング中は飢えさせる）と言っている。

159

Another way I have to man my haggard,
To make her come and know her keeper's call, 175
That is, to watch her, as we watch these kites
That bate and beat and will not be obedient.
She ate no meat today, nor none shall eat.
Last night she slept not, nor tonight she shall not.
As with the meat, some undeservèd fault 180
I'll find about the making of the bed,
And here I'll fling the pillow, there the bolster,
This way the coverlet, another way the sheets.
Ay, and amid this hurly I intend
That all is done in reverend care of her. 185
And, in conclusion, she shall watch all night,
And if she chance to nod I'll rail and brawl
And with the clamor keep her still awake.
This is a way to kill a wife with kindness,
And thus I'll curb her mad and headstrong humour. 190
He that knows better how to tame a shrew,
Now let him speak. 'Tis charity to show. *Exit*

[ACT IV, SCENE II]

Enter Tranio [as Lucentio] and Hortensio [as Litio]

TRANIO Is't possible, friend Litio, that mistress Bianca
Doth fancy any other but Lucentio?
I tell you, sir, she bears me fair in hand.
HORTENSIO Sir, to satisfy you in what I have said,
Stand by and mark the manner of his teaching. 5

Enter Bianca [and Lucentio as Cambio]

LUCENTIO Now, mistress, profit you in what you read?
BIANCA What, master, read you? First resolve me that.
LUCENTIO I read that I profess, *The Art to Love*.

174. man 「(鷹を) 人に慣らす」

　haggard ＝ female hawk（ここではキャタリーナのこと）

176. watch her ＝ prevent her from sleeping, in order to tame her　この watch も鷹狩りの用語。(*OED v.* 16)

177. That bate and beat ＝ that flutter and flap　関係代名詞 that の先行詞は kites。

180. underservèd fault 「責め立てるほどでもない落ち度」次行 find の目的語。

182. bolster　pillow を載せる長枕。

183. coverlet ＝ bedspread

184. hurly 「大騒ぎ」commotion, uproar（*OED n.¹*）

　intend ＝ assert, claim

185. in reverend care of her 「彼女をうやうやしく大切に扱うために」

186. watch ＝ stay awake

187. rail and brawl 「大声で騒ぎ立てる」

189. to kill a wife with kindness　⇒後注

192. 'Tis charity to show　じゃじゃ馬のもっと良いならし方を知っている人が知識をシェアしてくれれば、それは慈善行為になると言っている。シェイクスピアの時代の発音では、前行の shrew と最後の show が韻を踏んで二行対句 (couplet) になっていた。

〔4. 2〕あらすじ・・・

　家庭教師に扮したルーセンシオとビアンカが馴れ馴れしく親しげにしている様子を見て、ホーテンシオは怒ってビアンカへの求婚をやめ、裕福な未亡人と結婚すると宣言する。トラーニオは通りすがりの人物をルーセンシオの父親に仕立て上げ、ビアンカとルーセンシオの結婚に関する父親同士の取り決めを結んでしまおうと画策する。

・・・

2. fancy ＝ love

3. bears me fair in hand ＝ is letting me have an expectation

4. satisfy ＝ convince

6. read ＝ study an academic subject（学問の対象にする）

7. resolve me that ＝ answer that (for me)　me は ethical dative（心性的与格）　*cf.* Induction 1. 46

8. that ＝ what　　**profess** 「専門にしている」

　The Art to Love　オウィディウスの主著のひとつ *Ars Amatoria*（『愛の技法』）　*cf.* Induction 2. 48-52, 1. 1. 33 および 3. 1. 28-29

Bianca   And may you prove, sir, master of your art.

Lucentio   While you, sweet dear, prove mistress of my heart.   10

Hortensio   Quick proceeders, marry! Now tell me, I pray,
    You that durst swear that your mistress Bianca
    Loved none in the world so well as Lucentio —

Tranio   O, despiteful love, unconstant womankind!
    I tell thee, Litio, this is wonderful.   15

Hortensio   Mistake no more, I am not Litio,
    Nor a musician as I seem to be,
    But one that scorn to live in this disguise
    For such a one as leaves a gentleman
    And makes a god of such a cullion.   20
    Know, sir, that I am called Hortensio.

Tranio   Signor Hortensio, I have often heard
    Of your entire affection to Bianca,
    And since mine eyes are witness of her lightness,
    I will with you, if you be so contented,   25
    Forswear Bianca and her love for ever.

Hortensio   See how they kiss and court. Signor Lucentio,
    Here is my hand, and here I firmly vow
    Never to woo her more, but do forswear her
    As one unworthy all the former favours   30
    That I have fondly flattered her withal.

Tranio   And here I take the like unfainèd oath
    Never to marry with her though she would entreat.
    Fie on her! See how beastly she doth court him.

Hortensio   Would all the world but he had quite forsworn.   35
    For me, that I may surely keep mine oath,
    I will be married to a wealthy widow
    Ere three days pass, which hath as long loved me
    As I have loved this proud disdainful haggard.
    And so farewell, Signor Lucentio.   40
    Kindness in women, not their beauteous looks,

11. proceeder = a person who makes progress　Quick proceeders は「2 人の仲がずいぶん早く進んでいるんだな」という意味。また proceed には「学位を取る」という意味もある。ビアンカの master of your art（修士）という言葉からの連想でこの言葉が使われている。

13-14. ホーテンシオが文章を言い終わらないうちにトラーニオが興奮して（いるふりをして）話し始める。

14. despiteful = cruel, malicious　　**unconstant** = fickle, unsteady

15. wonderful = surprising, incredible

18. scorn = scorns　主語の I に引かれて scorn になっている。

19. such a one 「あんな女」（ビアンカのこと）　　**as** 関係代名詞で「…するような」

20. cullion = base fellow, low fellow　自分のような紳士をふって、家庭教師という身分の低い男を選ぶことに怒っている。

23. entire = sincere, unfeigned

24. lightness = unfaithfulness, inconstancy　日本語でも「尻軽女」という。

26. Forswear Bianca forswear は「誓って退ける」という強い言葉。このトラーニオの言葉に合わせて、ホーテンシオも ll. 28-29 で誓いの印として手を挙げて、vow と forswear という言葉を使って二度とビアンカに言い寄らないと宣言している。トラーニオは主人ルーセンシオのために、ライバルを 1 人放逐したことになる。

31. fondly = foolishly　　**withal** = with

32. unfainèd = sincere

34. beastly = like an animal　かなり強い言葉だが、トラーニオはホーテンシオを完全に追い払うためにあえて大袈裟に言っているのだろう。

court = flirt with

35. Would = I wish　　**all the world but he** = all the suitors except Cambio　ホーテンシオはあんな女に言い寄るのは身分の低い家庭教師だけになれば良い、つまりちゃんとした結婚はもうできないぞと、ビアンカへの捨て台詞を言っている。

36. that = so that

38. which = who　先行詞は a wealthy widow。ホーテンシオの結婚相手の未亡人は最終の場面にしか登場しない。ここで未亡人との結婚の話が出るのはいかにも唐突だ。じゃじゃ馬をならすというテーマの民話では、通常 3 人の女性が登場するので、その伝統に合わせたと考えられる。またこの劇では結婚が経済行為であることを強調する要素ともなっている。

39. this proud disdainful haggard ビアンカのこと。4. 1. 174 ではキャタリーナが haggard (female wild hawk) に喩えられていたが、ここではビアンカにも同じ比喩が使われている。

163

Shall win my love, and so I take my leave,

In resolution as I swore before.   [*Exit*]

TRANIO   Mistress Bianca, bless you with such grace

As 'longeth to a lover's blessèd case.   45

Nay, I have ta'en you napping, gentle love,

And have forsworn you with Hortensio.

BIANCA   Tranio, you jest — but have you both forsworn me?

TRANIO   Mistress, we have.

LUCENTIO   Then we are rid of Litio.

TRANIO   I'faith, he'll have a lusty widow now   50

That shall be wooed and wedded in a day.

BIANCA   God give him joy!

TRANIO   Ay, and he'll tame her.

BIANCA   He says so, Tranio.

TRANIO   Faith, he is gone unto the taming school.

BIANCA   The taming school? What, is there such a place?   55

TRANIO   Ay, mistress, and Petruchio is the master

That teacheth tricks eleven and twenty long

To tame a shrew and charm her chattering tongue.

Enter Biondello

BIONDELLO   O master, master, I have watched so long

That I am dog-weary, but at last I spied   60

An ancient angel coming down the hill

Will serve the turn.

TRANIO   What is he, Biondello?

BIONDELLO   Master, a marcantant, or a pedant,

I know not what, but formal in apparel,

In gait and countenance surely like a father.   65

LUCENTIO   And what of him, Tranio?

TRANIO   If he be credulous and trust my tale,

I'll make him glad to seem Vincentio

And give assurance to Baptista Minola

43. In resolution = determined

45. As l. 19 と同じ用法。

　'longeth = belongs

46. ta'en you napping 「油断しているところを捕まえた」(いちゃついている
ところを目撃したということを言っている) ta'en = taken
このあとわざわざ gentle love とビアンカに呼びかけているのは、自分が求婚
者だという演技の続きで、ふざけて皮肉を言っている。

50. lusty lively という意味と lustful という意味を兼ねている。当時の芝居の
中では、未亡人はしばしば性的に活発な女性と描かれていた。

52. God give him joy 結婚を寿ぐ祝福の言葉。祈願を意味する may が省略さ
れている。

53. He says so, Tranio 「まあ、そんなことを言っているのね」という皮肉と
解釈できる。やや座りの悪い台詞なので、F1 にはない疑問符をつけて、「あ
ら、そんなこと言っているの？」という疑問文として校訂する編者もいる。

54. is gone = has gone

57. eleven and twenty long l. 2. 32 でも使われていた one-and-thirty という
合計が 31 になることをめざすトランプのゲームへの言及。eleven and
twenty は 31 なので、「まさにぴったり」ということを表している。

58. charm 「魔法を使って静かにさせる」

60. dog-weary = exhausted 'as weary as a dog' ということわざからきて
いる。

61. ancient angel 「年老いた守護霊」 また angel は当時使われていた天使を
刻印した金貨の呼び方でもあったので、「金貨のように貴重な老人」と言って
いるのかもしれない。

62. Will serve the turn Will の前に関係代名詞 that が省略されている。「目的
のために役に立ちそうな」という意味。

63. marcantant ビオンデロは merchant をイタリア語っぽく言おうとしてい
る。正しいイタリア語では mercatante。

　pedant = schoolmaster

65. gait 「歩き方」

　countenance = appearance

67. trust my tale = believe my story

68. seem = pretend to be

As if he were the right Vincentio. 70

Take in your love, and then let me alone.

[*Exeunt Lucentio and Bianca*]

Enter a Pedant

PEDANT   God save you, sir.

TRANIO   And you, sir. You are welcome.

Travel you far on, or are you at the farthest?

PEDANT   Sir, at the farthest for a week or two,

But then up farther, and as far as Rome, 75

And so to Tripoli, if God lend me life.

TRANIO   What countryman, I pray?

PEDANT   Of Mantua.

TRANIO   Of Mantua, sir? Marry, God forbid!

And come to Padua careless of your life?

PEDANT   My life, sir? How, I pray? For that goes hard. 80

TRANIO   'Tis death for anyone in Mantua

To come to Padua. Know you not the cause?

Your ships are stayed at Venice, and the Duke,

For private quarrel 'twixt your Duke and him,

Hath published and proclaimed it openly. 85

'Tis marvel, but that you are but newly come,

You might have heard it else proclaimed about.

PEDANT   Alas, sir, it is worse for me than so,

For I have bills for money by exchange

From Florence, and must here deliver them. 90

TRANIO   Well, sir, to do you courtesy,

This will I do, and this I will advise you:

First tell me, have you ever been at Pisa?

PEDANT   Ay, sir, in Pisa have I often been,

Pisa renownèd for grave citizens. 95

TRANIO   Among them know you one Vincentio?

PEDANT   I know him not, but I have heard of him,

71. let me alone = rely on me

71. 2. *Enter a Pedant* ここで登場する人物がPedantなのか、Merchantなのかをめぐってはテクスト編纂上の厄介な問題がある。本版ではF1の通りにPedantとした。　⇒後注

73. are you at the farthest 「旅はここまでですか（これより遠くには行かないのですか）」

76. Tripoli トリポリ。北アフリカ（現在のリビア）の港町または東地中海（現在のレバノン）の港町のいずれか。*The Merchant of Venice*でも商人アントニオの商船の目的地として言及される。

77. What countryman = Where are you from?

79. careless of your life = regardless of your life

80. that goes hard = that is serious

83. Your ships マントヴァの船、マントヴァの旗をつけた船。（実際はマントヴァは内陸の都市。）

　stayed = held up, detained

　the Duke ヴェニスの公爵がパデュアも治めていた。

84. For private quarrel = on account of a personal quarrel

85. published = publicly announced

86. 'Tis marvel = it is remarkable

　but that = except that

　you are but newly come = you have only just arrived

87. else = otherwise

88. Alas 「ああ」など、悲痛や心配の気持ちを表す間投詞。強勢は第二音節にくる。

　than so = even than you think

89. bills for money by exchange 現金に変えられる手形、為替。

91. courtesy = favour

95. renownèd for grave citizens 1. 1. 10でも全く同じ表現が使われている。

A merchant of incomparable wealth.

TRANIO   He is my father, sir, and sooth to say,

In count'nance somewhat doth resemble you.   100

BIONDELLO   [*Aside*]   As much as an apple doth an oyster, and

all one.

TRANIO   To save your life in this extremity,

This favour will I do you for his sake —

And think it not the worst of all your fortunes   105

That you are like to Sir Vincentio.

His name and credit shall you undertake,

And in my house you shall be friendly lodged.

Look that you take upon you as you should.

You understand me, sir? So shall you stay   110

Till you have done your business in the city.

If this be court'sy, sir, accept of it.

PEDANT   O, sir, I do, and will repute you ever

The patron of my life and liberty.

TRANIO   Then go with me to make the matter good.   115

This, by the way, I let you understand:

My father is here looked for every day

To pass assurance of a dower in marriage

'Twixt me and one Baptista's daughter here.

In all these circumstances I'll instruct you.   120

Go with me to clothe you as becomes you.   *Exeunt*

[ACT IV, SCENE III]

Enter Katherina and Grumio

GRUMIO   No, no, forsooth, I dare not for my life.

KATHERINA   The more my wrong, the more his spite appears.

What, did he marry me to famish me?

Beggars that come unto my father's door

Upon entreaty have a present alms;   5

99. sooth = truth

101. as an apple doth an oyster　ことわざ 'As like as an apple is to an oyster' を下敷きにしている。

101-02. and all one　「それでも同じということにしておこう」　all one = the very same

103. extremity = extreme danger

107. credit = reputation, standing

　　undertake = assume, adopt　(*OED v.* 6)

109. Look that = see to it that

　　you take upon you as you should = you play your role properly

113. repute = esteem, value　　**114. patron** = protector

115. make the matter good = put the plan into action, carry out the plan

116. by the way = as we go along

117. looked for = expected

118. pass assurance of = make a formal agreement of

120. circumstances = details

121. becomes = be suitable to, befit

〔4. 3〕あらすじ‥‥‥‥‥‥‥‥‥‥‥‥‥‥‥‥‥‥‥‥‥‥‥‥‥‥‥‥‥‥‥‥‥‥‥‥‥

　食事を与えられず、睡眠を奪われて弱りきっているキャタリーナを、グルーミオがさんざん焦らした後で、ペトルーチオが食べ物を持ってきてキャタリーナから感謝の言葉を引き出す。しかし仕立て屋が持ってきたキャタリーナの帽子や衣装には難癖をつけて、キャタリーナの要望にはいっさい耳を貸そうとしない。強引にすべて自分の命令通りにさせようとするペトルーチオにキャタリーナも根負けし始める。

‥‥‥

0. F1 ではここに 'Actus Quartus. Scena Prima' とラテン語で第 4 幕第 1 場の始まりを示す幕・場割が印刷されている。The RSC Shakespeare 版（Jonathan Bate, Eric Ramussen 編）はこの F1 の幕・場割に従い、この場面からを第 4 幕としている。

1. No, no　このように会話の途中から場面を始めるのは、シェイクスピアが時々使う手法。一気に観客の関心を話の核心に引き込む効果を持つ。

　　forsooth = in truth

2. The more ... appears　「私がひどい目にあえばあうほど、彼はもっと意地悪になる」　**my wrong** = the wrong done to me　　**3. famish** = starve

5. have a present alms　「すぐに施し物をもらえる」　present = immediate

alms = money or food given to the poor

169

If not, elsewhere they meet with charity.
But I, who never knew how to entreat,
Nor never needed that I should entreat,
Am starved for meat, giddy for lack of sleep,
With oaths kept waking, and with brawling fed.   10
And that which spites me more than all these wants,
He does it under name of perfect love,
As who should say, if I should sleep or eat,
'Twere deadly sickness or else present death.
I prethee go and get me some repast,   15
I care not what, so it be wholesome food.

GRUMIO   What say you to a neat's foot?

KATHERINA   'Tis passing good. I prethee let me have it.

GRUMIO   I fear it is too choleric a meat.
How say you to a fat tripe finely broiled?   20

KATHERINA   I like it well, good Grumio, fetch it me.

GRUMIO   I cannot tell, I fear 'tis choleric.
What say you to a piece of beef and mustard?

KATHERINA   A dish that I do love to feed upon.

GRUMIO   Ay, but the mustard is too hot a little.   25

KATHERINA   Why then, the beef, and let the mustard rest.

GRUMIO   Nay then, I will not. You shall have the mustard,
Or else you get no beef of Grumio.

KATHERINA   Then both, or one, or anything thou wilt.

GRUMIO   Why then, the mustard without the beef.   30

KATHERINA   Go, get thee gone, thou false deluding slave

Beats him

That feed'st me with the very name of meat.
Sorrow on thee and all the pack of you
That triumph thus upon my misery.
Go, get thee gone, I say.   35

6. meet with = receive (*OED v.* 6)

9. meat = food in general（肉に限定されない）

10. with brawling fed　「もらえるものといったら怒鳴り声だけ」

11. spites = vexes, irritates

　wants = lacks　睡眠と食事が欠けていること。

12. under name of = in the name of

13. As who should say = as if to say

14. present = immediate

15. repast = meal

16. so = so long as

17. neat's foot　「牛の足」

18. passing = exceedingly

19. choleric = causing an excess of choler (*OED adj.* 2b)　「胆汁を増やして人を怒りっぽくさせてしまう」*cf.* 4. 1. 153　ペトルーチオも同じ理由でキャタリーナに肉を食べさせなかった。

20. tripe　「牛や羊の胃袋」　日本語で「ハチノス」とも呼ばれる。イタリア料理の「トリッパ」（ハチノスのトマト煮込み）がよく知られている。

　broiled = grilled

22. I cannot tell = I am not sure

26. let the mustard rest　「マスタードは持ってこなくていい」

28. Or else = otherwise　マスタードなしではビーフはあげられません、と言っている。

32. the very name = only the name

33. Sorrow on thee　「お前に不幸がふりかかればいい」may light が省略された祈願文。

　pack of you　「お前ら一味（にも不幸がふりかかれ）」　pack = confederacy for a bad purpose

34. That　関係代名詞で先行詞は thee and all the pack of you。

Enter Petruchio and Hortensio with meat

PETRUCHIO How fares my Kate? What, sweeting, all amort?

HORTENSIO Mistress, what cheer?

KATHERINA   Faith, as cold as can be.

PETRUCHIO Pluck up thy spirits, look cheerfully upon me.
Here, love, thou seest how diligent I am
To dress thy meat myself and bring it thee.   40
I am sure, sweet Kate, this kindness merits thanks.
What, not a word? Nay then, thou lov'st it not,
And all my pains is sorted to no proof.
Here, take away this dish.

KATHERINA   I pray you, let it stand.

PETRUCHIO The poorest service is repaid with thanks,   45
And so shall mine before you touch the meat.

KATHERINA I thank you, sir.

HORTENSIO Signor Petruchio, fie, you are to blame.
Come, Mistress Kate, I'll bear you company.

PETRUCHIO [*Aside to Hortensio*] Eat it up all, Hortensio, if
thou lovest me.   50
—Much good do it unto thy gentle heart.
Kate, eat apace. And now, my honey love,
Will we return unto thy father's house
And revel it as bravely as the best,
With silken coats and caps, and golden rings,   55
With ruffs and cuffs and farthingales and things,
With scarfs and fans and double change of bravery,
With amber bracelets, beads and all this knavery.
What, hast thou dined? The tailor stays thy leisure,
To deck thy body with his ruffling treasure.   60

Enter Tailor

Come, tailor, let us see these ornaments.

36. sweeting = sweetheart, darling

　all amort = dejected, dispirited　おそらくフランス語の à la mort (to death) から来ている言葉。

37. what cheer? = How are you?

　as cold as can be　ホーテンシオの挨拶の言葉の cheer には food という意味もあるので、キャタリーナは「すっかり冷え切っている」と答えている。

38. Pluck up thy spirits = summon up your courage, cheer up

40. dress = prepare　　**meat** = food

41. merits = deserve, be worthy of（*OED v.* 2a）

43. all my pains = all my labour　　**is sorted to no proof** = proved to be to no purpose, has been performed in vain

44. stand = remain

45. The poorest service is repaid with thanks　「どんなささやかなことでも何かしてもらったら感謝で報いるものだ」

46. mine = my service　　shall mine be before となるべきところだが be が省略されている。

48. to blame = at fault, blameworthy

49. bear you company = join you

51. Much good ... heart　一般的な祝福の言葉。may が省略されている。「この食事が心も満たしますように」という意。

52. apace = quickly

54. revel it = make merry, feast　　**bravely** = finely, splendidly　結婚式の日とは打って変わって、ゴージャスに祝宴をしようと言っている。

56. ruffs　「襞襟」レースを糊付けしてたくさんの襞にし、それを首の周りにきっちりと1周させた飾り襟。　　**cuffs**　飾りとして袖に縫い付けられたレース。
　farthingales　鯨の骨や細い木などで作った丸い輪を組み合わせ、その上からペティコートやスカートをはいて、腰の張りを強調するファッション。

57. double change of bravery　「豪華な衣装 (bravery) を2回着替えられるようにする」

58. knavery = illusion created by one's dress or jewellery（*OED n.* 2b）knavery は通常は「悪行」という意味だが、ここでは「これ見よがしな衣装や宝飾品」という意味で使っている。前行の bravery と韻を踏むための工夫。l. 55 からこの台詞の終わりまでは couplet（二行対句）を続けている。

59. stays = awaits

60. ruffing treasure　「ヒラヒラでキラキラの衣装」l. 56 にあるように 'ruff' は華やかな襟飾。ruffing はそういう飾りがたくさんついている「派手な」という意味。

Lay forth the gown.

Enter Haberdasher

What news with you, sir?

HABERDASHER   Here is the cap your worship did bespeak.

PETRUCHIO   Why, this was moulded on a porringer;

A velvet dish. Fie, fie, 'tis lewd and filthy.   65

Why, 'tis a cockle or a walnut-shell,

A knack, a toy, a trick, a baby's cap.

Away with it! Come, let me have a bigger.

KATHERINA   I'll have no bigger. This doth fit the time,

And gentlewomen wear such caps as these.   70

PETRUCHIO   When you are gentle, you shall have one too,

And not till then.

HORTENSIO   [*Aside*] That will not be in haste.

KATHERINA   Why, sir, I trust I may have leave to speak,

And speak I will. I am no child, no babe.

Your betters have endured me say my mind,   75

And if you cannot, best you stop your ears.

My tongue will tell the anger of my heart,

Or else my heart concealing it will break,

And rather than it shall, I will be free

Even to the uttermost, as I please, in words.   80

PETRUCHIO   Why, thou say'st true. It is paltry cap,

A custard-coffin, a bauble, a silken pie.

I love thee well in that thou lik'st it not.

KATHERINA   Love me or love me not, I like the cap,

And it I will have, or I will have none.   85

PETRUCHIO   Thy gown? Why, ay. Come, tailor, let us see't.

[*Exit Haberdasher*]

O mercy, God, what masquing stuff is here?

What's this? A sleeve? 'Tis like demi-cannon.

What, up and down carved like an apple tart?

62. 1. *Haberdasher* = hatmaker

63. bespeak = order

64. porringer　ポリッジ（オーツ麦や雑穀で作ったおかゆ）を入れるボウル、どんぶり。

65. A velvet dish　「まるでヴェルヴェットでできた皿みたいだ」

lewd and filthy = vulgar, disgusting

66. cockle　ザル貝というホタテ貝に似た二枚貝。ここでは「ホタテの殻みたいな帽子だ」と言っている。

67. knack = trifle, knick-knack「ガラクタ、おもちゃ」　この後に続く toy、trick もほぼ同じ意味。

69. fit the time = suit the current fashion

71. gentle　前行のキャタリーナの gentlewomen は「上流階級の女性」という意味なのに、ペトルーチオはわざと gentle women「穏やかな女性」という意味にずらしている。それを聞いてホーテンシオは、キャタリーナが穏やかになる日は「すぐには来ない」と言っている。

73. I trust = I believe

75. Your betters have endured me say my mind　「あなたより偉い人たちだって、私が自分の気持ちを話すのを許してくれた」　endure me say = tolerated my saying

76. best you stop = it would be best for you to stop

80. Even to the uttermost　「もっとも極端なことでも」

81. paltry = vile, contemptible

82. custard-coffin　カスタードクリームを入れるパイのケース。

bauble = showy trinket

silken pie　「シルクでできたパイ」

83. in that = because

86. 1 [*Exit Haberdasher*]　⇒後注

87. masquing stuff　masque は豪華な衣装や凝った舞台装置を特徴とする「仮面劇」のこと。masquing stuff はそうした仮面劇に使う衣装や装置のこと。「これじゃあ、まるで仮面劇の舞台衣装だ」とペトルーチオは怒っている（ふりをしている）。

88. demi-cannon　半キャノン砲。半とは言うものの大型の大砲で、口径が17センチほどある。「大砲みたいにでっかい袖だ」とペトルーチオは言っている。

89. up and down　「上から下まで」

carved like an apple tart　「アップルパイみたいに切り込みが入れてある」

175

Here's snip and nip and cut and slish and slash,   90
Like to a censer in a barber's shop.
Why, what a devil's name, tailor, call'st thou this?

HORTENSIO [*Aside*] I see she's like to have neither cap nor
    gown.

TAILOR You bid me make it orderly and well,
According to the fashion and the time.   95

PETRUCHIO Marry, and did. But if you be remembered,
I did not bid you mar it to the time.
Go, hop me over every kennel home,
For you shall hop without my custom, sir.
I'll none of it. Hence, make your best of it.   100

KATHERINA I never saw a better-fashioned gown,
More quaint, more pleasing, nor more commendable.
Belike you mean to make a puppet of me.

PETRUCHIO Why, true, he means to make a puppet of thee.

TAILOR She says your worship means to make a puppet of
    her.   105

PETRUCHIO O monstrous arrogance! Thou liest, thou thread,
    thou thimble,
Thou yard, three-quarters, half-yard, quarter, nail,
Thou flea, thou nit, thou winter-cricket, thou!
Braved in mine own house with a skein of thread?
Away, thou rag, thou quantity, thou remnant,   110
Or I shall so be-mete thee with thy yard
As thou shalt think on prating whilst thou liv'st.
I tell thee, I, that thou hast marred her gown.

TAILOR Your worship is deceived. The gown is made
Just as my master had direction.   115
Grumio gave order how it should be done.

GRUMIO I gave him no order; I gave him the stuff.

TAILOR But how did you desire it should be made?

GRUMIO Marry, sir, with needle and thread.

90. snip, nip, cut, slish and slash　いずれも「切る」ことを表す言葉。布に切り込みを入れ、その下の違う色の布をのぞかせるという装飾が、この時代の流行だった。

91. censer in a barber's shop　censer は「香炉」。香りを放出するための穴の開いた蓋がついているため、ここで比喩として用いられている可能性がある。しかしなぜ「床屋」の香炉なのかは判然としない。　⇒後注

92. a devil's name = in the devil's name　　**93. she's like** = she is likely

96. and did = so I did　　**if you be remembered** = if you remember

97. mar it to the time = ruin it by following the fashion

98. hop me ... home　「さっさと帰れ」という意。　me は ethical dative。*cf*. Induction 1. 46　　**kennel** = street gutter

99. hop without my custom = hop without my patronage, lose my patronage

100. make your best of it　「(こんな服はいらないから) お前の好きなようにしろ」という意。　　**102. quaint** = skilfully made, elegant

103. Belike = perhaps, it seems　　**make a puppet of** = make a fool of puppet は「意のままにあやつれる人形」。

106. thread, thimble　ここから「糸」「指抜き」など、仕立て屋の仕事に関わる言葉を並べ立てて、ペトルーチオは仕立て屋を威嚇する。

107. yard ... nail　布の長さの計り方を、長いものから順番に短いものへと並べ立てている。　yard = 3 feet (約91.4 cm)　nail = 1/16 yard (約5.7 cm)

108. flea, thou nit, thou winter-cricket　小さい虫を並べ立てている。nit はしらみの卵または幼虫。前行の短い寸法とともに、仕立て屋の背が低いことへのあてこすり。'Nine tailors make a man' (仕立て屋9人でようやく一人前) ということわざが広く知られており、仕立て屋は小柄というイメージがあった。小柄な役者または少年俳優が演じた可能性も高い。

109. Braved in mine own house with a skein of thread　「糸の束を振りまわしてこの俺様の家の中でふんぞりかえったのか」という意。　braved = defied, challenged　skein は糸を巻いて束ねたもの。

110. rag, quantity, remnant　「ボロ」「端切れ」「残り布」　いずれも布に関する言葉を軽蔑的に使っている。

111. be-mete　「長さを計る」という意味での mete と「お仕置きをする」という意味での mete out を重ねている。　　**yard**　「物差し」「これでお前の低い身長を測ってやる」と「これでお前を叩いてやる」の意味を重ねている。

112. prating = talking idly, prattling　ペトルーチオに酷い目にあわされて、仕立て屋は「くだらないおしゃべりする前にちゃんと考えるようになるだろう」と言っている。　　**117. stuff** = material

TAILOR   But did you not request to have it cut?   120

GRUMIO   Thou hast faced many things.

TAILOR   I have.

GRUMIO   Face not me. Thou hast braved many men; brave not
me. I will neither be faced nor braved. I say unto thee, I bid
thy master cut out the gown, but I did not bid him cut it to   125
pieces. *Ergo*, thou liest.

TAILOR   Why, here is the note of the fashion to testify.

PETRUCHIO   Read it.

GRUMIO   The note lies in's throat if he say I said so.

TAILOR   [*Reads*] 'Imprimis, a loose-bodied gown.'   130

GRUMIO   Master, if ever I said 'loose-bodied gown', sew me in
the skirts of it and beat me to death with a bottom of brown
thread. I said 'a gown.'

PETRUCHIO   Proceed.

TAILOR   'With a small compassed cape.'   135

GRUMIO   I confess the cape.

TAILOR   'With a trunk sleeve.'

GRUMIO   I confess two sleeves.

TAILOR   'The sleeves curiously cut.'

PETRUCHIO   Ay, there's the villainy.   140

GRUMIO   Error i'th'bill, sir, error i'th'bill! I commanded the
sleeves should be cut out and sewed up again, and that I'll
prove upon thee, though thy little finger be armed in a
thimble.

TAILOR   This is true that I say; an I had thee in place where,   145
thou shouldst know it.

GRUMIO   I am for thee straight. Take thou the bill, give me thy
mete-yard, and spare not me.

HORTENSIO   God-a-mercy, Grumio, then he shall have no
odds.   150

PETRUCHIO   Well, sir, in brief, the gown is not for me.

GRUMIO   You are i'th'right, sir, 'tis for my mistress.

121. faced　ここでは「(衣服に) 飾りをつける (adorn)」の意味。

123. Face not me　グルーミオは face を「立ち向かう (outface)」の意味にず
らしている。

　Thou hast braved many men　この braved は「衣装を着せて華やかにする
(make splendid)」の意味。

123-24. brave not me　この brave は「挑みかかる (challenge, defy)」の意味。

126. *Ergo*　ラテン語で therefore, consequently の意味。

127. note　「注文書」

129. lies in's throat = lie utterly　同時にグルーミオは l. 127 の note を「音
符」の意味にずらし「音は喉から出るものだ」とも言っている。

　he = it (the note を指す)

130. *Imprimis*　ラテン語で first の意味。　*cf.* 4. 1. 56

　loose-bodied　「ゆったりとした (loosely fitting)」という意味だが、次行の
グルーミオは「みだらな女用の (sexually loose woman)」という意味にずらし
している。

132. bottom　木製の糸巻きの心棒。

135. compassed　「円形にカットした」

136. confess = admit to　前行の compass と音を合わせている。

137. trunk sleeve　「たっぷりとした袖」

139. curiously「丁寧に (carefully)」と「凝った (elaborately)」の意味を重ね
ている。ペトルーチオは「凝った袖はいかん」と次行で怒っている。

141. bill　l. 127 の note (注文書) のこと。

143. prove upon thee = prove by fighting you

145. an = if　　**in place where** = in the right place「しかるべき場所に行け
ば」と言っている。仕立て屋は法廷で戦えばと言っているのだが、グルーミオ
は決闘することを考えている。

147. for thee straight = ready for you now

　bill　「注文書 (note)」と「矛槍 (halberd)」の意味を掛け合わせている。仕立
て屋には「注文書」と聞こえ、グルーミオ本人は「お前は武器を持ってもいい
ぞ」と言っているつもり。

148. mete-yard = yardstick

149. God-a-mercy　May God have mercy の崩れた形。

150. odds　「勝ち目」ホーテンシオは、仕立て屋が紙 (hill) でグルーミオが物
差し (mete-yard) を手にして戦うのであれば、仕立て屋には勝ち目はないと
言っている。

PETRUCHIO   Go, take it up unto thy master's use.

GRUMIO   Villain, not for thy life. Take up my mistress' gown
for thy master's use!   155

PETRUCHIO   Why, sir, what's your conceit in that?

GRUMIO   O sir, the conceit is deeper than you think for. Take
up my mistress' gown to his masters use? O, fie, fie, fie!

PETRUCHIO   [*Aside to Hortensio*]   Hortensio, say thou wilt see
the tailor paid.

[*To the Tailor*]   Go take it hence, be gone, and say no more.   160

HORTENSIO   [*Aside to the Tailor*]   Tailor, I'll pay thee for thy
gown tomorrow,

Take no unkindness of his hasty words.

Away, I say, commend me to thy master.   *Exit Tailor*

PETRUCHIO   Well, come, my Kate, we will unto your father's

Even in these honest mean habiliments.   165

Our purses shall be proud, our garments poor,

For 'tis the mind that makes the body rich,

And as the sun breaks through the darkest clouds,

So honour peereth in the meanest habit.

What, is the jay more precious than the lark   170

Because his feathers are more beautiful?

Or is the adder better than the eel

Because his painted skin contents the eye?

O no, good Kate, neither art thou the worse

For this poor furniture and mean array.   175

If thou account'st it shame, lay it on me,

And therefore frolic. We will hence forthwith

To feast and sport us at thy fathers house.

[*To Grumio*]   Go call my men, and let us straight to him,

And bring our horses unto Long-lane end.   180

There will we mount, and thither walk on foot.

Let's see, I think 'tis now some seven o'clock,

And well we may come there by dinner-time.

153. take it ... use 「キャトリーナのために作られた服を持って帰って、お前の主人の好きなように再利用しろ」とペトルーチオは言っているが、次行でグルーミオは「キャトリーナの着ているスカートをめくりあげて、仕立て屋の主人の好きなようにさせろ」と意味をずらしている。

154. not for thy life 「絶対そんなことは許さん」 そのあとの台詞については前行の注を参照のこと。

156. conceit = meaning, innuendo

157. deeper = more serious

  think for = expect

158. fie 強い不快、嫌悪を表す間投詞。

159. see = make sure

162. Take no unkindness of = don't be offended at

  hasty = quick tempered

165. honest mean habiliments = respectable and humble clothes

166. proud = puffed up

  our garments poor garments と poor の間に shall be が省略されている。

169. peereth = appears

  habit = outfit

170. What, F1 ではここにカンマがないが、カンマを入れて What は疑問詞ではなく感嘆詞と捉える方が適切であろう。

  jay カケス、カラス科の鳥。全体は茶色っぽいが、羽のところどころに美しい青い色が入っている。声はやかましい。

  lark ひばり。

173. painted = colourful

  contents = pleases, delights

175. furniture = equipment, clothing (*OED adj.* 2a)

  mean array = humble attire

176. account = esteem, think

  lay = blame

177. frolic = be merry, be joyous

  forthwith = without delay, immediately

178. sport us = make merry

180. Long-lane end 「ロング・レインのはずれ」 Long Lane は実際にロンドンに存在する通りの名前。シェイクスピアの時代には商店が立ち並んでいた。

181. thither = toward that place

183. dinner-time シェイクスピアの時代には dinner は１日のうちの主な食事（正餐）であり、午前の遅い時間から正午の間に食べられた。

KATHERINA I dare assure you, sir, 'tis almost two,
 And 'twill be supper-time ere you come there.   185
PETRUCHIO It shall be seven ere I go to horse.
 Look what I speak, or do, or think to do,
 You are still crossing it. Sirs, let't alone.
 I will not go today, and ere I do,
 It shall be what o'clock I say it is.   190
HORTENSIO Why, so this gallant will command the sun.

                                                      [*Exeunt*]

[ACT IV, SCENE IV]

 *Enter Tranio [as Lucentio] and the Pedant [, booted and] dressed
 like Vincentio*

TRANIO Sir, this is the house. Please it you that I call?
PEDANT Ay, what else? And but I be deceived,
 Signor Baptista may remember me
 Near twenty years ago in Genoa,
 Where we were lodgers at the Pegasus.   5
TRANIO 'Tis well, and hold your own, in any case,
 With such austerity as 'longeth to a father.

                    Enter Biondello

PEDANT I warrant you. But, sir, here comes your boy.
 'Twere good he were schooled.
TRANIO Fear you not him. — Sirrah, Biondello,   10
 Now do your duty throughly, I advise you.
 Imagine 'twere the right Vincentio.
BIONDELLO Tut, fear not me.
TRANIO But hast thou done thy errand to Baptista?
BIONDELLO I told him that your father was at Venice,   15
 And that you looked for him this day in Padua.
TRANIO Th'art a tall fellow. Hold thee that to drink.

185. supper-time supper（夕食）は夕方 6 時前後に食べた。

187. Look what = whatever

188. still = always　　**crossing** = contradicting, opposing

　let's alone = leave it（出発の準備はやめていい）

189-90. ere I do, / It shall be what o'clock I say it is 「俺が言ったとおりの時間に合わせるまでは、俺は出発しない」 ere I do = before I go at all

　shall は話者であるペトルーチオの意思を表しているので、「実際に出発するまでに、時間を言ったとおりにさせてみせる」という意味になる。

191. so = at this rate 「こういう調子なら太陽にまで命令するようになるぞ」という意。

〔4. 4〕あらすじ・・

　予定通り、トラーニオは教師にルーセンシオの父親役をさせ、バプティスタとの間でルーセンシオとビアンカの結婚を取り決める。結婚の条件を定めた正式な文書を用意する間に、ビオンデロに急かされ、ルーセンシオはビアンカとさっさと結婚する決意をする。

・・

0. 1. ⇒後注

1. Please it you = May it please you

2. what else = of course, certainly　　**but** = unless

4. Near = nearly

5. at the Pegasus 「ペガサスという名前の宿に」 Pegasus は神話上の翼のある馬。ペガサスはシェイクスピアの時代のロンドンに、よくある宿屋の名前の 1 つだった。　⇒後注

6. hold your own = play your part　　**case** = circumstances

7. such austerity as 'longeth to a father 「父親らしい威厳」という意。

　' longeth = belongs

9. 'Twere = It would be　　**schooled** = instructed how to act　（*OED v.¹* 2b）

　「芝居の振り付けを教えておいた方が良いのでは」という意。

10. Fear you not him = Don't worry about him

11. throughly = thoroughly

12. right = real

16. looked for = expected

17. tall = fine, worthy

　Hold thee that to drink = take this to buy a drink　こう言いながらトラーニオはビオンデロに駄賃を渡す。シェイクスピアの戯曲はト書きがきわめて少ししか書かれていないが、台詞の中に動作を示す箇所はたくさんある。

—Here comes Baptista. Set your countenance, sir.

Enter Baptista and Lucentio [disguised as Cambio].
Pedant [stands] bare-headed

TRANIO Signor Baptista, you are happily met.
—Sir, this is the gentleman I told you of.   20
I pray you stand good father to me now,
Give me Bianca for my patrimony.
PEDANT Soft, son.
—Sir, by your leave, having come to Padua
To gather in some debts, my son Lucentio   25
Made me acquainted with a weighty cause
Of love between your daughter and himself.
And, for the good report I hear of you,
And for the love he beareth to your daughter,
And she to him, to stay him not too long,   30
I am content, in a good father's care,
To have him matched. And if you please to like
No worse than I, upon some agreement
Me shall you find ready and willing
With one consent to have her so bestowed,   35
For curious I cannot be with you,
Signor Baptista, of whom I hear so well.
BAPTISTA Sir, pardon me in what I have to say.
Your plainness and your shortness please me well.
Right true it is your son Lucentio here   40
Doth love my daughter, and she loveth him,
Or both dissemble deeply their affections.
And therefore if you say no more than this,
That like a father you will deal with him
And pass my daughter a sufficient dower,   45
The match is made, and all is done:
Your son shall have my daughter with consent.

18. Set your countenance = put on the appropriate expression of a father

18. 2.　*bare-headed* ルーセンシオの父親に扮した教師は、バプティスタへの敬意を表すために、ここで帽子を脱ぐ。*cf.* 4. 4. 0. 1 後注

20. Sir 「お父さん」という呼びかけ。この行から父親役の教師に向かって語る台詞となる。　⇒後注

21. stand good father 「息子を想う父親となって」

stand = be, show yourself as

22. patrimony = inheritance 「遺産を保証してビアンカと結婚できるようにしてください」という意。

23. Soft = Just a moment

24. by your leave = if I may

having come = I having come

26. weighty cause = important matter

28. for = because of

30. to stay him not too long = in order not to keep him waiting too long

32-33. if you please to like / No worse than I = if you are as satisfied as I am

34. Me find の目的語。

35. With one consent = in unanimity

bestowed = matched, married

36. curious = over-particular, cautious (*OED adj.* 2b) 「(持参金のことは)事細かに騒ぎ立てたくない」という意。

42. Or both dissemble deeply their affections 「そうでないなら2人とも大嘘をついていることになる」という意。実際にバプティスタは大いに騙されているので、滑稽なアイロニーがこの台詞には含まれている。　or = otherwise

45. pass = hand over, transfer (*OED v.* 37a)

dower 「寡婦産」夫が亡くなったときに妻に与えられる財産。*cf.* 2. 1. 334

46. done = settled

185

TRANIO   I thank you, sir. Where, then, do you know best
   We be affied and such assurance ta'en
   As shall with either part's agreement stand?   50
BAPTISTA   Not in my house, Lucentio, for you know
   Pitchers have ears, and I have many servants.
   Besides, old Gremio is heark'ning still,
   And happily we might be interrupted.
TRANIO   Then at my lodging, an it like you.   55
   There doth my father lie, and there this night
   We'll pass the business privately and well.
   Send for your daughter by your servant here.
   My boy shall fetch the scrivener presently.
   The worst is this, that at so slender warning   60
   You are like to have a thin and slender pittance.
BAPTISTA   It likes me well. — Cambio, hie you home,
   And bid Bianca make her ready straight,
   And, if you will, tell what hath happenèd:
   Lucentio's father is arrived in Padua,   65
   And how she's like to be Lucentio's wife.   [*Exit Lucentio*]
BIONDELLO   I pray the gods she may, with all my heart.
TRANIO   Dally not with the gods, but get thee gone.
                                            Exit [*Biondello*]
   Signor Baptista, shall I lead the way?
   Welcome! One mess is like to be your cheer.   70
   Come, sir, we will better it in Pisa.
BAPTISTA   I follow you.   *Exeunt* [*Tranio, Pedant and Baptista*]

                    Enter Lucentio and Biondello

BIONDELLO   Cambio.
LUCENTIO   What say'st thou, Biondello?
BIONDELLO   You saw my master wink and laugh upon you?   75
LUCENTIO   Biondello, what of that?
BIONDELLO   Faith, nothing, but h'as left me here behind to

49. affied = formally betrothed

49-50. such assurance ... stand 「双方が合意できるような証書をかわす」の意。　　**ta'en** = taken　前に be が省略されている。　　l. 50 はわかりやすい語順に直すと As shall stand with either part's agreement「それぞれの側の合意と一致するような」という意。

52. Pitchers have ears　ears は水差しの「持ち手」だが、「耳」という意味を重ねて「水差しにも耳がある」ということわざ。日本語の「壁に耳あり」と同義。

53. heark'ning still　「常に聞き耳を立てている」　still = always

54. happily = haply　「ひょっとして」

55. an it like you = if it please you

56. lie = lodge

57. pass = settle, transact (*OED v.* 21)

58. your servant here　キャンビオ、すなわちルーセンシオのこと。

59. My boy　ビオンデロのこと。　　**scrivener**　「公証人」（正式な証書を作成する人）　　**presently** = immediately

60. at so slender warning = with such short notice

61. like = likely　　**thin** = scanty, poor　　**pittance** = food and drink

62. It likes me = it pleases me　　**hie** = hurry

63. make her ready = make herself ready

straight = straightway, without delay

65. is arrived = has arrived

66. like = likely

66-72. l　⇒後注

67. she may　後に be Lucentio's wife が省略されている。

68. Dally not with the gods　「神の名前をやたらと口に出すものではない」か「お祈りの言葉をならべてグズグズしているな」と言っているかのいずれか。

70. mess = dish, course of dishes　　**like** = likely　　**cheer** = hospitality, entertainment　「一皿だけのおもてなしになりそうですが」の意。

71. better = improve　「ピサではもっと良いもてなしをします」の意。

75. wink and laugh upon you　F1 にはこれに対応するト書きはない。l. 58 でルーセンシオをビアンカへの使いに出すようトラーニオがバプティスタに言ったあたりが、もっとも可能性の高い箇所であるが、いずれにせよ演出の裁量のうちである。

77. h'as = he has

expound the meaning or moral of his signs and tokens.

LUCENTIO   I pray thee moralize them.

BIONDELLO   Then thus: Baptista is safe, talking with the   80
deceiving father of a deceitful son.

LUCENTIO   And what of him?

BIONDELLO   His daughter is to be brought by you to the
supper.

LUCENTIO   And then?   85

BIONDELLO   The old priest at Saint Luke's church is at your
command at all hours.

LUCENTIO   And what of all this?

BIONDELLO   I cannot tell, expect they are busied about a
counterfeit assurance. Take you assurance of her, *cum*   90
privilegio ad imprimendum solum. To th'church, take the priest,
clerk and some sufficient honest witnesses. If this be not that
you look for, I have no more to say, but bid Bianca farewell
for ever and a day.

LUCENTIO   Hear'st thou, Biondello?   95

BIONDELLO   I cannot tarry. I knew a wench married in an
afternoon as she went to the garden for parsley to stuff a
rabbit, and so may you, sir. And so, adieu, sir. My master
hath appointed me to go to Saint Luke's to bid the priest be
ready to come against you come with your appendix.   *Exit*   100

LUCENTIO   I may and will, if she be so contented.
She will be pleased, then wherefore should I doubt?
Hap what hap may, I'll roundly go about her.
It shall go hard if Cambio go without her.   *Exit*

[**ACT IV, SCENE V**]

Enter Petruchio, Katherina, Hortentio [and Servants]

PETRUCHIO   Come on, a God's name, once more toward our
father's.

78. moral = meaning, significance (*OED n.* 3c)

　tokens = signs

79. moralize = interpret

80. safe = safely taken care of

87. command = service

90. counterfeit assurance = fake marriage contract

　Take you assurance = make sure

90-91. *cum privilegio ad imprimendum solum* ラテン語で「出版独占権」を
示す定型文。英語訳は with the privilege for printing only。印刷出版にビ
オンデロがここで言及しているのは、同じもの (copy) を作る印刷と、自分と
似ているもの (copy) を産む結婚の共通点に着眼しているため。

92. sufficient = of adequate wealth, having a competence (*OED adj.* 4)
「証人としての財力や能力が十分ある」という意。

92-93. that you look for = what you look for

96-98. a wench married ... to stuff a rabbit 「畑に行ったと思ったら結婚し
た」というのは、つまりあわただしく駆け落ちしたことを言っている。ビオン
デロはさっさと秘密結婚してしまえとルーセンシオをけしかけている。

98. so may you = you also can do it

　My master トラーニオのこと。

100. against you come = in preparation of your coming

　appendix = addition, adjunct　花嫁のこと。ここではビアンカ。

103. Hap what hap may = whatever may happen

　I'll roundly go about her 「まっすぐにあたってみるぞ」という意。

　roundly = straightforwardly, without hesitation

104. go hard = be hard luck, be unfortunate

〔**4. 5**〕あらすじ……………………………………………………………………

　バプティスタの家に向かう途中、ペトルーチオはキャタリーナが自分の発言に
一言でも異を唱えると、怒って動こうとしなくなる。やむなくキャタリーナはペ
トルーチオの言いなりになる。たまたま老紳士と出会っても、ペトルーチオがこ
の人は若い女性だと言えばその通りだと同意し、老人だと言い直せば再びその通
りと同意する。この老人がルーセンシオの父のヴィンセンシオだとわかり、一行
は一緒にパデュアに向かう。

………………………………………………………………………………………

1. a God's name = in God's name

Good Lord, how bright and goodly shines the moon!

Katherina   The moon? The sun! It is not moonlight now.

Petruchio   I say it is the moon that shines so bright.

Katherina   I know it is the sun that shines so bright.   5

Petruchio   Now by my mother's son, and that's myself,

It shall be moon, or star, or what I list,

Or e're I journey to your father's house.

[*To Servants*]   Go on, and fetch our horses back again.

Evermore crossed and crossed, nothing but crossed.   10

Hortensio   Say as he says, or we shall never go.

Katherina   Forward, I pray, since we have come so far,

And be it moon, or sun, or what you please.

And if you please to call it a rush-candle,

Henceforth I vow it shall be so for me.   15

Petruchio   I say it is the moon.

Katherina   I know it is the moon.

Petruchio   Nay, then you lie. It is the blessèd sun.

Katherina   Then God be blest, it in the blessèd sun,

But sun it is not, when you say it is not,

And the moon changes even as your mind.   20

What you will have it named, even that it is,

And so it shall be so for Katherine.

Hortensio   [*Aside*]   Petruchio, go thy ways. The field is won.

Petruchio   Well, forward, forward! Thus the bowl should run,

And not unluckily against the bias.   25

But soft, company is coming here.

Enter Vincentio

[*To Vincentio*]   Good morrow, gentle mistress, where away?

—Tell me, sweet Kate, and tell me truly too,

Hast thou beheld a fresher gentlewoman?

Such war of white and red within her cheeks!   30

2. goodly ＝ beautifully

7. list ＝ please, choose

8. Or e'er ＝ Before 「好きなように呼ぶまではお父さんの家に向かって出発しないぞ」と言っている。

10. crossed ＝ contradicted

　but ＝ except

14. rush-candle 　獣脂の中にイグサを浸して芯にした粗末な蠟燭。

15. Henceforth ＝ From now on

20. the moon changes even as your mind 　満ち欠けする月は「変わりやすさ」の象徴。'As changeful as the moon' ということわざを元にした台詞であるとともに、月の影響が狂気の原因となると信じられていたので、ペトルーチオが「狂っている」という意味も匂わせている。

21. What ＝ Whatever

23. go thy ways 　「その調子で進め」

　The field is won 　「戦況はもうこちらのものだ」という意。　field ＝ battle, battlefield

24-25. ローン・ボウリング (lawn bawling) の比喩が用いられている。ローン・ボウリングは芝生の上で球 (bowl) を転がし狙った場所にとめようとするゲーム。転がした時にカーブするように、球には重心が片側にずれるように重りが入れてある。その重りの作用でカーブすることを bias という。against bias はその自然な傾きに反すること。ペトルーチオはキャタリーナをボウリングの球になぞらえ、「自然なコースからずれずにちゃんと進んでいくべきだ」と言っている。

26. soft ＝ wait a moment

　company ＝ somebody

27. where away ＝ where are you going

29. fresher ＝ more youthful

30-32. 若い女性の美しさを讃える際に、白い肌や血色の良い頰を赤白のバラに喩え、目の輝きを星に喩えるのは、ソネットなどで多用される常套句。

30. war ＝ contest 　白バラを記章とするヨーク家と赤バラを記章とするランカスター家が王位継承をめぐって内乱を繰り広げたバラ戦争 (War of the Roses, 1455-1485 年) への言及も重ねられている可能性がある。

191

What stars do spangle heaven with such beauty
As those two eyes become that heavenly face?
—Fair lovely maid, once more good day to thee.
—Sweet Kate, embrace her for her beauty's sake.

HORTENSIO [*Aside*] A will make the man mad, to make the   35
woman of him.

KATHERINE Young budding virgin, fair and fresh and sweet,
Whither away, or where is thy abode?
Happy the parents of so fair a child;
Happier the man whom favourable stars   40
Allots thee for his lovely bedfellow.

PETRUCHIO Why, how now, Kate, I hope thou art not mad.
This is a man, old, wrinkled, faded, withered,
And not a maiden, as thou say'st he is.

KATHERINE Pardon, old father, my mistaking eyes   45
That have been so bedazzled with the sun
That everything I look on seemeth green.
Now I perceive thou art a reverend father.
Pardon, I pray thee, for my mad mistaking.

PETRUCHIO Do, good old grandsire, and withal make known   50
Which way thou travellest: if along with us,
We shall be joyful of thy company.

VINCENTIO Fair sir, and you my merry mistress,
That with your strange encounter much amazed me,
My name is called Vincentio, my dwelling Pisa,   55
And bound I am to Padua, there to visit
A son of mine, which long I have not seen.

PETRUCHIO What is his name?

VINCENTIO   Lucentio, gentle sir.

PETRUCHIO Happily met, the happier for thy son.
And now by law, as well as reverend age,   60
I may entitle thee my loving father.
The sister to my wife, this gentlewoman,

31. spangle ＝ shine

32. become ＝ suit, look good on

35. A ＝ He (ペトルーチオを指す)

35-36. make the woman　1632 年の第 2 二つ折本 (F2) では a woman と校訂されている。a woman であれば「女にしている」ということであるが、the woman であれば、「女役をやらせている」という意味になる。

37. budding ＝ blooming
　virgin ＝ young woman

38. Whither away ＝ Where are you going
　abode ＝ home

40. whom ＝ to whom

41. Allots ＝ Appoints　s がついているが主語は favourble stars。三人称複数を主語としながら、動詞に s がつく例は F1 にはしばしば見出せる。

47. green　「緑色」という意味と、「若々しい」という意味を重ねている。

48. reverend ＝ worthy of deep respect

50. grandsire ＝ old man (*OED n.* 4)
　withal ＝ at the same time, together with this

54. encounter ＝ style of greeting

55. my dwelling Pisa　Pisa の前に is が省略されている。

61. may ＝ can
　entitle ＝ call
　father ＝ father-in-law

Thy son by this hath married. Wonder not,
Nor be not grieved. She is of good esteem,
Her dowry wealthy, and of worthy birth; 65
Beside, so qualified as may beseem
The spouse of any noble gentleman.
Let me embrace with old Vincentio,
And wander we to see thy honest son,
Who will of thy arrival be full joyous. 70
VINCENTIO But is this true, or is it else your pleasure,
Like pleasant travellers, to break a jest
Upon the company you overtake?
HORTENSIO I do assure thee, father, so it is.
PETRUCHIO Come, go along and see the truth hereof, 75
For our first merriment hath made thee jealous.

Exeunt [all but Hortensio]

HORTENSIO Well, Petruchio, this has put me in heart.
Have to my widow, and if she froward,
Then hast thou taught Hortentio to be untoward. *Exit*

63. by this = by this time　ペトルーチオはこの時点では、トラーニオをルーセンシオだと思っている。トラーニオ扮するルーセンシオが「すでに」ビアンカと結婚したと知るはずはない。本物のルーセンシオとビアンカが教会に向かうのも次の場面である。明らかな齟齬だが、観客は気がつきにくい。*cf.* l. 74 後注

64. esteem = reputation

66. qualified = furnished with qualities, possessed of qualities　(*OED adj.* 3a)　　**beseem** = befit

69. wander = travel, go

　　thy honest son　コミカルな効果を持つアイロニー

70. of = at

71. or is it else = or else is it

72. pleasant = merry, humorous

　　break a jest = play a joke, make a joke

74. I do assure thee, father, so it is　⇒後注

75. hereof = of this

76. jealous = suspicious

77. put me in heart = encourage me, restore my spirits

78. Have to my widow = Now I will go to my window

　　froward = difficult to deal with, perverse

79. untoward = unmannerly, unruly

195

[ACT V, SCENE I]

Enter Biondello, Lucentio [as himself] and Bianca. Gremio is out before

BIONDELLO   Softly and swiftly, sir, for the priest is ready.
LUCENTIO   I fly, Biondello. But they may chance to need thee
   at home, therefore leave us.   *Exit [Lucentio with Bianca]*
BIONDELLO   Nay, faith, I'll see the church a' your back, and
   then come back to my master's as soon as I can.   *[Exit]*   5
GREMIO   I marvel Cambio comes not all this while.

Enter Petruchio, Katherina, Vincentio, Grumio, with Attendants

PETRUCHIO   Sir, here's the door, this is Lucentio's house.
   My father's bears more toward the market-place;
   Thither must I, and here I leave you, sir.
VINCENTIO   You shall not choose but drink before you go.   10
   I think I shall command your welcome here,
   And by all likelihood some cheer is toward.

He knocks

GREMIO   They're busy within. You were best knock louder.

Pedant looks out of the window

PEDANT   What's he that knocks as he would beat down the
   gate?   15
VINCENTIO   Is Signor Lucentio within, sir?
PEDANT   He's within, sir, but not to be spoken withal.
VINCDENTIO   What if a man bring him a hundred pound or
   two to make merry withal?
PEDANT   Keep your hundred pounds to yourself. He shall need   20
   none so long as I live.
PETRUCHIO   Nay, I told you your son was well beloved in
   Padua. — Do you hear, sir? To leave frivolous circumstances,
   I pray you tell Signor Lucentio that his father is come from

〔**5. 1**〕あらすじ・・

　ルーセンシオとビアンカがこっそり教会に行って結婚している間に、ペトルー
チオ、キャタリーナ、ヴィンセンシオたちの一行はルーセンシオの家にやってく
る。しかしヴィンセンシオに扮した教師とルーセンシオに扮したトラーニオがい
るせいで、ヴィンセンシオは牢屋に送られそうになる。事態を知らされたルーセ
ンシオが教会から戻ってきて、事情をすべて話し、ビアンカと結婚したことを告
げる。一同の大騒ぎをそばで見ていたペトルーチオとキャタリーナは、最後に仲
良くキスをする。

・・

0. 1. ⇒後注

0. 1. *Gremio is out before* 「グレミオは先に登場している」　グレミオの後に
　登場するビオンデロ、ルーセンシオ、ビアンカは、グレミオに気がつかれない
　ように、そっと後ろを通りながら一言台詞を語って退場する。

4. a' your back = at your back　「2人が結婚式を挙げるところを後ろから見守
　る」とビオンデロは言っている。

6. I marvel = I am surprised, I wonder why　キャンビオが来ないと言ってい
　るグレミオのすぐ後ろをキャンビオ(ルーセンシオ)が、たった今、通り抜け
　ていったばかりというアイロニー。

8. My father's = My father's house
　bears = is situated　(*OED v.¹* 33)

9. Thither = To that place

10. You shall not choose but = You must　shall は話者の意思を表す。ここ
　では「ぜひ飲んでいってもらいますよ」というヴィンセンシオの気持ちを表し
　ている。

11. your welcome = welcome for you, hospitality for you

12. some cheer is toward = some food is to be expected

13. 1. *Pedant looks out of the window*　おそらく二階舞台を使ったものと推
　測できる。　⇒後注

17. withal = with

19. make merry = have fun　**withal** = with

23. frivolous = slight, trivial
　circumstances = formality, ceremony

24. is come = has come

Pisa and is here at the door to speak with him. 25

PEDANT Thou liest. His father is come from Padua, and here looking out at the window.

VINCENTIO Art thou his father?

PEDANT Ay, sir, so his mother says, if I may believe her.

PETRUCHIO Why, how now, gentleman! Why, this is flat 30 knavery to take upon you another man's name.

PEDANT Lay hands on the villain. I believe a means to cozen somebody in this city under my countenance.

Enter Biondello

BIONDELLO [*Aside*] I have seen them in the church together. God send 'em good shipping! But who is here? Mine old 35 master Vincentio! Now we are undone and brought to nothing.

VINCENTIO Come hither, crack-hemp.

BIONDELLO I hope I may choose, sir.

VINCENTIO Come hither, you rogue. What, have you forgot 40 me?

BIONDELLO Forgot you? No, sir. I could not forget you, for I never saw you before in all my life.

VINCENTIO What, you notorious villain, didst thou never see thy master's father, Vincentio? 45

BIONDELLO What, my old worshipful old master? Yes, marry, sir, see where he looks out of the window.

VINCENTIO Is't so, indeed?

He beats Biondello

BIONDELLO Help, help, help! Here's a madman will murder me. [*Exit*] 50

PEDANT Help, son! Help, Signor Baptista! [*Exit from above*]

PETRUCHIO Prithee, Kate, let's stand aside and see the end of this controversy.

26. is come from Padua 「父親が現れるならパデュアからだ」つまり「父親な らとっくにパデュアにいる」という冗談まじりの返事をしていると考えられ る。あまり気の利いたジョークとは言えないので、to Padua、from Pisa、 from Mantua などに改変している版もある。

30. flat = downright, outright

32. a = he **cozen** = cheat

33. countenance = appearance, look (*OED n.*^{*1*} 2a)

35. God send 'em good shipping 幸運を祈る定型的な表現。直訳すれば、「2 人が良い航海にめぐまれますように」となる。

36. undone = ruined

38. hither = to here, to this place

　crack-hemp hemp はもともと植物の麻だが、ここでは麻で作った絞首刑用 のロープ (halter) のこと。それを引きちぎってしまうような悪党という意味 であろう。*OED* ではこの台詞が唯一の用例として引用されている。また *OED* は crack-halter を同義語とし、その初出の用例としてギャスコインの *Supposes* からの引用を挙げている。crack-hemp はそこから連想してシェイ クスピアが造った言葉の可能性も高い。

39. I hope I may choose = I hope I can do as I choose 「言われるとおりにし なくてもいいですよね」という意。

44. notorious = notable, remarkable

49. madman will madman と will の間に関係代名詞 that を補って読む。

50. l. F1 にはビオンデロの退場を示すト書きはない。l. 92 でビオンデロがルー センシオとビアンカとともに登場するので、ここで慌ててルーセンシオに事態 を伝えるために退場すると考えるのが妥当である。

51. l. [*Exit from above*] l. 53 で教師は再び登場するので、ここでいったん退 場する。above は二階舞台から退場することを示す。*cf.* l. 13. 1

52. Prithee = please ここでペトルーチオとキャタリーナは舞台の傍に移動 し、本物と偽物のヴィンセンシオたちが繰り広げるドタバタを眺めることにな る。ひとつの舞台の上に、見る側と見られる側が同時に存在する場面は、シェ イクスピアの戯曲にしばしば表れる。

[*They stand aside*]
Enter Pedant with servants, Baptista and Tranio [*as Lucentio*].

TRANIO   Sir, what are you that offer to beat my servant?

VINCENTIO   What am I, sir? Nay, what are you, sir? O immortal   55
gods! O fine villain! A silken doublet, a velvet hose, a scarlet
cloak, and a copatain hat! O, I am undone, I am undone.
While I play the good husband at home, my son and my
servant spend all at the university.

TRANIO   How now? What's the matter?   60

BAPTISTA   What, is the man lunatic?

TRANIO   Sir, you seem a sober ancient gentleman by your
habit, but your words show you a madman. Why, sir, what
'cerns it you if I wear pearl and gold? I thank my good father,
I am able to maintain it.   65

VINCENTIO   Thy father? O villain, he is a sail-maker in
Bergamo.

BAPTISTA   You mistake, sir, you mistake, sir. Pray, what do you
think is his name?

VINCENTIO   His name? As if I knew not his name! I have   70
brought him up ever since he was three years old, and his
name is Tronio.

PEDANT   Away, away, mad ass! His name is Lucentio, and he is
mine only son, and heir to the lands of me, Signor Vincentio.

VINCENTIO   Lucentio? O, he hath murdered his master! Lay   75
hold on him, I charge you, in the Duke's name. O my son, my
son! Tell me, thou villain, where is my son Lucentio?

TRANIO   Call forth an officer.

[*Enter an Officer*]

Carry this mad knave to the jail. Father Baptista, I charge
you see that he be forthcoming.   80

VINCENTIO   Carry me to the jail?

54. offer ＝ dare, presume

56. fine ＝ richly dressed　　**doublet**　男性用の体にぴったりと密着した上着。
cf. Induction 2. 8　　**hose**　膝丈までのズボン　doublet and hose はシェイ
クスピアの時代の標準的な紳士服。

56-57. scarlet cloak　赤いマントは王侯貴族の着るものだった。

57. copatain　*OED* によれば a high-crowned hat in the form of a sugar-
loaf を指す。円錐形の丈の高い帽子は 16 世紀に流行した。リボン、羽飾り、
宝石などをつけた贅沢な服飾品だった。

58. good husband ＝ careful housekeeper　ここでの husband は「夫」では
なく「節約家」という意味。

62. sober ＝ decent　　**ancient** ＝ having the experience and wisdom of
age, venerable　(*OED a.* 3)

63. habit ＝ dress

63-64. what 'cerns it you ＝ what concern is it of yours

65. maintain ＝ afford

67. Bergamo　ベルガモはロンバルディア中部にある都市。内陸のため 'sail-
maker' がいるとは考えにくく、ここでも地理に関する正確な知識について
のシェイクスピアの鷹揚さが出ている。ただしコメディア・デラルテの特徴で
ある類型的な「ずる賢くて粗野な召使い」という道化は伝統的にベルガモ生ま
れとされた。コメディア・デラルテの道化の系譜に属するトラーニオをベルガ
モ生まれとすることは、この点で妥当である。

74. mine only son　my が mine となっているのは、次に続く言葉が母音で始ま
るから。

78. officer ＝ constable

78. 1. [*Enter an Officer*]　F にはこのト書きはないが、l. 82 でグレミオが警吏
に向かって、牢屋には連れて行くなと呼びかけているので、登場させる必要が
ある。

80. see ＝ ensure　　**forthcoming**　「出廷する」

GREMIO   Stay, officer. He shall not go to prison.

BAPTISTA   Talk not, Signor Gremio. I say he shall go to prison.

GREMIO   Take heed, Signor Baptista, lest you be cony-catched
in this business. I dare swear this is the right Vincentio.   85

PEDANT   Swear if thou dar'st.

GREMIO   Nay, I dare not swear it.

TRANIO   Then thou wert best say that I am not Lucentio.

GREMIO   Yes, I know thee to be Signor Lucentio.

BAPTISTA   Away with the dotard; to the jail with him!   90

VINCENTIO   Thus strangers may be haled and abused. O
monstrous villain!

Enter Biondello, Lucentio and Bianca

BIONDELLO   O, we are spoiled, and yonder he is! Deny him,
forswear him, or else we are all undone.

Exeunt Biondello, Tranio and Pedant as fast as may be

LUCENTIO   Pardon, sweet father.

Lucentio and Bianca kneel

VINCENTIO   Lives my sweet son?   95

BIANCA   Pardon, dear father.

BAPTISTA   How hast thou offended?
Where is Lucentio?

LUCENTIO   Here's Lucentio,
Right son to the right Vincentio,
That have by marriage made thy daughter mine
While counterfeit supposes bleared thine eyne.   100

GREMIO   Here's packing, with a witness, to deceive us all.

VINCENTIO   Where is that damnèd villain, Tranio,
That faced and braved me in this matter so?

BAPTISTA   Why, tell me, is not this my Cambio?

BIANCA   Cambio is changed into Lucentio.   105

LUCENTIO   Love wrought these miracles. Bianca's love

84. cony-catched = deceived, tricked　cony (または coney) はもともとウサギだが、「お人好しで簡単に騙される人」の比喩でもあった。cony-catching は「詐欺」、cony-catcher は「詐欺師」。　*cf.* 4. 1. 36

88. thou wert best say = you would better say

90. dotard = an old man in his dotage

91. haled = dragged about

93. spoiled = ruined

93-94. Deny him, forswear him　いずれも「彼は父親ではないと断言する」という意味。

96. How hast thou offended?　「何か悪いことをしたのか」という意。

100. counterfeit supposes　counterfeit は「偽物」、supposes も「代理を本物だと思わせること」という意で、ほとんど同じ意味の言葉の繰り返し。シェイクスピアは材源としてジョージ・ギャスコイン (George Gascoigne) の喜劇 *Supposes* を利用した。その連想から、この言葉をこの喜劇的クライマックスで使ったのであろう。

bleared = make (the eyes) watery

eyne は eyes の古い形。　bleared thine eyne は「（涙で目が曇るように）事実を見えなくしてしまった」の意。

101. packing = plotting, conspiracy

with a witness = with clear evidence, without a doubt　(*OED n.* P6)　「明らかな策略だ」と非難している。

103. faced = bullied, outfaced

braved = defied　*cf.* 4. 3. 109

105. Cambio is changed into Lucentio　Cambio は change という意味のイタリア語なので、この台詞は語呂合わせになっている。

106. wrought　work の過去形の古い形。

Made me exchange my state with Tranio
While he did bear my countenance in the town,
And happily I have arrived at the last
Unto the wishèd haven of my bliss.   110
What Tranio did, myself enforced him to;
Then pardon him, sweet father, for my sake.

VINCENTIOI   I'll slit the villain's nose that would have sent me
to the jail.

BAPTISTA   But do you hear, sir? Have you married my daughter   115
without asking my good will?

VINCENTIO   Fear not, Baptista, we will content you. Go to. But
I will in to be revenged for this villainy.   *Exit*

BAPTISTA   And I, to sound the depth of this knavery.   *Exit*

LUCENTIO   Look not pale, Bianca, thy father will not frown.   120
                                    Exeunt [Lucentio and Bianca]

GREMIO   My cake is dough, but I'll in among the rest,
Out of hope of all but my share of the feast.   *[Exit]*

KATHERINA   Husband, let's follow to see the end of this ado.

PETRUCHIO   First kiss me, Kate, and we will.

KATHERINA   What, in the midst of the street?   125

PETRUCHIO   What, art thou ashamed of me?

KATHERINA   No, sir, God forbid, but ashamed to kiss.

PETRUCHIO   Why, then let's home again.
   [*To Grumio*]   Come, sirrah, let's away.

KATHERINA   Nay, I will give thee a kiss. [*She kisses him*]   130
Now pray thee, love, stay.

PETRUCHIO   Is not this well? Come, my sweet Kate.
Better once than never, for never too late.   *Exeunt*

⌈ACT V, SCENE II⌉

*Enter Baptista, Vincentio, Gremio, the Pedant, Lucentio and
Bianca, [Hortensio] and Widow, [Petruchio and Katherina,] Tranio,
Biondello and Grumio with Servingmen bringing in a banquet*

107. state = status, social position

108. bear my countenance = assume my identity　countenance = appearance　*cf.* 5. 1. 33

113. I'll slit the villain's nose　「鼻を削ぎ落とす」ことは復讐の印とされていた。

116. asking my good will = asking for my consent

117. content = satisfy　**Go to** = Come!　「さあ！」と人を促すときに使う。

118. I will in = I will go inside　退場のきっかけとなる台詞。

119. I　この後に will in が省略されている。　**sound** = probe　「この悪事の深さを測る」と言っている。

121. My cake is dough　私のケーキは種のままだ（ふくらまなかった）、つまり「私のもくろみがはずれた」という意味。*cf.* 1. 1. 108

122. Out of hope of all = With no hope of anything　**but** = except

123. ado = hustle and bustle（大騒ぎ）　*cf. Much Ado about Nothing*

124. kiss me, Kate　この表現が出てくるのは 2. 1. 315 に続いて 2 回目。

127. God forbid　「とんでもない！」

133. Better once than never, for never too late　'Better late than never' と 'It is never too late to mend' の 2 つのことわざを 1 つにして使っている。ここでの once は sometime の意味。「いつか実現すれば良い、遅すぎることはない」という意。また Kate と late は韻を踏んで、場面の締めくくりの couplet となっている。

〔5. 2〕あらすじ……………………………………………………………………………
　ルーセンシオとビアンカの結婚式の後、一同が全員そろって宴の後の談話を楽しんでいる。機知の応酬のあと妻たちが退室すると、ペトルーチオたちは誰の妻が最も従順に夫の指示を聞き入れて宴席に戻ってくるかをめぐって賭けをする。予想を裏切りキャタリーナだけが、夫に言われた通り部屋にやってくる。キャタリーナはさらに命じられるまま他の妻たちを連れてきて、妻たちに夫に対する服従の義務を説く。ペトルーチオのじゃじゃ馬ならしの腕前を称えて劇は終わる。
……………………………………………………………………………………………

0. 1-3.　⇒後注

0. 3.　*banquet*　宴会という意味ではなく、宴会の後に食べる、お菓子、フルーツ、ワインなどのこと。

Lucentio   At last, though long, our jarring notes agree,
   And time it is when raging war is done
   To smile at scapes and perils overblown.
   My fair Bianca, bid my father welcome,
   While I with selfsame kindness welcome thine.   5
   Brother Petruchio, sister Katherina,
   And thou Hortentio, with thy loving widow,
   Feast with the best, and welcome to my house.
   My banquet is to close our stomachs up
   After our great good cheer. Pray you, sit down,   10
   For now we sit to chat as well as eat.
Petruchio   Nothing but sit and sit, and eat and eat.
Baptista   Padua affords this kindness, son Petruchio.
Petruchio   Padua affords nothing but what is kind.
Hortensio   For both our sakes, I would that word were true.   15
Petruchio   Now, for my life, Hortensio fears his widow.
Widow   Then never trust me if I be afeard.
Petruchio   You are very sensible, and yet you miss my sense.
   I mean Hortensio is afeard of you.
Widow   He that is giddy thinks the world turns round.   20
Petruchio   Roundly replied.
Katherina   Mistress, how mean you that?
Widow   Thus I conceive by him.
Petruchio   Conceives by me! How likes Hortensio that?
Hortensio   My widow says, thus she conceives her tale.
Petruchio   Very well mended. Kiss him for that, good widow.   25
Katherina   'He that is giddy thinks the world turns round.'
   I pray you tell me what you meant by that.
Widow   Your husband, being troubled with a shrew,
   Measures my husband's sorrow by his woe.
   And now you know my meaning.   30
Katherina   A very mean meaning.
Widow   Right, I mean you.

1. long = after a long time　　**our jarring notes agree**　音楽の比喩。「合っていなかった音がちゃんとしたハーモニーになった」という意。

3. scapes ＝ escapes from danger　　**overblown** ＝ that have blown over, that have passed away

5. kindness　「優しさ」(affection) という意味と「血のつながり」(kinship) の意味を兼ねている。

8. with the best ＝ on the best food

9. close our stomachs up　「お腹の隙間を埋める」という意。　close ＝ fill

10. great good cheer　「(結婚を祝う) 大宴会」　おそらくバプティスタのところで祝宴を開き、その後、ルーセンシオの家で食後の banquet を楽しんでいるという想定であろう。

13. affords this kindness ＝ can afford this hospitality

14. affords nothing but what is kind ＝ yields nothing that isn't affectionate
バプティスタが「パデュアはこれくらいのおもてなしはできます」と言ったのに対し、ペトルーチオは「パデュア生まれの者はみな優しい」と、違う意味にずらして切り返している。

16. for my life ＝ upon my life
Hortensio fears his widow　ペトルーチオは「ホーテンシオは奥さんのことを恐れている」という意味で言ったが、それを未亡人は「ホーテンシオは奥さんのことを怖がらせている」の意味で受け取った。

17. never trust me if I be afeard ＝ I can assure you that I am not afraid of him

18. sensible ＝ reasonable, judicious　　**my sense** ＝ my meaning

20. He that ... round　自分の目が回っているのに、世界の方が動いていると勘違いしてしまう、つまり自分の物差しで他人のことも理解してしまう、という意味のことわざ。

21. Roundly ＝ outspokenly, bluntly
how mean you that ＝ what do you mean by that

22. Thus I conceive by him　未亡人は「ペトルーチオの言葉をこういう風に理解した」と言っているが、ペトルーチオはわざと conceive の意味をずらして「俺のせいで子供を身ごもっただと！」と切り返している。

24. thus she conceives her tale　⇒後注

25. mended ＝ rectified, remedied　　未亡人の下品な発言をうまく修正したなとペトルーチオは言っている。

28-29.　⇒後注

31. mean meaning ＝ nasty meaning　　同音異義語を使った言葉遊び。

KATHERINA   And I am mean indeed, respecting you.

PETRUCHIO   To her, Kate!

HORTENSIO   To her, widow!

PETRUCHIO   A hundred marks, my Kate does put her down.   35

HORTENSIO   That's my office.

PETRUCHIO   Spoke like an officer. Ha' to thee, lad.

He drinks to Hortensio

BAPTISTA   How likes Gremio these quick-witted folks?

GREMIO   Believe me, sir, they butt together well.

BIANCA   Head and butt? An hasty-witted body   40
Would say your head and butt were head and horn.

VINCENTIO   Ay, mistress bride, hath that awakened you?

BIANCA   Ay, but not frighted me; therefore I'll sleep again.

PETRUCHIO   Nay, that you shall not. Since you have begun,
Have at you for a better jest or two.   45

BIABCA   Am I your bird? I mean to shift my bush,
And then pursue me as you draw your bow.
You are welcome all.   *Exeunt Bianca* [, *Katherina and Widow*]

PETRUCHIO   She hath prevented me. Here, Signor Tranio,
This bird you aimed at, though you hit her not;   50
Therefore a health to all that shot and missed.

TRANIO   O sir, Lucentio slipped me like his greyhound,
Which runs himself and catches for his master.

PETRUCHIO   A good swift simile, but something currish.

TRANIO   'Tis well, sir, that you hunted for yourself.   55
'Tis thought your deer does hold you at a bay.

BAPTISTA   O, O, Petruchio, Tranio hits you now.

LUCENTIO   I thank thee for that gird, good Tranio.

HORTENSIO   Confess, confess, hath he not hit you here?

PETRUCHIO   A has a little galled me, I confess.   60
And as the jest did glance away from me,
'Tis ten to one it maimed you two outright.

32. I am ... respecting you キャタリーナは mean の意味をさらにずらし moderate の意味で応えている。「あなたのことを考えれば、私なんかまだまだだわ」と言い返している。

33-34. To her 「やっつけろ」という闘鶏や狩猟で使われる動物へのかけ声。

35. A hundred marks 1 マルクは 13 シリング 4 ペンスに相当する。ペトルーチオはかなりな金額を賭けている。　　　**put her down** = defeat her

36. That's my office ホーテンシオは put her down を文字通り「彼女を押し倒すこと」と性的な意味にずらし、「それは夫である僕の役目」と答えている。

37. Spoke like an officer 「任務を果たす役人のような口調だ」

Ha' = Have　Ha' to thee で「君のために乾杯しよう」という意味。

39. butt = strike with the head like a horned animal 「丁々発止のやりとりで角を付き合わせていますね」という意味。

40. Head and butt = Head and tail　⇒後注

hasty-witted body = quick-witted person

41. your head ... horn 「あなたの場合、head and butt と言うべきところが head and horn になるでしょう」と言っている。*cf*. 4. 1. 23

42. hath that awakened you? 性的にきわどい意味の言葉が交わされる機知の応酬にビアンカも参戦してきたことに驚いて、ヴィンセンシオは「こんな話で目が覚めましたか」と言っている。

43. not frighted me 「目は覚めたけれど、恐れるほどのものではない」ということを言っている。

45. Have at you = Be prepared for

46-47. この 2 行以下、狩りの比喩が連続して使われている。　⇒後注

49. prevented = escaped, avoided by timely action

50. hit 狩りで狙いが「当たる」という意味と、性的に「女とやる」という意味を重ね合わせている。

51. health = toast

52. slipped = released from a leash (*OED v.*¹ 27a)

54. swift = quick-witted　　**something** = somewhat　　**currish** 「当意即妙の答えはうまいが、野良犬風だな」とトラーニオをからかっている。

56. your deer deer は同音の dear との言葉遊び (pun)。

at a bay「追い詰められた状態」「鹿（キャタリーナ）の方が狩人のあなたを追い詰めている」とトラーニオは切り返している。

58. gird = sharp remark, biting remark

60. A = He　　**galled** = wounded, hurt

61. glance away 「斜めに当たってそれる」「目標をかすめてそれる」strike obliquely upon and turn aside (*OED v.*¹ 1a)

62. ten to one = very likely　　**maimed** = hurt

BAPTISTA Now in good sadness, son Petruchio,
I think thou hast the veriest shrew of all.

PETRUCHIO Well, I say no. And therefore for assurance   65
Let's each one send unto his wife,
And he whose wife is most obedient
To come at first when he doth send for her
Shall win the wager which we will propose.

HORTENSIO Content. What's the wager?

LUCENTIO   Twenty crowns.   70

PETRUCHIO Twenty crowns?
I'll venture so much of my hawk or hound,
But twenty times so much upon my wife.

LUCENTIO A hundred then.

HORTENSIO   Content.

PETRUCHIO   A match. 'Tis done.

HORTENSIO Who shall begin?

LUCENTIO   That will I.   75
Go, Biondello, bid your mistress come to me.

BIONDELLO I go.   *Exit*

BAPTISTA Son, I'll be your half Bianca comes.

LUCENTIO I'll have no halves; I'll bear it all myself.

Enter Biondello

How now, what news?

BIONDELLO   Sir, my mistress sends you word   80
That she is busy and she cannot come.

PETRUCHIO How? 'She's busy and she cannot come'!
Is that an answer?

GREMIO   Ay, and a kind one too.
Pray God, sir, your wife send you not a worse.

PETRUCHIO I hope better.   85

HORTENSIO Sirrah Biondello, go and entreat my wife
To come to me forthwith.   *Exit Biondello*

63. sadness = seriousness

64. veriest = worst

65. for assurance = to make confidence greater　⇒後注

68. To come = in coming

70. Content = I am content; agreed!

　Twenty crowns　1 クラウンは 5 シリングまたは 1/4 ポンド。20 クラウンは 5
　ポンド。1590 年時点での 5 ポンドは職人の賃金にして 100 日分程度とされる。
　cf. 2. 1. 120

72. of = on

73. twenty times　twenty は具体的な数値ではなく、「とても多い」ことを示
　す。「妻のためならその何倍も賭ける」と言っている。

　A match = Agreed! (*OED n.*¹ 9)

78. Son = son-in-law

　half = one of two partners or co-sharers (*OED n.* 6a)　おそらくバプティ
　スタは掛け金も半分出すが、儲けも半分もらうと言っている。

82. How? = What?

85. I hope better = I expect something better

87. forthwith = immediately

PETRUCHIO   O ho, entreat her?
Nay, then she must needs come.
HORTENSIO   I am afraid, sir,
Do what you can, yours will not be entreated.

Enter Biondello

Now, where's my wife?   90
BIONDELLO   She says you have some goodly jest in hand.
She will not come. She bids you come to her.
PETRUCHIO   Worse and worse; 'she will not come'! O vile,
Intolerable, not to be endured!
Sirrah Grumio, go to your mistress.   95
Say I command her come to me.   *Exit Grumio*
HORTENSIO   I know her answer.
PETRUCHIO   What?
HORTENSIO   She will not.
PETRUCHIO   The fouler fortune mine, and there an end.

Enter Katherina

BAPTISTA   Now, by my holidame, here comes Katherina!
KATHERINA   What is your will, sir, that you send for me?   100
PETRUCHIO   Where is your sister, and Hortensio's wife?
KATHERINA   They sit conferring by the parlour fire.
PETRUCHIO   Go fetch them hither. If they deny to come,
Swinge me them soundly forth unto their husbands.
Away, I say, and bring them hither straight.   [*Exit Katherina*]   105
LUCENTIO   Here is a wonder, if you talk of a wonder.
HORTENSIO   And so it is. I wonder what it bodes.
PETRUCHIO   Marry, peace it bodes, and love, and quiet life,
An awful rule, and right supremacy,
And, to be short, what not that's sweet and happy.   110
BAPTISTA   Now fair befall thee, good Petruchio!
The wager thou hast won, and I will add

87. ho 「ほう」という驚きを表す間投詞。ホーテンシオが entreat（頼む）という言葉を使ったことへのあてこすり。

88. needs = of necessity

 I am afraid = I regret to say, I suspect

89. Do what you can = No matter what you do

91. goodly jest = excellent joke　もちろん未亡人は皮肉を言っている。

98. The fouler fortune mine = That will be worse luck for me

 there an end = that will be the end of the matter

99. by my holidame = by all that I hold holy　ここではバプティスタの驚きを表す「これは！」というような誓いの言葉。holidame は halidom と同じ。版によっては halidom の方を選んでいる。halidom はもともと holy place という意味だが，holy dame（Virgin Mary のこと）だと誤解され，holidame と綴るようになった。F1 では hollidam と印刷されている。

102. conferring = chatting

103. deny = refuse

104. Swinge me them soundly forth unto their husbands　me は ethical dative（心性的与格）。あえて訳せば「私のために」という話者の感情を表すために添えられている。*cf.* Induction 1. 46, 1. 2. 8, 4. 2. 7, 4. 3. 98　Swinge = beat, whip　soundly = severely　「2人を思い切りひっぱたいてでも夫のところに連れてこい」と言っている。

106. wonder = miracle

107. I wonder what it bodes　尋常ならざること (miracle) は何かの予兆だと信じられていた。ホーテンシオは「これから何が起きるのだろう」と恐れ入っている。　bodes = presages, portends

109. awful rule　「畏敬の念を抱かせるような権威」　awful = inspiring awe, commanding respect

 right supremacy　「夫が至上であるという正しい関係」

110. what not = everything

111. fair befall thee = good luck to you

Unto their losses twenty thousand crowns,
Another dowry to another daughter,
For she is changed as she had never been.   115
PETRUCHIO   Nay, I will win my wager better yet,
And show more sign of her obedience,
Her new-built virtue and obedience.

Enter Katherina, Bianca, and Widow

See where she comes, and brings your froward wives
As prisoners to her womanly persuasion.   120
Katherine, that cap of yours becomes you not.
Off with that bauble, throw it underfoot.

[She obeys]

WIDOW   Lord, let me never have a cause to sigh
Till I be brought to such a silly pass!
BIANCA   Fie, what a foolish duty call you this?   125
LUCENTIO   I would your duty were as foolish too.
The wisdom of your duty, fair Bianca,
Hath cost me five hundred crowns since supper-time.
BIANCA   The more fool you for laying on my duty.
PETRUCHIO   Katherine, I charge thee, tell these headstrong
   women   130
What duty they do owe their lords and husbands.
WIDOW   Come, come, you're mocking. We will have no telling.
PETRUCHIO   Come on, I say, and first begin with her.
WIDOW   She shall not.
PETRUCHIO   I say she shall. And first begin with her.   135
KATHERINA   Fie, fie, unknit that threatening unkind brow,
And dart not scornful glances from those eyes
To wound thy lord, thy king, thy governor.
It blots thy beauty as frosts do bite the meads,
Confounds thy fame as whirlwinds shake fair buds,   140

115. as she had never been = as if she had never existed 「かつてのキャタリーナなどいなかったかのように」 つまりまるで別人のように変わってしまったとバプティスタは言っている。

117-18. l. 117 の her obedience を強調するために、次行で Her new-built virtue and obedience とさらに詳しい言い方で繰り返していると解釈することができる。ただし2行の末尾がいずれも obedience で重複しているのは植字工が元になる原稿を読む際に、間違えて前の行を見てしまったことによるエラーではないかと考える編者も多い。

119. froward = difficult, perverse

121. that cap おそらく第4幕第3場で激しく非難したのと同じ帽子。

becomes = suits, looks good on

122. bauble = showy trinket ペトルーチオは4. 3. 82 でも同じ言葉を使って帽子をけなしている。

124. pass = predicament, embarrassing situation 未亡人は「こんな馬鹿馬鹿しいことをさせられたら嘆かざるをえない」と言っている。

126. I would = I wish

128. five hundred crowns l. 74 でルーセンシオが賭けた金額は 100 クラウンだった。そのため Capell 以来、多くの編者が one hundred あるいは a hundred に校訂している。しかし近年の第3アーデン版、マクミラン版は F1 をそのまま受け入れ、five hundred としている。本書もルーセンシオが腹立ちまぎれに大げさに言っていると考え five hundred とした。

129. laying = betting

132. you're mocking = you are joking

136-79. *The Taming of the Shrew* の中で最も長い台詞で、キャタリーナの「服従の演説」(speech of submission) と呼ばれることもある。　⇒後注

136. unknit = unwrinkle, smoothe　　**unkind** 「冷たい」(hard-hearted) と、「人としておかしい」(unnatural) の意味を兼ねている。

137. dart = shoot out, cast

139. blots = stains, defaces　　**meads** = meadows

140. Confounds thy fame = Destroys your reputation

And in no sense is meet or amiable.
A woman moved is like a fountain troubled,
Muddy, ill-seeming, thick, bereft of beauty,
And while it is so, none so dry or thirsty
Will deign to sip or touch one drop of it.   145
Thy husband is thy lord, thy life, thy keeper,
Thy head, thy sovereign: one that cares for thee,
And for thy maintenance commits his body
To painful labour both by sea and land,
To watch the night in storms, the day in cold,   150
Whilst thou liest warm at home, secure and safe,
And craves no other tribute at thy hands
But love, fair looks and true obedience;
Too little payment for so great a debt.
Such duty as the subject owes the prince,   155
Even such a woman oweth to her husband.
And when she is froward, peevish, sullen, sour,
And not obedient to his honest will,
What is she but a foul contending rebel
And graceless traitor to her loving lord?   160
I am ashamed that women are so simple
To offer war where they should kneel for peace,
Or seek for rule, supremacy and sway,
When they are bound to serve, love and obey.
Why are our bodies soft, and weak, and smooth,   165
Unapt to toil and trouble in the world,
But that our soft conditions and our hearts
Should well agree with our external parts?
Come, come, you froward and unable worms,
My mind hath been as big as one of yours,   170
My heart as great, my reason haply more,
To bandy word for word and frown for frown.
But now I see our lances are but straws,

141. in no sense = in no way   **meet** = appropriate

142. moved = angered, annoyed   **troubled** = disturbed, stirred up

143. ill-seeming = ugly, unpleasant in appearance

  thick = not clear, turbid   **bereft** = void of

144. none so dry or thirsty = no one no matter how dry or thirsty

145. deign = condescend, stoop, lower himself

146-47. Thy husband ... thy sovereign　『新約聖書』「エペソ人への手紙」第5章 22-23 節を反映する言葉遣いになっている。*cf.* ll. 136-79 の後注

148. F1 では And for thy maintenance. Commits his body と印刷されている。この句読法をできるだけ残そうとすれば、for thy maintenance は cares に続き、夫とは「妻と妻の扶養を心にかける人」という意味になる。一方、for thy maintenance を動詞 commits を修飾する副詞句と考え、And for thy maintenance commits his body とすることも可能である。本書では maintenance の後に息継ぎの入らない、このより長いフレーズの方がキャタリーナの淀みない雄弁さが引き立つと考えた。

149. painful = hard, gruelling

150. watch = stay awake durign

151. secure = free from care or apprehension

152. craves　主語は l. 147 の one   **153. But** = Except

155-56. Such duty ... her husband　『新約聖書』「エペソ人への手紙」第5章 24 節を反映する言葉遣いになっている。*cf.* ll. 136-79 の後注

155. prince = sovereign ruler

157. peevish = obstinate

158. honest = honourable, virtuous

159. but = except   **contending** = warlike, making war

160. graceless = impious, sinful   **161. simple** = foolish

162. offer = venture, dare

163. sway = power of rule, control

164. serve, love and obey　『一般祈禱書』で定められた結婚式の誓いの言葉を反映している。*cf.* ll. 136-79 の後注

166. Unapt = unfit

167. But that = if not so that（その理由はまさに以下のようなことだ）

  conditions = constitutions

169. unable worms = weak little creatures

170. big = proud, arrogant   **one of yours** = that of either of you

171. heart = courage   **haply** = perhaps

172. bandy = exchange, strike (a ball) to and fro

173. but straws = only straws

Our strength as weak, our weakness past compare,

That seeming to be most which we indeed least are. 175

Then vail your stomachs, for it is no boot,

And place your hands below your husband's foot:

In token of which duty, if he please,

My hand is ready, may it do him ease.

PETRUCHIO Why, there's a wench! Come on, and kiss me,

Kate. 180

LUCENTIO Well, go thy ways, old lad, for thou shalt ha't.

VINCENTIO 'Tis a good hearing when children are toward.

LUCENTIO But a harsh hearing when women are froward.

PETRUCHIO Come, Kate, we'll to bed.

We three are married, but you two are sped. 185

[*To Lucentio*] 'Twas I won the wager, though you hit the white,

And being a winner, God give you good night.

Exeunt Petruchio [*and Katherina*]

HORTENSIO Now, go thy ways; thou hast tamed a curst shrew.

LUCENTIO 'Tis a wonder, by your leave, she will be tamed so.

[*Exeunt*]

174. past compare = weaker than anything else

175. That seeming ... are　seeming（見かけ）と are（実態）の対比はシェイ
クスピア劇にしばしば現れるモチーフ。which we indeed least are「実際は
ごくごく小さいもの」を seeming to be most「最大に見せようとしている」
という意味。文章の構造がやや不明瞭なのは、前行の末の compare と are で
韻を合わせることを優先しているから。ここから劇の終わりまで couplet が
続く。

176. vail = lower, let fall　　　**stomachs** = pride, arrogant spirit
boot = profit, advantage

178. In token of which duty = As a gesture of my obedience

179. may it do him ease　「もしこの手がお役に立つものであれば」という if が
省略された節か、あるいは「どうかこの手がお役に立ちますように」という祈
願のいずれか。

180. kiss me, Kate　この表現が出てくるのは 2. 1. 315, 5. 1. 124 に続いて 3 回
目。

181. go thy ways = well done!　祝福の言葉　　　**ha't** = have it「勝利を摑ん
だ」という意味。ha't は前行の Kate と韻を合わせている。

182. a good hearing = a good news, a good thing to hear
toward = obedient, compliant（froward の逆）

183. a harsh hearing　前行の a good hearing の逆。
froward = perverse

185. sped　speed の過去分詞。ここでの speed は bring to the undesired end
の意味。(*OED v.* 7b)　you two are sped で「君たち 2 人は残念な結果だっ
たな」という意。

186. hit the white　アーチェリーで的の真ん中の白い部分を射たという意味。
「狙った的を射た」という意味だが、同時に Bianca はイタリア語で white と
いう意味があるので、「ビアンカを射抜いた」という意味も重ねている。また
hit には性的な意味合いも含まれている。

187. being a winner = as I am a winner　ギャンブルで勝った人はツキのある
うちに早めに退場するものという言い伝えがあった。

188-89.　シェイクスピアの時代の発音では shrew と so は韻を踏んでいた。*cf.*
5. 2. 28-29

189. by your leave = if I may say so

付録：*The Taming of A Shrew* より抜粋

The Taming of the Shrew（*The Shrew*）では、Sly および Sly に悪戯をしかけた領主たちは、第1幕第1場を最後に台詞がなくなる。また *The Shrew* は本来、劇中劇であったはずのルーセンシオやペトルーチオの結婚をめぐる喜劇が終わったところで終わっている。

一方、*The Taming of A Shrew*（*A Shrew*）では、何度か Sly たちの場面が差し挟まれ、劇の終わりも冒頭部分と整合する形で、眠りから目覚めた Sly の場面で終わっている。以下は *A Shrew* から、Sly の登場する場面を抜粋したものである。

〔**1**〕

SLY　Sim, when will the fool come again?

LORD　He'll come again, my lord, anon.

SLY　Gi's some more drink here. Zounds, where's the tapster?
　Here Sim, eat some of these things.

LORD　So I do, my lord.　　　　　　　　　　　　　　　5

SLY　Here Sim, I drink to thee.

LORD　My lord, here comes the players again.

SLY　O brave, here's two fine gentlewomen.

〔**2**〕

SLY　Sim, must they be married now?

LORD　Ay, my lord.

Enter Ferando and Kate and Sander

SLY　Look Sim, the fool is come again now.

〔**3**〕

Pylotus and Valeria runs away
Then Sly speaks

SLY　I say we'll have no sending to prison.

LORD　My lord, this is but the play, they're but in jest.

SLY　I tell thee, Sim, we'll have no sending to prison,

〔1〕••

　この直前には Aurelius（ルーセンシオにあたる）の召使い Valeria（トラーニオにあたる）を音楽教師に変装させ、Kate がリュートのレッスンをしている間に、妹の Phylema（ビアンカにあたる）に恋心を伝えようとする計画が語られる。*The Shrew* には完全に一致する場面はないが、第 2 幕第 1 場と第 3 幕第 1 場の間に相当する部分で、このスライと領主の短いやりとりが挿入される。

••

1. Sim = Simon　領主は召使い Simon に扮して、スライに仕えているふりをしている。　**the fool**　Ferando（ペトルーチオにあたる）の召使い Sander を指す。スライは道化が演じるお笑いの場面を最も気に入っている。

3. Gi's = Give us　**Zounds**　「ちぇっ」という軽いののしりを表す間投詞。God's wounds が短くなった形。

8. two fine gentlewomen　実際にこの台詞を受けて登場するのは音楽教師に扮した Valeria と Kate。スライが見当はずれなコメントをして笑いを誘うという意図ではないかと思われる。

〔2〕••

　Aurelius と Phylema、Polidor（ホーテンシオにあたる）と Emelia（未亡人にあたる）の二組の結婚が決まり、4 人が愛を語りあう場面と、Ferando と Kate が月か太陽かを言い争う場面の間で、この 3 行のやりとりがなされる。*The Shrew* の第 4 幕第 4 場と第 5 場の間に相当する。

••

1. they = Aurelius, Phylema, Polidor, Emelia の 4 人
3. the fool = Sander

〔3〕••

　Aurelius と Phylema が結婚し、Aurelius の父親に扮した Phylotus（教師にあたる）と Aurelius に扮した Valeria が嘘を並べ立てているところに、本物の父親 Duke of Sestos（ヴィンセンシオにあたる）がやってくる。本物と偽物の父親が顔を合わせ、Aurelius が本物の父に謝罪の言葉を述べているさなか、Valeria と Phylotus はこそこそと逃げ出す。*The Shrew* の第 5 幕第 1 場に相当する場面の途中でスライが口を出す。

••

1. prison　*The Shrew* ではヴィンセンシオが逮捕されそうになるが、*A Shrew* で投獄されそうになるのは、偽物の父親 Phylotus と主人に扮していた召使いの Valeria。スライはそれを見て、殿様気分で牢には入れるなと言っている。

2. but = only

221

That's flat.

Why, Sim, am not I Don Christo Vary?   5

Therefore, I say they shall not go to prison.

LORD   No more they shall not, my lord. They be run away.

SLY   Are they run away, Sim? That's well.

Then gi's some more drink and let them play again.

LORD   Here, my lord.   10

Sly drinks and then falls asleep

〔**4**〕

Sly sleeps

LORD   Who's within there? Come hither, sirs.

[Enter servants]

My lord's

Asleep again. Go take him easily up,

And put him in his own apparel again,

And lay him in the place where we did find him,

Just underneath the alehouse side below,   5

But see you wake him not in any case.

BOY   It shall be done, my lord. Come, help to bear him hence.

〔**5**〕

*Then enter two bearing of Sly in his own apparel again,
and leave him where they found him, and then go out.
Then enter the Tapster*

TAPSTER   Now that the darksome night is overpast,

And dawning day appears in crystal sky,

Now must I haste abroad. But soft, who's this?

What, Sly? O wondrous, hath he lain here all night?

I'll wake him. I think he's starved by this,   5

But that his belly was so stuffed with ale.

4. That's flat 「それで決まりだ」 a defiant expression of one's final resolve or determination (*OED a.* 6b)

5. Don Christo Vary スライは自分の権限を発揮して、2人の投獄を防ごうと、自分の名前に Don というスペイン語の敬称をつけて権威付けをしている。Christo Vary は Christopher をスペイン語風に訛らせたもの。ただし *A Shrew* ではスライのファースト・ネームの Christopher は一度も出てこない。*The Shrew* の Induction 2 では、急に領主扱いされたスライが戸惑って、自分は Christopher Sly ではないのかと何度も確認するが、それにあたる台詞は *A Shrew* にはない。Sly という名前も終幕に Tapster から呼ばれるまで出てこない。

9. gi's = give us

〔4〕••

Aurelius が父親に謝罪し、Duke が皆を許して和解が成立する場面が終わると、スライは眠りこんでいる。*The Shrew* の第5幕第1場と第2場の間に相当する部分に置かれた場面。

••

6. see = ensure

〔5〕••

劇の終わり、すべての登場人物が退場した後に置かれている場面。

••

0. 3. *Tapster* *The Shrew* では Induction の冒頭でスライを酒場から追い出すのは Hostess だが、*A Shrew* では Tapster である。

1-21. Q(1594) ではこの場面は最初から最後まで韻文の形で印刷されている。しかしかなり不規則で、不自然な lineation になっている。ll. 1-7 と ll. 20-21 の Tapster の台詞はスライに比べると明らかに韻文の調子がはっきりしているので、ここでも韻文とした。それ以外は、やや韻文調の部分も含め、すべて散文とした。

3. haste abroad = go out in a hurry 　　**soft** = stop, just a moment

5. by this = by this time

6. But that = Unless

What ho, Sly, awake for shame.

SLY Sim, gi's some more wine. What's all the players gone? Am I not a lord?

TAPSTER A lord, with a murrain. Come, art thou drunken still? 10

SLY Who's this? Tapster! O Lord, sirrah, I have had the bravest dream tonight that ever thou heardest in all the life.

TAPSTER Ay, marry, but you had best get you home, for your wife will course you for dreaming here tonight. 15

SLY Will she? I know now how to tame a shrew. I dreamt upon it all this night till now, and thou hast waked me out of the best dream that ever I had in my life. But I'll to my wife presently, and tame her too an if she anger me.

TAPSTER Nay tarry, Sly, for I'll go home with thee, 20
And hear the rest that thou hast dreamt tonight.

Exeunt omnes

10. with a murrain = with a pestilence　驚きや軽蔑を表す表現として使われている。(*OED*. *n.* 2b)

13. bravest = most excellent

14. you had best = you should

15. course = trounce, thrash (*OED*. *v* 4)

19. presently = immediately　　**an if** = if

後注

Ind. 1. 0. 0. INDUCTION 1　F1 では *Actus primus. Scoena Prima* とラテン語で「第 1 幕第 1 場」と表記されている。以下、*The Taming of the Shrew* の幕場割りは F1 では 4 か所のみである。シェイクスピアの全戯曲を 5 幕形式の古典劇の伝統に合わせて幕場割りを行ったのは Nicholas Rowe（1709）である。舞台装置の使用がきわめて少なく、スピーディな場面展開を特徴とするシェイクスピア劇では、幕という大きな区切れを想定するよりも、場の連続として作品をとらえるほうがふさわしいという考え方に基づき、幕割りをしない版本もある。本書は幕場割りをした方が、場面の参照の際にわかりやすいという便宜上の理由を優先し、現在までにもっとも一般的に用いられているものに合わせた幕場割りをした。

　また幕開けのスライの登場する場面を Induction（インダクション）とするのは 1723 年の Alexander Pope の版本からの慣行である。シェイクスピアの時代の演劇で Induction という言葉が用いられている例には、劇を見る人物たちと、その人物たちが見る劇という入れ子構造の「外側」の部分を指す場合と、劇の進行に合わせて、前口上や解説、コメントなどの形で劇に「介入」してくる場合と、大きく分けて 2 種類がある。*The Taming of the Shrew* のスライと領主の場面は、前者の典型と言える。

　The Taming of the Shrew でのスライの登場は F1 では第 1 幕第 1 場の終わりが最後であり、その後はいっさい登場しない。その点でスライの場面について、「じゃじゃ馬ならし」という劇中劇を導入するための「序幕」という言葉を使うのも妥当であるが、*The Taming of A Shrew* に見られるような、断続的な介入や劇中劇の終了後の締めくくりの場面があった可能性も考慮して、本書ではスライの場面を「インダクション」と呼ぶ。

Ind. 1. 0. 1. ***Enter Christopher Sly***　F1 では *Enter Begger and Hostes, Christophero Sly* となっている。またこの後に続く台詞につけられた人物名も一貫して Beg である。当初、登場人物として想定されていたのは Beggar だったが、その Beggar が劇中で自分の名前を口に出すことがわかり、後から冒頭のト書きに Christophero Sly という名前が付け加えられて印刷されたのではないかと想像される。

　また *A Shrew* では *Enter a TAPSTER beating out of his doors SLY, drunken* となっている。F1 のようにこの役を Hostess として、同様にスライを酒場から叩き出すのであれば、「乱暴者の女」がインダクションと劇中劇を結ぶ共通点となる。また実際の上演でも、スライとペトルーチオ、酒場のおかみとキャタリーナを同一の役者が演じることもある。1995 年の RSC での上演

は酒場のおかみをスライの女房という設定に変え、劇中劇は妻になじり倒され
た夫が見た夢という演出だった。

Ind. 1. 1.　feeze　F1 では pheeze という綴りになっている。もともと drive
away という意味のゲルマン語系の語源を持つ言葉で、シェイクスピアはこの
The Taming of the Shrew と *Troilus and Cressida* で各 1 回ずつ使っているの
みである。*Troilus and Cressida* ではエイジャックスが I'll feeze his pride と、
アキリーズの高慢さをなじる際に使っている。

　　I'll feeze you という *The Taming of the Shrew* の開幕第一声のこの台詞は、
A Shew 幕開け早々にもほぼ同じ形で出てくる。酒場の店員に追い出されたあと、
スライは Tilly vally, By crisee, Tapster, I'll feeze you anon(1. 4) と怒鳴り返す。
The Taming of the Shrew の冒頭で、使用頻度の低いこの言葉を、あえて使っ
ているのは、先行作品である *A Shrew* からシェイクスピアが気に入った部分
だけを、いわば「つまみ食い」して自作に生かした結果かもしれない。

Ind. 1. 4.　Richard Conqueror　1066 年、ノルマン人がイングランドを征服し、
ノルマンディー公がイングランド国王となった。この征服王ウィリアム
(William the Conqueror) と、プランタジネット朝の獅子心王リチャード
(Richard the Lion-Hearted) とをスライは混同している。うろ覚えの知識をひ
けらかしながら、スライ家は中世からの歴史を持つ古い家系であると主張して
いる。

Ind. 1. 5.　*paucas pallabris*　*pocas palabras* は当時、人気のあった芝居『スペ
インの悲劇』(*The Spanish Tragedy*) に出てくる表現である。主人公の復讐者
Hieronimo が自分の復讐の意図を隠すために、*Pocas palabras,* mild as the
Lamb「言葉少なに、子羊のごとく穏やかに」と自らに言い聞かせる台詞である。
シェイクスピアの他にも、Thomas Dekker, Thomas Middleton, Thomas
Heywood がそれぞれ戯曲の中で引用している。Thomas Kyd (1558-94) の復
讐悲劇 *The Spanish Tragedy* は 1592 年から 1633 年の間に 10 回も版を重ねる
大ヒット作だった。初演は 1587 年頃と推測されている。スペインの宮廷人
Hieronimo が殺された息子のために、復讐を果たした後、自らも自害すると
いう悲劇だ。復讐者が狂気を装ったり、復讐の手段として劇中劇が利用される
など、*Hamlet* をはじめとするエリザベス朝の復讐劇の定型を確立した作品と
言える。血生臭い殺戮のテーマや、復讐を訴える亡霊など、セネカの悲劇の影
響を強く示している。

Ind. 1. 5.　Sessa!　フェンシングやハンティングで使われる「さあ行け！」と
いう掛け声、あるいはフランス語の cessez からくる「やめろ」という意味で
はないかと推測されている。シェイクスピアは *King Lear* でも 2 度、この言
葉を使っているが、それ以外の使用例は *OED* には挙げられていない。

Ind. 1. 7.　Saint Jeronimy　『スペインの悲劇』の台詞 Hieronimo, beware!
go by, go by! を引用しようとしながら、ここでもスライは主人公の名前

227

Hieronimo と Saint Jerome（聖ヒエロニムス）を混同している。

Ind. 1. 7-8.　go to thy cold bed and warm thee　ここも『スペインの悲劇』の台詞 What out-cries pluck me from my naked bed のもじり。スライは「この冷たき地面で寝るとしようぞ」と、芝居じみた口調で自分に向かって語りかけている。

Ind. 1. 9.　thirdborough　F1 では Headborough となっている。headborough も thirdborough と同様、下級警吏を意味する言葉である。しかし次行でスライが Third, or fourth, or fifth borough（3 番目だろうと、4 番目だろうと、5 番目だろうと）と言い返しているので、そのやりとりの面白さを明確にするためには、thirdborough と校訂する方が適切である。secretary hand（書記体）と呼ばれる書体で書かれた手書き原稿では head と third の区別がつきにくいことによる植字工のミスである可能性が高い。

Ind. 1. 12.　tender well my hounds　ここから 24 行目まで、猟犬の働きぶりについて詳しく語られている。*A Midsummer Night's Dream* の 4. 1. 101-24 でも、猟犬の鳴き声について詳細に語られる台詞がある。*Macbeth* の 3. 1. 91-99 でも猟犬のさまざまな種類や特徴が並べられている。シェイクスピアの時代、狩猟は王侯貴族の楽しみであった。これらの台詞からうかがえる猟犬についての詳しい知識から、作者は貴族階級の生活に詳しかったはずだと考え、貴族がシェイクスピアの名前を使って劇作をしたのではないかと推測する、「シェイクスピア別人説」の根拠のひとつにもなっている。

Ind. 1. 13.　Breathe　F1 では Brach で、Breathe とするのは 1954 年の Sisson 以来の校訂。brach は雌の猟犬の意味で、「猟犬メリマン」でも問題はないが、文章の最後も同一の言葉となるのが不自然であるため、Sisson を踏襲して Breathe への校訂を採った。

Ind. 1. 19.　cried upon it at the merest loss　at a loss は狩猟の用語。having lost the track or scent の意。*OED* の loss, *n.*[1] 2b.

Ind. 1. 84.　SECOND PLAYER, Soto　F1 ではこの台詞を語る役名は Sincklo と印刷されている。シェイクスピアが所属した国王一座 (King's Men) の役者 John Sincklo のことを指すと考えられる。また John Fletcher の *Women Pleased* という芝居には Soto という名前の農夫の長男が登場する。ただし Fletcher の *Women Pleased* は *The Taming of the Shrew* よりずっと後の 1620 年の作品である。おそらく Fletcher が材源とした先行作品があって、それに Sincklo が Soto の役で出演し、現在では失われたその芝居についてここで言及していると推定される。この台詞はその芝居の上演についての観客の知識を前提としており、楽屋落ちの一種と考えられる。

Ind. 2. 0. 1.　*Enter aloft*　aloft は gallery とも呼ばれる二階舞台 (upper stage) のことと考えられるが、F1 に印刷されているこのト書きをめぐってはさまざまな議論がある。登場人物の数や水盤 (basin) や水差し (ewer) などの小道具

が運び込まれることを考えると、小さく客席から見えにくい二階舞台が実際に使われたのかどうか疑問の余地がある。また劇中劇が始まり、スライたちの台詞がなくなった後も、このインダクションに登場した人物たちがそのまま舞台上に残るのか、退場するのかについても、意見は分かれている。

Ind. 2. 12.　humour　シェイクスピアの時代には、体の中を流れる 4 つの体液 (four humours) のバランスで心身の状態が決まると考えられていた。そのバランスが崩れたせいで、スライの精神は変調をきたしていると領主は言っている。「こんな無意味な妄想を語る病状に神が終止符を打ってくださいますように」という祈りを領主は口にしている。

Ind. 2. 17.　Burton Heath　シェイクスピアの生まれ故郷ストラットフォード・アポン・エイヴォン (Stratford-upon-Avon) から 25 キロほど離れた村 Barton-on-the-Heath を指すのであろうと考えられている。シェイクスピアの母方の伯母が住んでいた。

Ind. 2. 19.　Marian Hacket　Wincot に Hacket という姓の家族が住んでいた記録は残っている。l. 87 でも Cicely Hacket という名前が出てくる。

Ind. 2. 20.　Wincot　ストラットフォードの南 6 キロほどのところにある小さな村。これらの村や町を含むウォリックシャー (Warwickshire) は羊毛業が盛んであり、l. 18 の cardmaker も地元の経済に結びついている職業である。

Ind. 2. 36-37.　the lustful bed ... Semiramis　アッシリアの伝説上の女王セミラミスは、官能的な美しさで知られていた。

Ind. 2. 48, 52, 55.　Adonis, Io, Daphne　これらの人物が登場する物語はいずれもローマの詩人オウィディウス (Ovid, 43B.C.-A.D.18) の詩集『変身物語』(*Metamorphoses*) の中で語られている。オウィディウスはラテン語教育にも使われ、ルネサンス期のイングランドで絶大な人気を博していた。代表作である『変身物語』は英訳もされており、『ヴィーナスとアドーニス』をはじめ、シェイクスピアに大きな影響を与えている。シェイクスピアはラテン語と Arthur Golding の英訳 (1565-67) の両方でこれらの物語に馴染んでいた。『変身物語』は古典的な教養の書であるとともに、エロティックな欲望をかき立てる官能文学としても、当時のイングランドの文学に大きな影響力を与えた。無教養な庶民の一人であるスライは、よくわからないながらも、次々とエロティシズムを感じさせる言葉を浴びせかけられ、次第にその気になっていく。3. 1. 28-29 の後注参照。

Ind. 2. 61.　in this waning age　アダムとイヴが暮らしていたエデンの園の完璧さを失い、人類の歴史は次第に暗い時代へと向かっているという歴史観が、シェイクスピアの時代には受け入れられていた。

Ind. 2. 91-92.　Stephen Sly ... John Naps ... Peter Turph ... Henry Pimpernell　実在の人物名を台詞の中にちりばめることで、彼らを直接知っている人には楽屋落ち的なおかしさを感じさせることができただろう。またご

く平凡な名前が並ぶことでスライにはイングランドの庶民のひとりとしての実在感が与えられる。これによって、イタリアのパデュアに舞台が設定され、イタリア語の名前の人物たちが登場する本編と、インダクションとの間の違いがはっきりとし、劇中劇の構造が明確になる。

Ind. 2. 91.　Greece　この言葉についてはいくつかの説がある。(1) ストラットフォードからそれほど遠くない Greet という村の名前をスライが Greece と呼んだのではないか。(2) シェイクスピアが Greete と書いたのを植字工が Greece と誤読したのではないか。(3) 傭兵としてイングランドに来ていたギリシア人の名前を英語化して John Naps としたのではないか。いずれも決定的な証拠はない。

Ind. 2. 97.　thou shalt not lose by it　スライは従者のひとりに感謝を述べているが、it が何を指すかは曖昧。自分の病気回復を喜んでくれた Amen という言葉に感謝しているのか、あるいは病気中世話をしてくれたことを感謝しているのかもしれない。ペンギン版の編者 Hibbard は One gives Sly a pot of ale というト書きを加え、それに対する謝辞と解釈している。

1. 1. 2.　fair Padua, nursery of arts　1222 年に神聖ローマ皇帝フリードリヒ二世によって大学が創設され、学問の都として知られていた。*The Merchant of Venice* でも Portia はパデュアの学識ある博士に扮して Shylock を裁く。

1. 1. 2.　arts　古代ギリシアにおいて自由民にふさわしい教養という考え方が始まり、ローマ時代末期にその教養科目は文法 (grammar)、修辞学 (rhetoric)、論理学 (logic)、数学 (arithmetic)、幾何学 (geometry)、音楽 (music)、天文学 (astronomy) の 7 学科によって構成されると限定された。中世の大学においては、神学、法学、医学を学ぶための予備教育としてこれらの教養科目が教えられた。その影響はルネサンス期にも強く残っていた。

1. 1. 3.　Lombardy　パデュアは正確にはロンバルディア州の一部ではない。当時のイングランドの人々は、ロンバルディアは北イタリア地方というおおざっぱな捉え方をしていたようだ。

1. 1. 13.　come of the Bentivolii　実在のベンティヴォリ家はピサではなくボローニャの有力者である。

1. 1. 19-20.　happiness / By virtue ... achieved　徳によって幸福をめざすという考え方はアリストテレスの倫理学の中心的な思想のひとつである。

1. 1. 42.　come ashore　実際はパデュアは内陸の都市である。「上陸する」という表現が使われている理由として、次のような議論がなされている。1) パデュアを港町にしたのは紛本として利用したギャスコインの *Supposes* の影響である。2) 運河での到着を想定している。3) arrived を意味するイディオムとして come ashore とした。これらの説のいずれかかもしれないが、単にシェイクスピアが地理的な正確さに無頓着であった可能性もある。*The Winter's Tale* におけるボヘミアの海岸が代表的なものだが、シェイクスピアは地名や

時代考証でしばしば「間違い」をおかしている。

1. 1. 93-95.　music, instruments and poetry　音楽、詩、外国語といった社交上のたしなみに役立つ教育を娘に施すため、住み込みの家庭教師を雇うのは、シェイクスピア時代のイングランドではごく一部の特権階級に限られていた。バプティスタは貴族ではなく商人だ。これはシェイクスピアの時代のロンドンで、貴族と同様の子女教育をする、きわめて富裕な市民階級が登場し始めていたことの反映である。

1. 1. 106.　Their love　校訂上の問題となる箇所。Their は women を指すと考え、「女の愛情を勝ち得ること」という意味と解する立場を取る校訂者たちがいる。一方、There, とすべきところを、印刷工程のミスで Their になってしまったと推定する校訂者もいる。この場合、there は「やれやれ」というような意味の間投詞である。

1. 1. 233-38.　So could I ... your master Lucentio　主人の恋愛成就のための忠義という口実で、召使いのトラーニオは主人に扮する。召使いの地味な青いユニフォームから、派手な主人の衣装に着替えたトラーニオの嬉々とした気分が、調子の良い韻文の口調ににじみ出ている。l. 233 の after と l. 234 の daughter はシェイクスピアの発音では韻を踏んでいる。その後に続く4行も二行対句。これらの二行対句には主人に代わってビアンカに求婚するトラーニオの浮かれた気分が表れていると論じる批評家もいる。ラテン喜劇の「賢い召使い」の系譜につらなるトラーニオは、ともすれば忠実な召使いの立場を踏み超えて、主人との取り違えを楽しみ過ぎる危険な可能性を秘めている。

1. 2. 1.　Verona　*The Two Gentlemen of Verona* と *Romeo and Juliet* の舞台ともなっている。特に「ジュリエットの家」と称される14世紀に建てられた石造の家は観光名所にもなっている。

1. 2. 7.　rebused　グルーミオのように背伸びして難しい語彙を使おうとして誤用してしまうことを malapropism と言う。*Much Ado about Nothing* に登場する道化的な巡査ドグベリーは malapropism の連続で笑いを誘う。その前の knock もペトルーチオは「ドアをノックしろ」と言ったのに、グルーミオは「誰をひっぱたくのですか」と（わざと）意味を取り違えて答えている。グルーミオの道化的なキャラクターが登場早々はっきりと示されている。

1. 2. 8.　knock me here　シェイクスピアの時代、here と ear の発音は同じだったとされる。グルーミオはペトルーチオの言葉をわざと 'knock my ear' と聞き取って、「横っ面をひっぱたくんですか？」と仰天しているという解釈も可能である。

1. 2. 50.　Where ... in a few　F では Where small experience grows but in a few となっており、これでも「故郷でもわずかな経験はできるが、ただしそれはごくわずかな人間だけだ」という意味に解釈できる。しかし1733年の Theobald の校閲を継承し、grows. But in a few とする編者が多い。

1.2.108.　in his rope-tricks　この部分の解釈をめぐっては諸説あるが、グルーミオは rhetoric と言うべきところを rope-tricks と言い間違えたとする説が比較的有力。それだと「旦那独特の言い回しでわめきちらす」という意味になる。グルーミオがふざけて意図的に間違えたという解釈も成り立つ。あるいは「ロープで絞首刑にするのがふさわしいほどの大言壮語」という意味で rope rhetorics と言おうとしたのだとする説もある。また tricks を字義どおり「（女房をこらしめる）技」と解し、「絞首刑になるほどの荒技で」と解釈することも可能。

1.2.242.　Paris　パリスは愛の女神アプロディテ（ヴィーナス）の力を借りてスパルタ王の妻となっていたヘレネをさらってトロイに連れ去った。このことが原因でギリシアとトロイが 10 年に渡って繰り広げたトロイ戦争が起こった。

1.2.243.　out-talk　おそらくシェイクスピアの造語と考えられる。*OED* は John Cooke の喜劇 *Greene's Tu Quoque* (1611) を初出としているが、シェイクスピアの *The Shrew* の方が創作年代は先である。

1.2.244.　jade　この芝居のタイトルからしてすでに女性が馬に喩えられているが、劇中でもしばしばキャタリーナが欠陥の多い馬に喩えられている。ここではトラーニオが駄馬に喩えられているが、男性にこの比喩が用いられることは稀であると、*OED* が指摘している。(*OED adj.* 2c)

2.1.0.1.　[*with her hands tied*]　手を縛られて登場するという説明は F1 にはないが、l.4 で示されるように、明らかにビアンカは手を縛られている。シェイクスピア劇には女性同士の喧嘩はあまり出てこない。*A Midsummer Night's Dream* のハーミアとヘレナの口論は、激したハーミアがヘレナを爪で引っ掻こうとするところまで描かれているが、キャタリーナは実際に肉体的暴力を使ってしまっている。またキャタリーナが妹を thou で呼び、姉をなだめようとするビアンカが you を使っているのも、この場面でのキャタリーナの横暴さを示している。

2.1.73.　Baccare　英語の back にラテン語動詞の不定形語尾の -are をくっつけて作った言葉ではないかとされる。シェイクスピアの創作ではなく、Nicholas Udall の *Ralph Roister Doister*、John Lyly の *Midas* にもふざけて使う言葉としての用例が残っている。(*OED int.*)

2.1.112-25.　Signor Baptista ... on either hand　ペトルーチオとバプティスタの会話には、当時の結婚の慣習が反映している。花嫁の父親は財産を分与して、持参金として娘の結婚相手に与えなければならなかった。一方、もしも夫が先に死んだ場合、妻が夫の財産から受け取れるのは寡婦年金分だけで、地所は相続人のものとなった。バプティスタからの持参金の「地所半分と 2 万クラウン」(ll. 120-21) はかなり大きな財産で、キャタリーナのような厄介な娘と結婚してもらうために、たっぷりと持参金をつけるという意図が見える。それに呼応して、自分の死後「地所と借地権すべて」(l. 123) を妻に与えるという

ペトルーチオの条件も、当時としては破格の手厚い条件だった。

2.1.179. Petruchio 「ペトルーチオよ」と自分に呼びかけているが、このように自分を第三者として呼びかける台詞はシェイクスピア劇にたびたび出てくる。自己演出の意識が強調される「キメ」の台詞で、ときとしてそれだけで滑稽になる。

2.1.180-271. ペトルーチオとキャタリーナが激しい舌戦をかわし、互いに相手を言い負かそうと機知の鋭さを競いあう。こうした喜劇的な場面は wit combat（機知合戦）とも呼ばれる。2人は相手の言葉尻を捕まえて巧みに意味をずらしたり、同音異義語を利用した言葉遊びを次々と繰り広げる。この場面の lineation について、近年の版本でも編者たちの意見は分かれている。韻文における渡りの台詞ととらえるか、散文的な短い言葉の投げあいととらえるか、判断の難しい部分もある。韻律が整わない doggerel 風な部分も混じる。本書ではペトルーチオとキャタリーナの言葉のテンションの高さとリズム感に一体感があり、一気呵成に進む調子の良さを重視し、できる限り韻文として処理した。

2.1.180. Kate 開口一番 Kate となれなれしく呼びかけるのもペトルーチオの戦術のひとつ。この場面だけでペトルーチオは Kate という愛称を30回近く連発する。

2.1.184. bonny F では bony と印刷されているが、F4 で bonny とされており、A Shrew の対応する部分でも bonnie となっていることから、ほとんどの版で bonny が採られている。

2.1.186. Kate Hall 具体的な邸宅等の名前を引き合いに出したものではなく、単に「ケイト館のケイト様」というからかい気味の呼びかけであろう。

2.1.197. Assess are made to bear キャタリーナが「ロバが荷物を背負う」という意味で用いた bear をペトルーチオは次行で、「(性行為で男の体の重み)に耐える (bear) のは女」、さらに「女は子供を産む (bear) ようにできている」という意味にわざとずらしている。

2.1.204. be ペトルーチオはキャタリーナの言葉尻の be の意味を同音の bee（ハチ）にずらして、buzz（ブンブンうるさい）と言い返している。buzz には「噂話をしあう」という意味もあり、ペトルーチオは「自分について言われている噂に耳を貸した方がいいぞ」とあてこすっている。

2.1.204. buzzard 字義通りだと鷹狩りのイメージで「よれよれのくせによく捕まえたわね」という意味になる。しかし buzzard には「役立たず」、さらには「噂をまき散らす人間」の意味もあり、それらの意味も重ねてキャタリーナはペトルーチオをからかっている。

2.1.214. with my tongue in your tail 「'my tongue in your tail' という言葉で話を終えてしまうのか？」という意味だが、同時にかなり卑猥なことを言っている。tail は vagina の意味も持つ。

2.1.246. brown in hue ペトルーチオはキャタリーナをほめそやす言葉のひとつとして brown in hue と言っているが、シェイクスピアの時代には、雪のように白い肌が理想とされ、黒い髪や小麦色の肌は望ましくないものだった。*Love's Labour's Lost* でビルーンと丁々発止の機知合戦をするロザラインも肌の色の濃い女性とされているので、キャタリーナとロザラインは同じ少年俳優が演じた可能性が高い。

2.1.315. kiss me, Kate *The Taming of the Shrew* の劇中で、ペトルーチオがキャタリーナに「キスして、ケイト」と命じる台詞はこの部分と、第5幕第1場、第5幕第2場の3回ある。コール・ポーター作詞作曲のブロードウェイ・ミュージカル『キス・ミー・ケイト』(1948) のタイトルは、ここから取られている。『キス・ミー・ケイト』は『じゃじゃ馬ならし』を劇中劇にし、舞台裏で繰り広げられる別れた夫婦のドタバタを描いている。

3.1.28-29. ここで引用されているオウィディウスの『ヘロイデス』(*Heroides*) は神話上の女性たちが夫や恋人に宛てた書簡の形を取りながら、女性の心理を巧みに描いた詩集である。第4幕第2場では、ルーセンシオがビアンカに同じくオウィディウスの『愛の技法』(*Ars amatorial*) を読ませている。Induction. 2.48, 52, 55 の後注参照。

3.1.45. HORTENSIO F1 ではホーテンシオの台詞の2行目以下、ll. 46-56 の台詞の振り分けが大きく乱れている。1728年の Pope の第2版以降、広く受け入れられている振り分けを本版でもそのまま踏襲している。

3.1.72-76. ut, re, mi, fa, sol, la という音の呼び方は、'Ut queant laxis / Resonare fibris / Mira gestorum / Famuli tuorum / Solve pollute / Labii reatum / Sancte Iohannes' という聖ヨハネの賛歌の各行の冒頭の音から取られている。11世紀のカトリックの修道士 Guido d'Arezzo が考案した。

3.1.79. odd F1 では old となっている。odd は1733年の Theobald の校訂。

3.1.80-82. Mistress, ... day この台詞は F1 では Nicke という人物にあてられている。シェイクスピアの所属していた劇団 The King's Men の主要俳優のリストの中にいた Nicholas Tooley ではないかと考える研究者もいるが、3行しか台詞のない役のために、シェイクスピアが特定の役者を念頭に置いて書いたとは考えにくい。

3.2.30. old news F1 では Master, master, news, and such news as you never heard of となっており、old という言葉が使われていない。しかし次行のバプティスタの受け答えから old を入れる必要がある。本書では1842年の Collier 以来の such old news という校訂を採用した。

3.2.42. jerkin 16世紀から17世紀の男性用上着。袖がなく、体にぴったりとしていて、丈は短め。しばしば革で作られた。

3.2.42. thrice turned 布が擦り切れてくると裏返して使う。そちらも擦り切れてきたので、再度、裏返すということを3度繰り返した。

3. 2. 47-48.　mose in the chine　意味が不明瞭な一節。mose は mourn の間違いではないかと推測する研究者もいる。chine は「背骨」。「病気が進んで末期症状になりかけている」という意味ではないかとされる。

3. 2. 85.　Were it better, I should rush in thus.　この 1 行は F1 では Were it better I should rush in thus: となっており、さまざまな校訂がなされてきた。Barbara Hodgdon によるアーデン第 3 版 (2010 年) は Were it better I should rush in thus? と疑問文にしている。着飾ったトラーニオを thus と指差しながら、「こんなふうに着飾ってやってくる方が良かったかな？」と言っているという解釈だ。また H. J. Oliver によるオックスフォード版 (1982 年) は、意味の通りと韻律とを考慮し、Were it not better I should rush in thus? としている。これだと「こうして急いでくる方が良いじゃないか」という意味になる。本書は F1 の読みをできるだけそのまま残す方針で、Were it better, I should rush in thus. を選択した。

3. 2. 122.　But, sir, to love　この場面の切り替えの唐突さには何かしらのテクスト上の乱れがあることがうかがえる。3. 2. 120 までのトラーニオの台詞をすべてホーテンシオの台詞と考えればかなりすっきりする。その場合、トラーニオとルーセンシオは第 3 幕第 2 場の冒頭で登場するのではなく、一行全員が退場した l. 120 の後で会話をしながら登場すると考えればつじつまがあう。またここから始まる 20 行ほどの台詞の間に、ペトルーチオとキャタリーナの結婚式が済んでしまうことも不自然であり、本来あった場面が削除されている可能性を推測する研究者もいる。

　また F1 ではこの部分は But sir, Love となっている。これでは意味が通じない。本書は 1838 年の Knight の校訂にならって to love とした。Capell は to her love としていてこの方が意味はより明瞭だが、音節数を優先して to love を採った。

3. 2. 225.　my ox, my ass, my anything　『旧約聖書』の「出エジプト記」20 章のモーセの十戒の 10 番目、他人の所有物を貪らないようにという戒めを下敷きにしている。'Thou shalt not covet thy neighbour's house, thou shalt not covet thy neighbour's wife, nor his manservant, nor his maidservant, nor his ox, nor his ass, nor any thing that is they neighbour's.'

4. 1. 1.　F1 ではここには幕の区切れを示す表記はない。しかし明らかにここで場面はパデュアから別の地に移動している。またキャタリーナとペトルーチオの結婚の前と後という大きな区切れもここである。それらを考慮し、Pope はここからを第 4 幕第 1 場とした。以降、多くの版がそれを継承した幕・場割りを行っている。本書もそれにならう。

　グルーミオの愚痴からこの場面は始まる。いかに寒いかを強調するグルーミオの台詞は、場面が冬であることを観客に伝えている。舞台装置や照明のないシェイクスピアの時代の劇場では、天候や時刻などの情報は台詞の中に書きこ

まれていた。

4. 1. 15-16.　fire, fire, cast on no water　当時よく知られていた輪唱歌の歌詞 'Scotland's burning / See yonder! See yonder / Fire, fire! Fire, fire! / Cast on Water! Cast on Water!' の最後の部分を、（わざと）間違えて引用している。

4. 1. 74.　Nathaniel, Joseph, Nicholas, Philip, Walter, Sugarsop　ここでは 6 人の召使いの名前が挙がっているが、この後、さらに Gregory (l. 103)、Gabriel (l. 114)、Peter (l. 115)、Adam, Rafe (l. 117) と合計 11 名の召使いの名前が言及される。ここにグルーミオとカーティスが加わると、全部で 13 名になる。名前が挙げられた全員に台詞があるわけではない。テクストが乱れている可能性もあるが、名前を並べあげることで召使いの多さを強調し、ペトルーチオの財力を示す目的だったのかもしれない。

4. 1. 189.　to kill a wife with kindness　ことわざになっている 'to kill with kindness' は「甘やかしてダメにする」という意味。しかし実際にペトルーチオのやろうとしていることは逆なので、大いに皮肉になっている。また同時代の作家 Thomas Heywood に *A Woman Killed with Kindness* と題した家庭悲劇がある。市民階級の、理想的と思われた夫婦の関係が妻の不貞によって破綻し、妻は自ら飲食を絶って死んでいく。

**4. 2. 71. 2.　*Enter a Pedant*　**F ではここで Pedant が登場し、この後の台詞も Pedant が語るよう指定されている。しかし *A Shrew* やシェイクスピアが材源として利用した George Gascoigne の *Supposes* では、対応する人物は Merchant である。また台詞に bills of money（為替手形）の話題が出てくることや遠隔地まで旅することから、このシェイクスピアの *The Shrew* でもこの登場人物は商人とすべきと考え、ケンブリッジ版 (1984) の編者 Ann Thompson とアーデン版 (2010) の編者 Barbara Hodgdon は人物名を全面的に Merchant に変えている。しかし本版では F1 をそのまま受け入れ Pedant とした。その理由は次の通りである。1) ビオンデロが ll. 63-64 で「商人か教師か、何かわからないがちゃんとしている人」と言っている台詞を、そのまま受けて Pedant としただけではないか、つまり「何かわからない人物」を指す言葉として仮に Pedant という役名が与えられているだけだと考えられる。2) 各地を訪ね歩くなど、商人かもしれないと思わせる台詞はあるが、職業が教師では絶対に成立しないわけではない。以上の理由から、F1 に残された役名をあえて変える必要はないという判断をした。ただし上演する際に、この役を「商人」に設定することは十分に妥当なことだと考える。だがテクストの編纂と、上演台本の決定は別の作業であり、本書では古版本の F1 を、現在でも読めるテクストとして編集することを目指した。

4. 3. 86. 1.　[*Exit Haberdasher*]　F1 では帽子屋の退場を指示するト書きはどこにもない。帽子を欲しがるキャタリーナを無視して、ペトルーチオが服の話をし始めた。さんざん帽子のデザインの悪口を言われたうえ、手持ちぶさたに

なった帽子屋が退場するとしたら、この86行目の後のタイミングであろう。ただし所在ないままずっとこの場面に帽子屋が居続けることで、さらにぎこちない雰囲気になるという演出も可能である。

4. 3. 91.　censer in a barber's shop　第3アーデン版の Hodgdon は cithern「シターン」（ギターに似た弦楽器）と校訂した。床屋がシターンを奏でることはよくあり、またシターンに付けられた凝った装飾が、仕立て屋の持ってきた服の凝ったデザインへのあてこすりになりうる。またオックスフォード版（またそれを元にしたノートン版）の全集は scissor「はさみ」と校訂している。これなら、あちこちに切り込みを入れているデザインへの揶揄として成立する。いずれにせよどの校訂も、はっきりとした典拠はなく、推測の域にとどまる。

4. 4. 0. 1.　F1 では Pedant の登場のト書きが場面の冒頭と18行目の2回ある。2回目の登場は明らかに間違いだが、そこには *Pedant booted and bare headed* という服装についての指示が書かれている。旅行用のブーツを履いており、バプティスタに挨拶するため帽子を脱ぐという意図のト書きと解釈できる。それらの情報を整理し、場面冒頭の登場のト書きに *booted* という説明を加え、*bare headed* は l. 18 のタイミングのト書きとして残した。

4. 4. 5.　Where we were lodgers at the Pegasus.　F1 ではこの1行はトラーニオの台詞になっている。Pedant の台詞としたのは Theobalt.

4. 4. 20.　Sir　l. 19 のピリオドは F1 ではコロン。その場合 l. 20 以降の3行も前行から続いてバプティスタに向かって実の父親を紹介する台詞という解釈になる。l. 21 の father は father-in-law の意味となり、「（保証人の父親を連れてきたのですから、）義父として私にビアンカをください」という意味になる。

4. 4. 66-72. 1.　バプティスタから娘への使いを命じられたルーセンシオの退場が F1 では示されていない。Rowe は l. 67 の台詞をルーセンシオのものと校訂し、この台詞のあとにある人名の指定のない *Exit* をルーセンシオの退場と考えた。つまり変装したルーセンシオが、「ビアンカがルーセンシオの妻になれるといいですねえ」と言ってから退場するという流れだ。この Rowe の校訂も捨てがたい選択肢だが、それだとビオンデロはずっと舞台の上にいることになり、l. 72 の後にある *Enter Lucentio and Biondello* と矛盾してしまう。本書では l. 72 の後の2人の登場をそのまま生かすために、バプティスタに命じられたタイミング (l. 66) にルーセンシオの退場を書き加え、ビオンデロの退場はトラーニオに「さっさと行け」という命令 (l. 68) の後へと1行分遅らせた。

　また F1 には l. 68 の後に *Enter Peter* というト書きがある。ルーセンシオの召使いが食事の支度ができていることを伝えにきた、あるいはペトルーチオの召使いが一行の到着を伝えにきたなどの推察はなされているが、いずれも決定的なものではない。本書ではエラーによって残ってしまったト書きと考え、削除した。

4. 5. 74.　I do assure thee, father, so it is　第4幕第2場でトラーニオ扮す

るルーセンシオはホーテンシオとともに、ビアンカへの求婚をやめると宣言している。ホーテンシオがここでペトルーチオの言ったとおりルーセンシオがビアンカと結婚したと断言するのは、l. 63とともに展開上の明らかな齟齬である。シェイクスピアがうっかり間違えた可能性もあるが、いずれかの時点でホーテンシオの役まわりについての改変がなされ、その結果としてテクスト上の乱れが生じている可能性が高い。実際の舞台では、演出上、この台詞をキャタリーナに語らせることで矛盾を解消する工夫がなされることもある。

5.1.0.1. F1では第5幕の開始は次の場面からになっている。しかし舞台がパデュアに戻るこの場面から第5幕が始まるという幕・場割の方が妥当だと判断し、18世紀のWarburtonおよびTheobald以降、ここで幕を区切っている。本書もこの幕割を踏襲した。

5.1.13.1. ***Pedant looks out of the window*** *Othello*の第1幕第1場でロダリーゴの呼びかけに応じてブラバンシオが窓から顔を出して答える場面には*Above*というト書きがついている。おそらく同様の舞台の使い方をしたのではないか。*The Comedy of Errors*第3幕第1場にも本物のアンティフォラスが帰宅したのに、そっくりな双子が中にいるために門を開けてもらえず閉め出されるというよく似た場面がある。この場面でも二階舞台を使った可能性がある。

5.2.0.1-3. F1ではここから第5幕が始まっている。冒頭のト書きには複数の乱れがある。登場する人物の中に、ホーテンシオ、ペトルーチオ、キャタリーナの名前は欠けており、トラーニオの名前が2回出てくる。この部分に関しては印刷の底本となった原稿に問題があったことは確実である。

また直前の場面で退場したばかりのペトルーチオとキャタリーナがすぐに登場するのも、シェイクスピア劇の通例に反する。2人は舞台から退場せずに残り、他の人物たちが登場して2人に加わるという可能性もある。

5.2.24. **thus she conceives her tale** ホーテンシオは「妻は君を見て自分の発言を思いついただけだ」と言っている。taleはtailと同音で、tailはvaginaの隠語にもなっている。ホーテンシオは妻をかばいながら、同時にペトルーチオの下ネタに合わせているとも解釈できる。

5.2.28-29. シェイクスピアの時代にshrewはwoeと韻を踏むように発音されていた。coupletを使った決め台詞で未亡人はキャタリーナに答えている。

5.1.40. **Head and butt** ビアンカはグレミオのbuttという言葉をbuttock, bottomの意味にずらして、「head and buttのbuttと言いたいのですか」と言っている。さらに次行では寝取られ亭主の額に生えるhornという言葉まで口にしている。下ネタ混じりのジョークの応酬に参加してくることで、ビアンカの「おしとやかなお嬢様」というイメージが崩れ始める。

5.2.46-47. **your bird** 「あなたが狙う鳥」（私に向かって機知の効いたジョークを言おうとしているの、とペトルーチオに聞いている。） **I mean ... your bow** この時代の野鳥狩りは木にとまっている鳥を弓矢で狙った。もし

も鳥が別の木に移ると (shift my bush)、弓を引きながら別の場所に移る
(pursue me as you draw your bow) 必要があった。

5. 2. 65.　for assurance　F1 では sir assurance となっているが、手書き原稿
の secretary hand で書かれた s が f と判別しにくいため、植字工が for を sir
と読んでしまった可能性がある。F2 では for assurance である。現代ではこ
の F2 の読みを採る版と、F を生かして Sir Assurance と校訂する版に分かれ
ている。Sir Assurance とした場合、キャタリーナが一番のじゃじゃ馬だという、
バプティスタの自信たっぷりさを皮肉って、Sir Assurance (「過信殿」といっ
たところか) と呼んでいるという解釈になる。

5. 2. 136-79.　キャタリーナの長い「服従の演説」には、シェイクスピアの時代
の観客にとって聞きなじみのある表現が散りばめられている。イングランド国
教会の儀式を定めた『一般祈禱書』(*Book of Common Prayer*) は、結婚式で
の妻の誓いの言葉を次のように定めている。新婦は wilt thou obey him and
serve him, love, honour, and keep him, in sickness and in health? という問い
かけに I will と答え、服従を誓う。そして結婚式の締めくくりとして最後に読
み上げられる教えでも、主に仕えるように妻は夫に仕えるべしと繰り返し命じ
ている。

Ye women, submit yourselves unto your own husbands as unto the Lord:
for the husband is the wives' head, even as Christ is the head of the Church.
And he is also the saviour of the whole body. Therefore, as the Church or
congregation is subject unto Christ, so likewise let the wives also be in
subjection unto their own husbands in all things.

イングランド国教会が信者の教化のために編纂した『説教集』(*Homilies*)
の中の、「結婚に関する説教」(Homily of the State of Matrimony) でも、同様
に妻の絶対従属を説いている。

Ye wives, be ye in subjection to obey your own husbands ... them must
they obey, and cease from commanding, and perform subjection. For this
surely doth nourish concord very much, when the wife is ready at hand at
her husband's commandment, when she will apply herself to his will, when
she endureth herself to seek his contentation, and to do him pleasure, when
she will eschew all things that might offend him:

これらの教えの元にあるのは『新約聖書』「エペソ人への手紙」第 5 章
22-24 節である。

Wives, submit yourselves unto your own husbands, as unto the Lord./ For
the husband is the head of the wife, even as Christ is the head of the church:
and he is the saviour of the body./ Therefore as the church is subject unto
Christ, so let the wives be to their own husbands in everything.

これらの結婚式の時に繰り返し唱えられる祈禱の言葉や、教会でたびたび読

み上げられる説教は、馴染みの言葉として社会の中に定着している。キャサリンの大演説はそうした「当たり前」と化した定型句の列挙と言える。キャサリンのこの演説が、家庭の調和と妻の従属という結婚イデオロギーを是認し、さらには強化する方向で作用したのか、はたまた「当たり前」をあえて滔々と論じることによって喜劇的効果をあげ、イデオロギーの形骸化を暴いて見せていたのかは、議論の分かれるところである。

　第3アーデン版の編者 Hodgdon は、本来、教会内で男性聖職者が伝えるべきイデオロギーを、女であるキャタリーナが劇場で教える側に立つ点に、通俗的な社会規範に収まりきらない要素が見出せると論じている。第3ケンブリッジ版の Thompson は、*A Shrew* での同箇所の演説が天地創造や女の原罪に言及した宗教色のより色濃いものであるのに比して考えれば、*The Shrew* のキャタリーナの演説には男女が一種の社会契約を結ぶという、よりリベラルな結婚観が見て取れると論じている。

　Hodgdon や Thompson の議論は、シェイクスピアの時代におけるこの演説の意義がどのようなものであったかを問うものである。一方、女の従属が「当たり前」ではなくなった時代に、この大演説にどのような意味を与えていくか、そしてそれをいかに舞台上で表現するかは、当然ながらまったく別問題である。

［編注者紹介］

前沢浩子（まえざわ　ひろこ）

1961年生まれ。津田塾大学英文科卒業、同大学大学院文学研究科博士課程単位取得満期退学。文学修士。東京医科歯科大学准教授を経て、現在、獨協大学教授。
［著書］NHKカルチャーラジオ『生誕450年シェークスピアと名優たち』（NHK出版）
［訳書］スタンリー・ウェルズ『シェイクスピアとコーヒータイム』（三元社）、ジョン・ネイスン『ニッポン放浪記―ジョン・ネイスン回想録』（岩波書店）、マーティン・ウォデル『森かげの家』（PARCO出版局）、他

〈大修館シェイクスピア双書 第2集〉

じゃじゃ馬ならし
©Hiroko Maezawa, 2023　　　　　　　　　　　NDC 932／xii, 240p／20cm

初版第1刷――2023年9月1日

編注者―――前沢浩子
発行者―――鈴木一行
発行所―――株式会社 大修館書店
　　　　　　〒113-8541 東京都文京区湯島2-1-1
　　　　　　電話 03-3868-2651（販売部）　03-3868-2293（編集部）
　　　　　　振替 00190-7-40504
　　　　　　［出版情報］https://www.taishukan.co.jp

装丁・本文デザイン―――井之上聖子
印刷所―――広研印刷
製本所―――ブロケード

ISBN 978-4-469-14265-5　Printed in Japan

大修館 シェイクスピア双書 (全12巻)
THE TAISHUKAN SHAKESPEARE

大修館 シェイクスピア双書 第2集 (全8巻)
THE TAISHUKAN SHAKESPEARE 2nd Series

アントニーとクレオパトラ	*Antony and Cleopatra*	佐藤達郎 編注
ヘンリー四世 第一部・第二部	*King Henry IV, Parts 1 and 2*	河合祥一郎 編注
尺には尺を	*Measure for Measure*	佐々木和貴 編注
ウィンザーの 陽気な女房たち	*The Merry Wives of Windsor*	竹村はるみ 編注
リチャード二世	*King Richard II*	篠崎　実 編注
じゃじゃ馬ならし	*The Taming of the Shrew*	前沢浩子 編注
タイタス・アンドロニカス	*Titus Andronicus*	清水徹郎 編注
冬物語	*The Winter's Tale*	井出　新 編注

シェイクスピア，それが問題だ！

シェイクスピアを読み解くための百問百答

井出 新 著

「勉強は得意だった？」「年収と資産は？」「好きな食べものは？」「犬派？
猫派？」といった人物像から、「当時、演劇はどんな娯楽だった？」「観劇代
はいくら？」「熊いじめって何？」「寝取られ亭主になぜ角が生える？」
「無韻詩とは？」など作品理解に役立つ当時の風習や英文の読み方まで、
シェイクスピアにまつわるあらゆる Q に答える 1 冊。

四六判・144 ページ・近刊

ゴーストを訪ねるロンドンの旅

平井杏子 著

世界でもっとも幽霊人口の多い国、イギリス。ウェストミンスター寺院や
バッキンガム宮殿、大英博物館、ロンドン塔など、ロンドンの有名な観光
地を巡りながら、そこに出現すると噂される幽霊のエピソードとその背景
を紹介する。英国史に名を残す人々の幽霊を通してイギリスの歴史と文化
を知る、カラー写真満載の 1 冊。

A5 判・224 ページ　定価 2,530 円（税込）

ガーデニングとイギリス人

「園芸大国」はいかにしてつくられたか

飯田 操 著

修道院の思索の庭から、権勢誇示のため贅を尽くした整形庭園へ、そして
不屈のイングランド精神を主張する風景庭園から、「古き良きイングラン
ド」の象徴であるコテージ・ガーデンまで、何世紀もかけて、岩だらけの
島を花いっぱいのエデンの園に変えてきた、「ガーデナー」の国民と庭園
とのつきあいの歴史をたどる。

四六判・360 ページ　定価 3,630 円（税込）

2023 年 6 月現在　定価は消費税 10% 込み

ビアトリクス・ポターを訪ねる
イギリス湖水地方の旅
ピーターラビットの故郷をめぐって

北野佐久子 著

ピーターラビットなど、今も世界中で変わらぬ人気を博している絵本を描いた作家ビアトリクス・ポター。彼女が暮らし、作品の舞台として描いた湖水地方を巡りながら、自然保護・菌類研究・牧羊と様々なことにチャレンジしたビアトリクスの人生を辿る。

A5 判・218 ページ　定価 2,530 円（税込）

聖書でたどる英語の歴史

寺澤 盾 著

英米人の生活・文化と深く関わってきた英訳聖書。各時代の聖書の記述を比較しながら、過去 1500 年の間に英語に起こったさまざまな変化をたどる。時代の変化を"体感"しながら学ぶ英語史。

A5 判・262 ページ　定価 2,420 円（税込）

挿絵画家の時代
ヴィクトリア朝の出版文化

清水一嘉 著

挿絵画家ジョージ・クルックシャンクと小説家ディケンズの活躍を軸として、「挿絵の時代」と呼ばれる、19 世紀イギリス出版界に生きた挿絵画家、小説家、木版職人、出版社、貸本屋たちの愛憎劇に満ちた人間模様を描く。挿絵版画約 100 点。カラー口絵つき。

四六判・310 ページ　定価 2,640 円（税込）

2023 年 6 月現在　定価は消費税 10% 込み